# *Destiny's Crucible*

## Book 2

# The Pen and the Sword

## Olan Thorensen

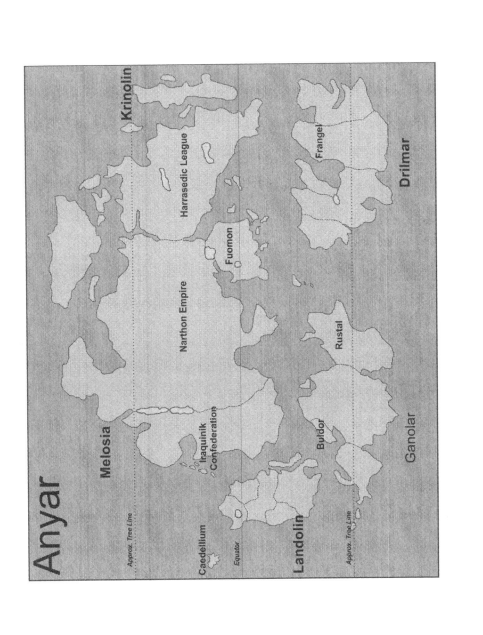

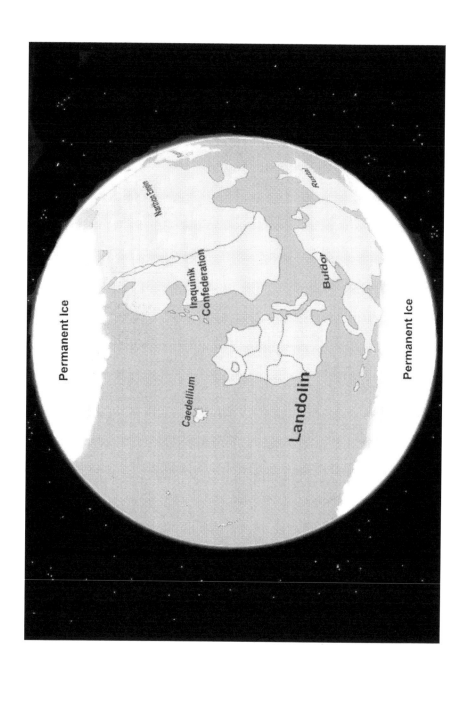

# Caedellium

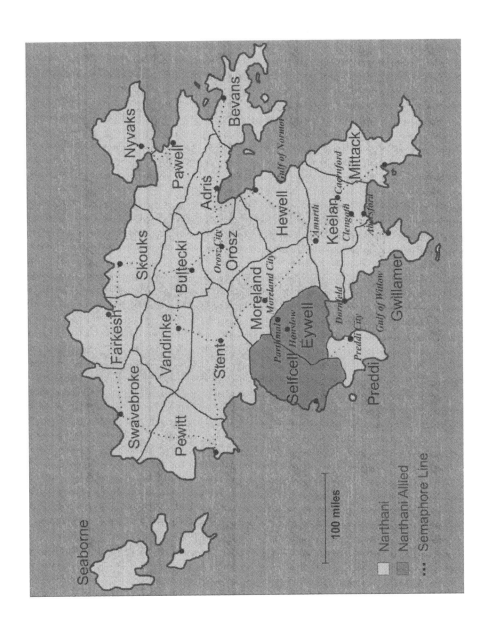

## Acknowledgments

Thanks to my wife, Kathleen, for encouragement, tolerating my sequestering away for endless hours writing and revising, and for reading drafts. Thanks to editors Felicia Sullivan and Patricia Waldygo for contributions and teaching me those things about writing and grammar that I didn't learn in school. Cover by Damonza.com.

A list of major characters is given in the back of the book.

# CONTENTS

"*The word is mightier than the sword.*"—7th-century BC, Ahiqar (Assyrian sage)

"*The pen is mightier than the sword.*"—1839; taken from the play *Richelieu* by Edward Bulwer-Lytton

"*There are only two powers in the world, saber and mind; at the end, saber is always defeated by mind.*"—Napoleon Bonaparte.

"*Anyone who thinks the pen is mightier than the sword has not been stabbed with both.*"—Lemony Snicket.

"*The quill may be mightier long term, but the sword wins short term.*"—Yozef Kolsko

# PROLOGUE

To others, an enigma paced the room, the click of his heels on the polished plank floor synchronized to alternate heartbeats. Yet *he* didn't think of himself as an enigma but as an imposter.

None of them knew the truth. How could they? Or maybe he was a mirage, something they wanted to exist so badly that nothing would shake their unwavering belief.

A light appeared in the corner of his vision. He turned his head toward the source—a full moon peeking through an open window. The second moon had already set. The scent of coralin vine flowers, pungent and sweet, wafted into the room. Once he thought the odor alien, but now he pulled the aroma deep into his lungs, anchoring himself.

"If just once to see the one big moon again, the one I was born under, or to smell jasmine or pines," he whispered to the night. At times, the longings were a probing knife, though only a pang this night.

"We'll be ready in a few minutes," called a woman's voice from the next room.

"That's fine," he responded.

*Take all the time you want, take forever, or go without me.*

He turned from the window and strode to stand before a full-length mirror framed in fine-grained kaskor wood. A stranger stared back, wearing a plain but finely tailored dark brown suit of clothes over a sturdy physique marred by a scar from his forehead edge to above the right ear and a sudden limp, as both men turned to complementary side views. They each raised one hand to gently stroke their head scars, while their other hands reached down to rub the shins below the knees.

"Nothing we can do about the head scar," they'd told him. "The limp and ache in your leg will fade with time, although you may notice it during cold and damp weather."

Not mentioned was the third scar, angry across his left side, the injury healed after his nearly dying. He remembered all three moments, the impact on his leg and the pain that only came later, a searing sensation as a jagged wood fragment slashed his head, and the flash of light and then darkness, awakening to agony. Three scars and a limp as lifelong companions, the scars always visible and the limp and ache recurring enough for him to . . . remember.

More voices. Soon they would come for him. He looked deep into the eyes in the mirror, eyes that could hold anyone's focus: a rare pale color that in different lights changed chameleon-like among shades of blue, gray, and sometimes an unidentifiable hue, unsettling the object of their attention. Not that the man realized the effect.

The man standing before the mirror had brown hair. It had darkened in the first year after his arrival, now with only streaks of the original color left. How his hair darkened, he didn't know, although he assumed it was tied to what the Watchers had done to him. He also remembered himself as young, with an unassuming form, a confident pleased-with-himself manner, a secure and comfortable future, and no urge for noble commitments. A man who knew his place in life and was content. In contrast, while the man in the mirror might appear young, a closer look belied the impression. Not that the face was older, merely . . . more lived. A determined face, a face with responsibilities, with resignation, with apprehension, a face foreseeing an unchosen future.

The man standing before the mirror remembered who he *had* been, while part of the man in the mirror longed for the same, someone with a quiet, unexciting life. Someone without monumental responsibilities. A different life from that of the man in the mirror; the man before the mirror had seen much, accomplished much, and lived thirty years in the last four. He was a man who knew his life would not be quiet. It would be a meaningful life, one with joys and darkness, a life of making a difference, but also a life of burdens as heavy as a mountain. Both men recognized an irrevocable moment; after today, there was no turning back. The parting smile needed no words, because the men knew they would not see each other again. A smile of melancholy farewell. As they stared at each other, the man before the mirror morphed until the two men became one. He shifted his shoulders to adjust the new suit of clothes.

Voices again. The women's voices he recognized, one in particular. She and others had told him this day was stirring, exhilarating, inspirational, and other words holding no weight for him. They were words he didn't want to hear, words whispering "duty," even if not voiced. She chided him for behaving as if it were an appointment to have his teeth pulled. In her annoyed remonstrations, she would never understand the depth of his reluctance. His acceptance would never be matched by any yearning for what others assumed for him—or themselves.

Questions. There would always be questions: *Did all this really happen? Am I insane? Has it been nothing more than a dream? A nightmare? Who am I? Do I even exist? Will there ever be answers?* A wry smile followed the last question and a gentle shake of head attested to his expectation. No, there would be no answers. There was only to be.

# CHAPTER 1

# WORRY

*A musket ball splintered a wooden crate twelve inches from where Yozef Kolsko crouched for protection. He might have cried out, though if he did, the sound vanished within the cacophony of hundreds of screaming voices, musket and pistol fire, and the clash of metal.*

*Blood splashed across his arm, after the battle axe wielded by the man next to him at the barricade cleaved a raider from neck to navel. Yozef stared at the warm, bright red coating on his arm, calmly satisfied the blood came from someone else.*

*He looked up to see a scarred, tattooed man charging with a spear leveled at his gut. Although time slowed, his reflexes betrayed him. He'd only just brought his own spear around to ward off the blade when a jolt of searing agony enveloped his midriff. He looked down at a blade end attached to the spear shaft, the rest of the blade buried in his flesh, blood spraying outward.*

Yozef Kolsko jerked upright in bed, gasping, hands covering his abdomen, sweat running down his face. His heart pounded against his ribs and subsided only when he recognized his bedroom.

He had thought the nightmares were behind him. The attack on the abbey happened a month ago. Thirty-six Anyar days. After the attack, his dreams relived the terror and blood of that awful day.

He threw back the covers, stood naked by the bed for a moment, then pulled on a robe and walked out to the veranda. A weather front had pushed through hours earlier, and now the sky blazed with stars undimmed by competing lights of civilization. Around the town of Abersford, after the sun set and while hard-working people slept, no lights marked human presence.

After he took several deep breaths, his pulse eased, and his sweat turned chill. He recognized the Anyar night sky but would never quit missing the constellations of Earth. Whatever the distance to Earth, it was far enough that the shifting view lost any terrestrial star pattern—no Orion, Big Dipper, Southern Cross.

A flash caught his eye, streaking briefly before burning up. It took him a moment to recognize a meteor and not a vehicle of the Watchers, as he had named them.

*I wonder if they're up there looking down on Anyar the way they said they studied Earth?*

It wasn't the first time he'd had this thought. When Joseph Colsco's San Francisco to Chicago flight accidently collided with the alien vessel, the occupants saved him but wouldn't return him to Earth. His only contact had been with an artificial intelligence—Harlie, he named it—created to communicate with him. Despite his pleading, Harlie never wavered that Yozef couldn't return to Earth, because he had knowledge of the Watchers' existence.

Harlie's creators were studying the mystery of who transplanted humans to other planets and why. The AI gave Joe the options of either being terminated, as presented in its dry and toneless voice, or being placed on another planet inhabited by humans. Despondent and afraid, he chose to live and awoke in the care of strangers who'd found him unconscious and naked on a beach.

His mind drifted from the Watchers to his new life. The first months were hard. Torn from his life and cast among a strange people and society, he'd adjusted and found a place, albeit drastically different from his previous life. In introspective moments, he wondered which life was better—the comfortable, mundane one on Earth or the one here in the town of Abersford, Keelan Province, Island of Caedellium, on planet Anyar.

Yozef shook his head. *Well*, he thought, *it certainly isn't always a safe life, but I can't say it isn't interesting.*

He rubbed the scar on his lower left leg. The medicants had removed the stitches two sixdays ago—two Anyarian weeks—but the leg was still tender. He'd been lucky. The musket ball ricochet tore a two-inch gouge that nicked the shinbone. They said the wound wasn't serious, but the leg might ache after sudden weather changes or when he got older. The former effect was already evident.

Finding himself in the middle of a musket-and-blade battle was one more shock in the last two years. He had accepted his fate enough to start a new life, had found friends, had had an affair with a local farm woman, had introduced technology unknown on Caedellium, and was on the way to becoming wealthy by local standards, when the harder reality of this world was thrust on him by a mercenary raid.

The night air brought shivers. Enough wondering for tonight. The nightmare faded. Yozef Kolsko walked back to the bedroom, lay down, pulled the covers over himself, and let sleep come again.

Others were also awake and thinking of recent events. Culich Keelan, hetman and leader of the sixty-thousand-member Keelan clan, sat in his study, rereading reports about the raid on St. Sidryn's abbey and the adjacent town of Abersford. The raiders were Buldorians, freebooters from the Ganolar continent, yet the real enemy was the Narthon Empire. Caedellium and its twenty-one clans had seemed too distant to be threatened by conflicts plaguing the rest of Anyar. The Caedelli had blithely assumed their large island, off regular trading routes and not near major continents, prevented temptations for annexation. They were wrong. The Narthon Empire coveted their island.

The aggressive Narthani had roared out of the northern reaches of the Melosia continent two hundred years earlier and systematically subjugated people and nations until a coalition of neighboring realms stopped their expansion. When the Narthani first appeared on Caedellium seven years ago, it was in the guise of mere traders. The naïve Preddi Clan accepted Narthani presence and was oblivious, until too late, to the surreptitious plan to enthrall the island. With shocking speed, the Narthani destroyed the Preddi Clan, usurped their province for Narthani colonists, and coerced two adjacent clans, Eywell and Selfcell, into alliance. Culich Keelan feared that only time separated similar threats to other clans.

The Buldorian raids carried out under Narthani tutelage reinforced his fears. Although the attack on St. Sidryn's was the first overt move on Keelan Province, Culich suffered no illusions it would be the last. More trouble brewed. The Buldorians were only a foretaste; the main thrust was yet to come. No one clan could withstand the Narthani, and he chafed at his failure to convince enough of the other clan hetmen of the threat level he foresaw.

As with too many nights, Culich's sleep had eluded him. Rereading reports was better than lying in bed, trying to avoid looking to the future and fearing an abyss might stare back.

A hundred and sixty feet away in Keelan Manor, another person was awake. Maera Keelan lay in bed, covers pulled up to her chin, eyes open. She couldn't hear her father, but somehow knew he was awake and worrying. Everything her father knew about the Narthani threat, so did Maera. She had been his scribe and assistant the last five years, sitting as recorder on important meetings and drafting much of his correspondence. It was an unusual role for any Caedelli female, and even more so for one only twenty-three years old (twenty-one Earth years). However, Meara wasn't just anyone. The hetman's eldest daughter possessed a brilliant mind restrained by acceptable roles in Caedelli society.

If she had been a son, everyone would assume her destined to be the next hetman. But there were no hetwomen. Instead, she helped her father where she could, studied Caedellium history, taught herself languages of other peoples of Anyar, and played the role of hetman's daughter. She was already late in performing one duty to her father and clan, a duty she had accepted all of her life. There would be a marriage advantageous to the clan, and she would produce children. Because her father had no sons and Maera was who she was, everyone, including her, expected one of her sons to be the next hetman. That she hadn't yet performed this duty was partly due to the prospective suitors' reluctance to take a wife who was too intelligent, too opinionated, and too assertive, no matter the advantages of a familial liaison to a clan as important as Keelan.

Tonight, her fears about the Narthani intertwined with thoughts about marriage and children. She wasn't as reticent as her father to look toward the future, but for her, the abyss also threatened any future children of *her* body.

In Preddi City, General Okan Akuyun slept fitfully until rising to go to his study. While the commander of all Narthani on Caedellium was not a habitual worrier, even *he* suffered doubts, most of which he shared with his wife, Rabia, but not all.

The Buldorian raids had gone as planned, except for the last, the first raid on Keelan Province. He didn't know the details of the raid's failure, because the Buldorians had sailed for home without reporting back to Akuyun. That one failure didn't matter. The successful raids, plus other actions meant to destabilize the Caedelli clans, had proceeded well enough that he and his command staff were near deciding it was time to move to the next phase—direct action against the clans. The first steps would be to ratchet up raids by Eywell and Selfcell, forcing the neighboring clans to concentrate on defending their own provinces and minimizing aiding one another. Soon, Akuyun would commit his Narthani troops to invade and force the islanders to fight open field battles, where his professional troops could use combined infantry, artillery, and cavalry to crush enough of the clans to compel the others to accept Narthani suzerainty.

Despite acceptable progress, Akuyun believed it his duty to worry. Any failure fell eventually to him, in both his own mind and that of the Narthani High Command in Narthon, but he reassured himself that nothing seemed to stand in their path, barring unforeseen factors that couldn't be accounted for in any plan.

# CHAPTER 2

# WHO IS YOZEF KOLSKO?

**Keelan Manor, Caernford, Keelan Province**

Culich pushed aside reports scattered across his desk, as Maera entered his study. He had reread the accounts so many times, he could recite many of them from memory. No matter whose perspective had produced the descriptions, the common thread was a sense of the miraculous that the people of St. Sidryn's and the neighboring town of Abersford had beaten off the Buldorians, despite being short of fighting men. Not mentioned in all accounts, but prominent in those of St. Sidryn's abbot and Denes Vegga, senior militiaman leading the defense, was the role of Yozef Kolsko.

Culich already knew of Kolsko from reports of his mysterious discovery, lying unconscious on an Abersford beach, and his subsequent introduction of novel products. Culich had personal experience and appreciation of the new kerosene lanterns whose light was so much brighter than the older whale oil models. He also grudgingly converted to new soaps and toilet papers after cajoling by his wife, Breda, and he likewise admitted the new whiskeys rolled smoother on the tongue. He had no experience with other products whose value he accepted without personal experience, not needing to avail himself of new medical procedures or the "kotex" Breda assured him that all younger women treasured.

What was new from St. Sidryn's were reports that Kolsko had suggested not to defend the abbey walls against the raiders but to let them into the abbey courtyard and a trap. Everyone outside St. Sidryn's and Abersford, including Culich Keelan, had thought the idea insane. However, those who knew Kolsko were not so sure, and, more important, Denes Vegga had listened and followed the advice. Whether the successful defense was due to Kolsko's mad idea, sheer luck, or a miracle from God was actively argued, but it convinced Culich he needed to meet this outsider to Caedellium.

"Yes, Father, you wanted to see me?" queried Maera.

"Yes, there's something I wanted to discuss with you. First, though, you've seen all the reports coming out of Moreland about more and more sightings of Eywellese crossing the clan border into Moreland and now several small raids. Do you have any thoughts?"

She was blunt, as always. "The Narthani will try to take Moreland. The province is in the center of Caedellium, and once under Narthani control, they'd have a foothold in the island's heart. All indications are Moreland is their next target. The only question is *when* they move, and it's only a matter of time. If I guessed, I'd say a year, at most."

He grunted, having hoped for a different conclusion from his own.

"All the more important is the outcome of the conclave at Orosz City. The other clan hetmen need to understand what's happening and prepare their people for what may come. The conclave is the best chance to convince them."

"Do you really expect such recognition at this meeting, Father?"

Although her voice may have sounded like she was asking for an answer, he knew her opinion. "You're right. This is more a meeting out of duty and hope, rather than expectations. However, I'm obliged to try." Culich's face drew down into discouragement. "Since it's not a formal All-Clan Conclave, attendance by all hetmen isn't mandatory, nor do they even need to send a representative. The best I hope for is that two-thirds of the clans will be there and half of the hetmen. That's my hope, though my prediction is lower."

"A great Caedellium philosopher once said that all a man can do is his best," said Maera.

Culich smiled. It was something he himself was fond of saying. "Obviously, a great thinker."

"Obviously," replied Maera innocently.

He could always count on her to lift his mood. *God, what will I do if she marries and moves away?*

"And the reports from St. Sidryn's?" asked Culich. "You've read all those as well. I'm particularly interested in the references to the mysterious stranger who washed up near Abersford and is cutting quite a swath around St. Sidryn's and now farther afield. Sounds like something out of a child's story."

"True, but the fruits of his coming are evident here in Caernford and throughout the province. With the Narthani stopping trade for the poppy powder, you can understand how many would consider the ether of Kolsko an answer of prayers to God. And all the other things he's introduced, like kerosene. Everyone is switching to the new kerosene lamps as soon as they're available."

"Yes, it's amazing, though I admit I've been too occupied to pay enough attention to everything. But now, with the reports of the St. Sidryn's raid, I wonder again just who *is* this Yozef Kolsko?"

"Obviously, you need to meet him for yourself."

"That's what Abbot Sistian suggested when he was here after the raid, that I go to Abersford and evaluate for myself this mystery person, this Yozef Kolsko."

Maera raised an eyebrow. "*You* should go *there* to meet *him*. Not *he* come *here?*" Her tone conveyed her surprise that the clan hetman would consider traveling to meet a commoner who wasn't even a clan member.

"I have the impression Sistian is concerned that Kolsko might refuse to come. Certainly, Sistian has cautioned me several times to remember the man is not from Caedellium and has peculiar ideas. He also believes Kolsko is more comfortable where he is, and I should see him in that environment first, whatever that means. I know, it sounds odd and somehow mysterious in itself, but there you are."

"Well," she replied, "Abbot Sistian isn't one to play games, so I'd be tempted to follow his advice."

"I agree, and I've been thinking more and more about such a trip. Of course, that's not possible for a few sixdays, because I leave soon for the conclave meeting. What I'm thinking is that since you're always interested in rummaging through St. Sidryn's library, you could go in my place. I might then consider a visit sometime in the next few months after I hear your impressions."

Maera's normally serious expression morphed into delight, something that lightened his mood.

"Oh, Father, that would be wonderful. I love Sistian and Diera dearly and haven't visited the abbey in over two years."

Culich knew Maera would devour any new books the library had obtained since her last visit, and she was always interested in the medicant profession, St. Sidryn's being acknowledged as one of the best sites for medicant training and housing a modest-sized, though influential, group of scholastics. If she had been born into a different family, he suspected Maera might have entered either the medicant or the scholastic order, although such a vocation was impossible, given her family position.

"Plus, Father, I confess I'm interested in seeing this Yozef Kolsko myself. I have had several letters from Diera, and they often sound almost euphoric. Not just the ether, but other pieces of knowledge Diera believes will revolutionize treatments for illnesses and injuries. She didn't give details, which means I'm dying to learn more."

"It's settled then," he said. "Go ahead and plan your trip. I'll probably be gone three sixdays, so let's say we plan your visit to last a month."

# CHAPTER 3

# THE SWORD

The nightmares became less frequent, although they reinforced Yozef's trepidation about open warfare breaking out with the Narthani. He ruminated over what knowledge from Earth might help the islanders survive. Although he wasn't optimistic, his plans coalesced one evening while walking from Abersford to his house. The darkness and the alien stars helped focus his mind, there being no way to ignore, even for a moment, that this wasn't Earth. He had to act to survive.

As he walked the half-mile to his house, those stars provided the only light. The smaller of Anyar's two moons, Haedan, would rise soon. The larger moon, Aedan, wouldn't be seen until early morning. Even with both moons visible, they reflected a quarter of Luna's light at full phase. Compensating, more stars filled the Anyarian night than on Earth. He could see several prominent star clusters and the Anyar version of the Milky Way, here called the River of Stars, high in the sky. One tight star cluster looked as though it had scores of stars, which Yozef suspected meant it contained hundreds, with most stars not bright enough to be seen under the blaze of their bigger brethren. Even without the moons, the star array gave enough illumination that, once his eyes adjusted, making his way down the roads and the paths was easy.

The stars, the sea air drifting onshore this time of evening, and firefly-like Anyarian insects, of which several sizes flashed yellow or green, together often provided a reflective time in preparation for a night's sleep.

But not tonight. His thoughts refused to divert from the raid and future implications, and he spoke them aloud in English, a habit he indulged in when no Caedelli was within hearing.

"A raid is one thing, but what if the Narthani move on the other clans with an army? From what I can learn, the Caedelli have no direct experience with real warfare and seem naïve. Their idea of a battle is masses of horsemen charging one another. What would be the Narthani methods of war? If the military tactics here are on a similar timeline to the general levels of technology I've seen, then the Narthani have infantry formations, cannon, cavalry screening, reconnaissance and pursuit, and maneuvering tactics. War is a strict taskmaster. A mainland realm like Narthon will have developed sophisticated tactics.

"Just think of cannon alone. From descriptions I've heard, the Narthani warships mount cannon, so their army must use them, too. What about the Caedelli? I've neither heard nor seen anything about cannon. *Are* there any cannon or cannon making on Caedellium?

"And what about me? Lord knows, I wasn't ready to defend myself against anyone, much less experienced Buldorian mercenaries. There weren't many sword or musket fights in Berkeley. I'm lucky I survived with only the scar on my leg and the occasional limp.

"Carnigan didn't joke when he handed me that spear and told me not to stick him with it."

The volume of his voice had increased, as he continued talking out loud to himself. He stopped, afraid to arouse the Faughns and have them wondering what was wrong with him. However, somehow his mind had cleared. He had used the spear but didn't fool himself. Alone against a real opponent, he would have died quickly and in agony. He had to accept where he was and a level of potential violence far beyond anything he would have experienced in his old life. Worse, he had a bad feeling the raid on St. Sidryn's wouldn't be the only time it happened.

He shook his head, as if discarding conflicting thoughts and leaving clarity. No. There it was. He'd have to learn the basics of handling weapons. Maybe Carnigan or Denes could be persuaded to give lessons.

And what about the islanders? He'd introduced ether, pure alcohol, kerosene, and new soaps and papers, all from elementary aspects of chemistry. He should be able to come up with things that go bang, like cannons, grenades, mines, and rockets. He hoped.

## Cannon

The next morning, he hustled toward his shops clustered between Abersford and St. Sidryn's, eager to gather information. Cadwulf Beynom was his first target. The eldest son of Abbot Sistian and Abbess Diera Beynom was a mathematics prodigy who soaked up everything Yozef could remember about mathematics and was writing a textbook Cadwulf believed would revolutionize Anyarian mathematics. He was also Yozef's friend and the manager of the Bank of Abersford, the B of A, as Yozef insisted on referring to another of his innovations, the first formal bank on the island. Yozef found him at the bank talking with two staff members.

"Yes, I know what cannon are. I've seen them on ships, and Preddi City had cannon defending the harbor to discourage pirates, but the Narthani control Preddi now."

"No others?"

"Not that I'm aware of."

"Are any made on Caedellium?"

"No. Why do you ask?"

"Just some thoughts I've had. We need cannon in case of more raids, or worse, but you have to cast bronze or iron to make them."

"Casting? You mean like we use to make the bells for abbeys? They were all made in Preddi City before the Narthani came. New ones aren't possible since the Narthani took over Preddi Province."

*Hell, I should have thought of that. Bells and cannon! Both are casting chunks of metal. If you can make a bell, you should be able to use the same techniques for cannon . . . maybe.*

Yozef left Cadwulf to his ledgers and walked to Abersford. He now knew the concept of metal casting existed on Caedellium. He went straight to the alcohol distillery building and found Brellen Nyfork, the Preddi who'd escaped the Narthani with his family and now ran the alcohol and whiskey production. Brellen was working with two other men, cleaning one of the distillation set-ups, when Yozef motioned him aside.

"Brellen, do you know what a cannon is?"

"Of course. Why do you ask?"

"I understand that none are made on Caedellium, but that bells were made in Preddi City before the Narthani came. Did you know anything about the process?"

"No. I daily passed by the building where they were made in Preddi City and was inside a few times. Besides bells, they did metal work of all kinds— grills for windows and doors, decorative grillwork, cooking pots, wagon parts, and other smaller objects. As for the bells, I never saw how they did it."

Yozef's face fell. He had expected it unlikely Brellen knew bell making but had hoped for luck.

"Maybe my cousin Yawnfol would know."

"Who?"

"Yawnfol Nyfork is also an escaped Preddi. He lives in Clengoth and worked in a Preddi City metal shop for a few months before his family fled the Narthani. I'd ask him about bell making."

*Bingo!*

Five days later, Yozef returned from Clengoth, accompanied by a twenty-year-old Preddi as a technical "expert." Although Yawnfol Nyfork had worked for the Preddi City metalworker only two months, he had absorbed much of the basic knowledge required for metal casting. Not that he had practical experience casting cannon, but Yozef figured that would come with making mistakes.

A new workshop was built near Abersford in the "industrial park" alongside Yozef's workshops for ether, ethanol, kerosene, papers, and soaps. Nyfork and Cadwulf hired three more workers, and the cannon foundry began work.

The first goal was to produce a useable swivel gun, a small cannon mounted on a moveable stand or point to allow rapid pointing in different directions. Typically, they were a yard long, with a bore of no more than two and a half inches, and were used as a large shotgun to fire musket balls. While of no use against ships or any serious shielding, they *were* effective against personnel.

To Yozef's frustration, he couldn't remember the fine details of cannon making on Earth. When his airplane had collided with the Watchers' spacecraft, his injuries were so severe they had used microscopic autonomous machines, nanomachines, to help repair the injuries. They had also modified his mitochondria, the subcellular organelles that generate energy for metabolism, to compensate for Anyar's heavier gravity. A side effect of these treatments was his ability to recall sections of texts he had read. Unfortunately, the enhanced memory was sporadic. He could recall whole chapters of organic chemistry and the instruction manual for a strategy video game but could dredge up only a few details on cannon making. He would advise the workers, then would have to trust to trial and error.

After Yozef had a session with Yawnfol and the three other workers assigned to this new project, they decided on a two-inch bore and two-and-a half-foot barrel. They used bronze, the alloy of copper and tin. Yozef remembered that bronze was preferred over iron in early cannon, because iron tended to burst annoyingly often, with less than desirable consequences for gun crews. Until they had more experience, bronze was safer, plus the cannon firing the same charges could be lighter than the same bore iron cannon, an advantage for both horse artillery and manual maneuvering of the guns. The shop Yawnfol had been lured from in Clengoth specialized in bronze products, so Yozef arranged with copper and tin sources to obtain sufficient metal for experiments.

He also recalled that most bronze cannon on Earth were cast as a solid piece and then the bore drilled out. The problem was what to drill with. He assumed the best option would be drill bits of the hardest iron possible. However, since Yawnfol had explained how bells were cast hollow, Yozef figured they would try a single-step cast, and then any drilling would be to smooth out imperfections in the barrel's bore. To hold the position of the bore, the mold would be placed vertically and a hard-baked clay cylinder positioned inside the mold where the bore would be. They poured molten bronze into the mold, and when cooled, the clay center was drilled out. Next, they assessed if the bore were centered in the barrel by inserting a wooden rod the diameter of the bore into the barrel, any significant slanting of the bore could be seen by rolling the barrel and noting whether the rod stayed in approximately the same angle. If not, they'd melt down the barrel and recast.

Although Yozef cringed at the whole process, it worked. If the bore was uniform, a crude iron bit drilled the bore's internal surface reasonably smooth. They then drilled a vent in the closed end of the barrel to allow firing, and the barrel clamped to an immovable block to test-fire. They decided that if a barrel didn't rupture after ten firings, they would assume success.

It sounded simple and *was*, in principle. Performance of the simple was the problem. The twenty-fourth cast produced the first swivel barrel to survive mounting on a carriage. The second success came eleven casts later, the third on the next seventh cast, and after the fourth they were successful half of the time.

Yozef planned on eventually casting 12-pounder cannon—field pieces firing twelve-pound projectiles: round shot, two-inch grapeshot, or canister-holding musket balls—the standard cannon for Napoleon's armies and modified versions used by both sides during the U.S. Civil War. The first dozen 12-pounder casts were such disasters they gave up and tried 9-pounder barrels, with no better results.

They moved to 6-pounders, which Yozef remembered were used effectively by the United States in the Mexican War of 1846–1848 and in the U.S. Civil War as horse artillery—cannon mobile enough to accompany cavalry units. Anything smaller wouldn't be appreciatively better than the swivels his foundry already produced.

By the twenty-eighth pour, no 6-pounder bronze barrel was successful. Although Yozef thought they could eventually work through the problems, instinct told him time was running out for testing, with rumors and reports of increasing incursions into clan territories, and a new Preddi escapee detailing large-scale movements of combined infantry, cavalry, and artillery. If the Narthani moved soon, the only cannon Yozef and his men had produced were the swivel guns.

The next problem was how the swivels would be used in field operations and not just in fixed defense. They had to be mobile. In his overconfidence that they would succeed in producing 12-pounder cannon, Yozef had assigned a crew of carpenters and blacksmiths to make carriages and limbers with two and four spoked wheels, respectively. The two-wheeled carriage mounted the barrel on a crosspiece with bronze nubs, trunnions, on each side of the barrel, allowing the barrel to tilt up and down using a screw assembly between the barrel and the trail piece protruding back to the ground. The limbers would hold shot, powder, and an attachment for the gun carriage trail, and a team of six horses would pull the assembly.

A single swivel gun mounted on a carriage meant for a 12-pounder looked both ridiculous and of dubious impact in a field battle. Yozef had the workers mount three swivels to a single carriage after widening the cross piece between the wheels. An obvious problem glared with the first tests. The guns had to be reloaded and fired rapidly to be useful. Yozef was chagrined that he hadn't considered the reloading procedure when mounting three swivels to a single carriage. It simply wasn't possible for all three swivels to be simultaneously reloaded; there wasn't enough space in front of the muzzles. The two outer barrels could be reloaded at the same time, but the middle barrel had to wait for the two outer guns to be reloaded.

Disgusted, Yozef stood with Yawnfol and shook his head. "We'll have to stick to two barrels."

"What do we do with the two other carriages already built for three swivels?"

"It's too late to change those. We have seven barrels finished, so go ahead with two more," Yozef replied after a moment of thought. "Those nine swivels can finish the three carriages already built. Further carriages will just have two swivels. Make four of those, then go back to trying to figure out why we can't cast the 6-pounder barrels."

It wasn't as if he had any more advice to give on casting. At this point, the workers knew as much as he did.

Yozef switched his attention to what the swivels would fire. He had envisioned 12-pounders firing round shot at Narthani artillery batteries and canister at infantry. Using the swivels as counterbattery fire was out of the question, since whatever size and caliber the Narthani cannon, he couldn't imagine them not outranging the swivels. Against infantry, the swivels might have utility, but a single swivel canister charge fired only thirty musket balls. Given that the cone of balls coming out of the gun would result in many balls going over the heads of any targets or into the ground, only ten balls might actually hit infantry formations. Yozef had Yawnfol try balls smaller than the standard musket size. They would have less range and impact but more projectiles. He settled on a powder charge and a ball size that allowed eighty balls in a 2-inch bore canister round. The resulting weapon had a shorter effective range than Yozef had planned and penetrated less, but it was a compromise.

For maximum firing rates, the powder charges and the canister had to be pre-made. The first designs on Earth used cloth bags for the charge. The bag was rammed in, followed by the round shot. For canister, a container with the projectiles followed the charge bag, the container made of cloth, wood, or metal, depending on the type of shot and the level of technology. Wooden or metal cylinders were more efficient, but Yozef didn't want to wait for the development of cylinder production and settled on heavy cloth bags for both canister and grapeshot.

To produce the bags, Yozef thought of Buna Keller's clothing shop and her seamstresses. He had had a brief affair with Buna a few months earlier, broken off by her, to his relief, because she considered him too different from Caedelli men. For the task of making cannon powder and shot bags, she was perfect—hard working, meticulous, and venal. She'd do it, if paid well.

With everything assembled, the finished product might have looked pathetic to Yozef, although the Caedelli were suitably impressed with the results at the nearby test range. Ten man-sized straw dummies were placed at one hundred yards and covered with paper on the side facing the cannon to count canister hits. The dummies represented the distance covered by a line of fifty infantry standing shoulder-to-shoulder. Their three complete triple swivel carriages fired an initial salvo of 720 canister balls. All ten dummies showed at least one hit—most had three or more.

During the next sixday, they ran a series of test firings to determine effective ranges and optimal charges. A hundred and fifty yards seemed the maximum range to get enough hits to be effective, and they adjusted the charges to allow the musket balls to penetrate thick leather, simulating leather protection that Preddi escapees reported was worn by Narthani soldiers.

With a supply of ammunition on hand, they worked out a firing cycle. The powder bag was shoved into the open end of the barrel and rammed home with a wooden dowel, followed by the canister bag and a second application of the dowel. The carriage was faced toward the target, the barrels' elevations adjusted by screws, and gunpowder from a powder horn tapped into the firing vents. A thin wooden rod was used to ignite the powder in the vent; its end was kept glowing in an ember chamber carried by one of the crew. The barrels were fired sequentially and the carriage quickly repositioned after each recoil. After firing, a rod with a wet cloth on the end was run down each bore to quench any embers, preparing the barrels for the next firing cycle.

As soon as the first triple-gunned carriage was ready, Denes selected eight men as potential gun crew leaders. While trials had shown that a six-man crew was the minimum necessary for an optimal rate of firing, Yozef insisted on an eight-man crew. He didn't elaborate that in battles, inevitable casualties meant crews needed enough men to ensure the guns were manned and fired as long as possible.

The original eight men drilled for days until they could operate the guns blindfolded and fire the outer barrels every thirty seconds. Denes appointed the original eight men as gun crew leaders and they, in turn, trained other men, half from the Abersford area and the other half brought in from Clengoth. Within another two sixdays, eighty gun crew members were trained, hopefully well enough not to kill themselves or others on their side, if forced into a battle.

## Gunpowder

Successful development of the swivel gun carriages led to unanticipated discoveries, as Yozef had found with many projects. This time, it was Denes who broke the news after witnessing another test firing.

"I can see how these 'swivel' guns, as you call them, might be useful in some circumstances, but they must use a lot of gunpowder, which is in short supply."

"Short—!" Yozef turned to Denes with dumbfounded look. "I guess I hadn't thought where the gunpowder is coming from. Yawnfol! Come here."

The young foundry supervisor trotted over. "Yes, Yozef, a good test. Every Narthani dummy was hit at least once."

"Yawnfol, where do you get the gunpowder for the tests?"

"Oh, yes, that's been a problem. We ask around for anyone willing to part with a few spoonfuls, and traders as far as Hewell Province know to look for any sources. The cost is more coin than we expected, but you told us not to worry about that."

"Well, Jesus Christ! Can't anything go easy?" a red-faced Yozef yelled.

Denes and Yawnfol both stepped back, startled, neither man knowing what Yozef said, because he'd used English, and they'd never witnessed such a display from him.

Yozef stomped away forty feet and stared at the eastern peaks, fuming to himself. *I've got to stay sharper. I'm getting too involved in the details of my brilliant ideas and ignoring obvious issues. With the cannon, first I was oblivious to the loading problem with three barrels, and I'm just now learning about the gunpowder shortage. Such mistakes will get me or others killed.*

With a cooler head, he walked back to the puzzled Denes and Yawnfol, hearing the former tell the latter, "Don't worry, he's not mad at you, he's just Yozef Kolsko and acts odd at times."

"I'm sorry, I was only surprised to hear we're short of gunpowder. Isn't it made here on Caedellium?"

"Of course," said Denes, "many know how to make it. It's just that the crystal ingredient is scarce. No one likes to dig around voiding pits or animal manure piles, and even that source is becoming harder to find. Much of the gunpowder was imported by traders to Preddi City until the Narthani took control."

Potassium nitrate. Those were the crystals Denes referred to. The other two ingredients, carbon and sulfur, were easier to find, but the islanders didn't seem to know about mineral deposits or guano. Here was where Yozef's fertilizer project would pay off.

He had discovered deep guano deposits covering the cliffs of an inlet and offshore rock formations a two-hour hike west of Abersford along the unpopulated coast toward Gwillamer Province. Although the islanders used manure as fertilizer, the use of guano had been unknown. Cadwulf had been correctly dubious that Keelan farmers would be interested, because they already had trouble selling excess crops now that the Narthani had blocked off-island trade. However, Yozef persisted, asserting that the time would come for increased yields, either for restarted trade or unforeseen needs for food.

What he hadn't told Cadwulf or anyone else was that guano was a source of potassium nitrate and sodium nitrate, both of which could be used to make black powder. He had kept that use in the back of his mind and now used it to salve his self-castigation.

"I think we can solve the gunpowder shortage problem. I believe I know how to prepare a substance to replace the crystals."

"How would you—" blurted Yawnfol, before Denes elbowed him sharply in the ribs.

"If Yozef says he knows how, it's best to just stand back and watch what happens. His ideas don't always work, but enough do to reserve judgment."

"All right," said the Preddi worker, rubbing the impact point. "No reason to beat on me."

Yozef had ignored the interchange. Lost in thought, he spoke aloud. "Let's see, charcoal's the easy ingredient, and the people here know of sulfur, so there must be deposits. Nitrates are the limiting factor. They're the main component of gunpowder and provide rapid oxidation for the reaction. Here come my guano deposits at Birdshit Bay."

The aforementioned locale was descriptive of large guano deposits from Anyarian murvors, the local flying creatures filling the niche of terrestrial birds. After he had stumbled on these guano deposits, he had registered ownership of the area. Tests of the guano as fertilizer and elementary chemical tests had confirmed high levels of nitrates, in both the sodium and the potassium forms. Both could be used to make gunpowder, although the sodium version absorbed moisture, and the resulting gunpowder needed to be used within weeks or stabilized by coating the gunpowder grains with graphite, a natural mineral he knew existed on the island, because it was commonly used as a lubricant on wheel axles.

"I'll need to get a staff to work on this," Yozef continued in a mix of English and Caedelli, the meaning equally obscure to the two listeners. "Probably apothecaries or their apprentices. I can give them clues on how to purify nitrates from the guano and convert the sodium form to potassium, if necessary. I don't know the exact composition of the guano, so they'll have to experiment with various precipitations and leachings."

The free flow continued, with Denes bemused and Yawnfol confused.

"Is he talking to us?" queried the Preddi worker.

"No. To himself. I think. Although . . . " Denes didn't continue, having given no credence to rumors of Yozef communicating with the unseen. While the militiaman wasn't religious, one could never be sure.

"Once we have the gunpowder source licked, we can experiment with rockets, grenades, and mines." Yozef's voice radiated excitement.

Within two sixdays, one more shop was added to Yozef's cluster. The gunpowder facility was located several hundred yards distant from the others and within a circle of large boulders, supplemented with masonry walls in gaps. If the experiments went well, he figured to set up a larger production facility far enough distant that accidents would be confined to a single facility.

Yozef hired four apprentices, two from Caernford and two from a Hewell Province abbey whose scholasticum specialized in apothecary knowledge. Yozef wrote out everything he could remember about gunpowder production, provided the staff with connections to sources of materials, drilled them to distraction on safety, and turned them loose. Two months later, after one rebuilding of the shop structure, several minor burns, one broken arm, one worker replaced when he decided the work was too dangerous, and only occasional peeks on progress by Yozef, the shop produced the first gunpowder using murvor guano as the nitrate source.

Yozef put aside dreams of rockets, grenades, and mines when he decided that more development of fuses was needed before handing such products to the islanders. He ordered a larger facility built a mile from Abersford and focused on gunpowder for muskets and cannon.

It was time to better prepare himself for the Narthani.

# CHAPTER 4

# SELF-DEFENSE

Life in Abersford and St. Sidryn's returned to a semblance of normal, yet *only* a semblance. Tradesman worked in their shops, farmers farmed, mothers mothered, and smithies smithed. Yet confidence in what was normal didn't recover. Faces were sterner, arguments erupted faster, Godsday services were more heavily attended, and the three pubs in Abersford boomed.

Another difference in daily life was that most men and some women now bore one or more weapons. They could have gone armed before the raid, but there had been no sense of imminent danger. No longer. The people felt safer having a weapon at hand, although the comfort was tempered by not forgetting why they carried a pistol, a sword, or a knife.

Another change was increased formal martial training. The existing three Thirds, the local levy of fighting men, expanded to add farmers and miners farther distant than before and required them to take part in training and minimal drills. In addition, the population of the Abersford area continued to grow to fill Yozef's need for workers. Eighty men now composed each Third, compared to the previous fifty. Also organized was a reserve militia of younger and older men, plus weapons training for able women, the latter eliciting controversy among some men until the majority of women made it clear they, too, were defenders of family and clan.

Neither was Yozef immune from a changed attitude. He understood that luck had carried him through the courtyard fight with only the leg scar. If he'd faced one of the Buldorians by himself for even a few seconds, he would have died in the courtyard. Yozef had helped protect Carnigan's flank, yet he was only slightly more effective than bales of hay.

This wasn't Berkeley or San Diego, his previous home and where he grew up, respectively. It was hard enough accepting what had happened and finding a new life, but more was needed. While he prayed that the raid was the last real fight he would experience, he needed to be better prepared for even an elementary defense of himself.

On yet another morning he woke to the nightmares and cold sweat dampening the bed, as he remembered those abbey courtyard minutes that had seemed to last hours: the yells, the screams, the firearms, the whistling of musket and pistol balls passing nearby, the clash of metal, the "sssst" of blades swinging and missing, and, worse, the sound of blades meeting flesh.

He got out of bed naked and looked at himself in a mirror, not for the first time. The man in the mirror only *resembled* Joseph Colsco. In his previous life, he had never been an active person and had told himself muscles weren't needed in a tech society. Then, his only concern was keeping an eye on an incipient pot belly. That wasn't who looked back at him now. This body had clearly defined musculature. He made the classic poise to display biceps. The knotted muscle existed where it hadn't on Earth. Harlie had said that the changes the Watchers made to him would help compensate for Anyar's higher gravity. Was that what he saw?

He looked harder at the face in the mirror, by now accustomed to seeing and caring for the beard, but the color had changed. His mousy light brown hair had turned a darker brown in the first months on Anyar, the original shade existing only in a few lighter streaks.

He kept staring. Hair, beard, physique. This wasn't who he had been, it was who he *was*. He needed to discard lingering past images.

Standing there in the early morning, with light coming through the windows, he decided to survive on Anyar to as old an age as possible, and to pass on as much knowledge as he could, he needed to be better prepared, both in body and in minimal weapons training.

The first objective was the easiest. On Caedellium, physical condition counted more than it did on Earth. He needed to be as fit as he could make himself, including both basic strength and endurance, the latter having the additional benefit of being able to run away farther and faster.

Setting up a "weight room" contributed to the stories circulating.

"You want what?" asked a puzzled Brak Faughn.

"A room about fifteen-feet square added to the house off my bedroom. It should connect to the bedroom and have a door to the outside."

"That's easy 'nough, but why do you need another room?"

Yozef had prepared an answer for this expected question. "My people believe that to remain healthy, especially men, the body needs to be used and used vigorously. Most people get this through their everyday work."

Brak nodded approvingly. "Yes, the *Word* sez God blesses those who toil by the sweat of their brow."

"Very true," said Yozef. "As you know, I spend most of my days meeting with workers and overseeing shops and seldom do hard work. Since it is impractical for me to spend enough hours at honest hard work to stay healthy, the only solution is to spend shorter times in vigorous activity. By spending a few minutes several times a sixday lifting heavy weights by methods my people have developed, I can maintain better health and come closer to what the *Word* says."

Brak looked dubious. "I guess I cun see it, but I never heard of it here on Caedellium. Sum of the shopkeepers could use doin' the same."

"The weights will help, but, of course, I won't sweat as much as if I was working in a field or a smithy. So, to let myself sweat more and to help strengthen my heart, I'll also run occasionally."

"Run? Run where?"

"Oh, just around here. Maybe to the village or the abbey and back. Maybe out to the beach."

"Everyone gonna think you've gon' mad. That or there's somethin' wrong. Like another raid."

"They'll get used to it. If anyone asks, you can explain why I'm doing it."

The cannon foundry made the weights, to the similar confusion of the workers there and with the same explanations as he gave Brak. However, because it was "Yozef acting strange," to which they had all become accustomed, the rationale passed with a shrug.

By necessity, the running placed Yozef in full view of any citizen along his route of the day. The initial stares and the guarded behavior soon devolved into cheerful acceptance of one more of his eccentricities.

## Using Weapons

Arranging for weapons training took less explanation, the ability to defend oneself and others being taken for granted. Never having touched a firearm before—and hundreds of hours at *Call of Duty* and other video games didn't qualify—made familiarity a priority. Instruction from Filtin Fuller, his worker and friend, provided enough basics to continue practicing with flintlock muskets and pistols on his own, and Yozef soon decided it was fun.

Not so with blade weapons. Merely looking at the edges of swords, axes, spears, and everything else that could be put to such use made him queasy. But *needs* ruled. He *needed* to have a remote chance of survival should occasion arise where familiarity was critical.

Again, he required an instructor. Cadwulf was out, because he was too young, and Yozef couldn't imagine him being experienced at dicing someone. Carnigan was out as an instructor, since his fighting ability was tied to his prodigious strength. However, Denes provided a lead when Yozef explained what he wanted and pointed him to Wyfor Kales, a scrawny, fiftyish man of Yozef's height, missing a few teeth, bearing several prominent scars, and with a mean look to his eyes. Kales was one of the few islanders to have spent time off the island, including over twenty years of employment, doing what no one knew the details.

"Trust me, Yozef. If you want to learn about blades, Kales is your man." Denes was right.

Carnigan directed Yozef to Kales one evening in the Snarling Graeko.

"Hello, Ser Kales. We've never met before. I'm Yozef Kolsko."

"As if anyone 'round here doesn't know who you are," deadpanned Kales.

"Yes, well, Denes Vegga recommended you."

"Vegga, huh. He's not bad," Kales said grudgingly. "And why would he point you to me?"

"I'm not from Caedellium, and in my homeland I never learned to use weapons, particularly blades. You know . . . swords, spears, whatever. The recent raid showed me I need to learn enough to have a chance to defend myself and others. When I asked Denes who he would recommend instructing me, he suggested you."

Kales stared at Yozef with a blank face. A minute passed. Yozef could feel a sheen of sweat forming on his forehead.

Had he insulted Kales? Maybe this wasn't such a good idea.

"I can pay you quite well for any instruction," Yozef blurted.

Kales's mouth twitched. "Vegga. He's all right. On the other hand, they say you're *very* odd, but it's been a more interesting place to live since you arrived. As for the raid, too bad I wasn't here, instead of in Clengoth. I coulda taken care of myself, but I have family here, brothers and their kids. People say you helped beat off those Buldorian shitheads, plus my brother Elrin here in

Abersford tells me your medicines saved his wife. So I'll teach you the fundamentals, enough to keep you alive for a few seconds, if you find yourself facing an average man."

Yozef exhaled.

*I guess that means he's not going kill me outright for some insult or intrusion. And a few seconds? Well, that's something. Sometimes you only need a few seconds to run.*

"You won't need to pay me. I got plenty a coin. An hour a day, three days a sixday. Just before midday meal. I'll set the days. You either come those days, or we forget it. We start tomorrow."

With those words, Kales picked up his stein of beer and walked to a table with several men playing an Anyar card game. Yozef stood and watched.

*Okay, so social graces aren't his strong point, but I hope his fighting instruction is.*

Thus began instruction on the mayhem that could be done with anything sharp. Kales seldom had a friendly word, being matter-of-fact in the means and consequences of the violent application of sharp instruments to a human body. During the raid, Yozef had clumsily stuck a Buldorian with his spear, but in the turmoil and his fear, he didn't recollect details. Kales corrected this oversight. At the third session, Kales had several burlap bags of wet sand and had Yozef practice stabbing with knives of various designs.

"It gives a good first impression of what it feels like to run a blade into someone. The wet sand has about the same resistance to a blade as a man's body," Kales explained in a tone Yozef might have used to clarify a law of chemistry—cool, objective, and authoritative.

Yozef didn't have the nerve to ask how Kales knew the feeling of sticking a knife into a human body.

A month later, when Yozef arrived for his session, Kales had a live yearling calf. At first, Yozef was afraid Kales expected him to kill it, but Kales cut its throat and hung it in a tree to let Yozef get the look and feel for driving a knife and a sword into a flesh-and-blood body.

The training was intense, and Kales had no compunction against inflicting pain when they sparred with wooden copies, each hour leaving Yozef with a collection of bruises from stabs and slashes. He was surprised at the complexity of using a spear, as Kales disillusioned Yozef's preconceptions in the first session. Swords were even more difficult. It took only seconds for Kales to either disarm Yozef or make a mock fatal touch.

"Don't be discouraged," Kales said, after noting Yozef's frustration. "You're not likely to get in a sword fight with anyone as good as me. If you can get so you can survive ten seconds of my attacking, you'll be good enough to defeat almost anyone."

Yozef didn't know whether Wyfor was bragging but applied himself diligently, accepting the bruises. Then one day Kales broke off his attack, stepped back, and smiled—a rarity.

"Nicely done, Yozef. You've done better than I expected. I told you the goal was to last ten seconds, and you just doubled that."

It was with knives where Yozef exceeded both of their expectations. To Kales, "knives" meant two men with knives using those plus every part of their bodies. Yozef's familiarity with the concepts of martial arts from movies and TV, even if with no direct personal experience, meant Kales didn't have to explain why fists, elbows, foreheads, knees, and feet were important in a knife fight. Yozef's bigger size and increasing strength helped compensate for Kales's speed and experience. Yozef still lost every mock knife fight, though Kales needed more time to win and came away with bruises of his own. The time it took Kales to win also increased, and several times Yozef thought, in error, that he was about to win.

Finally, one day Yozef arrived for his lesson to find Kales grinning.

"I think I've taught you enough to satisfy your goal: being able to minimally defend yourself and others. You're actually much better than that. You're strong for your size and unusually quick. Your biggest weakness is lack of experience in actual fighting, something I can't give you. We could continue, and you would improve, but considering who you are and the unlikelihood you would need to improve to that degree, I doubt your time is well spent with more lessons, though I'll spar with you occasionally if you like."

"You say I'm good. Then why am I always the one to get killed every time we spar?"

Kales looked genuinely amused.

"That's because you're facing *me*. Nothing personal, but you stand no chance against me, nor would most anyone else here on Caedellium. Maybe Carnigan, because he's so huge and strong, but for him I'd just stay out of his reach, and he couldn't catch me."

"In that case, I'll be sure to always try to stay on your good side," quipped Yozef.

Kales's smile broadened. "I doubt that'll be a problem. I've grown a little fond of you, in a way. Goodbye."

With that surprising statement and terse dismissal, Kales walked away, and Yozef's lessons in blade fighting were over.

# CHAPTER 5

# WHAT HAPPENED AT ST. SIDRYN'S?

Two months had passed since the failed Buldorian raid on Keelan. General Akuyun walked along the harbor piers with Assessor Hizer, as they stretched their legs and took in sea air. Each man thought himself too tied to his office.

"Still no solid information on what happened on the Keelan raid?" Akuyun asked.

Hizer shook his head. "Only what our agents in place transmit and our own suppositions, since the Buldorians vanished back home, I assume, after the raid. All we can say is that the main action was an assault on the local abbey of . . . what was it? Yes, St. Sidryn's. Of no particular military significance, but one of the most respected of their abbey complexes, particularly for their medicant training and the reputation of the abbey's abbot . . ." He thumbed through his memory. "Sistian Beynom. Also a known lifelong friend of the Keelan hetman and an unofficial advisor.

"Fragmented reports indicate a high number of Buldorian casualties and relatively few islanders. Whatever happened, it was a rout, and the Buldorians withdrew and headed for home."

"Do you see any relation to our conclusion that the Keelanders and their allies are the most potentially troublesome for our overall mission?"

"Nothing we can definitively determine," replied Hizer. "It may just be bad intelligence on their defenses, mistakes on the part of the Buldorians, or who knows what else?"

"What about putting more agents in place in Keelan?" asked Akuyun.

"Worth considering, but there's the danger of alerting them to those already in place. We'd need to balance the potential gain of more information versus the losses if they realize our agents are among them, and they root them out."

"For more information alone I'd be hesitant, but I'm inclined to be in favor of more Keelan agents in place, if we decide to eliminate their hetman."

"That's my own thinking," said Hizer. "Once we move on Moreland, everything will change, anyway."

"All right. See if you can insert a couple more agents into the Keelan capital. Obviously, these will have to be capable of more direct action than the others, in case we move against their hetman."

## Sowing Confusion

The two men stopped when a work crew of twenty men rounded a corner. The brown tunics and the leather collars identified them as slaves, either Preddi or imported from other conquered peoples. They weren't shackled, and a single guard led them, signaling they were docile enough not to require more security or supervision.

"Sir!" exclaimed the infantry non-com soldier with cavus rank markings. "Sorry, sir. Didn't see you coming."

"No problem, Cavus . . . Keznak, isn't it?" said Akuyun.

"Yes, sir!" said the non-com, thrusting out his chest farther at the mission commander who knew his name, though they'd never spoken.

"Carry on. I'm sure you have important work for these men. I'm always glad that experienced soldiers like you are with me on missions."

Hizer smiled, as the non-com hustled the slaves off. "Of course, Okan, if he was that valuable, his unit would have him leading twenty men typical of the cavus rank, not slaves."

"Yes, but he's still valuable, no matter what his assignments, and there's no reason for him not to think the officers don't appreciate his efforts, no matter how high their positions."

They walked out to the end of a pier and watched a recently arrived cargo ship being unloaded of general supplies, mail, and dispatches from Narthon— and a new shipment of gunpowder, if Akuyun remembered the manifest summary he'd seen first thing that morning.

"Well, I think we've put off enough sitting on our butts at our desks for today. I have some paperwork to do, before riding with Zulfa this afternoon to witness a field exercise, so we'd better head back," said Akuyun. "While we do, anything new from your agents?"

Hizer was an assessor, tasked by the Narthani High Command to give independent evaluations on mission progress and commanders' performances. While not in the formal chain of command, Akuyun had asked him to serve as the intelligence coordinator for the mission, a somewhat unusual arrangement, but within the scope of Akuyun's and Hizer's assignments, as least as they both agreed to define those scopes. Akuyun's query involved efforts to suborn Caedellium clans through deception of true intentions by means of disinformation, false rumors, decoy military movements, bribes, facilitation of conflicts between clans, promises of substantial long-term rewards for cooperation, and implied threats for non-cooperation following the inevitable Narthani victory.

"Nothing new," said Hizer. "We've both seen Admiral Kalcan's reports of the ongoing raids and patrols along the entire Caedellium coast. According to my agents within several of the coastal provinces, we're having varying levels of success in tying down available clan fighting capabilities. I'm reasonably confident that the Pewitt and Swavebroke clans have put too many of their fighting men at coastal posts to contribute to a coalition against us.

"I also believe we've been successful in neutralizing the Nyvaks and Pawell clans. Nyvaks is geographically connected to the island only by a narrow isthmus, which probably contributed to their feeling less cultural connection to the other clans. They've historically chafed at their territory. Their histories and legends say the clan was chased there by stronger clans in the early century of settling the island. Concurrently, the Pawell Clan, which sits on the other end of that isthmus, is justifiably wary of Nyvaks. We've given both clans bribes and promises to the Nyvaks hetman that we intend no interest in his province or the others in the northeast portion of Caedellium, and we wouldn't object to a future where Nyvaks expands into several neighboring provinces. We also continue to trade with Nyvaks, essentially a continuing bribe—the only clan where such trading is still ongoing, I'll add, and only possible to be kept hidden by their geographic remoteness from the other clans.

"With Pawell, we continue to spread rumors and false information about the Nyvaks planning an invasion that, when combined with the Admiral Kalcan's operations, will freeze Pawell from any action outside their province.

"Similar fomenting of distrust between clans has been less successful elsewhere, although we've raised suspicions in Swavebroke about Farkesh intentions. Swavebroke is also isolationist. Their hetman is on the dull side and wouldn't understand any strategy or tactic beyond his own borders, so Swavebroke is not expected to respond.

"We're uncertain about the Skouks Clan on the north coast of Caedellium. The only agent we have in place there has reported strong disagreements between the hetman and a majority of the boyermen, with the hetman more inclined to oppose any move by us on other clans, while the boyermen agree only if a neighboring clan is directly threatened.

"Less encouraging are the failures with the other northern provinces—Farkesh, Vandinke, and Bultecki. These, along with Skouks and Nyvaks, are descended from a different migration to the island than the other clans, and there remains friction between the descendants of these two migrations. These clans also have a longer history of inter-clan conflicts. We expected to be more successful, but Farkesh and Vandinke may join a coalition at some point, while Bultecki has close ties to the Orosz Clan and would follow their lead. However, for the immediate future we see none of these clans as major factors.

"There's also an irksome report out of Adris. Their hetman was an isolationist, but he died last year, and his son is different. He's held several meetings with other hetmen, particularly Hetman Keelan. We don't know the topics of the meetings, but I'm not ruling out Adris forming a tighter connection to the Keelan and the two clans in their Tri-Clan Alliance."

"And you still think it unlikely that more than four or five clans will come to Moreland's aid?"

"I now think the number could go as high as six or seven, but that should still pose no problem. I've estimated to Zulfa that the number of horsemen he might face is between eight and fourteen thousand. And that's all horsemen. They still aren't familiar with infantry tactics, plus they lack artillery."

"I agree," said Akuyun. "Eight to fourteen thousand horsemen could be handled, but we need to keep it at those numbers. Even without infantry and artillery, should all the clans commit with every available man, we'd face upward of fifty thousand light cavalry. Once we move, it needs to be quick."

"I've seen no sign of a unified front against us, but you're right, we need to be expeditious once you decide it's time to move to the next phase."

## Aivacs Zulfa

General Okan Akuyun and Brigadier Aivacs Zulfa rode back the six miles to Preddi City after spending part of the afternoon inspecting two infantry units, one unit drilling in mixed pike and musket defense and assaults and the other unit building a bridge to a newly opened copper mine. Akuyun could have listened to or read reports of both units' activities, but he got out of his office whenever possible. He also wanted to hear Zulfa's thinking directly about their coming move against the other clans. As troop commander, Zulfa would plan campaign details. Akuyun would offer advice but intervene only if he foresaw major problems. He believed in carefully picking his subordinates and letting them do their jobs.

"So that's my summary plan, Okan." They were on a first-name basis when alone or with the other senior officers.

"Appears to be a solid plan, Aivacs. You have the men shaping up nicely. The drills we saw this morning may not be as smooth as either of us would like, but considering the quality of men we have and the need to integrate two different sets of men sent to us, all in all, I think they'll do fine."

"It just chafes me to be drilling them with pike formations. They'll only have to all be retrained with all muskets when they return to Narthon. I know the High Command didn't see the need to change for this mission, since the Caedelli pose no serious threat, but why bother with pikes at all? I thought the Battle of Three Rivers against the Fuomi settled that. Their solid musket blocks decimated our pike formations."

"While I can't say I disagree," Akuyun said, "they had already committed the units to our mission and saw no need to change. Again, we may question the High Command's wisdom, but it's our job to work with what they give us."

"I know, I know, and we'll perform as necessary, still . . ."

"No 'stills.' This unit and others will do well, and that's to your credit. However, I think I have a pleasant piece of news for you. The unit building the bridge we looked at is almost finished, and it'll be the last such assignment for them or any other unit. From this point on, all focus will be on training for the coming campaign."

Zulfa pumped a fist. "Yes! Finally, stop with the digging and hammering."

Although their troops' primary mission was to subdue the Caedelli clans, the massive influx of Narthani settlers required military support in developing infrastructure. The mission included larger-than-normal engineering sections, but the engineers needed workers to build bridges, roads, canals, structures, and defenses. Although slaves were useful, some projects needed more disciplined workers. In the previous year, the number of Narthani civilians rose beyond a hundred thousand, and the troops had spent a third or more of their time supporting the engineers, to Zulfa's annoyance.

"It's been too hard getting larger units together for any length of time. Now we can work more on unit cohesion and coordination."

The two men and their escorting guards rode through the streets of Preddi City to the Narthani headquarters. As always, Akuyun kept to rigid schedules, and they arrived at the end of the hours slotted to Zulfa and time for a meeting with Admiral Morfred Kalcan, who waved as he walked to greet them.

"Okan, Aivacs, I assume you've been on those horses for hours. How you stand it, I don't know. Stupid, smelly creatures that look to throw you off at any opportunity." Kalcan's aversion to horses was even worse than most sailors', for good reason. His horsemanship was atrocious, with the admiral falling off even the tamest horse, as witnessed by both Akuyun and Zulfa.

"Nonsense, Morfred. If you'd practice a little more, you'd stay on longer."

"By that logic, you should sail around on my ships more often to cure your seasickness." Zulfa was the antithesis of a sailor and got queasy crossing a lake.

Both men laughed. It was a routine exchange.

"Well, I'll be off then, General Akuyun," said Zulfa, switching back to formal mode.

"Gentleman, unfortunately, we don't have a general staff meeting for another sixday, but before we part, I, and I'm sure Morfred also, want to offer congratulations to Brigadier Zulfa. I understand from my wife, Rabia, that a child was born in the Zulfa household from your woman, Panira."

Admiral Kalcan slapped Zulfa on the back, shouting, "Good going, Aivacs! That's two from Panira, if I recall."

A broad smile broke on the face of the usually impassive Zulfa. "Yes, first a boy, Turmin, who's now almost two, and yesterday a girl, Nizla. Both baby and mother are doing well."

Zulfa could have brought his family with him when he posted to the Caedellium mission, but his wife had been heavy with child, and one of their other three children had a long-term weakness that needed constant attention. He hadn't realized the posting to Caedellium would last more than two years. He and his wife had agreed he needed a woman, neither expecting him to remain celibate.

Zulfa's wife played a central role in choosing a seventeen-year-old girl, Panira, the daughter of one of Zulfa's retainers back in Narthon. Her family was honored to accept the offer to have one of their daughters join the Zulfa household. Her position would be as a "second wife"—effectively a concubine. There could be many such second wives, but resulting children were formally the children of the first wife. For Panira, her children might not be major inheritors of the father, but would have education, contacts, and more opportunities than otherwise possible. It was an accepted and respectable position in Narthani society, particularly for a lower-caste Narthani family, descendants of a people absorbed into the Narthon Empire eighty years previously. They were of the core of Narthani society, yet had no expectations of rising into higher levels for another generation or more, without associating with the higher levels of society, of which Zulfa's immediate and extended family was part.

The daughter, once informed of the arrangement, acquiesced, as expected. Not that she had a choice, but Zulfa wouldn't have taken her if she were unwilling. It had proved a good decision. The girl managed his Caedellium residence, which included several local slaves and the aides and the guards of Zulfa's who resided within the villa he had appropriated from a wealthy Preddi family

Akuyun's wife, Rabia, was a friend of Panira's, an uncommon connection between a wife and a concubine in another household, but Rabia and Akuyun both approved of the young woman and the stability she gave Zulfa, allowing him to focus on his duties.

The two years Zulfa had expected stretched into four. He exchanged letters with his wife, but his children were growing up without him. The separation hit him hard recently when his oldest son, now eight years old, began writing letters to a father he hardly remembered. If he didn't get back soon, Zulfa wondered whether the children at home would ever form the level of connection he had had with *his* father.

# CHAPTER 6

# THE PEN

The islanders often reinforced Yozef's opinion of their acumen and industry. They might be backward in technology compared to Earth, yet once given direction, they ran with it. None of his earlier shops needed his attention. The Caedelli supervisors and staff implemented his initial instructions and developed further products and processes by experimentation. He seldom stopped at the workshops for ether, alcohol, papers, or soaps, while devoting only moderately more time to keeping abreast of progress on the cannon and gunpowder projects. Business details he left to Cadwulf and the staff at the Bank of Abersford.

It was after a meeting to discuss expanding kerosene production that Cadwulf commented on Yozef's recent activity.

"Yozef, I hope you don't mind my asking, but recently you're spending most of your time preparing for fighting. Not that I don't think it important to do whatever we can in case the Buldorians or the Narthani come again, but I've seen you more as the scholastic type."

"I am, but we can't always do what we want. My people have a saying: 'The quill is mightier than the sword,' though it's more a philosophical proposition than one rooted in the real world. While I agree that over time, often what a person writes can have more influence than another person's conquests, time and the effect of the present can't be ignored. The quill may be mightier long term, but the sword wins short term.

"To do what I'm best at, I and everyone here have to survive whatever the Narthani plan. I hope my projects can help both Keelan and me to survive."

What Yozef didn't tell Cadwulf was that in this case, the "quill" was his journals. He needed time to write as much as he could remember. Soon after he'd recovered from the shock of being cast away on Anyar, he recognized that his knowledge of Earth science would advance human civilization on Anyar by centuries. The problem was that there was no way to suddenly incorporate what he knew into the existing civilization. Knowledge didn't exist in a vacuum. Each piece needed to fit into a society's existing knowledge base and philosophical principles.

Added to this problem was fear for his own safety, if he attempted to introduce knowledge violating religious or cultural precepts he didn't even know existed. As a science student, he knew of the fate of early scientists who contradicted the Catholic Church's teachings on astronomy around 1600 AD: Giordano Bruno, a Dominican friar, was burned at the stake for heresy, and Galileo, thirty years later, was threatened with the same fate, until he recanted. Yozef had estimated Anyarian technology to be at approximately Earth's level around 1700, so he treaded lightly at first.

As time passed and he gained more confidence, he had used elementary chemistry to introduce new products and processes without experiencing serious repercussions. Mathematics had also been safe, because it was seen as more abstract than something that directly impacted beliefs. The Caedelli were not yet aware of how it permeated everything else.

He had also given St. Sidryn's medicants, members of the medical order of the Caedelli service society, ether, ethanol as an antiseptic, and knowledge of the body's organs and physiology, being very careful not to introduce too much too soon and retreating into feigned ignorance at warning signs.

Still, these were minor advances. He assumed he would transfer only a fraction of what he knew within his life span. To reach beyond that time, he wrote in English two sets of secret journals. One set recounted how he had come to Anyar and everything he could remember about Earth history. He intended that no one read this set while he lived, but he wanted there to be a record of what had happened to him to tell future Anyarians where they came from.

The second set of journals he also wrote in English, but it was everything he remembered about science and mathematics. The Watchers, aliens who had saved him after colliding with his airliner, had modified his DNA for more efficient energy production and utilization. The AI, Harlie, said it was to compensate for Anyar's gravity being higher than Earth's. Whether intended or not, a side effect was enhanced memory for previous experiences. Concentrating brought forth entire pages of text and lessons from his undergraduate and graduate courses. There were annoying gaps, paragraphs, or pages missing from a chapter, but the totality was more advanced than anything likely to exist on Anyar for a century or more, especially in physics, geology, biology, biochemistry, and, most of all, chemistry—his specialty.

He spent many hours with quill and ink filling blank bound journals with carefully stroked words, equations, and diagrams. Page after page, journal after journal. His latest efforts focused on electromagnetism and Maxwell's equations and a second journal on the elements of molecular genetics and the structure of DNA. He hadn't time to translate everything into Caedelli, so he expanded the English/Caedelli dictionary, which he'd begun when first learning the language, to include a Caedelli explanation of English grammar—the dictionary and the grammar to be stored with the science journals. At some future time, whether in his lifetime or not, the science journal set would be available. Initially, he'd thought the time to reveal this set would be after his death, but after the raid on St. Sidryn's and his own narrow escape, he became impatient. He needed to push knowledge forward faster, but it required more people to understand and extend what he knew. Cadwulf's enthusiasm for the new mathematics and Brother Wallington's epiphany on using the first microscopes to study previously unknown realms of animal and plant life encouraged Yozef to bring in more Caedelli scholastics. He envisioned expanding St. Sidryn's scholastic staff, the Caedellium version of academics, into a university. These were dreams to which he could devote the rest of his life.

However, the university would succeed only with the abbot's approval and backing. He had procrastinated, but the time had come. He spent two days thinking, and then one mid-afternoon, after seeing the abbot enter the cathedral, he knocked on Sistian's door.

"Enter." Sistian sat behind his cluttered desk. "Ah, Yozef, what can I do you for today?"

Yozef jumped right in. "If you have time, I'd like to discuss expanding the scholastic staff here at St. Sidryn's."

"Expand? How do you mean expand?" asked the abbot, waving for Yozef to sit.

"I'm thinking about the number of scholastics. I understand there are fourteen scholastics here, plus several of the brothers and sisters are medicants and have interests that might be considered scholastic oriented. The experience of my people is that scholastics are more efficient in learning when their number is higher and represented by many different areas of knowledge."

*We'd call it a "critical mass," but if he asked where the phrase came from, how would I explain about nuclear chain reactions?*

Sistian nodded. "I understand, Yozef, but how many scholastics can there be in one place?"

"As many as possible."

"Then how are they supported? An abbey like St. Sidryn's is doing well to provide for its fourteen scholastics. Even so, some of the medicant and theophist brothers and sisters chafe at even the fourteen as being too many."

Yozef had learned early on that the Caedelli service society included three orders: medicants to tend the body; theophists, to the spirit; and scholastics to study God's world. Sistian was St. Sidryn's abbot and head theophist, while his wife, Diera, was abbess and the head medicant. This was the first Yozef had heard of tension among the orders.

"Obviously, it takes more coin as the number of scholastics increases," Yozef said, "which is why I wanted to speak with you. My people strongly believe in the value of scholastics and willingly provide such support, but what about the people here? I assume to expand the number of scholastics on Caedellium would require considerable additional coin."

Sistian sat back in his chair and folded hands over a stomach that had been growing the last few years, as Diera had mentioned to him numerous times. "And how would you see such support happening here?"

"The people are already taxed, the funds going first to the district boyermen and then part to the clan hetman. It would require using part of that tax to increase the scholastic staff."

"I hope you understand you would need to convince not only the hetman and the boyermen. The people would also have to believe in the value of supporting more scholastics. As much as I love all Keelanders, most are concerned with the here and now, and getting them to understand the longer-term value of scholastics is always difficult."

"I appreciate the problem, but what do *you* believe? Given all the uses for available coin, how do *you* value scholastics, compared to all the other needs?"

The abbot was quiet for a moment, his eyes on Yozef, the fingers of his hands now tapping his stomach as he thought. "Before you arrived, I thought I was allotting as much of St. Sidryn's resources to our scholastics as was possible, and possibly more than I should. Now... after the ether, kerosene, the mathematics you've shown Cadwulf, the medical knowledge you've shared with Diera, I've been wondering . . ."

"Tell me, Yozef, how many scholastics are found at one site in your land?"

Yozef could hardly tell him thousands to tens of thousands—if you counted professors, post-docs, graduate and undergraduate students. It needed to start slowly, here. Too grandiose for Caedelli standards, and he'd lose the abbot.

"Our scholastics aren't part of abbeys such as here on Caedellium. They gather in what we call a university, where they can number several score, and at some of the more important universities, hundreds."

Sistian jerked in his chair. "That many! And your people support such a number?"

"Yes. Naturally, people being people, there are always arguments over whether that's too many or not enough, but certainly many more than on Caedellium."

"University," Sistian repeated. "I suppose I appreciate the value of getting scholastics together in larger numbers, although I'm dubious about it here on Caedellium. I know there are such centers on some of the mainland realms—the Fuomi, for example, and some Iraquinink states. Diera spent several years in medicant training on Landolin in a large center. Here? I doubt the hetman and the boyermen would even consider such a proposal."

"I agree, which is why I came to you. What if we start by increasing the scholastic staff here in St. Sidryn's? You already have fourteen scholastics. Plus, I suspect Cadwulf would reasonably be considered a scholastic in mathematics. What I propose is that since the abbey has increased coin from its share of the ether and kerosene trades, and since my enterprises are doing so well, that we jointly support establishing a small university."

Sistian sat thoughtfully, considering. "And if we did this, how much would the abbey need to provide?"

"We can discuss it, but I suggest the abbey provide one-fifth of the coin, and I would provide the rest."

"Such an uneven share," said the surprised abbot. "I expected you to propose we share the cost equally."

"Realistically, I probably have more available coin than the abbey, plus the abbey would provide not only one fifth of the coin, but also its existing scholastics, the prestige of the abbey, and, let's be honest, the reputation of, and regard for, the abbot."

Sistian smiled at the compliment and waved it off with a hand motion.

"Over time," Yozef said, "the boyerman, the hetman, and hopefully the people will come to understand the value of supporting the university here and possibly other ones elsewhere in Keelan and the other clans."

Sistian raised a hand. "That's getting too far ahead for now. Some clans hardly support any scholastics at all, although I'm inclined to be positive about trying one of these universities. Would it need to be housed here in the abbey complex or outside, and how many additional scholastics would you envision?"

"I suggest a new building near the abbey, and I was thinking of adding twenty-five additional scholastics. With your permission, we could call it the University of Abersford."

"Hmmm, I think the abbey could manage that. Would you envision specific topics of study?"

"I suggest three broad areas. One would be what my people call 'biology,' the study of living organisms. Included would be topics related to medicant knowledge and agriculture."

*And an avenue to introduce more physiology, anatomy, biochemistry, genetics, and everything else I can dig out of my memory.*

"The second would be mathematics. My impression from Cadwulf is that there're several of the better mathematics scholastics scattered around Caedellium he thinks we could convince to move to Abersford, thereby giving us a strong group right from the start."

*And mathematics is a core knowledge that feeds into many other fields, a way to introduce physics, more astronomy, and God knows what else.*

"The third area would be the study of other realms on Anyar—their history, customs, languages, and how they are ruled."

The abbot raised an eyebrow and scratched his chin. "This 'biology' I realize the value of, and perhaps the mathematics. Certainly, Cadwulf pestered Diera and me enough over the years about how mathematics relates to so much of the world and our lives, but the third one I'm not sure I understand why it's important enough to emphasize."

"It's because of the Narthani," said Yozef. "Caedellium's isolation from the rest of Anyar is over. Oh, there was trade before the Narthani came and some travel, such as Diera's studying in Landolin. However, for most of the people of Caedellium, it's as if the rest of Anyar doesn't exist. I'm sure you know this has changed forever. The Narthani aren't going away, not on their own. How they took over Preddi and got Selfcell and Eywell to ally with them is partly due to your clans not knowing about the rest of the world and how the Narthani have probably done the same with other peoples. The more that's understood about them, the better Caedellium's chances to resist."

A grimmer-faced abbot grunted. "I grasp your point. We've considered the Preddi stupid for allowing the Narthani in, but you suggest ignorance is an equally plausible excuse. And as for knowing more about the Narthani . . ."

"My people would say to 'know your enemy.'"

*And a nucleus of intelligence on the Narthani, if what I fear happens. We'll need to know everything possible about them.*

"St. Sidryn's has two scholastics who study the history of Caedellium," said Sistian.

"Yes," said Yozef. "They'll form part of a group of scholastics to study and compare all the peoples of Anyar, including those of Caedellium and Narthon."

A thought came unbidden into Sistian's mind. *Maera. By God's creative finger, she would be a perfect scholastic for such a study! She knows as much about the history of the clans as anyone, plus she's studied several of the mainland languages and histories, including Narthon and Fuomon. Of course, she's the hetman's eldest daughter, which complicates matters, unless this university was in Caernford. She'll be visiting soon, and I can discuss it with her, then.*

The abbot decided. "You've convinced me, Yozef, to give all of this some serious thought about the possibility and implications. Also, I may be the abbot, but I need to speak with the other brothers and sisters for their opinions. I already know Diera's."

Thus was born, in principle, the University of Abersford.

# CHAPTER 7

# MAERA VISITS ST. SIDRYN'S

### Jacarandas

The hills west of Abersford sheltered diverse valleys and dells that almost could have evolved in isolation. Yozef knew it was simply the jumble of Earth and Anyar plants intermixing or dominating, depending on happenchance, but he fantasized each landscape a different world. The ground was a jumble of rock, sand, and loam. Although Yozef wondered what geological history had created this terrain, he knew why it was unpopulated. More fertile and convenient land still existed on Caedellium to attract farmers and herders.

When occasionally a solitary mood ensued, walking or riding the hills proved meditative. Today he walked in a new area for the first time. He had just climbed a hill and started down a grass-covered slope when, before him, in a small dale, towered a single mighty oak, or a tree he imagined to be an oak, alone in the middle of the grass, with no other tree in view. Where had this single tree come from? Did a bird drop a seed, an acorn, or whatever propagation mechanism it used here, and it sprouted and took root? Its massive trunk had to be eight feet in diameter, with a broad canopy of leaves nearly reaching to the slopes on all sides.

Why had it not seeded offspring trees around it? Was it lonely? Although it was magnificent in its stature, Yozef felt sad for it. He paused next to the trunk, leaning on it with one hand, as if to feel a heartbeat. The thought flashed through his mind, as if he were whispering to the tree, *I am here . . . you are not alone. I will remember you and the route here. I will visit you again.* Yozef laughed at himself. *Maybe the tree'll talk to me next time.*

He left the shade of the oak and worked his way up the next slope to strewn rocks at the crest of the next hill. Boulders taller than himself coated the top, and as he came around one cluster, he stopped in his tracks. He expected each valley or dale to reveal novelty, but this time he was thunderstruck.

*Jacaranda trees! As I live and breathe, jacaranda trees!*

Yozef stood next to a boulder, amazed at the spectacle. As far as the eye could see, starting from the valley floor and rising to the tops of the surrounding hills, a forest of blue-flowered jacaranda trees was coming into bloom. He had never seen so many, and why here?

At the bottom of the valley, California poppies covered scattered patches of open ground, their golden flowers just emerging. An artist or a landscape architect couldn't have designed a more perfect setting.

He soaked in the scene for ten minutes, before slowly walking down the slope, wondering, as he often did, at the haphazard distribution of Earth and Anyar life forms. Why jacarandas and not dogwoods? Dogs and not cats? Horses and cattle but not sheep or goats or camels? California poppies and not bluebells? Orioles and not robins? Butterflies and not moths? Dragonflies, but no mosquitoes? Not that he complained about the latter option.

Whoever or whatever had transplanted Earth's organisms, did they have a plan, a rationale, or was it random? Would the distribution elsewhere on Anyar be the same as on Caedellium or different? Maybe the Melosia continent had dogwoods and cats, but not jacarandas or dogs?

He sat on the ground, his back against an isolated jacaranda trunk, feet amid poppies growing in the sandy soil and reaching for the sun through the characteristic sparse foliage of the tree. Full bloom would be in another sixday or two and likely last a month. He hadn't brought a lunch, and the first hunger pangs growled. He sat under the tree for a few more minutes.

*Tomorrow. I have to come back tomorrow. Or soon. Full-bloom won't be for a month or more. I'll bring a lunch and spend a whole day here before the bloom fades.*

Reluctantly, he headed back to Abersford, carefully noticing landmarks. He was nearing his shops when he spied a carriage and accompanying riders turn off the main road and continue to the abbey. He watched them until they passed through the abbey's main gate. The carriage looked fancier than most, with a symbol on the doors that reminded him of ones he had seen around the abbey and the village. *Some kind of higher muckety-muck,* he thought. Four outriders preceded the carriage and appeared more military than the men hereabout, with similar clothing that might pass as house livery—blue jackets and pants, brimmed hats held on by chin straps. He thought he could make out short muskets and swords attached to their saddles.

Over beers that evening at the Snarling Graeko, he learned from Carnigan that the symbol he saw was for the Keelan Clan and the hetman's family. The big man didn't know who occupied the carriage, but another patron said the hetman's daughter had come to visit St. Sidryn's.

## Beynom's House, Yozef meets Maera Keelan

Two days later, Cadwulf passed on to Yozef an invitation to mid-day meal at the Beynoms' the following Godsday after services. The house lay outside the abbey's main walls and atop a nearby low hill. Although spartan, the house was tastefully furnished, and what it lacked in size, it made up for with a view. A wide veranda faced downhill toward the abbey complex and the shore and the ocean beyond. The day was perfect: a blue sky with isolated clouds moving in off the ocean, carried on what on Earth would have been called a trade wind.

The two Beynom children still living at home were not in attendance, and four people sat around a table outside. Diera introduced Yozef to the other guest, a slender young woman with brown hair and penetrating green eyes. They ate under overhanging vines with red-and-yellow-striped flowers that reminded Yozef of trumpet vines. Culich and Diera sat opposite each other, as did Yozef and Maera Keelan. The meal was typical: fresh rolls, butter and preserves, several cheeses, a greenish-fleshed melon, tangerines, candied figs, a fruit juice mixture of unknown composition, and kava.

They passed the meal talking of trivial matters, including the weather, the prospects for crops that year, stories from the history of the Beynoms and the Keelans, and probes by Maera Keelan to Yozef, trying to tweeze tidbits of information about his past. He had gotten so used to deflecting or misdirecting that he hardly noticed her questions, which was worrisome, because inconsistencies could be picked up.

He answered Maera's questions about his family. As usual, he stuck to basics without giving details that might raise suspicions. He described his siblings, parents, and studies in general terms. He didn't elaborate on details, such as although his younger brother played an instrument, it was in an amateur heavy metal band.

Yozef deflected more detailed questions about his family by asking Maera about her siblings. She described three sisters, with obvious love. Yozef thought he detected special warmth for the youngest of the three, a hint of exasperation about the next youngest, and a touch of . . . something, when she mentioned the oldest sister being courted by suitors.

When the meal started, the Beynoms facilitated the conversation, though by the end they quieted while Yozef and Maera interacted more and more. The hosts finally excused themselves with calls of duty: Diera, to check on patients at the hospital, and Sistian, to prepare for a ride to a neighboring village, where the village chief had asked him to preside at a wedding that afternoon.

Rising, Sistian said, "Please. It's a beautiful day. The two of you continue to enjoy it and regale each other with family stories. Also, Yozef, Maera is interested in learning more about your various shops and enterprises."

Somehow finding themselves without the older couple's presence changed the atmosphere, as if they had served as a buffer or a framework for the two guests.

Maera played with her napkin, as the silence extended. Then . . . "As Sistian said, Ser Kolsko, I would like to see your projects and have them explained."

"Anytime you wish, Sen Keelan. I'm afraid I have meetings this afternoon, but we could begin tomorrow morning, starting with the distillation facility, if you'd like to accompany me."

The plan settled, Yozef excused himself.

Maera returned to her room in the Beynom's house to write her initial impressions. She stared at the paper as she gathered her thoughts.

*Something of a disappointment. With all the stories and reports I was expecting . . . what? An impressive intelligence or a warrior figure with a dominant presence?*

She tried to be wary of preconceptions, but his average size and mild manner didn't fit her expectations.

*Not a handsome man or a masculine one, I guess would describe it.*

The brown hair and beard were nondescript, except for odd highlights she first thought reflections of light until she recognized a few lighter hair strands. Not gray, which would be early for someone his age, but a lighter brown, beige even. Then there were the eyes. Brown and green were the most common, and occasionally blue, though a darker blue than Yozef's.

*His eyes are lightest blue I've ever seen. More like a light gray. They're his most distinguishing feature, and when they turned at me was the only time I sensed there was something more than common there.*

She returned again to the paper and willed herself to write her first impressions.

The sun played hide-and-seek with the clouds the next morning when Maera met Yozef in front of the cathedral. She wore an ankle-length yellow dress of fine linen, covered by a light green–colored smock. She'd replaced the slippers at the Beynoms' lunch with leather shoes, and her brown hair was nestled in a bun behind a wide-brimmed straw hat. Yozef noticed that although the dress and the shoes displayed workmanship beyond the means of most Keelanders, the smock was utilitarian and showed unsuccessful attempts to remove ink spots.

The Beynoms had assigned their son Cadwulf as her local guide. He excused himself when assured that Yozef would shepherd her.

"Remember," Cadwulf murmured into Yozef's ear, "she's the hetman's daughter. You can't just leave her on her own. If you and she finish touring the shops, bring her to the bank, and I'll look after her from there on."

How they would travel between the abbey and the workshops never entered Yozef's mind. Cadwulf rescued him with a ready one-horse dray with two passenger seats and a driver. Silence ruled the six-minute ride, while Maera sat primly, looking around and occasionally nodding to citizens they passed. A few women curtsied, and one man awkwardly bowed.

Only when they entered the distillation building did Maera first sense something truly new was ongoing in Abersford. Five workers were diligently working on apparatuses whose purposes she had no clue. What struck her immediately were the level of activity and the mood of the workers. All were engaged in tasks she didn't recognize, and from their voices, there was a sense of "play," instead of "work."

Yozef called out to a worker, who waved. "Hey, Yozef. About time you showed up for work. Who's the young woman? Have you been holding out on us?" The man said something to the other workers and walked over to clasp forearms with Yozef.

"Filtin, this is Maera Keelan. She's here visiting the Beynoms and is interested in seeing what we're doing."

Filtin stiffened and made a short bow. An expression of respect and reservation replaced his previous good humor. Maera wasn't surprised. Being a member of the hetman's immediate family accustomed her to such responses.

"Sen Keelan, pardon my comment. An honor to meet you and show you our work."

Maera accepted the distance her position placed between her and most clanspeople and regretted it, when she noticed. However, today, curiosity ruled her attention. Yozef explained the basics of distillation and the equipment Filtin and his crew worked on. The next hour served as a crash course in distillation and an occasion for Maera to demonstrate her quick grasp of new concepts. She stopped the explainer, be it Yozef or Filtin, whenever she didn't fully grasp any aspect. It made for a slow beginning, though progress accelerated as her understanding grew.

Once the explanations and her questions slackened, they went into an adjacent room to witness a production run of ether. Now that she had heard the principles of distillation and seen the ether condense on top of the glass column, then the rivulets as they ran down and dripped into the collection receptacle, she smiled and clapped her hands in appreciation. By this time, Filtin's manner had relaxed in his eagerness to explain to an interested outsider what to him was obviously a work of love, and the banter she'd witnessed when they first arrived gradually returned. Maera had not been around many common workers, except at Keelan Manor, and she remained surprised at the workers' level of enthusiasm and their casual camaraderie with their employer.

Filtin accompanied them to other shops, and they finished briefer tours of the kerosene and soap facilities by mid-day.

"Would you like to return to the abbey for mid-day meal, Sen Keelan?" asked Yozef. The dray and the driver remained near the distillation shop.

"I believe the cannon foundry is next," said Maera, "and then gunpowder and the bank. Perhaps there's somewhere to eat here in the Abersford. Where were you planning on mid-day meal?"

"Oh, I usually just drop in on whatever shop is next, and the men and women give me something."

*Give him something? How odd.*

"In that case, if they could spare a little more, perhaps we should just proceed to the next demonstration."

"Okay," said Yozef and turned away to a worker checking a new glass column.

*Oh-kay?*

Filtin saw her puzzlement. "It's an expression from Yozef's homeland, Sen Keelan. *Okay* means something like 'yes' or 'in agreement' or generally positive. You'll find the expression has become common here in Abersford."

"Thank you, Ser . . . er . . . I didn't get your family name."

"Fuller, Sen Keelan. Filtin Fuller."

"Thank you, Ser Fuller."

Maera hadn't missed Fuller's surprise when she suggested she eat with Yozef and the workers at the foundry. Her forthrightness came to the fore. *If you want to know something, silly—ask!*

"Ser Fuller, you looked surprised when I suggested I accompany Ser Kolsko to the foundry to eat there. Please tell me why?"

Fuller was obviously ill at ease with the question. She looked straight at him and waited, with the "I'm the hetman's daughter and you need to answer" look she had cultivated.

"Well, you're the *hetman's* daughter. One doesn't expect someone like you to eat mid-day meal with workers, particularly sharing their food."

"But Ser Kolsko does it?"

"Yes, but Yozef is . . . different."

Maera could tell she was on to something. *What* she didn't know, but her instincts told her she needed this man to open up.

"I'm very curious, Filtin . . . may I call you Filtin?" she said, in as friendly a voice as she could manage.

Filtin blinked several times in surprise that the hetman's daughter wanted to call him by his first name, something usually reserved for when persons were better acquainted.

"Why . . . that's fine, Sen Keelan." It never occurred to either of them that he would use *her* first name.

Confident that she had established personal rapport with Filtin, she continued. "So, Filtin, obviously Yozef is an important person, not only here in Abersford but for all of Keelan, due to the many innovations he has introduced. Yet all the workers seem more familiar with him than one might expect. Why is that?"

"Well, he's just . . . Yozef," drawled out Filtin. "I don't know, exactly. I know he gets annoyed if we are too formal with him."

"So, he prefers the familiarity, that's it?"

Filtin's defensive posture and tone changed to ones more assertive, though still respectful. "Pardon me if I seem presumptuous, Sen Keelan, but Yozef doesn't see himself as of a higher stature than anyone else. He's just Yozef. He's respected for what he does and who he is but doesn't expect different treatment. Pardon again, Sen Keelan, but many people expect to be treated differently, if only because of their station."

Maera was momentarily taken aback. This was the bluntest statement she had heard of the distance among the different peoples of Keelan by status. She didn't like what Filtin said but recognized that he might be taking a risk in being so blunt with her.

*Is Fuller's forthrightness the influence of Kolsko?*

"I appreciate your honesty, Filtin. I also recognize such honesty may not always be welcomed by the receiver, but I assure you that's not the case with me. I'm curious, though, and I'd like similar honesty: is my family treated with respect only because my father is the hetman?"

Filtin shook his head. "Certainly, that's part of it, but there are few people of Keelan who don't recognize how fortunate we are to have Culich Keelan as hetman. We hear too many stories from other clans not to appreciate him and know his dedication isn't common everywhere."

Filtin hesitated, then continued, "You're given respect and deference because you're of the hetman's family, and respect for him transfers to you. Of course, there's always awkwardness for some people when they interact with people of status well above their own. What you don't see in Keelan is deference given out of fear of angering someone of higher status. And then there are those who will act cautiously around you, because they're uncertain about saying something or acting inappropriately."

*Hmmm . . . this needs some careful thinking.*

"Thank you, Filtin. Again, I truly appreciate your honesty."

As Fuller had indicated, the mid-day meal started awkwardly. Kolsko escorted Maera to the cannon foundry, where his five workers were joined by the soap-making staff, and the men paused in their work to eat. Maera's reservation about eating food donated by the workmen was ameliorated when, on the way, Kolsko stopped at a bakery and bought several loaves of fresh bread and fruit at a street market. Their arrival at the foundry was greeted with a similar welcome as in the distillery shops, with casual and friendly greetings to Kolsko, followed by a more distant manner when he introduced her.

They sat on boxes around a temporary table made out of sawhorses and boards. Kolsko broke out the bread and the fruit, and friendly banter ensued, while he "bartered" for cheese and dry sausage. They ate, while he gave Maera a briefing on what they were attempting at the foundry and their progress. As he did, different workers added updates and comments, and before long, Maera felt they had forgotten her presence and engaged in their usual working discussion.

*Interesting. He laughs when he recounts what he sees are mistakes he made, and he readily listens to his workers. It's like they work together and not for him.*

As for the cannon project, Maera could see the arguments Kolsko summarized on why cannon could be important, but she hadn't the experience or the basis to evaluate the ideas.

*Father needs to hear more about this. Father and Vortig Luwis.*

After the foundry, Kolsko walked Maera to the bank and left her with Cadwulf, who explained the rationale for a "bank." Cadwulf also strongly expressed the need to have formal procedures for handling the coin coming in from Kolsko's trades. It was the first time she had any clue about his finances.

*Merciful God! This Kolsko might already be the wealthiest man in Keelan, and getting more so all the time! He might even have as much coin as our family's direct possessions. The extent of his workshops here is only a shadow of all his enterprises now that he "franchises," as he calls it, to shops elsewhere in Keelan and other provinces. I doubt Father has any clue to any of this and needs to be more aware of what is happening here in Abersford.*

Maera had also recognized the prosperous look of the entire area. Not just Abersford, but the farms and the abbey complex.

*It must all be interrelated. From what Cadwulf says, most of the coin that comes in goes right back out for Kolsko's different shops and projects. Certainly, the foundry is not bringing in any coin, but he supports it, because he thinks it may be important in the future. That's something Father might do, but few other hetmen.*

After her introduction to Kolsko's finances, the rationale and operation of the bank, loan procedures, and double-entry bookkeeping, Maera returned to the abbey, escorted by Cadwulf. There she spent the rest of the day in the abbey library. Her intention to read faltered, as she stared out a window for several hours and went over in her mind what she had seen that day.

Her impression of Sen Kolsko had definitely changed. At mid-day meal yesterday, when the Beynoms introduced them, she'd thought him quite unimpressive. That was wrong. Maera still didn't have a strong feeling for him as a person, but what he'd accomplished here in Abersford in a relatively short time was nothing short of extraordinary.

*Father ABSOLUTELY needs to pay attention to what's happening here and meet this Kolsko.*

## Genes

Maera discussed Kolsko often with Diera Beynom. The abbess was simultaneously enthused and frustrated by the new knowledge that dripped from him.

"Yes," said Diera, "the ether putting patients to sleep and ethanol for antiseptic have been God's blessings to us, not to mention what he's told us of his people's understanding of the human body."

"I hear a big *but* in your voice, Diera."

"Yes, *but* it's also maddeningly frustrating dealing with him. Sistian and I both believe him honest and honorable, yet half the time I think he's hiding pieces of knowledge from us. Why, I don't know. The other half . . ."

"The other half, what?"

Diera shook head. "I don't know. He acts like single pieces of information suddenly come to him. I've heard it said that it seems he's hearing something no one else does, although I think it may be he's searching his memory. At times, he says he simply can't remember the answer to one of our questions, and he's always apologetic when that happens.

"Sistian told me that Yozef once came to him for advice about revealing beliefs and knowledge of his own people and how not to arouse trouble here on Caedellium if he did. He worried for both his safety and disturbing our society. Sistian and, more recently, I have advised him. I think you'd find it interesting to come to a meeting tomorrow with me, Yozef, and one of our scholastics, Brother Willwin Wallington, who studies Anyar's animals and plants. Yozef has had Willwin growing peas to study their flower colors. They've both been secretive, although Willwin is floating on air recently. They've asked to show me the results of whatever they're doing."

The four met in a small greenhouse, another of Yozef's introductions. Pots covered one table, each one growing a single pea plant with white or purple flowers.

Brother Wallington spoke, with Yozef standing to one side, his face impassive.

"Yozef came to me one day and asked how we thought characteristics are passed from generation to generation. There are practical examples of how we assume this to be. A herder breeds with a specific bull because the offspring are better than those of other bulls. A wheat farmer saves the seed of better-yielding plants, in hopes future generations will also have higher yields.

"He posed the question of how to explain the basis of these expectations. It was hardly a novel question, and one neither I nor, as far as I know, anyone else has a good answer. This led to a related question dealing only with humans. How can a husband be certain his wife's children are his? Ignoring simply her word she's been faithful."

Wallington shuffled his feet and stole a glance at Maera. "I hope I don't offend you, Sen Keelan, but this gets into facts about the relations between men and women."

Maera smiled. "Please don't worry, Brother Wallington. I've studied medicant texts, plus I've been around animals at Keelan Manor enough to know the basics are the same for humans and animals."

Wallington blushed. "Yes, well, anyway . . . a common belief, first proposed by the great Landolin scholastic Churnwicmon, is that the essence of the fetus is in the male's semen and transferred to the female's womb to be nourished and grow. In this proposition, everything that the new life is to be is contributed by the male. However, there are obvious fallacies."

"I know of Churnwicmon's proposition and the counterarguments," said Maera. "I can see them in my own family. I and my two younger sisters look more like our mother than our father, while my sister Ceinwyn clearly has our father's nose and ears. And when our stable master breeds horses, he doesn't just consider the sire, but also the mare."

"Right," enthused Wallington, "and that brings us to the fundamental problem of explaining how both the father *and* the mother contribute to offspring. That's when Yozef came to me and suggested breeding this wild pea you see on the table." He waved his left arm over the plants. "In fields, we see these two colors in different ratios, depending on location, but only these two. Yozef showed me how to breed pea plants and urged me to keep detailed records of the offspring. Peas grow fast, and it's only taken four generations of data to see three clear relationships. When I showed my results to Yozef, he confirmed them the same as found by one of his people, a man named Mendel."

"Gregor Mendel was his full name," said Yozef. "Diera, you and Sistian will be interested that Mendel was a monk, a position among my people that's similar to a theophist. He also did scholastic studies."

"Yes," Wallington gushed, "and this Mendel declared three laws of inheritance. Naturally, since he discovered them first, we'll keep his names."

Wallington and Yozef went on to describe Mendel's laws of segregation, dominance, and independent assortment. Diera listened carefully, but Maera was intense.

"That's all very interesting," said Maera, "but it's descriptive. It doesn't tell us how the essence of the color trait is transmitted. What *is* it that confers color?"

"The exact question I asked," said Wallington, and all three turned to Yozef.

"Color and all traits are conferred by what are called 'genes.' They're tiny particles within the pollen or the semen, which is how they're transferred to the female."

"If both male and female contribute, the female must also contain these particles in her womb," said Maera. "Does that mean that only one of the male or the female has the particle for the trait, like pea color?"

Yozef started his next words with the phrase he used to describe what he couldn't yet explain to the Caedelli. "As far as I remember, every person has two genes for every trait. One gene comes from the mother and the other from the father. It's the combination that confers the final characteristic."

"Of course!" shouted Wallington. "That explains how Mendel's three laws work and how both parents contribute."

Maera's scrunched her forehead, gnawing on a knuckle. "No, there's still something missing. The two pea colors might be explained by your Mendel's laws, but not all traits are so specific . . . countable. I don't know an exact description of what I'm thinking."

Yozef was impressed. He'd seen that Maera was clever and curious, but she had cut to the heart of more advanced genetics.

"I believe you're getting to an important point. With pea color, we see only a single gene pair, one gene each from both parents, which controls a trait, but many traits involve multiple genes—two, five, or even more."

"My God," said Wallington. "The complexity!"

They continued for three hours, going over the pea experiments once more, then back to discussing genes, Mendel's laws, future pea experiments with more traits, and equal contributions by both parents. Yozef didn't introduce DNA, that some traits involved thousands of genes, or that it was the female egg and not the womb that provided genes from the mother.

However, he came away with further evidence that Maera Keelan was an intellect not to be underestimated.

## Maera Investigates the Raid

It was several days before Maera saw Kolsko again. She busied herself with intended library readings and studiously interviewed participants in the abbey's defense against the Buldorians.

Sistian was of little help. As good an abbot as he was and as important an occasional advisor to her father as he had been, the raid was his first direct experience with life-and-death fighting on that scale. More informative was Denes Vegga, the local magistrate and titular area military commander. He had organized the defense, and for the first time, Maera got a clearer picture of Kolsko's role. Vegga hadn't thought there'd be any chance of repelling the raiders until Kolsko's suggestion to trick the Buldorians into the abbey courtyard saved them all. There, the defenders stood behind hastily thrown up barricades and fired from three sides into the knot of raiders pouring through the main gate. The fight had been short but vicious. Eleven defenders died behind the barricades, but more than one hundred Buldorian bodies carpeted the courtyard.

The rest of the raiders withdrew to the beach, possibly assuming the abbey's defenders more numerous than anticipated. Whatever their thinking, the Buldorians reboarded their ships anchored offshore and sailed away.

Vegga shook his head, still disbelieving they had survived.

Maera made careful notes and drawings of Vegga's description of the action; her father would want as much detail as she could gather. He already had numerous written and verbal reports, but he'd tasked her to prepare her own evaluations.

The details of the battle itself were as different as the people she spoke with, as all of them focused on what was right in front of them. She'd wondered whether Yozef had martial experience elsewhere on Anyar. How else would he have recognized how to defend the abbey? There, information was sparse. Few had any recollection of Kolsko's role in the fighting, except impressions that he'd been at the barricade and wielded a spear. The only direct comments she got were from an enormous man named Carnigan Puvey, who implied that Kolsko had no familiarity with weapons and had said sardonically that Yozef had helped defend Puvey at one point and hadn't killed anyone on their side.

After searching for other witnesses to Kolsko's role, she stumbled on a menacing-looking man named Wyfor, who had not been present for the raid but had trained Kolsko to blade fight months later.

"Oh, I don't doubt Yozef was essentially useless during the defense," said Wyfor, "but Carnigan says Yozef stood right there by his side, even though scared shitless. Pardon my language. That tells you something. Shows you Yozef has guts or is stupid, depending on how you view someone with no idea what he's doing, standing in front of charging Buldorians.

"It was later when he came to me to learn how to defend himself. I don't think he'd ever touched a blade before, to do anything except use a knife at meals. I thought him hopeless at first, but there was never any doubt about his determination. I beat him something fierce for several months, but he kept coming back."

"So he *did* learn to fight? He's not as helpless now as you say he was?"

Wyfor stared at her face for moments. She could almost see his mind evaluating what to say next.

"I didn't say this to him, and you shouldn't either. He learned faster than I thought possible. There's no substitute for real fighting, but he's as dangerous a person as possible for someone with no experience. Besides being smart and determined, he's fast and strong for his size. By the time we finished, I would've had no hesitation fighting along with him. I didn't praise him too much to keep him worried, in case he ever gets into another situation where even the littlest confidence could get him killed."

Everything Maera learned went into written reports for her father and a copy she kept.

# CHAPTER 8

# DISAPPOINTMENTS

### Conclave Hall, Outside of Orosz City

The square stone building sat atop a hill a mile outside the old walls of Orosz City. The only use of the structure was to house meetings of the clan leaders, once a year for the mandatory All-Clan Conclave, and whenever a hetman called for another meeting. In the latter case, attendance wasn't required unless a majority concurred. The building's single room sufficed to hold twenty-one hetmen and two or three aides each. That the Conclave Hall was not within the city proper signified that the Orosz Clan had no special stature. The meetings had to be held somewhere. Orosz Province was central enough, and the clan's history neutral enough in past conflicts for the hall to serve as a compromise location, when two centuries earlier the clans had agreed to the site. Hetman Orosz served as the host to start the meetings and, when necessary, attempted to cool ardor if discussions became too heated among individual clans or factions. In return, Hetman Orosz never took sides in disagreements.

The meeting called by Hetman Keelan had just ended, with the Narthani threat to Caedellium the only topic, as it had been in other meetings during the last years, since the Narthani crushed the Preddi Clan and forced alliances with the Selfcell and Eywell clans.

Culich Keelan's prediction that not all clan hetmen would attend came true: of the eighteen clans not under Narthani control, twelve clans sent representatives, including nine hetmen. Six hetmen gathered in a semi-circle around Orosz. The other clan representatives had already left the room.

"Don't be too discouraged, Keelan. The tide is slowly turning to recognize the threat," said Cadoc Gwillamer. The hetman of the Gwillamer Clan could have used Culich's first name, their being leaders of allied clans and lifelong acquaintances, but the custom at conclaves was to address only clan names.

"But slowly is the problem," rejoined Keelan. "I'll admit the turnout was better than I feared it would be, but every instinct tells me time is running out to convince the others."

"We have to work with what we have, not what we wished we had," said Tomis Orosz. "You know as well as any of us, Keelan, that there are some hetmen who will only wake up when the Narthani are at their own doors." While the Orosz hetman maintained neutrality during conclave sessions, he wasn't required to be oblivious.

Without intent, the seven hetmen stood in positions reflecting their relations. The three members of the Tri-Clan Alliance, Keelan, Mittack, and Gwillamer, stood beside one another. Facing them and separated by Orosz were Stent, Hewell, and Adris. The last two were in the process of joining the Alliance, so their presence was expected. Stent was of a like mind concerning the Narthani, but the Stent Province was on the opposite side of the island and bordered Selfcell, one of the Narthani client clans.

"Maybe it's because I feel so isolated," said Welman Stent, "but I'm buoyed by Bultecki and Farkesh coming around. While I know nothing is certain, I think both will join in response to a serious Narthani move against other clans."

"Bultecki, certainly," said Orosz. "However, Farkesh is north and would have to cross the lands of clans not yet committed, so it's difficult to see them sending aid."

"Yes," said Keelan. "Still, that they support a united resistance is encouraging, *especially* Farkesh. Maybe they can influence Skouks and Vandinke."

Those three clans, along with Bultecki and Nyvaks, were descendants from the first wave of colonists to Caedellium from the mainland continents five centuries ago. Although their exact origin remained unknown, two centuries later a second wave of colonists arrived from the Landolin continent. The original peoples on Caedellium were slowly pushed northward, and cultural and attitude differences were still evident in clans with descent from either of the two colonization waves. In contrast, the clanspeople of Swavebroke were a mixture from both waves.

"If that happens," continued Keelan, "then Swavebroke would have to join, leaving Pewitt no choice, because they could be surrounded by committed clans. As for the three eastern clans, I think Bevans would join, as would Pawell, if they could be assured that Nyvaks was no danger."

"That would be the most we could hope for." Orosz looked around at the other six. "Seaborne might want to help, but being on their islands off the western coast and with the waters controlled by the Narthani, it's hard to see them contributing. As for Nyvaks, who knows what they would do, and who would trust them?" Nyvaks Province connected to the rest of Caedellium by only a narrow isthmus, and its solidarity to the other clans was just as tenuous.

The hetmen stayed within their own thoughts about Nyvaks, until Keelan summarized, "So, we think Moreland will likely be the next target, with eight, possibly nine clans coming to Moreland's aid."

Stent turned his head and spat onto the floor. "As much as it galls me to try to save Moreland, we have to do it, no matter what any of us think of that ass, Gynfor Moreland. If his clan falls, the Narthani will be in position to move in any of several directions and could cut the island in two."

Sour expressions supported Stent's fear.

"Then let's return home and do what we can to get ready," said Keelan.

"And pray," said Orosz. "Pray that we've been too pessimistic and pray that the rest of the clans come to their senses soon."

"And hope we don't have to pray for a miracle from God," ended Hewell.

## Keelan Manor, Caernford, Keelan Province

Culich Keelan's rear ached from the 180-mile carriage ride from Orosz City to Caernford. He had pushed his drivers and escort, and they made it back in two long days, stopping overnight at a Hewell village. As always, his wife, Breda, waited on the manor's front veranda. He had updated her on his progress via semaphore before leaving Orosz City and at several semaphore stations en route. When she saw the carriage, she rose and walked down the steps.

The carriage hadn't completely stopped in front of the manor when Culich stepped out. In his rush to get off, he forgot and landed first on his bad leg. The knee buckled, and Breda steadied him before he tumbled.

"Damn! Too much in a hurry to get off my sore ass. Good thing you were here. Wouldn't do for people to see their hetman falling on his face."

Breda let go of his arm and hugged him. "Oh, they'd not worry, except to know you were all right. I suppose coming inside and sitting is not likely?"

"Let me stand for a few minutes, and then I'll sit, but only on the softest cushion we have. Even with the new seats you had made, after that many miles they still felt like stone. I even rode a horse for a while, but that only lasted a few miles until my knee made me stop. What I'd really like right now is a beer."

"Then come on in, and I'll send Alindra to the deep cellar."

They entered the manor and walked arm in arm to the main parlor. She called and a young woman appeared, listened to Breda, and scurried away. Culich leaned against the back of one chair, while his wife sat opposite him.

"So, don't leave me in suspense. How did the conclave go?"

"Better than I'd feared and worse than I'd hoped. While none of the staunch isolationist clans wavered from that idiocy, there's a firm commitment from eight clans to come to the aid of anyone attacked. Most of us believe it'll be Moreland, so naturally Gynfor Moreland didn't commit to helping any other clan. He even boasted that Moreland could take care of itself and didn't need help from any other clan. I wouldn't have thought it possible, but he acted even stupider than usual."

Breda thumped the chair arms with her fists. "God's mercy! What about his boyermen? Surely, some of them must feel differently. A hetman can always be replaced."

"In theory, yes, but lack of common sense seems to be endemic to too many of the Morelanders. Rumors are that half of the boyermen would move against him, though not enough to prevent fighting among factions, which would be disastrous. It would give the Narthani the perfect opportunity to take Moreland during the turmoil. No. We're stuck with Gynfor Moreland. I find myself wishing he'd suffer some fatal accident or illness and depart this world, God forgive me, though even that might not help. His eldest son, Heilrond, is just as bad.

"Now it's back to Keelan business. Our boyermen meeting is next sixday. I'll need to get the summary of the last meeting from Mae . . ." Culich's voice trailed off, as he remembered Maera was at St. Sidryn's.

"Yes, dear, she's still there, although it's about time for her to return." Breda became pensive. "Now that I think of it, she hasn't said in her last letters when she planned on coming home. She only sent her usual sixday report of her observations, plus letters to me and her sisters, nothing about her plans."

"I'll write her. Now that I'm back, I can use her help, especially with the boyermen meeting coming up. She's been there long enough. I doubt there's much left to hold her there. I'm sure she's eager to come home."

## Preddi City, Narthani Headquarters

Sadek Hizer drummed the fingers of his left hand on the wooden table, his lips thinned and eyes glaring, although not at Akuyun, sitting opposite him in the general's office.

"I'd thought we had a good chance to keep the clans from uniting, but the reports on the hetmen meeting confirm at least six of the clans have committed to a common defense. Neither of our agents could give details; however, it's evident Keelan pulled three to four other clans along."

"We expected that, didn't we, Sadek?" Akuyun asked.

"Yes, though not the surprises. The Orosz hetman came out in favor of the commitment, something we were led to believe wouldn't happen. The Caedelli custom has been for Orosz to stay neutral in any discussion. He's broken that custom and sided with Keelan and Stent on a collective defense.

"What's just as disturbing is that Farkesh hinted he was leaning to joining. We'd thought the northern clans would be the least likely to cooperate, there being historical animosity between them and the southern clans. While we already suspected Bultecki would break from the others, if Farkesh does, too, it's only a matter of time before the other northern clans join. That would only leave the outliers, Pewitt, Nyvaks, and Pawell," Sadek said in a disgusted grating tone. "Not a satisfying outcome for the time and effort we put into trying to divert the clans from uniting."

"Now, Sadek, it's not like we were counting on our efforts to keep them apart. It was always a secondary strategy."

Akuyun was right but was also pleased that Hizer took personally their failure to subvert clan cooperation. It was a sign of Hizer's commitment to the mission. Akuyun believed himself fortunate to have an assessor of exceptional ability and one willing to be incorporated into the mission's areas of responsibility, even if informally.

Although the news disappointed Akuyun, he wasn't discouraged. "No, Sadek, we might wish the Caedelli make it as easy as possible for us, but it just means we're back to the basic plan. We will ratchet up our pressure on their coasts and the neighboring clans and then launch a drive into their heartland with our troops. If the clans hadn't agreed to come to one another's aid, we'd simply have crushed Moreland and then moved on to Orosz. By cutting the island in half, the time when they could have presented a united front would have been over. Now, when we invade Moreland and other clans rush to help, it gives us the opportunity to bring all of this to closure faster. If we can entice them into an open field battle, their defeat will weaken multiple clans at the same time. As a result, those clans and others not participating will be more likely to come to terms. Either way, we succeed. It's just a matter of the details and timing."

Hizer sighed, then his eyes narrowed as he took in the mission's commander. "No, Okan, you're right. I know I'm flagellating myself unnecessarily, though I also wonder about our roles. I'm supposed to be the one giving you encouragement when necessary, yet why do I feel it's the other way around? Makes me wonder sometimes if I'm doing the assignment I'm here for."

"Nonsense. Both of our tasks are to bring Caedellium into the empire. That we work well together is a bonus for us both and is only good for the mission. Let's put the consequences of your agent's report aside. One advantage is that now we don't have the distraction of multiple avenues forward. We'll continue preparing our men and, at the right moment, move to crush whatever force the Caedelli can assemble."

## Akuyun Family Villa, Preddi City

Okan Akuyun arrived at his family's villa, expecting a relaxing evening. He was disappointed. His wife, Rabia, met him at the door, her mouth set and arms crossed tightly in front of her.

There was no preamble. "You need to speak to Ozem," she said. "He's become too full of himself. Too arrogant. Too stupid is all I can call it."

"I assume there are particulars you're referring to. What exactly has he done?"

Their eleven-year-old son was bright and energetic. Sometimes Okan thought him too bright for his own good, without having learned proper respect and discipline. His twin sister, Lufta, was also intelligent but lacked the drive of her brother. They had accompanied their parents to Caedellium, while their two older brothers stayed in Narthon as junior army officers and had their own growing families.

"It's gotten worse the last month. He is disrespectful to the guards, lords over Lufta, and is constantly denigrating the servants and the slaves. Today I heard him tell Lieutenant Jurnor to fetch him his coat. His coat! As if the officer of our guard was a servant or a slave. I'm also sure he's been on the verge of disobeying me several times and barely restrained himself. I doubt that restraint will last much longer."

Rabia unclenched her arms and took Okan's hand. "I'm sorry, dear, but I didn't mention any of this earlier. I thought it a phase he was going through and I could deal with it. Now I'm worried it's more serious."

Okan put an arm around her and squeezed. "Not to worry, dearest. I'll speak to him."


He found his son lounging in his room. Rabia had sent him there to await his father.

"Stand up!"

Ozem jumped to his feet, face flushing, eyes morphing from insolence to fear.

"You may be an Akuyun, but don't forget you're still a child and have not earned the right to behave in any way of your own choosing, even if it's to act stupid."

"Father, I—"

"Shut up! I'll let you know when you can talk."

Ozem's mouth snapped shut, and he stiffened to attention.

"You put Lieutenant Jurnor in a bad situation to no purpose. His duty is maintaining security of the villa and reporting to your mother when I'm not here. To order him to fetch your coat is the act of a spoiled child not worthy of the Akuyun family or your two brothers, who never behaved in such a manner. Jurnor's an officer in the Narthon army and due respect. *You* have no authority over him, and *you* have done nothing to earn respect. If you have such delusions, get them out of your mind. I'll be confirming to the lieutenant that he's under no obligation to listen to anything you say. Is that clear?"

"Yes, Father, I'm sorry I—"

"Did I say you could speak? As for the correct treatment of servants and slaves, while they're bound to our family and must obey, it's stupid to treat them badly unnecessarily. Think of how you treat your horse. You brush it and give it treats but are stern in its training. In return, it gives unquestioned obedience. Disciplining people is often necessary, though is never done for trivial reasons unrelated to their duties. Your mother tells me you struck a maid because she forgot to mend your favorite riding pants, and she wasn't even the one you told to do it. While we expect them to obey, in return they need to know they'll be treated fairly within the bounds of their station. To punish unnecessarily corrupts the bond between master and underlings, be they subordinates, common people, servants, or slaves."

Okan paused. Although he wasn't as mad as he tried to sound, the boy needed a strong lesson. He didn't think there was a major problem, but if there was, he needed to nip it quickly.

"I don't want to hear any excuses. I thought you've been taught better. If not, it's my fault. I expect better from you in the future. I'm *very* disappointed."

Ozem's face fell.

*Good,* thought Okan. *He wants my approval. I think Rabia's right, he's going through a phase.*

He expected this short session would show results. If not, stronger measures could always be taken.

# CHAPTER 9

# LIFE

### A New Life

Yozef was talking with Filtin about trying to make napalm, when a message arrived from a farm north of Abersford. Bronwyn had given birth. A boy. Both mother and baby were in good health. He read the message several times, while Filtin waited, then became curious.

"Bad news, Yozef?"

"No. Good news. Bronwyn gave birth, and everyone's fine." Filtin knew of Yozef's past connection with the farm woman and that a child had resulted.

"You don't *look* like it's good news."

"No, really, it *is* good news. It's just that having a son—and a son nearby whom I won't raise myself—only now seems real."

Yozef hadn't seen Bronwyn during the last two months, not since the Godsday when he sat in a back pew and saw Bronwyn, her sister, her husband, and three children walk down the right aisle and find a space in the middle of the cathedral. She was obviously pregnant and the family group looked . . . domestic? Yozef felt a pang, exactly why he wasn't sure. Not continuing with Bronwyn? He didn't think so. The child? Not being a daily part of its life felt wrong, although, looking at her family, he couldn't argue there was any other option. Maybe it was just the "family." He had made friends, but there was still a disconnected feeling.

Now the child had arrived, and Yozef still didn't know how he felt, except for one clear question: *I wonder what they named him?*

### Music

Yozef only occasionally attended the Godsday service at the cathedral. He wasn't a believer, on Earth or Anyar, but considered regular attendance both politically wise and a time to hear music that didn't assault his ears, as most

Caedelli music did. An ensemble of strings and wind instruments blended into calming arrangements, and some of the brothers and the sisters formed a choir with pieces reminiscent of Gregorian chants. Often, he listened only half-heartedly to the abbot's message, losing himself in the musical interludes.

The cathedral services weren't the only place Yozef heard Caedelli music. For Keelanders, music was an everyday feature of life. Walking through Abersford, he often heard half a dozen different voices singing or humming tunes. Besides the abbey's small ensemble, instruments, both in groups and solo, were everywhere at festivals, parties, pubs, and anywhere individuals or groups were in the mood.

What hadn't happened yet on Caedellium was standardization of instruments, although four basic types existed—percussion, wind, horn, and string. With all four types, the variety was such that at first Yozef wondered whether it was the custom for *every* instrument to be unique.

While the music itself varied, it was usually performed solo or, if with multiple instruments, played one person at a time. Combined playing was mainly restricted to small groups at festivals and pubs, with the Godsday service ensemble the only formal permanent grouping. There was also elementary standard notation, but Yozef thought it was in the early stages of development, where only the main melody line was written down, with the expectation that the musician would improvise the bass line or variations.

Some of the local music Yozef found appealing, particularly a few of the pub songs and Godsday music. Other pieces were downright strange, and even the same piece could be in either category, depending not just on the quality of the musician, but on how he chose to play the piece or what instrument he used. A melodic, meditative Godsday piece played by several strings with a soft drumming background didn't sound the same when played on something like a small bagpipe.

Yozef had initially contributed to the Caedellium music scene at the Snarling Graeko with rough translations of "I've Got Friends in Low Places," by Garth Brooks, Roger Miller's "Chug-a-lug," and the Irish song "Molly Malone." Other songs were less appreciated. Blank looks responded to his translation of the Beach Boys' "I Get Around."

He was in a good mood one day, while going over his bank accounts, which seemed on a steady rise, no matter how much he paid out in salaries, supplies, and new projects, most of which failed. He was unconsciously humming parts of the choral movement from Beethoven's Ninth Symphony when a voice interrupted.

"Say, Yozef, what's that you're humming?"

He looked up to see Pernel Horton, one of the bank's clerks.

"Ah, Pernel. It's a tune known to my people in America. Part of Beethoven's Ninth Symphony."

"Beethoven? Symphony?"

*Shit. I need to watch speaking without thinking.*

"A man named Beethoven created the music, and it's played by a group of musicians who together are called a symphony."

"I heard you humming, and the melody grabbed me right away. Wait a moment while I get my curnyx."

Pernel returned with an instrument that looked like a large kazoo. Yozef had seen and heard them at harvest festivals and Godsday services. Depending on sizes and shapes, the bulbous instrument's output reminded him of flutes and oboes.

"I play at Godsday services, and we're always looking for new music—if it's appropriate, of course. Please hum again, and let me try to copy."

Yozef hummed, Pernel blew, and work in the bank stopped, as workers and customers gathered to listen. Within minutes, the clerk could repeat everything Yozef remembered of the Ninth Movement.

"You said this music is played by a group. How large?"

"Perhaps as many as thirty musicians." Yozef didn't say large symphony orchestras could approach a hundred members.

"This is exciting. I'll speak with the others who play at the services and see if we can use this tune. I'm sorry I didn't think to ask you before, since I like some of the songs you gave us at the Snarling Graeko. I imagine you must know other music from your people?"

The two men walked out of the bank to let business resume. In a tree grove, Yozef obligingly whistled and hummed a number of tunes for Pernel, who was eager to adapt a few for a planned Godsday service, in honor of the memory of those who had fallen in the defense of St. Sidryn's.

During the next month, they worked sporadically on adapting novel tunes from Yozef, and the final memorial service ended up with ten musical pieces, six traditional Caedellium ones and four from Yozef that were based very loosely on the Schubert "Ave Maria," "Il Pensieros" by Verdi, "O Holy Night," and, of course, the same choral movement from the Ninth Symphony. When blended with the Caedellium tunes and words added to be sung by the small choir, the totality developed into a story starting as a somber reflection on the losses, progressed to asking for God's grace, then showed the unity of the community struggling together, and finally had a triumphal ending. Without intending to, they created the first Caedellium opera, a series of musical pieces telling a story.

Yozef insisted the music needed to be performed with a reduced variety of instruments, at least those pieces he contributed. After some arguments, they settled on a dozen that simulated an Earth orchestra. Five bowed instruments, taking the roles of violin, viola, and cello, were accompanied by a curved metal horn (French horn), three bulbous wind kazoos, two plucked strings (harp and guitar), and a drummer using drums of several sizes and tones.

Rumors of something unusual spread, so that when the Godsday for the memorial arrived, the cathedral was filled, with hundreds unable to get in, even by packing the hall in every available space. Sistian solved the problem by declaring that they would perform the entire memorial service twice. When this included the introductory traditional Godsday songs and sermon and the special musical performance, the entire service lasted two hours. Despite the tradition that services in the cathedral were solemn and quiet affairs, at the conclusion the throng shouted, clapped, and wept, and conversation broke out throughout the hall. Sistian finally had to ring a two-handed bell to quiet them, thank the musicians, and then ask the people to exit, so they could repeat the entire event for those left outside. People who missed the first performance filled perhaps two-thirds of the cathedral, which filled again to overflowing with those who wanted a second chance.

At the end of the second performance, Sistian again thanked the musicians, but by then he knew something extraordinary had happened that day, and he took additional time to thank the lead musician, Pernel Horton, and Yozef Kolsko. Horton, in turn, attributed much of the credit to Yozef, who, much to his discomfort, ended up having to come forward to general shouts of approval.

After eagerly exiting the hall, Yozef was thanked by people wanting to clasp arms, slap him on the back, or, most awkward for Yozef, reach out to *touch* him as he passed. Yozef had nearly escaped, when Brother Carllin Wye pushed aside several people and threw his arms around Yozef in a fierce hug, then stepped back with tears in his eyes.

"Ser Kolsko," Wye said huskily, "please forgive me for ever thinking you were an agent of the Evil One sent here to entice us to dark ways. Forgive me."

*Agent of the Evil One?*

Yozef knew the dour brother didn't approve of him, but this was the first time he realized there were still some who thought of him as a demon.

Wye hugged him again.

*Okay, Wye, enough with the hugging.*

Sistian rescued him by leading Brother Wye away, and Yozef made his escape.

Maera Keelan had been at St. Sidryn's two sixdays and knew of Wye's opinion of Yozef. She saw the performance twice, and the music and the words touched her more than she would have thought possible. The prolonged *story* and evolution of the music were something she hadn't experienced before. She closely observed Brother Wye's apology and Yozef's obvious discomfort and wondered.

## Maera Teaches Yozef

The Godsday memorial, tours of Yozef's projects, witnessing him explaining inheritance to Brother Wallington, and interviews with anyone who interacted with this strange man let Maera learn facts and impressions, but the information flow was one-way—from or about him to her. The opportunity presented itself to go in the other direction: her teaching Yozef.

They both attended a dinner reception at the abbey with senior brothers and sisters, the mayor of Abersford, Vegga as the magistrate, and two dozen other prominent men and women.

After the meal, the guests moved to a large room off the cathedral and engaged in what resembled a mixer, guests standing or sitting, sipping beverages, nibbling on tidbits, and circulating from one group and discussion to another.

It didn't take long for Yozef to become bored, until he drifted over and stood near Maera and six others talking about the history of Caedellium. After a few minutes, the group members dispersed, until only the two of them remained.

"Sen Keelan, I listened to your discussion, and I see you've quite an extensive knowledge of not just Keelan and its history, but of all the clans on Caedellium. I've done reading in the abbey library and have discussed this with

Abbot Sistian, but I'd like to learn more. I wonder if we could arrange to meet and you tell me more about the island and its history."

Maera nodded without expression. "Of course, Ser Kolsko."

Thus began daily hour-long sessions in the abbey library. Yozef took copious notes, while Maera talked, and she suggested several readings that he had missed in the abbey library. She also said there were other books in the St. Tomo's library at Caernford, but they didn't allow these to be taken from the library. Yozef said he was willing to pay to have a few of her highest recommendations copied, and she offered to write to the St. Tomo's abbot to see whether it could be arranged.

During the third sixday of such sessions, Kolsko made a suggestion. They had continued using each other's formal address. Maera had made an effort to be more familiar with several locals, but the relaxation hadn't occurred between her and Kolsko.

"Sen Keelan, since we've spent considerable time together, I wonder if we might dispense with the last names and use our first names, if that's appropriate and with your permission."

The question initially startled Maera. It was the first time someone had suggested *to her* that they use first names. She had always been the one who made the offer. A flash of indignation passed quickly at Kolsko's guileless query. After all, he was *different*, in Filtin Fuller's words.

"Of course . . . Yozef. You have permission to call me Maera."

For the rest of the month, Maera continued to pay visits to Yozef's enterprises and took voluminous notes on distillation, soap and paper making, banking, and other activities that had yet to come to fruition. These times, plus teaching Yozef about Caedellium, and their attendance at several meals with the Beynoms and other locals, resulted in their spending more time together than she had planned. At the social affairs, she noticed that they seemed to gravitate toward each other. She told herself it was because he was the most interesting person attending.

A month into her visit, reciprocal "lessons" began, this time with Yozef as the instructor. The topic was Yozef's views of Caedellium. It was her first experience in delving deeply into how someone from outside the island viewed Caedellium and its peoples, and it uncovered a new window overlooking a known world. Some of his ideas deserved longer thought, such as the inevitability of Caedellium being ruled by a single central authority. He asked several pertinent questions: Even if the Narthani left, wouldn't one of the mainland realms attempt the same, if only to stymie the Narthani? Perhaps not soon, but someday? Could Caedellium always exist as a collection of independent, jealous clans?

"I'm not convinced, Yozef, that Caedellium needs such a change. For one thing, I don't see the clans all agreeing."

"But isn't the Tri-Clan Alliance, soon to be the Five-Clan Alliance, as I hear you say, a step in such a consolidation? I'd predict that the advantages in defense and trade will be so obvious that it's only a matter of time before other clans join. My people would call it the 'domino effect,' where other clans see the advantages and, as more join, the pressure on the others will increase. Then, over time, central authority would grow."

"Who would rule? No clan will agree to be under the authority of another clan's hetman."

Yozef described different forms of governing; many Maera understood, but others, where the ordinary people had more decision-making power, seemed implausible. He assured her all of the systems had been tried in the past, some successfully and others failing. The variety was strange to her, but Anyar was wide and its history long enough that who knew what had existed or did exist elsewhere? In addition to everything else she'd learned about Kolsko, he never failed to give her more to think about.

She also found herself more and more relaxed, both in Abersford and particularly around Yozef. Without realizing it, she looked forward to their times together and was disappointed when a day passed without seeing him.

## Maera Learns to Properly Toast

The time for Maera to return to her family had come and gone. She'd already delayed a sixday longer than planned and was surprised that she wasn't eager at the thought of going home.

She was leaving her room at the Beynoms' house, heading for the dining area for morning meal, when Cadwulf burst into the house.

"Father! Mother! I—oh, Sen Maera, pardon my yelling."

Cadwulf's parents appeared, Sistian from his study and Diera from their bedroom.

"What's happening, son?" said Sistian. "Is there an emergency!?"

The young man flopped into a wooden chair, putting a hand to his chest. "Sorry. Sorry. I didn't mean to alarm anyone. It's just . . . just . . . *so* exciting! I spent the whole night at Yozef's house in his workroom. I don't think any of you has been inside, but he has blackboards covering two walls of the room. We ate last evening, and afterward he started explaining to me how to calculate the orbits of planets. We already do this, but he went further to show me the work of two scholastics of his people, one named Yohanes Kepler and the other Izak Newton. Kepler determined rules of how planets behave, and Newton provided the mathematical proof. Plus, Newton explained why things fall and how to calculate their speed and acceleration. It's called gravity, and there are equations for it, too!"

The parents and Maera looked at one another, perplexed by Cadwulf's exuberance and with no idea what he was talking about.

"You spent the entire night on this?" asked Diera.

"I did, not Yozef. He went to bed. I was too excited and spent the whole night going over the equations from Yozef to find faults. I couldn't. He said they could determine the paths of thrown objects, then fell asleep before he could give me details. It took me all night, but I derived them myself, and he's right. Tell me how fast an object is thrown and at what angle, and now I can tell you exactly how far it will travel."

Although Cadwulf tried explaining in more detail, Sistian was immediately lost. Diera lasted longer, but it was Maera who followed Cadwulf far enough to be impressed.

Later, she met Yozef for another general discussion session. She didn't mention Cadwulf's experience, though they rambled for three hours and veered over topics from the Narthani to other Anyar realms, the birds and animals of Caedellium, the relative merits of traditional Caedellium pancakes and Yozef's French toast, and on and on. They never seemed to run out of things to talk about.

*Odd*, thought Maera.

The abbey bell rang, signaling the traditional end of the workday and time for evening meal. Both of them were surprised how quickly time had passed. Maera had a sudden desire for the day to continue.

"What are your plans for evening meal, Yozef?"

He smiled. "I'm meeting Carnigan and Filtin at the Snarling Graeko for food and beers."

The warmth of his smile and obvious anticipation made her not look forward to her own meal with the Beynoms. Diera and Sistian were wonderful people, and she loved them dearly, but after a month and a half, their conversation was getting boring.

"Would it be possible for me to come, too?" she blurted without thinking.

"To the pub?" asked a surprised Yozef.

"Yes. While I've never been in a pub, I understand both men and women go, isn't that correct?"

He stared for a moment. *Grew up on Caedellium and doesn't know such details of common life? I guess being the hetman's daughter sheltered her.*

"Oh, yes. Customers are mainly men, but there are always a few women." There were no cultural prohibitions on Caedellium against women in pubs; it just seemed that the inclination was more with men, as on Earth.

"I caution that the manner and language are less genteel than you may be used to, Maera."

"I'm sure there won't be anything I haven't heard before."

*Well, why not?* Yozef mused. *No one will act inappropriate with the hetman's daughter. Anyway, Carnigan, Filtin, and I will be there.*

"Fine, Maera, we'll be happy to have you join us."

However, "happy" was not the initial response of the pub's patrons, including Yozef's friends: surprise, astonishment, reservations, annoyance, confusion, astonishment, yes, but not happiness. The pub was already full of customers when the two of them arrived. As they walked to Carnigan's regular table, the din died away, first to silence and then a low buzz. At their table was the big man, plus Filtin and his wife, Nerlin, who occasionally joined them. Yozef thanked the fates for another woman besides Maera. Filtin's face bordered on shock when he spotted Maera. He jumped to his feet and pulled out a chair for her. Carnigan's response was even greater—for him—a raised eyebrow and another generous quaff from his stein.

"Sen Keelan, what a surprise," Filtin stumbled.

"Thank you, Filtin. I prevailed on Yozef to invite me. I have heard tales of pubs but have never been to one before."

"They're the most honest place on Caedellium," offered Carnigan. "If not before a few steins, then after. People tend to be who they really are."

Maera nodded politely, not quite sure what to make of the comment. Filtin and Yozef just stared at Carnigan. It was the most philosophical comment either had ever heard him make.

The barmaid made her way around tables to their location, all the time pushed from behind by the pub owner. At the table, the woman curtsied, and the owner made a nervous bow.

"Sen Keelan, an honor to have you in my establishment. Please let Paola here know whatever it is you wish."

Maera, oblivious that not all customers were curtsied and bowed to, looked at the steins on the table. "Whatever they are having is fine, Sen," she said, smiling brightly.

"Same here," said an amused Yozef.

The next hour was initially quiet on a scale usually only associated with the pub being closed, but as customers downed a few rounds, and nothing else unusual was happening, the decibel level slowly increased to near normal. Paola still curtsied every time she stopped at or passed their table. Maera was no stranger to beers and ales, though on a more modest scale than she was currently consuming.

By the time the pub served the meal of the evening, she was, if not inebriated, definitely relaxed and convinced she was "just one of the customers." The aforesaid meal that evening was, by chance, another of Yozef's introductions. Noodles of various kinds were common on Caedellium, as were a type of medium-sized tomatoes, transfers from Earth. They tasted more bitter than he was used to, but adding a little sugar more closely approximated tomatoes sufficient for sauces. Thus, it was not an off-putting food innovation, but more a different combination than local custom. No one questioned why he called the dish "spaghetti." Why would they? Yozef Kolsko called it that, so that it was. When served, no one on Earth would have used the word *spaghetti*, but Yozef figured what did the Caedelli know? Broad, thick noodles, a tomato-based sauce, local spices that were not basil and oregano but "sort of" and added a similar flavor, and meatballs more usually served in a thick gravy. It had become a regular offering at the Snarling Graeko but had not yet spread to the rest of Keelan.

The meal finished, another stein or so consumed, and most customers had forgotten or didn't care any longer about the hetman's daughter's attendance. As usual, when Yozef was in the pub, at a certain point in the evening friends or patrons pressed him for a story. Maera looked on with a quizzical eye, as the shouts for "Yozef, Yozef!" rang through the hall. He had long quit telling more than one per evening, because even with his apparently improved memory, his recall wasn't limitless. They had finished the spaghetti and meatballs when the call came that evening, and the food jogged his memory.

As soon as he acquiesced, they found their table surrounded by an anticipating crowd.

"A married man was having an affair with a widow, all unbeknownst to the man's wife. One day the widow comes to the man and tells him she's pregnant. Not wanting to ruin his marriage, the man convinced the woman to move to a different town. In return, the man, who had a very prosperous business, promised that he would send generous coin regularly to the woman for her and the child. To signal to him that the child had arrived, she was to send him a letter with only the word *spaghetti*. Sure enough, many months later the man arrives home to a puzzled wife.

"'Husband,' she says. 'A strange letter arrived today. I opened it, and all the letter says is 'Spaghetti, spaghetti—one with meatballs and one without.'"

Although the customers had seemingly adjusted to the hetman's daughter's presence, and "ribald" was a reasonable description of the culture, there were only subdued snickers and choked-back laughs, as eyes tracked a flushing Maera. Only when she started laughing did the others let loose.

An hour later, Filtin and Nerlin Fuller excused themselves to collect their children at her sister's. They bid the others good evening and walked the quarter mile to their home.

"Filtin, did you notice how Yozef and Maera got along?"

"Huh? What do you mean?"

"I don't know. Yozef is, you know . . . Yozef. He's odd, and people don't always feel comfortable with him. With Maera Keelan, it was different. Oh, she's the hetman's daughter and all that, so you don't expect her to be like common folk, but the two of them seemed so comfortable with each other."

"And that means, what?"

Nerlin sighed and rolled her eyes. "Let's get the children."

Another hour later and after the last beer, a wagon appeared at the pub, and Carnigan and Yozef drove Maera to her hosts' house near the abbey. Diera was sitting on a bench, obviously concerned about her visitor. Only when the three happy singing people pulled up and Carnigan jumped off the wagon to lift a tipsy Maera onto the ground did the abbess smile warmly and shake her head. With a friendly wave goodbye, the two men headed off, as Diera put an arm around giggling Maera and helped her into bed. While there was no question in the abbess's mind that anything inappropriate had happened, she had conflicting thoughts. On one hand, such behavior would *not* have been approved of by the hetman, and, on the other, she wondered whether Maera had ever been drunk or had as a good time as Diera suspected.

# CHAPTER 10

# AN OUTING

## Maera Probes

Maera had been at St. Sidryn's past the planned month, when her father wrote to inquire about her return date in words she interpreted as pushing her to come home soon. To her surprise, she regretted the time had passed so quickly. Her time at St. Sidryn's had been relaxing in an unexpected manner, as if moving to an alternative lifestyle that was appealing in ways she didn't fully understand.

She had anticipated delving into St. Sidryn's library, one of the island's more comprehensive collections of books, letters, and other writings on the island's history, clan politics, and the events that led to establishing the Clan Conclave at Orosz City. While the original agreement that brought relative order to the island's clans was on display at the conclave site in Orosz, a signed copy lay behind glass at St. Sidryn's.

She had worked through an impressive list of readings during the visit, but there were still many more left unread. She prioritized readings she would ask her father to pay to have copied. She didn't doubt his acquiescence.

Another reason for her reticence to return home was Yozef Kolsko. Although she had started with a cautious attitude to her father's assignment to assess this stranger making multiple impacts on Keelan, she became more and more interested in understanding him personally and his influence on the people of Abersford and St. Sidryn's.

Objectively, he still looked ordinary, of average height and build, though with a relaxed manner. She agreed with the general impressions that he was "odd." His different interpretation of events from what the clanspeople saw was one example. Another was his belief in the value of what he called "exercise." The first time Maera had seen him "running," she thought something was chasing him. A village boy matter-of-factly told her that every other day Yozef ran six miles from his house past the abbey and the village, then down to the beach and along the sand back home. People ran if being chased, or children ran at play. Men might play various games that required running, though usually young men and in groups.

The weights she'd only heard others tell of witnessing. Why lift weights, unless for work? It seemed somehow almost perverse, like descriptions in books of mainland religious sects that scourged themselves to atone for sins. Had Yozef committed some great sins? After all, he was a stranger, and who knew what customs or religion his people followed?

The explanation for the exercise came from Yozef himself. Maera, as was her custom, simply asked.

"Yozef, why do you do this exercise you're so diligent about? Is it part of the customs of your people?"

"There are two main reasons. Well, actually three, I suppose. The first is for general health. Our bodies are made to be used. Consider different people and their professions or work. Often, you can guess what kind of work they do by the shape of their bodies. If you see a rotund person, you'd guess they worked standing or sitting, without much movement. You seldom see farmers with large bellies, because they move and work their bodies. No matter what your work, running or fast walks get the heart pumping and the blood moving faster. You wouldn't expect someone who never lifts heavy weights to do it suddenly, so neither should you expect your heart and veins to be fully capable, unless they have also had their exercise."

"And the weights?"

"They're less for general health than for having strength and personal feelings. Naturally, overseeing my projects doesn't require strength. However, you never know when a little more strength will be important. I hope never again to experience anything like the Buldorian raid, but if it happens again, my chances of surviving and helping others will be better if I'm stronger.

"Then there's the personal reason. I feel better about myself when I exercise. Other children considered me a weakling, and my feelings about that have evidently lasted into adulthood."

Yozef didn't elaborate that "Yozef the First" was the stereotypical unathletic nerd for as long as he could remember. "Yozef the Second" had potential, and it pleased him that the new version could do what the earlier one couldn't have.

Maera accepted Yozef's explanation without further comment, although she discussed it later with Diera, who had had similar discussions with Yozef and come to suspect he was right about the advantages for general health. Maera still thought the running and the weights strange, as well as peculiar habits.

More interesting was his depth of novel knowledge. Often, sometimes out of thin air, Yozef would reveal bits of knowledge that proved useful or gave the impression the listener was the one who didn't appreciate the significance.

She accepted that Yozef was more interesting than anyone she'd ever met. Most of all, however, he *listened* to her. And not just listened but expected her to have ideas of her own. At first, it made her uneasy, though by now she had begun to feel exhilarated during their discussions. He also was a sponge for information and seemingly had no problem that the person satisfying his craving was a woman. Thus, when she settled on leaving for Caernford in three days, she found herself melancholy.

Her time at St. Sidryn's was an end, and she began preparing mentally and gathering her things together. She and Yozef had taken to eating mid-day meal together with workers in one of his shops, in Abersford or in one of the abbey gardens, if they were working in the library. It was only days before she would leave when she realized that he was occasionally missing for hours, and no one could find him.

## Picnic

"Yozef, I've noticed you sometimes disappear, often for hours or a whole day, and no one knows where you've gone. It's becoming part of the rumors about the mysterious Yozef Kolsko. Is it a secret? Some people suspect you're somehow magical and vanish to who knows where? I hope I'm not intruding. I'm only curious."

Yozef hesitated, then answered, "Sorry to disillusion fantasies about me, but on occasion I like time alone. I'm talking and working with people all day most days. Sometimes I need to be away from people for a day or a few hours."

"Where do you go to be 'away'?"

Yozef grinned a shy, little-boy grin. "Into the hills. They rise sharply west of the village and down to the ocean. Within the hills are an amazing variety of terrains and plants. Hardly anyone goes there, which is unfortunate for them but good for me, since it's so quiet. I found a path up the first escarpment. At the top, there's a great view of the village, abbey, and shore. Sometimes I just sit there, if I don't have much time. Otherwise, I continue on where the land is rugged, and there's a series of valleys and dales. Each one is different."

Yozef paused, and his eyes took on a faraway focus. "One valley especially is quite amazing. I found it recently, and I've gone back once. Although the flowers are past their peak bloom, it's still beautiful."

*He's lonely*, Meara thought. *With all that's going on, all his projects, the obvious high regard everyone has for him, I wonder if everyone forgets that he was cast away here on Caedellium, never to see his home again.*

Without thinking, Meara blurted, "Would you take me there?"

Yozef was taken aback. As much time as they had spent together these last sixdays, it had been mainly time exchanging information and attitudes.

Yozef hadn't spoken before regrets at her impetuousness washed over her. *What was I thinking? Quick, what do I say to withdraw my silly question?*

Yozef looked at her with a different eye than before. He *liked* her. Somehow, showing her his special places wasn't an issue.

"I'd like that. But would it be appropriate for someone of your position? And what would the abbot and the abbess say? They might have reservations about you going to such a place without appropriate accompaniment."

*Does he mean go off with men without proper chaperone or guards? It probably* would *be inappropriate. And how exciting! Besides, I can take care of myself.* Excitement gave way to apprehension. *Maybe he doesn't want to take me. Maybe he doesn't like me. Oh, good God, here I am, confused and what's my mind doing?*

Suddenly, a day away from being "Maera Keelan" and seeing some of Yozef's special places were the most appealing thoughts she had had in forever.

"They can be managed," she said.

"Are you sure about the abbot and the abbess?"

"I'm the hetman's daughter, and they aren't my guardians." Then she smiled. "Besides, I'll make it up to them somehow, and I'll let Diera know I'm safe with Yozef and Carnigan."

Yozef looked disappointed. "Carnigan would go with us?"

Maera grinned mischievously, something that made her look very different and young. "I won't say Carnigan will be with us *all* the way to your valley, assuming you can get him away for the day."

Yozef grinned back. "I'll see if I can convince him."

They didn't plot further the next day, but as their paths crossed the following morning, Yozef slowed and whispered, "Tomorrow after morning meal, in the grove of trees in back of the abbey grounds. Wear clothes and shoes for riding and walking."

She nodded conspiratorially and kept going.

The next morning, Yozef and Carnigan waited in the grove with three horses, food, and water for the day. The morning coolness was fading when a slim figure in a reddish-brown hooded robe carrying a bag came furtively up the path from the rear door of the complex's stone wall.

"Gracious, I wonder who this could be," said a sardonic Carnigan.

"Little Red Riding Hood?" mumbled Yozef.

"Who?"

"Never mind."

The figure walked quickly, head tilted forward to further hide the face. She walked between the trunks of two large trees and stopped, her head turning in several directions. Then, apparently not seeing well, she pulled back the hood. Maera caught sight of them and hustled over to where they held the horses. She was flushed, with an expression that reminded Yozef of his older sister's three-year-old daughter and a look the niece had when about to do something she wasn't allowed.

"Yozef, Carnigan," she greeted them. "I told Diera we'd be back an hour before sundown at the latest. She promised not to tell Abbot Sistian unless we were late."

"That shouldn't be a problem. Where we'll go is not that far, and we'll take the horses first toward a beach, one of my favorite spots."

Maera nodded and accepted Carnigan's gesture to help her mount the older, gentle mare he'd chosen for her. While Maera was an accomplished rider, Carnigan was taking no chances with the hetman's daughter. She sat on the Caedellium version of a woman's side-saddle, her robe covering everything, except the foot and the calf of the left leg resting in one stirrup.

Yozef rode his gentle, gray gelding, Seabiscuit, while Carnigan's horse made the other two appear like ponies. The Percheron-like horse stood nineteen hands high and was stoutly built. It took a steed of such dimensions to accommodate Carnigan's bulk.

When they mounted, Yozef indicated to Carnigan, "We're set. Lead on, McDuff."

Carnigan ignored the Shakespeare misquote, accustomed to pretending indifference to odd utterances from his strange friend.

They started off in single file, Carnigan in the lead, followed by Maera, with Yozef deliberately trailing to get into Seabiscuit's rhythm before Maera saw him still trying to remember how to ride. He needn't have worried, because Seabiscuit still knew more about riding than he did.

They followed a winding game trail through the woods for a mile, before it opened onto a narrow road they followed few hundred yards and then onto another two-mile trail through brush. They reached a dry ravine and followed it down to a beach four hundred yards wide with whitish-cream sand and gentle waves breaking twenty to thirty yards across the flat expanse. Yozef's cove and retreat house lay only a half-mile away, but he wasn't ready to share *every* special place.

Yozef thought the day perfect—skies with scattered fluffy clouds breaking up the solid blue, gentle winds coming off the sea, and an occasional gull or flyers that looked and sounded like gulls.

As they rode along the sand, Yozef let Seabiscuit come next to Maera's horse.

"I remember visiting one of my mother's relatives several times when I was young. They lived near the sea, and they would take my cousins and me to a beach. The adults would sit under shade and talk about adult topics, while the kids played in the sand and the water. I always wondered why the adults didn't come and play, too, because it was more fun than sitting and talking. Even now, I wonder whether children don't have a deeper insight sometimes than adults."

Maera smiled. "I also remember that age. Several times a year, we'd travel to a shore. I loved to take off my shoes and run in the surf." Her voice was gentle, as she retrieved a fond memory.

"Here's your chance, Maera. We have enough time, and who knows what the surf will be like on the way back?"

"My chance?"

"To run in the surf again."

"I was a child then," Maera protested.

"What? You're too stuffy now as an adult to have fun?"

Maera glared at Yozef, who stared back unrepentant. Seeing he was unimpressed by her glare, she finally sighed. "All right, so maybe it *does* sound appealing. And I'm not stuffy."

Carnigan grunted ahead of them.

"I heard that, Carnigan Puvey! I am *not* stuffy."

When there was no response from Carnigan, she asked, "Well, am I?" a little plaintively.

"You're stuffy," asserted their chaperone.

Maera harrumphed, then was silent for a few moments.

"Well, I don't think I'm stuffy. But Yozef's right. If here's an opportunity to walk in the surf and I don't take it, then maybe I'll have to reconsider my *stuffihood.*"

She laughed, reined in, stepped off the saddle, and gave the horse to Carnigan, who had followed her in dismounting and accepted the reins with a quizzical expression. Maera walked out toward the water into shallow waves running up the beach. When the first push of water reached her, she skidded back until the water slowed and stopped. She reached down, slipped off her shoes and stockings, and carried them farther away from the water to a washed-up log. She returned to the water, but this time let the water sweep past her, holding up the robe to avoid getting it wet—a futile attempt, since by the fourth wave she spent most of her time holding up its soaked bottom.

Several unladylike exclamations erupted, followed by, "Well, curse it all! If I'm going to do this, I might as well do it properly!" She gave Yozef and Carnigan a threatening glare. "If you tell anyone about this, you'll wish the Narthani had gotten hold of you!"

She raced back to the log and shucked off the robe, then folded it into a quick ball and ran back to the water. Yozef whistled softly, while Carnigan raised an eyebrow and smothered a laugh, almost. Under the robe, she wore a short, printed dress more decorative than usual for Caedellium women and probably expensive enough to explain why similar garments were not common. The print depicted large colored flowers against an off-white background. Maera walked into the water, out to where it washed halfway up her calves.

*Nice legs*, Yozef observed to himself, still sitting on his horse.

"Why are you still sitting there like some statue?" huffed Carnigan, who tilted his head in Maera's direction.

Yozef grinned. "Good point." He dismounted and handed his reins to Carnigan, who walked the three horses farther away from the water to a grove of trees, where he could tie them up, sit in the shade, and watch the children.

Yozef shed his boots and socks, rolled up his pant legs, and walked after Maera. She was fifty yards away and obviously enjoying the moment. Yozef hesitated to interrupt, so got to within twenty yards and simply followed her. One larger wave surprised her, and she gave a squeal of delight as she raced away from it. When she turned back to the water, she saw Yozef following for the first time. She froze for a second, then relaxed.

"Oh, Yozef, I haven't done this for ever so long. Appropriate or not, I should thank you for the prompting, even if I am stuffy."

"I think you just occasionally forget to simply have fun."

Her bright manner faded. "I think you're right. It's just that there always seems to be something serious weighing on me every moment."

"Life is full of serious moments, but I don't believe God wants us to forget the moments of joy and pleasure. One of our philosophers believed that pain and joy were complementary and that without both you couldn't understand either."

Maera furrowed her brow and rubbed the back of her neck. "I can see the argument. No matter what, there should always be time for joy and hope. Otherwise, what's the purpose of it all?"

They walked side by side along the beach, talking like close acquaintances, though not touching. At the end of the beach, they turned and walked toward where Carnigan sat against a tree, dozing.

"So much for our guard," chuckled Maera.

"I imagine if anything happened, Carnigan would be on the spot before you might think."

"He's an imposing figure. I didn't know men came that large, until I saw him the first time."

"When was that?" asked Yozef, as they reached the log and their shoes.

"Three years ago, if I remember correctly," she answered, brushing off her feet and donning her shoes. "It's not clear to me what his exact role is at the abbey. He's not a member of any of the orders. I asked Abbot Sistian, but he was evasive. I suspect he's a probationer."

"A probationer?" Asked Yozef.

"A person who has committed some deed that got him in front of a magisterial court and is sentenced to the custody of someone to watch him, until the court or the custodian determines he can either resume normal Caedellium life or be banished from the island. I suspect the abbot is the custodian, so whatever Carnigan did must have been serious."

"Somehow, I can't see Carnigan doing anything to get into that much trouble. He's one of the nicest persons I've ever met."

"Carnigan Puvey? Nice!? Everyone's afraid of him!"

"Just because people are afraid of him doesn't mean there's any reason to be."

She glanced at Yozef quickly, then back to her shoes. Yozef was one of the smartest people she'd ever met, though he hid it behind general affability. She also suspected he was one of the deepest persons, though she had no idea what was in those depths. If he thought Carnigan was "nice," maybe she should take a closer look at his huge friend.

They walked to Carnigan and the horses, woke the man, and mounted, after Maera pulled a smock from her bag and tied the robe to the back of the saddle. They rode another mile to a cliff cutting off the beach, led the horses up a half-hidden game trail to the top of the bluff, and left Carnigan and the horses. Off they went, Yozef carrying a backpack and Maera a smaller bag she'd pulled from her larger one. It took another hour to reach Yozef's special place. As they crested a hill, the sun shone straight up at high noon. The sky was still clear, except for the scattered clouds, and they heard only their footsteps and breathing, the slight whisper of wind across their ears, and occasional nearby avian calls.

They stood on the crest for several minutes. For Yozef, it was his third visit, but was Maera's first. Though the bloom was past peak, Maera took in the scene, amazed. A stream meandered through the valley floor and scattered jacaranda trees, with golden poppies not quite carpeting the valley floor. The sandy soil was perfect for the poppies, as long as there was sufficient rain, which there had been more than enough of this year. The only difference on this trip was a native white flower now interspersed with the poppies.

They walked down the hill, stepping on and through carpets of gold and white flowers. Maera initially attempted to avoid stepping on them but soon gave up and strode through them, copying Yozef. At the floor of the valley, they picked a spot near the stream and under one of the more impressive trees, with a trunk three feet across and branches spread so wide the canopy width was greater than the tree height. As with all jacarandas, the foliage was sparse, so that even with a tree of this size, the filtered light danced beneath it, as the leaves moved in the breeze.

Yozef pulled a thick linen cloth out of his pack and started to spread it on the ground. Maera hastened to the other end, and they laid it out, so Yozef could set the pack on it and begin pulling out the mid-day meal.

"You said your people call this a 'picnic'? Why is there a separate name?"

"Most meals are more formal affairs, even if the food is plain and little of it. A picnic is when you eat outdoors and usually in a family or group setting. It's considered a fun thing to do, and the typical foods on a picnic also make it a little different."

Not having fried chicken, potato salad, and watermelon on hand, Yozef had improvised with what *was* available. A roll of hard sausage, hunks of three different cheeses, olives, a loaf of dark bread baked that morning, large green grapes, a hunk of sweetbread, and a flagon of grape wine that would have scandalized his wine-snobbish father. He assumed the wine was made from descendants of wild North American grapes, because the wine had the musty essence called foxy.

They sat on the linen, nibbled on the food, sipped the sweet wine, and simply talked as two acquaintances with no other references to the outside world. Two hours passed. Normally, she wasn't a prodigious eater, but today Maera's appetite surprised her.

They talked about her family, his family, his efforts to adjust to Caedellium and accepting he would probably never see his family again, and her frustrations at the limited roles of women, a topic she had seldom spoken of with anyone, particularly men.

"I can see it would be difficult here for women of your intelligence," Yozef remarked.

She eyed him pointedly. "You think I'm intelligent?"

"Maera," he chided, "anyone but an idiot could tell you're one smart cookie."

"Cookie?"

"Sorry. A phrase from home. Think of it as saying you're one of the smarter people around."

Maera flushed, not from embarrassment, but from appreciation. "Yozef, that's the first time in my life that anyone besides my parents has directly said that to me."

"I'm sorry if this offends you, but your people are backward . . . some would say stupid . . . not to acknowledge women of ability."

"*I'm* not offended, although I'd caution you to say such things carefully. Our customs are old and mean well, but we're only slowly allowing women more roles—Keelan more than many clans. I take it, then, that your people have different customs?"

"Some different and some similar. After all, we're all humans with the same needs and wants, even we if try to fulfill them in different ways. My people believe that there's nothing a woman should be restricted from doing, if she has the ability and desire. Anything less means that society is deliberately losing all of the contributions women could make."

"But men and women are *not* the same," Maera said. "There are roles that one fills that the other cannot. No man is going to bear and birth children. And men are generally much stronger and do the heaviest work and fighting."

"Having different roles doesn't require predetermined limitations. A woman can have children and still fill an important role outside the family, at least at some time in her life. It should also be the decision of the woman what roles she *wants* to fill. If it's her wish to be a traditional wife and mother, then fine. However, it should also be fine even if she doesn't want to marry or have children."

"Not marry and no children!" exclaimed Maera. "Then *what* is she? Who *is* she?"

"I am not saying it's a good thing or bad, only that it should be her choice and not forced on her."

"Although I appreciate what you are saying, things aren't that way here on Caedellium. While I would wish more opportunities for myself, I still want children and a family."

Yozef patted her hand sympathetically. "It must be terribly hard for you. Most people would imagine an attractive hetman's daughter would have everything she could desire and suitors beating down the doors. I'd hate to imagine you hiding who you are to fit roles not of your own choosing."

Maera, to her astonishment, found herself tearing up. It was the first time anyone in her life had come close to understanding how out of place she felt and the conflict between being who she *was* and who she was *supposed* to be. She placed her other hand on Yozef's briefly, then withdrew it and tried to change the subject.

"These cheeses are a specialty of the district. The brownish one doesn't look good, but put a piece on your tongue and just let it sit there until all the flavors come out." She reached past him for the cheese and came within a few inches of his face. He put a hand on her shoulder, making her stop and meet his eyes. Maybe it was the wine, the food, the perfect setting, or exposing themselves in the last few hours, but he drew her to him and kissed her.

She was startled and drew back slightly. When she didn't draw back farther, Yozef pulled her to him again and *they*, not just he, kissed. Their lips massaged each other, first pressing urgently, then softly, then moving over each other's lips. Her breathing deepened, as he drew her tighter until they pressed together from waist up. A hand that had been stroking her back moved slowly across her side to a breast. Maera jerked back suddenly and jumped to her feet.

Yozef looked up at her. *Oh, shit, maybe that wasn't a good idea.*

"I'm sorry, Maera. Please excuse me. I didn't mean to offer offense."

She said nothing, her mind a vortex of conflicting thoughts and feelings. *He's sorry he kissed me? Should I be offended? I didn't give him permission for the kiss. Am I sorry I pulled back? Does he think he has privileges with me, in spite of our difference in station? Does he like me? Do I like him? Was it offensive that he touched my breast? Why did it feel exciting when he did? What am I thinking, and how am I supposed to react?*

"It is getting late. We need to be back before Diera worries, and I still have packing to do." With that, she began gathering up their picnic food.

"Maera, please excuse me. I didn't mean to offend you. Let's talk about this."

"Time to go," she only repeated and wouldn't say another word, as they collected the remains of their picnic and walked back to Carnigan, who immediately sensed something was amiss. He scowled at Yozef, who answered with a shrug and a two-handed motion that indicated lack of knowledge. No one spoke during the entire ride back to the abbey.

# CHAPTER 11

# DILEMMA

### Maera Leaves the Abbey

Two days later, Maera left to return to Caernford. As arranged by her father, a carriage, a driver, and four outrider escorts had come to Abersford the previous day. She hadn't seen Yozef since their excursion and wondered whether he would be present at the farewell. Considering all of the time they spent together, his absence would be noticed by the Beynoms.

Her feelings about the events were confused. Should she be angry at him for effrontery? What would she say when they met again? She had no answers.

Maera rose early and finished packing. She traveled light, not seeing a need for too large a wardrobe. She left with the same amount of baggage as on her arrival, balancing presents she had brought from her family to the Beynoms with gifts from the Beynoms she was taking back to her family. The other major item was her satchel with notes and diagrams, mainly details of the raid and pages of observations, much of which related to Yozef.

After a final morning meal with the Beynoms, with baggage loaded on and in the carriage, she made her goodbyes. The parting party was small—the Beynoms, their two sons, several abbey brothers and sisters she had interacted with, and Yozef Kolsko, standing to one side.

Diera hugged her firmly. "It was wonderful you could visit this long, child. We hope not as much time passes before we see you again."

"Same with me, Diera," said Maera. "The next time Sistian travels to Caernford, you should come with him and stay awhile."

"I'd like that, but no promises, since there never seems to be a time when there aren't a thousand things here I need to do."

"Well, make the time. You're the abbess. Take advantage of it once in a while," Maera chided, then turned to Sistian.

The abbot was still grumpy about how she'd slipped away without escorts or guards and then steadfastly declined to tell him what she had done that day.

"I'm still angry at you," he said in a tolerant tone, spoiled by smiling and enveloping her in his arms, her forehead buried in his beard.

When she resurfaced, she whispered apologetically, "Sorry, Sistian, but occasionally you need to be someone else, even if for only part of a day."

She then turned to Yozef, who had edged his way forward, his face impassive.

"A pleasant journey home, Sen Keelan."

"Thank you, Ser Kolsko. I enjoyed our conversations and will report to my father about all of your interesting projects."

The two using formal addresses had passed over the abbot's head, but Diera's eyes narrowed. Had she missed something here? They'd been on a first-name basis for the last several sixdays. It was curious.

Maera made polite thanks and farewells to several others gathered by her carriage, then climbed through the carriage door held open by one of her escorts. He then remounted, and the party exited the main complex gate, turned left toward Abersford and the road junction leading to Clengoth, and on to Caernford farther inland.

The farewell grouping in the courtyard dispersed to their regular lives, but it didn't pass a now alert abbess that as Yozef walked back toward Abersford and his shops, he kept looking at the carriage party. Only when they were out of sight did he stop following their progress.

## Arriving Home

The trip back to Caernford took one long day's travel to cover the fifty miles. Normally, Maera would have spent the time alternately observing the countryside and attempting to read, despite the constant jostling on the dirt roads. Not this day. She causally noted passing terrain, but even when her head faced out the carriage windows, her mind was processing . . . something . . . that didn't quite rise to full awareness. Whatever went on in her thoughts, she arrived at Keelan Manor as if only a few hours had passed, instead of the entire day.

The first family member she saw was Mared. Her youngest sister sat on the front veranda, waiting to be the first to see Maera arriving so she could spread the news. As the party turned into the approach to the manor, Mared jumped up, waved both arms, and ran inside. By the time the carriage halted in front, Mared and Anid, the next-youngest sister, stood at the bottom of the stairs, her mother and father on top.

"Maera, Maera, you're home!" shouted Mared, rushing to hug her eldest sister the moment one of her feet met the ground.

"Yes, and I'm glad to see you, too," reciprocated Maera with a hug of her own, soon widened to include Anid—who, being four years older than Mared and considering herself more mature, waited until both of Maera's feet were on the ground.

"You've been gone *so* long!" said Mared. "You said it would only be a six sixday visit. It's been *eight* sixdays!"

"Turns out, there was more to do than I expected, but I'm glad to be home."

With her arms around her sisters, she climbed the stairs to her parents.

"Welcome back, Maera," said Breda with a twinkle, a kiss on the cheek, and a hug. "And yes, we all missed you terribly. Even your father, although he might not admit it."

"What do you mean, I won't admit it?" exclaimed Hetman Keelan and enveloped his daughter in a crushing hug. "I hadn't realized it until your mother told me, but this is the longest you've ever been away from home. I confess to all present that I missed you. Of course, mainly for assisting me in clan affairs." His smile and embrace belied the last words. After another round of hugs, the family went inside.

"Where is Ceinwynd?" asked Maera. "Still pouting?"

The next-oldest sister blamed Maera for their father's cool reception to potential Ceinwynd suitors. Statements by both parents that she was still too young did nothing to dissuade her belief that they were waiting for the eldest daughter to marry first. Maera suspected another reason was that her parents thought Ceinwynd too immature for that serious step but hadn't conveyed it convincingly to Ceinwynd. Maera also knew Ceinwynd considered herself unattractive and wanted a head start on getting a husband.

"Oh, you know Ceinwynd," said Breda. "Being put-upon by the world is her normal condition. I forget exactly what terrible imposition we put on her today, so she's in her room, sulking again."

"It's something to do with a new dress she insists is essential to her happiness," said Culich, resignedly.

"Oh, yes, now I remember," Breda said. "Anyway, she'll be down for dinner, and if the pattern holds true, she'll be close to normal by then."

## Home, but Not Present

Maera outwardly resumed her routine. She ate morning meal with various combinations of her three sisters or ate alone. When called on by her father, she helped prepare communications to his boyermen, to other hetmen, or with whomever he corresponded. She accompanied her mother and sisters on shopping in the city and exchanged letters with Anarynd "Ana" Moreland, her best friend, and whose family was distantly related to the Moreland hetman. In her rooms or the St. Tomo's library, Maera continued her studies of Caedellium history and books available about other lands on Anyar and refreshed her studies of several mainland languages. She arranged to copy several texts from St. Sidryn's library and walked the manor grounds. During that time, an astute observer would have noted that her walks lasted as long as an hour or more, instead of the usual quarter to half-hour. Breda Keelan was an astute observer.

"Have you noticed anything about Maera since she got back?" Breda asked Culich one evening, two sixdays after her daughter's return.

"Noticed what?"

"If she's acting different."

"Different?"

"Yes, different," she said in exasperation. "Your daughter, you know, the one away at St. Sidryn's for over a month."

Breda now had her husband's attention. His eyes focused on his wife, as he considered the original question. "Maera acting different. I assume you mean from before she went to St. Sidryn's?"

"Yes," said Breda, looking heavenward and shaking her head.

Culich reviewed the last few days since his daughter's return. *Was* she acting differently?

"Now that you mention it, she seems a little quieter than usual."

"And her dress?" Breda prompted.

"Her dress . . . her clothing . . . how she dresses, you mean? N-o-o-o, can't say I've noticed anything." Culich then smiled at his wife. "But I take it from the direction of this conversation that Maera's been acting different in several ways, including being quieter than usual and dressing differently, I'm sure you'll enlighten me about details I've missed."

Breda rapped him affectionately with her hand.

"I admit I may be imagining it, but I'd swear Maera is taking more care of her clothes and appearance. She's never fussed over such things, except on formal occasions when she has to be the 'hetman's daughter.'"

"I'll take your word in matters of Maera's clothing. Is it supposed to mean something?"

"With any other young woman, I might wonder if she's taken an interest in a young man."

Culich started. *Maera?* He was quiet, while he processed his wife's intuition. He couldn't find anything supportive in his memory, but he had long ago learned to listen to his wife about certain matters. His reasoning centers now took over. If Maera was interested in a man, who would it be? If someone new, she must have met him at St. Sidryn's. Nothing in her letters had—

Culich's internal dialogue churned, making new connections.

Wait . . . someone had been prominent. Not in her personal letters, but in her observations and reports.

*Yozef Kolsko?*

Breda watched her husband's face during his review. The expression "read like a book" might not be part of the Caedelli lexicon, but it would have been appropriate for her detecting when an idea coalesced in Culich's mind.

"You've thought of something, dear," she prompted.

"Just that if this happened while she was at St. Sidryn's, there's only one name that comes to me. A name of someone who caught her attention, although I wouldn't have associated the attention with anything personal—at least, without your original questions."

A light went on behind Breda's watchful eyes. "The mysterious stranger the Beynoms have written about? Yozef something or other?"

"That's the only name I can come up with. Of course, it could be someone different whom she never mentioned, all of this assuming there is anything to this at all and not just our imaginations."

Breda sat back in her chair, folded her hands in her lap, and stared off over Culich's head. He gave her the same time she had given him.

"You may be right," she said after a long moment. "It could fit. I've read you parts of her letters to me, and I've seen the ones to you. What I may not have shared with you is that at times, when referring to this Kolsko, her writing sounded enthusiastic. For Maera, anyway. Now that I recollect her words, perhaps a bit entranced, although she didn't come right out with it. She wrote that he listens to her and values her opinions and knowledge. They evidently spent many hours together, with Maera telling him about Caedellium's history and customs, and he explaining his various projects to her. I guess at the time when I read the letters, I was pleased that Maera kept busy and interested in the visit. Now . . ."

"I should talk to Maera about this," said her concerned father.

"No," said Breda, "*I* should talk with her first."

"You don't think they . . . you know?"

Breda snorted. "You should know your daughter better than that. If anything, Maera takes her duty to the family and clan *too* seriously. Did they bed while she was at St. Sidryn's? Definitely not. Whatever is going on inside Maera, however, it's something new for her. I'll see if I can tease it out of her. You know your daughter, though. If she doesn't want to tell us something, she won't."

## Letters

While Maera herself wasn't sure what she thought—or more accurately, *felt*, she knew the departure from St. Sidryn's had been too abrupt. If *she* had been confused at the time, what must Yozef be thinking? She decided she wasn't angry at him. However, Yozef might believe her offended by his effrontery at kissing a hetman's daughter.

Why had he kissed her? Did he think she'd encouraged him? She didn't see how, although her experience was limited, despite Ana's fruitless attempts to teach her the art of flirting.

As for Yozef, as much as he seemed to have adjusted to Caedellium, who knew whether the customs of his people and hers confused mutual understanding? Whatever Yozef's feelings and intentions, it was *she* who broke off communication. He had attempted to apologize if the kiss offended her. She had refused to speak with him after the kiss and had barely acknowledged his presence on the morning when she left to return to Caernford. Therefore, it was up to her to reinitiate contact.

Maera first wrote of her pleasure at having met him and thanked him for time spent showing her his shops and discussing issues of mutual interest. She closed the short, neutral letter with crafted questions about his projects and her arrangement to copy several books he'd expressed interest in reading. The questions implied a desire for answers and thereby a return letter to Maera. She omitted mention of their picnic or her departure.

Eight days later, a return letter arrived. Given that the quickest she might have received an answer was four days, after those four days she worried he wouldn't answer, and as each day's mail arrived, her anxiety grew. She found herself both relieved and unexpectedly nervous when Yozef's letter came. She tore open the outer paper and quickly scanned the letter, then relaxed and slowly read it again. He was pleased to receive her letter and learn she had arrived home safely. He had been happy to show her his shops and discuss issues and thanked her for arranging book copying. He answered her questions and countered with a couple of his own about her family, her studies, and how was the weather in Caernford? The exchange left open opportunities for future letters.

## Yozef Kolsko Is Different

It was two days after Maera's parents discussed her changed behavior and possible implications, when Breda Keelan sensed the opportunity had arrived to probe. In the early afternoon, mother and daughter sat on the back veranda finishing mid-day meal. The conversation had been about the usual: Mared's interests in learning, much as Maera had been at that age; Anid's chafing at scholasticum work; Ceinwyn's moping so much, her mother had finally taken her to task. They touched on news of the Narthani, Maera's latest letters from Anarynd, and wasn't this the nicest weather? With the preliminaries out of the way, Breda struck. Guilelessly, she hoped.

"I'm glad you met and became acquainted with this Kolsko fellow. He seems to be making quite a mark in Keelan and beyond. He sounds very mysterious."

"Mysterious? Yes, I suppose so. Mysterious sounds somewhat ominous, though." Maera paused for a moment. "Different? Definitely."

"How different?"

"Certainly, with all of the new ideas he's brought with him, particularly making things we didn't have on Caedellium before. Not just the ether and kerosene lanterns, but new soaps, papers, and yes, the kotex."

Breda smiled. "I have to say, it seems odd for a man to think of such a product. I can't imagine your father even discussing the topic. He'd be mortified. So how does Yozef Kolsko do it?"

"Mother, he just casually *knows* things. That was only one example. Diera is alternately ecstatic and chagrined at the new medicant knowledge she's learned from him. As with so much, it's not that he's an expert in any particular area. He seems to pull pieces of knowledge out of the air."

"So, it's not that he's that smart, just that his people have more general knowledge than we do?"

"Oh, it's assured his people know so much more, but he's smart himself."

"How smart, compared to other people?"

Maera considered. "Probably at least as smart as Diera and Sistian or any of the scholastics at St. Sidryn's and St. Tomo's."

Breda noted that Maera hadn't included her father in the list of the smartest people she knew. She wasn't offended. Culich Keelan never pretended to be an intellect. He wasn't dense, and his intuitions, skill at reading people, and ability to see long term, when combined with honesty and integrity, made him a formidable hetman.

"And what about yourself, Maera? Is he as smart as you?"

Maera looked sharply at her mother. She knew Breda understood that her eldest daughter was smart—very smart. Breda also had been comforting when Maera expressed frustration over dealing with others who couldn't follow or agree with her thinking. However, Breda had never directly asked for Maera's own evaluation, nor had Maera ever given it. Until now.

"No," said Maera. "I can't say he is. I've never met anyone smarter than me." She continued looking straight at her mother with a firm and only slightly defiant stare. "He's definitely more so than all but only a few men I've met, although he's smart in a different way."

"*How* different?" asked Breda, surprised at Maera's bluntness, boast, or honesty, depending on how accurate was her assessment.

"I couldn't put my finger on it, until I realized he didn't feel pride in his intelligence and knowledge. It just *was*. He simply takes it for granted and doesn't mind others disagreeing with him or showing more knowledge."

"Could one of those others be yourself?"

Maera's cheeks colored, though she continued to look straight at her mother. "Yes, it could. All my life people have thought of and looked at me as being somehow not quite correct. When I was young, at times I tried to hide that I was smart to get people to like me more, but it never worked. Even you and Father. Mother, I know you and he love me, but there's always a hint that you wish I was a little more like other daughters. As for Father, though he values my help, in his heart of hearts he wishes I'd been born a son and feels awkward that I'm a *different* kind of daughter."

"Oh, Maera," said her suddenly teary-eyed mother, "both your father and I have always loved you dearly. If we've ever made you think we wished you were anyone other than who you are, please forgive us!"

Maera patted her mother's hand. "I'm not blaming either of you. If anything, I'd blame God or myself. Him for making me a person who feels out of place or myself for not either somehow changing myself or just accepting the way the world is."

"And Yozef Kolsko, how does he see you?"

"I sense he accepts me as I am. Possibly because he's not from Caedellium and doesn't come with ideas of roles he expects me to fill. Maybe his people are just different from ours. Maybe *he's* different. I don't know the reasons, but I didn't feel I had to worry about what I said. If he didn't understand something I was telling him, he simply asked it to be explained again or in more detail, not that he had any problem with me knowing more. When I disagreed with him, we'd discuss our differences and either come to an agreement or resolve to disagree without the need for one opinion to win out. It was . . . exhilarating."

Breda could hear some of the exhilaration and perhaps a *relaxation* of spirit, in Maera's tone, and, on hearing it, pangs of regret saddened her that Maera was only now able to share such feelings.

"So, Yozef Kolsko brought all this out in you, dearest?"

"Yes," asserted Maera.

"And more?"

"More?"

"You know what I mean, Maera. More than just being comfortable with him. He's a man, you're a woman—what do *you* think I mean?"

The color on Maera's cheeks came again, spreading to more of her face. "I *like* him, Mother. He's nice, compared to most of the men I've met. Not that being a hetman's daughter, the eldest daughter, and one expected to produce an heir to Keelan has allowed me to meet all that many men. And let's be blunt, the last few years the few new men I've met have been potential suitors. They've been hetmen or boyermen's sons, and those roles constrain what kind of men they grow into. I've always assumed one day I'd marry one of them for the sake of the family and Clan Keelan. I'd hoped to find a marriage like yours and Father's, but I'd given up that dream. I know my duty, that the day will come when I'll have to marry and have children. It's just . . . I dreaded that day and the thought of living the rest of my life with one of those suitors."

"I take it it's different with Yozef?" Breda unconsciously switched to using only his first name.

Maera was quiet, as she looked off into the fields north of the manor. Her gaze moved over the green fields, groves of trees, and scattered patches of wildflowers. "I don't know exactly what I feel." Several moments passed. "But it occurred to me that if I *had* to marry him, I don't have the dread I did with the suitors. I can't say if that's love like between you and Father, but as different . . . yes, even strange . . . as Yozef is, I respect him and am comfortable around him. No, that's not quite right either. There were a few times when we were together at St. Sidryn's that I felt more at ease than I can remember for years, except when I'm with Ana."

"Let's look at this from another perspective, dear," said Breda, a conspiratorial tone creeping into her voice. "Just for discussion's sake, what would be the advantages to the clan if you married Yozef?"

Maera looked sharply at her mother. She recognized the tone of voice from when she was plotting to convince Culich of something he might not initially favor.

"Well, the obvious advantage is to produce heirs for the clan and, secondarily, quiet any growing murmurs about that lack."

"Yes to the first of those, but I doubt the second is much of a concern for our family, at least not yet. What else?"

"He's rich. I was astounded at the amount of coin coming monthly from his enterprises, even after all the coin he puts into setting up new trades and contributing to various causes. Moreover, it's only going to increase from the trades and the new products he's already introduced. Blessed God only knows what he comes up with next. He may already be one of the wealthiest men in Keelan and eventually possibly in all of Caedellium. It would clearly be to the family's and the clan's benefit for a close alliance with such a resource."

Breda noted that Maera was into her analytic mode and for the moment was not thinking of herself and her feelings.

"It's not just the status of his wealth that might help us, it's how some of his ideas and the knowledge he brings from his people might help against the Narthani. I see all the reports Father sees, and I know how much he worries about the future, but I wonder if even Father is aware of the severity of the Narthani threat. I think Yozef *is*, and he's spending coin to make gunpowder and cannon. Caedellium may need every bit of help it can get to survive as a people, and I have the feeling in my bones that Yozef will somehow make a difference. How I don't know, but all my intuition yells it at me."

"So," Breda summarized matter-of-factly, "correct me if I've not heard right. If you *were* to marry Yozef, there's a good chance you would be 'comfortable' with the idea, it would help begin to produce Keelan heirs, and it would bind to the family and clan a man of great wealth and knowledge. Am I missing something, or does this not sound like a reasonable argument for you to marry this Yozef Kolsko?"

Maera stared at her mother for several seconds, then sighed and sat back in her chair. "Yes, Mother, it's a reasonable argument. I would need time to understand what I'm feeling. This is all so new to me. I'm not accustomed to feeling confused."

"Maybe the best thing to do is to invite this Yozef here to Caernford for a visit," Breda stated. "That way, you can have more time to be around him, and it's an opportunity for your father to meet him."

Maera considered the suggestion briefly, then said, "Yes, I agree that's a good plan. Even aside from myself, Father needs to meet Yozef, so he can assess for himself if and how Yozef can be helpful and to better understand how Yozef is going to change all of Caedellium, in one way or another." Maera paused. "How much of this should I discuss with Father?"

"Oh, I think it best to stick with the value of him meeting Yozef for himself. Let's see how that goes and leave the other parts for later. No point in confusing your father with multiple ideas at once," Breda said with a twinkle. "Besides, who knows what ideas might come to your father, all by themselves?"

*And with some subtle tweaks by Mother,* Maera suspected.

"Although it's probably too soon to consider this," said Breda, "if you decided you wanted to marry Yozef, how would it be proposed?"

The question hadn't occurred to Maera. By custom, the man usually proposed marriage, either to the woman or to her family. The woman taking the initiative was not uncommon; however, this was not a common situation for any of the parties.

Maera sighed. "Oh dear, I think it would have to be either Father or myself. Yozef's still uncomfortable with his understanding of our customs, and I doubt he'd propose on his own. I see no reason to involve Father at first. To be truthful, I'm not sure Yozef would even be interested in marrying me."

"He hasn't ever shown such interest? Man to woman?" Breda watched her daughter blush.

"Well, there was one instance at St. Sidryn's. He kissed me."

Breda's eyes widened. This was the first she'd heard of this. "What did you do?"

Maera stared in her mother's eyes and said with a firm voice, "I kissed him back. Then he touched me elsewhere, and I guess I panicked. It was the day before leaving, and I didn't speak to him again. I'm afraid he worried that he'd violated some custom or law. So I wrote to him, and we've exchanged several polite letters."

"My dear, so far I've heard nothing to make me think we shouldn't take a good long look at this Yozef Kolsko of yours, and getting him to Caernford is the first step."

# CHAPTER 12

# A TRIP TO CAERNFORD

**Invited**

Maera had sent her father written reports while she was at St. Sidryn's, and once she returned, they frequently discussed her visit, particularly the raid and her impressions of Yozef. Now, she spent several days preparing a detailed written analysis of Yozef's introductions, estimations of his future status on Caedellium, and his contributions to the defense against the raid. She ended by suggesting that a more personal analysis by the Keelan hetman would be in order. She didn't give the final version directly to her father but placed it, along with several other pieces of reading, into a basket for non-urgent reading on the upper left corner of his desk.

Two days later, Culich reached Maera's report. He read through it quickly. Then read it again, thought for a few minutes, and picked it up. He walked to the west wing of the manor and Maera's quarters, three rooms serving as her office, sitting room, and bedroom. He would normally have knocked before entering, but he walked straight into the office. Maera was at her desk, smaller than Culich's and infinitely neater, arranged in a corner with windows on two sides for maximum light and views of the surrounding gardens.

Maera looked up as her father entered, and she identified the papers in his hand. She had estimated when he would reach the report and come to discuss it with her; her estimation had missed by half an hour.

"Interesting reading, Maera," he said, holding up the report. "I've heard and read much of this already, but it was useful to see it all together. I think you're right. I need to finally meet this Kolsko myself. Abbot Sistian already urged me to visit St. Sidryn's, since Kolsko wasn't up to traveling yet. I considered it before the hetmen meeting, which is one reason I asked you to visit St. Sidryn's in my place."

*One reason,* wondered Maera. *There were others? Hmmm.*

"I doubt there's a problem with Kolsko traveling, Father. Maybe when he first came to Abersford, but not now. I know he's traveled to Clengoth several times."

"That settles it, then," said Culich. "I'll draft a letter to Sistian to tell Kolsko to come up here as soon as possible. I'll do it right now, while I'm thinking about it, and give it to you to edit and tidy up." Without thinking any discussion was needed, he turned and left.

*That was easy. But Father telling the abbot to* order *Yozef to come?* She had doubts about such a directive's reception. No Keelander would have hesitated, but Yozef? As mild-mannered and agreeable as he seemed, he wasn't from Caedellium, and based on what she gleaned from their conversations, Maera had the impression his people gave less deference to their leaders. Might he refuse to come?

An hour later, Culich returned. "Here's the letter to the abbot."

Their custom was that she would read a draft, make changes she thought necessary, then rewrite the correspondence and return it to her father for his signature. As expected, the draft was a simple directive for Abbot Sistian to send Yozef to Caernford. Besides the implied order, there was no mention of the timing, the purpose, or the length of the visit or any indication where Yozef would stay.

Back at her desk, she perused the draft, then amended the letter to *ask* Abbot Sistian if he would speak with Yozef Kolsko and *request* his coming to Caernford. Another read, and she added wording that the purpose of the visit was to allow Hetman Keelan to discuss past and future issues important to the clan, that accommodation would be provided at one of the manor's guest houses, and that the hetman would appreciate Yozef's visit. All very polite.

Maera copied the modified letter on better paper and took it to her father. She held her breath as he took it from her, waiting to see if he read it before signing, and if he did, how he reacted to the changes. She exhaled slowly when he didn't read it, signed it, and handed it back to her. He returned to his other paperwork.

Maera all but snatched the signed letter from his hand, went back to her office, and sealed the folded letter inside the thicker outer paper. She addressed the correspondence and placed it with other outgoing mail. It would be picked up first thing the next morning and be in the mail pouch for the Abersford area later that day.

Even with the modifications of her father's letter, Maera wasn't sure of Yozef's response. She found herself both eager to see him again and nervous about his reply. She wrote a separate letter to show that *she* also wanted him to come and not just to meet her father. Her letter was even more carefully crafted than her changes to her father's letter. Maera would look forward to his visit, so they could continue their discussions in person. She would show him the local sights. One last addition to the letter she included, then removed, and finally put back in. *She* would be happy to see him again.

## Off to See the Hetman

For Yozef, Maera's departure day had confirmed that he'd unwittingly overstepped. Not that he was mad at himself or her. A pleasant day, a fine picnic with wine, and a woman he liked and who gave off reciprocal signals, by Earth standards. He was still learning the rules on Caedellium and had momentarily forgotten caution. As regretful as his lapse had been, there seemed to be no lasting consequences, because two sixdays had passed without repercussions. Thus, he was surprised and slightly apprehensive when a letter from Maera waited at home one evening, delivered from the local magistrate's office that also served as the postal station.

He read the letter carefully, looking for references to his evident indiscretion. Nothing. It was as if it had never happened. He interpreted that all was reasonably well between them. He answered equally politely and correctly to that first letter and the several that followed. Other than the letters, his thoughts had only occasionally lingered over her.

Besides regular stops in his various shops, he was dabbling with several ideas to improve communications. Although cannon and gunpowder were among the obvious tools of warfare, the ability to communicate and control were force multipliers. He was considering paying to construct a spur semaphore line into Abersford from the line between Caernford and Gwillamer Province. He also suggested changes to the semaphore system to allow faster and more complex messages, but so far his ideas hadn't caught on. Not that he worried about it, because he was working on a telegraph. He hoped to have a simple test system running within a year. When finished, he then planned to work on a wireless telegraph, the next step to real radio.

When not in his shops, he continued his workouts and weapons practice on his own and each day assiduously wrote an hour or more in his English journals. He'd recently completed 80 percent of an introductory organic chemistry text, all that his enhanced memory could recall, and he'd started on electromagnetism. Not that any human on Caedellium could have understood any of it. Someday they might, however, and who knew? Maybe elsewhere on Anyar, the science was further advanced than on Caedellium.

His routine was interrupted the day he returned home to a new letter from Maera and a note from the abbot, asking him to come to the abbey the next day. Maera's letter alerted him to the abbot's request from Hetman Keelan and was the clearest sign of no permanent damage from his indiscretion with her.

As warned, the next morning Sistian passed on the hetman's "request" that Yozef come to Caernford for a sixday. Yozef saw no reason to let the abbot know about Maera's letter, so he pretended the invitation—or order, depending on the point of view—was news to him. He took the rest of that sixday to tidy up details of ongoing enterprises, most of which were producing products for sale and could, by now, run perfectly well without him. Those projects under development had enough inertia for a sixday. The abbot passed his acceptance back to Culich, and Yozef left for Caernford four days later.

Yozef decided to make the fifty-mile trip in a single day. Horseback was still not his favorite mode of transportation, particularly since to make the trip in one day required a hard pace. He asked the abbot's permission to see if Carnigan was interested in accompanying him to drive a carriage Yozef had bought. Sistian was doubtful about Carnigan's willingness, as was Yozef, but the big man surprised them both by accepting. Although the carriage had a compartment intended for passengers, Yozef rode atop beside Carnigan, which offered better views and allowed the two of them to talk. This made Yozef feel less awkward, because he considered Carnigan a friend and not an employee.

The countryside to Clengoth was familiar to Yozef from his previous trips to register land and hire workers, and the terrain continued the same farther north on to Caernford, with low rolling hills flanking flat river valleys covered with farms and pastures. Beyond were higher hills leading up to significant peaks, visible particularly to the east, as they neared their destination.

They changed horses twice at stations spaced along the route. By custom, on round trips they would exchange the same horses on the return trip and end back at Abersford with their original team.

The sun touched the eastern peaks when they pulled into what Carnigan described as Keelan Manor. Yozef didn't know what to expect, yet the manor wasn't a castle, since there were no obvious signs of fortifications. Whatever the Caedelli called it, it wasn't your average Keelan home.

*Must be eight, ten thousand square feet,* Yozef estimated.

The manor appeared well maintained, with abundant windows, large verandas, and formal gardens covering perhaps three acres surrounding the house. To the right and the rear were buildings that on Earth he would guess were mother-in-law setups or guest cabins. *Maybe servants' quarters?* Also to the rear were a large barn and several other working-looking structures.

*Hmmm . . . large, but not extravagant, easily appropriate for the leader of sixty thousand clanspeople, according to Maera's numbers.*

She had expressed disdain of hetmen or their ancestors for constructing and maintaining more elaborate residences.

They reined in on the cinder driveway where stairs led up to the front veranda. One of the large double doors opened, and out came Maera, an older woman, and two girls. Her mother and two of her sisters, Yozef assumed. A man in workman's clothes appeared and held their team's reins.

He wondered whether he should have made the last part of the trip inside the carriage to look more substantial? Yet he didn't need to pretend he was someone he wasn't.

He climbed down from the top of the carriage and staggered only a step or two, as his bones and muscles tried to recover from the last fifteen nonstop miles. He walked around the horses, nodding and smiling to the workman he passed, and strode to the bottom of the stairs. Among Cadwulf's lessons in Caedelli etiquette was the custom of waiting for a verbal invitation before setting foot in a home.

"Welcome, Ser Kolsko. I'm Breda Keelan. Welcome to our home," said the older woman, confirming her as the hetmistress or whatever her title, if any. Yozef had a moment of panic when he realized he hadn't gotten clued in on how to address the hetman's wife. After a frantic few seconds of mental scrambling, he selected what he hoped was the least offensive response.

"Thank you. I appreciate the hetman's invitation, the opportunity to meet his wife and family, and your kind offer for me to stay here during my visit. Thank you again." He gave a slight bow to Breda Keelan and made himself look only at the mother, though he could see the three daughters from his peripheral vision.

Breda indicated another workman who magically appeared next to Yozef. "Norlin will see you to your rooms and give you a chance to rest from your trip. The hetman will be home in another hour, and someone will let you know when evening meal is ready." Her gaze moved from Yozef to the carriage and Carnigan. "We'll see to your horses and carriage, and will you need accommodations for your man?"

*My man?*

"This is Carnigan Puvey, a friend and a member of St. Sidryn's staff. He's much better at handling horses than I am and kindly drove the carriage. He'll be staying in Caernford." The comment established Carnigan as a friend and contained a slight rebuke to Breda's assumption.

"Until evening meal, then." She turned, and the four of them went back inside.

"You're sure you'll be all right?" he asked Carnigan.

"I think I can take care of myself," Carnigan assured him, with a slap on Yozef's back that only slightly jarred, because by now Yozef was accustomed to his friend's gestures.

"Just remember, I'll either be at St. Tomo's Abbey or the Galloping Horse Inn in Caernford. I'll check in at St. Tomo's and deliver letters from Abbot Beynom and may do work around the abbey, but I'll stay at the inn. Let me know when you want to return to Abersford or if you need me for anything."

With that, Carnigan shouldered his pack and headed back down the driveway, covering ground quickly with his long strides.

Breda and Maera watched the two men through lacy curtains on one of the manor windows.

"Well, Yozef looks undistinguished from my first impression. But by God, the Merciful, the *size* of that other man. Did you see how the carriage lifted higher once he got off? I don't know about Yozef, but the other one *needs* a wagon."

"Oh, he has a horse back at St. Sidryn's. Of course, it's a very *large* horse," Maera said with a laugh.

"Was I imagining it, or was your Yozef a little annoyed that I referred to . . . what's his name? Carnigan . . . as his servant?"

"As I've said, Mother, the customs of his people are different. Evidently, they discourage using address to establish social position."

"Hmmm, curious. I know the *Word* treats all people as equals, but some recognition of status seems appropriate. And Kolsko rode on top of the carriage, instead of inside. I suppose to be with his 'friend'?"

"Don't worry about it, Mother. Yozef doesn't make an issue out of any differences in custom from his people. However, he tries not to offend. You'll notice that once he's familiar with someone, including his servants and workmen, he reverts to his people's customs and treats them more as acquaintances, rather than by their positions."

## Evening with the Hetman's Family

The sun was long gone, and the smaller of Anyar's two moons had risen above the western hills when Yozef was summoned by a knock on his quarter's door. A voice he didn't recognize announced it was time for evening meal. When he opened the door, no one was there. He had been shown a tub of hot water in a room adjacent to the cottage when he arrived and had availed himself of it. He now donned what Cadwulf assured him was plain but well-made attire for general occasions. Expensive, but not ostentatious.

Although dark, there was enough light from the moon, the stars, and the glow from the manor house windows to walk along the stonework path to the front door. A knocker on the door gave him one of his increasingly infrequent flashbacks to Earth. It could be the door to any of hundreds of such doors he'd stood before. The reflection evaporated when he knocked, and a young girl about ten years old opened it so quickly, he guessed that she must have been waiting at a window and seen him coming. It was Mared, the youngest of the four daughters. Maera's description matched the mischievous grin on the young face.

She did a credible curtsey, then said, "Welcome, Ser Kolsko. Welcome to the Keelan Manor. Please come in."

*How do I address her?* wondered Yozef, in another of those moments when he had no clue about the custom. He had passed with the mother, but what about a hetman's child? In lieu of knowing and afraid of making mistakes, he was accustomed to admitting ignorance and throwing himself on the mercy of whoever he faced.

"Thank you for the invitation to come in. But pardon me. You know I'm a stranger to Caedellium and ignorant of many customs. I know you're Mared Keelan, Maera's sister and the hetman's daughter, but how should someone like you be addressed by someone like me?"

Mared giggled with a hand over her mouth, then leaned forward and in a conspiratorial tone whispered, "You just call all children by either Sem or Child until you're properly introduced."

Yozef whispered back, "Which is better for a hetman's daughter, Sem or Child? And which would you prefer?"

"Well," said his co-conspirator, "I *am* a hetman's daughter, so Sem Keelan would be proper. Here, where there are four of us, Sem Mared would also be appropriate."

"Thank you," Yozef whispered again. Then in a normal voice, said "Thank you, Sem Mared. Your family has a beautiful home, and any stranger would be honored to have the greeting given by one so charming."

Mared giggled again and motioned him to follow her into what he presumed was their version of the family parlor containing chairs of various sizes, tables, lanterns and, in this case, occupied by Maera and her mother.

"Welcome again, Ser Kolsko," offered Breda, rising from her chair. "You're just in time. Evening meal is ready. If you'll follow me? Maera, alert your father, if he isn't already on the way."

They went into the hall, down the beautifully grained and polished wood flooring and into a room with a table large enough for twenty people. Tonight there were only seven and spaced far enough apart to give a formal tone to the setting.

Hetman Keelan entered from another door seconds later, nodded to Yozef, and sat at one end of the table. Breda moved to the other end and indicated for Yozef to sit to one side of her. Maera sat between Yozef and her father, which made them far enough apart that they couldn't touch without rising from their chairs. The three younger daughters sat on the opposite side, facing Yozef and Maera. As soon as they were all seated, all of the Keelans placed a right hand over their hearts, closed their eyes, and lifted their heads slightly, and Culich recited the Caedellium common thanksgiving.

"We thank you, Merciful God, for the bounty of this world and ask your understanding of our weaknesses. Praise God."

"Praise God," echoed the rest of the Keelan family, and the meal was on. Immediately, a woman and a teenage boy appeared through a swinging door. Then, and later, Yozef could see into the next room, which appeared to be the kitchen, as the door opened and swung shut. First course was a brownish soup with what appeared to be rice with pieces of meat, heavy on spices. Warm fresh-baked bread filled an artfully woven basket, accompanied by dishes of butter that the Keelans lathered on bread slices. A grunt of appreciation came from the hetman, as he recognized the soup.

Next came an incredibly tender roast with browned potatoes, a tangy gravy, a vegetable resembling Chinese cabbage, and more warm bread and butter. Both water and wine glasses were refilled by the boy, as soon as the level got halfway. The wine was a surprise. Yozef expected one of the sweetish wines he had had so far, both from phila and other fruits, or the foxy wines he suspected were descendants of wild North American grapes. This wine had only a faint hint of sweetness, definite tannins, and a complexity reminiscent of *Vitis vinifera*, true wine grapes. He decided he needed to find out where it came from and either start his own vineyard or know the source where he could order this wine.

The constant refilling of glasses and keeping his attention focused on the family and maintaining his place in the conversation made him lose track of how much wine he'd downed. Once he realized he was getting a buzz, he left the wine glass alone and, whenever tempted, reached instead for water.

The final serving was a pie of mixed fruits adorned with whipped cream, something Yozef hadn't seen in his time on Anyar. On savoring a spoonful, he realized there was no reason not to have whipped cream; you just started with heavy cream and beat the hell out of it—by hand, presumably, there being no Kitchen-Aids, Oster blenders, or whatever, in this part of the galaxy.

The meal lasted just over an hour. Yozef held his own in the conversation and thought he acquitted himself satisfactorily. There were the usual questions about where Yozef came from, how he got to Caedellium, his family, his people, his enterprises, his opinions of Caedellium and Keelan Province, and on and on. By now, Yozef had his story down by heart, but he paid special attention this evening to keep to the official story and add no embellishments, which took focus after drinking too much Chateau L'Keelan. The hetman was polite, if cool, and though his questions to Yozef might have seemed unconnected, Yozef bet to himself the questions and the answers were carefully constructed and stored away. This guy might look and act like an English country squire, but Yozef had the feeling the hetman was not someone to underestimate.

Although some of the meal's accompanying conversation involved Keelan family and clan matters, Yozef was the main topic. The two youngest sisters kept up constant questioning of Yozef, while the third played the part of an aggrieved teenager during most of the meal. Breda also had questions and played the gracious hostess. Maera was there, though they hardly exchanged a word during the meal.

Yozef's uncertainty about the schedule following the meal was answered by Culich.

"A fine meal, Breda. We should have this more often."

"I'll make a note of it, Culich, although the balmoth meat isn't always available."

Yozef would never know that the meal had been carefully crafted of the hetman's favorite dishes. Breda and Maera took no chances on Culich's mood.

The hetman stood, followed by the rest of the family and belatedly by Yozef. The family repeated the same short prayer that started the meal. Yozef had seen this routine before at the Beynoms', although there the initial prayer was longer and with more elaboration. At the Keelans', it was more a rote recital, although Yozef couldn't decide whether it was perfunctory.

"Ser Kolsko, I'll accompany you to the veranda."

Yozef thanked the hostess for a lovely dinner, complimented her on her fine house and family, smiled, and told the younger daughters it was a pleasure to meet them. He then turned to Maera to say it was a pleasure to meet her again and winked his right eye, out of the line of sight of the other family members.

Maera jerked slightly from the unexpected gesture. They hadn't conversed since he'd arrived that afternoon. The wink gave her pause, but by the time he was out the door, she decided it was a friendly gesture, indicating he thought he'd played well his role as guest.

Once on the veranda, Culich was all business. "I've made time in my schedule tomorrow at mid-morning for us to meet in my office. Someone will come for you in your quarters when it's time."

With that, the hetman left Yozef alone, watching the back of Culich's dark green coat go through the front door.

*And thank you for coming so quickly, Yozef. I appreciate you taking time out of your busy schedule. And, if it's convenient for you, could we meet tomorrow to discuss world affairs, the Narthani problem, how you helped the economy in Keelan? Oh, and by the way, thanks for any help in repelling the raid on St. Sidryn's.*

*Oh, well. I guess it's not easy being green, and maybe the hetmen don't go to charm school.*

Yozef made his way back to his cottage. Because of the large meal and too much wine, especially after the ride from Abersford, he had barely undressed and pulled the bed covers up before he was asleep.

# CHAPTER 13

# MEET THE HETMAN

**Summons**

The next morning began with knocking. Yozef roused himself from under the covers when the sound wouldn't go away, and he reluctantly concluded it wasn't a dream. He'd drunk more wine the previous night than intended, and now his throbbing head wondered at the alcohol content. The headache was a puzzle, because neither the local beers nor the fruit wines had such side effects on him.

Throwing on clothes, he padded barefoot to the door and opened it to wince at the bright sunlight. There stood the same serving boy as the evening before, this time holding a basket.

"Good day. Your morning meal, Ser Kolsko," he said with a smile to the blurry-eyed, disheveled guest.

"Whether it's a good day I'll be the judge, eventually. One help will be if that basket contains kava."

"It does. Shall I lay it out for you?"

"Please."

The boy put the basket on a chair at the table and pulled out a cup and a steaming ceramic pitcher.

"You're my friend forever," said Yozef. Whatever the wine was, he needed to drink less of it. Still, he'd had far worse headaches after over-imbibing. While he poured himself a cup of kava, the boy finished bringing out several woven bowls containing fruit, rolls, hunks of cheese, a dish of butter, and another of a jam.

"Will this be sufficient, Ser Kolsko, or is there anything else you would like or prefer?"

"No . . . what's your name?"

"Norlin, Ser Kolsko."

"No, Norlin, this looks fine. What do I do with whatever I don't eat and drink?"

"Do? You don't do anything," Norlin said, puzzled. "I'll return later when you're out and remove it when I check for any clothes you need cleaning."

"What do you know, a multi-service establishment."

Norlin looked blankly at Yozef, who had unconsciously spoken in English but now switched back to Caedelli.

"If I had any such clothes, where would I put them?"

"Why, in the sack," Norlin said, pointing to a heavy-cloth bag hanging by a hook.

"Oh, yes, I didn't see the bag." *And wouldn't have known what it was for, if I'd seen it.*

"Hetman Keelan told me to inform you he'll send someone for you when he's ready to meet. It will be sometime in mid-morning."

*Meaning, hang around for when the high muckety-muck deigns to have you come to his presence.* Even when grumbling to himself, Yozef knew he was being unfair. *Well, grouchy anyway.*

What was he supposed to do while waiting? Stare at the walls?

"Once I eat, and I'm awake, could you show me around the grounds so I can stretch my legs?"

"I understand Sen Maera is planning on doing that this afternoon, Ser Kolsko."

"Yozef," he mumbled, sipping the kava. "Call me Yozef."

The boy shifted his weight between his feet. "It would be inappropriate for me to address a guest of the hetman by his first name, Ser Kolsko."

"Okay. I wouldn't want you to get in trouble. But I'm the guest, and I prefer my first name. How about we agree that when other people are around, you call me Ser Kolsko, but when we're alone like this, I'm Yozef."

"Well. All right," said Norlin unconvincingly and then excused himself and exited in a hurry.

Yozef sat and focused on the kava. His earlier inquiries about the source of the coffee substitute revealed it came not from a root, as he'd first suspected, but from a truly impressive tree that often reached 150 feet in both height and breadth. The tree's four-to six-inch-long nuts fell after an enclosing husk split, and the ground under a tree was often covered with nuts. When ground fine, mixed with water and a little salt, and then boiled several hours, it turned into kava. Its effect was similar to coffee, leading him to suspect it contained alkaloids similar, if not identical, to caffeine. This kava batch was especially good and reminded him of Kona coffee, not his favorite back on Earth, but it was familiar tasting and smelling and had the same physiological effects.

Once more awake, he found himself famished and devoured most of the rolls with butter, several fruits, and much of the cheese. He tried the jam. It tasted like overripe figs and leather.

Alert and sated, he had to fill the next few hours. On Earth, he'd carried a paperback for "hurry-up-and-wait" occasions. On Caedellium, he used any available slack time to work on whatever science he dredged from his memory, so he often carried paper, quills, and ink for free moments. Later, he would transfer the notes to bound journals and burn the loose-leaf drafts. This morning, he moved the eating table closer to a window with sunlight coming through the panes, laid out his materials, and delved into copying from his memory a text on thermodynamics. As usual, there were gaps—sections that, for whatever reason, hadn't survived in his memory and whatever the Watchers had done to him. However, he managed to reproduce major sections as if he saw the open book in front of him. He was well into a chapter on statistical entropy and ruing that he didn't have the recall ability when taking courses at Berkeley, when another knock on the door found him finishing a theorem proof and accompanying diagrams.

"The hetman is ready for you," said Norlin. "Please follow me."

So he did. Down the same path to the house, through the double doors, and this time down a different hall to a door where Norlin knocked and waited.

"Come in," called the hetman.

They entered a spacious den-like room. As elsewhere in the house, the exquisite woodwork was made from a variety of woods. From the walls hung paintings, one of which depicted a stylized battle he assumed to be from clan history and another version of a ubiquitous theme he'd seen many places— God creating humans. Bookshelves and drawers occupied much of the rest of the wall space. The most prominent piece of furniture was a large desk, behind which sat the hetman. Elsewhere were two tables, one for six to eight people and a smaller table sitting in a bay window, along with three leather and cushion chairs at different points of the room.

"Thank you, Norlin. Come back at mid-day bell to retrieve Ser Kolsko."

Norlin bowed and left, closing the door quietly.

*That means he expects this meeting to last around two hours?*

Culich rose and motioned to the table in the window. "Let's sit here, Ser Kolsko. I always like the sunlight."

They sat and looked at each other for a few seconds.

"You've made quite an impression on Keelan, since they found you on the beach near Abersford, Ser Kolsko. I know of the new products you introduced and use a few of them myself," the hetman said, motioning to four kerosene lanterns scattered about the room. "Maera is very impressed with you and tells me you were open and helpful in showing her your workshops."

"It was my pleasure, Hetman. Sen Maera is bright and insightful. It's always good to get outside impressions, since we get locked into patterns of thinking. I remember one day when Sen Maera visited the kerosene shop . . ." Yozef continued describing a problem-solving session and how Maera had provided suggestions that Yozef and the workers had missed.

"Anyway, Hetman, I'm happy to share what I know with your people. It's only befitting I repay the care given me when I arrived and the place that the people of Abersford and St. Sidryn's have allowed me to fill in their community. Also, the information exchange with your daughter wasn't one way. Sen Maera was kind enough to educate me on many aspects of Caedellium culture and history, and many of her insights have been very useful."

"Hmmm, yes," said Culich. "It was probably good fortune you found yourself near St. Sidryn's. The Beynoms and the others at the abbey might be more understanding of your strange arrival and innovations, whereas in some other places even in Keelan Province, much less other provinces, not to mention elsewhere on Anyar, things might have turned out badly for you."

Thus ended the polite phase, and the hetman launched into the real interrogation. His arrival, his origin, how did he get to Caedellium— questions like he had already answered the previous evening. Yozef was sure Keelan had already been briefed by Sistian, Diera, Denes, Boyerman Vorwich, Maera, and who knew who else?

*Why do I sense this is not so much an information-gathering session as much as a test to see if I can keep my story straight?*

Once again, he focused on keeping the details few but consistent. He told himself he was handling the meeting well, though was relieved when the hetman moved to other topics.

"I've read the reports about the raid and the battle at St. Sidryn's and talked with Abbot Beynom and Denes Vegga. I've also discussed it with some of my other advisors, including Vortig Luwis, my military advisor. A consensus is to wonder why, for God's mercy, did you suggest letting the Buldorians enter the abbey? Ser Vegga is emphatic they couldn't have held the walls with the number of men available and is even more forceful in his opinion that trying to trap the raiders inside the abbey courtyard would *never* have occurred to him. Same with Vortig Luwis. So the question is, why did *you* think of it? One possibility is that you've had more experience and training in such matters than you've led anyone to believe." The hetman paused and looked expectantly at Yozef.

"I understand that suspicion occurring to you, but all I can say is that I'd never been part of anything like that day. In fact, I've never seen blood spilled, except for common accidents and certainly not in deadly fights like that. As to why I thought of what I did, it seemed logical at the time. Denes told the abbot there was no way they would hold the walls. In that case, and I accepted Denes's estimation, my mind struggled for other options. If we couldn't drive them off from the walls, then wasn't the only other option to let them in and trap them inside the barricades? Remember, it was Denes who organized the defense, once he got his mind off the walls. I would've had no idea what to do next. I've thanked the people of Abersford for their gratitude, but I've pointed out it was Denes who deserves most of the credit."

Culich shook his head dismissively. "Even if true, the fact remains the original ideas came from you. I still don't understand how that happened. Events happened so fast, it's puzzling that you came up with such a radical idea so quickly."

"All I can say, Hetman, is it just popped into my head."

"Popped into your head, you say? This sounds like one of Abbess Diera's comments about you, that it seems to her sometimes that ideas just 'pop into your head' from out of nowhere."

Yozef was silent. What could he say? Most of Diera's observations were related to knowledge he was careful about revealing, but the raid situation was different. Culich was also silent, waiting for more from Yozef, who sensed he needed to say something more to assuage the hetman's suspicions.

"Well, there's one other possibility. Although I've no personal experience with combat or planning for such things, I assume you're aware I was studying to be a scholastic?"

"Yes, yes. Abbot Beynom told me about your claim that your people have vast amounts of knowledge, more than we on Caedellium, and that your people value longer years at study."

"Not just studying to older ages than here, but we also believe in breadth of knowledge. I was a problem for my mentors in our scholasticums for reading *too* widely and not focusing more in my last few years. One interest was history and particularly histories of warfare. Although I have no practical experience, those readings might explain my sudden insight and suggestions to Denes."

That much was true. Yozef *had* read a lot of military history and read a few of the classic strategy books. He suddenly wondered whether he should try to recall some of those.

He knew there was no way to tell the hetman he probably had more "military" experience than any Caedelli, if one considered all of the readings and the video and board strategy games he'd played. Granted, they weren't real-world experience, but he had neither heard nor read evidence that the Caedelli knew anything about real warfare or battle tactics—an enviable situation as long as no one such as the Narthani showed up.

Culich didn't look convinced but gave the impression of filing away Yozef's speculations. "In that case, I wonder what your ideas might be as to the purpose of these raids that the Buldorians, and now the Narthani, have been carrying out along our coasts."

"It's only been since the raid that I've paid attention to the Narthani," said Yozef. "Coming to Caedellium, adjusting to no expectation of ever seeing my family or homeland again, and then working on a place for myself took all of my focus until the raid. That's changed, of course. The Narthani *definitely* have my attention."

Culich noted the last sentence. It was as if Kolsko had stated a threat—a threat to the Narthani, now that they had this strange man's attention.

"And what does your attention say?"

Yozef's expression was solemn. "That the Narthani are an 'existential' threat to the clans."

"Existential? A word I'm not familiar with." Yozef had used the English word.

"Pardon, Hetman. I couldn't think of a Caedelli word, so I used one from my own language. *Existential* relates to something's existence. For Caedellium, the Narthani are a literal threat not just to the lives of every single Caedelli, but to the very existence of your people and their history."

Culich's expression was more attentive than before, as for the first time he became more interested in what was being said than who was saying it.

"I'll admit I share your worry that the Narthani are an 'existential' threat, as you say. Something I'm afraid few other hetmen and not all my boyermen share with me. How is it you came to this conclusion?"

"Remember, I've only recently learned details of the Narthani and so may be wrong, but when I take what I learned from Brother Sistian and Maera and combine that with previous examples from my people's histories, the obvious conclusion is that the Narthani intend to subjugate the entire island and turn it into a piece of the Narthon Empire. Consequences for all the clans can be seen in what's happened so far. The Preddi resisted and were destroyed. The Selfcellese and the Eywellese are fooling themselves that they're allies of the Narthani. Once the Narthani control all the island, the individual clans will disappear, and the Narthani will absorb the clans so completely that within two or three generations, there'll be only a memory of Caedellium as it is now, and the name Keelan will vanish."

Culich's face got grimmer with Yozef's words, which gave substance to the hetman's deepest fears. Fears so deep he hadn't given them full credence even to himself until now. He passed a hand over his face to rest on his chin, elbow on the tabletop.

"If this grim scenario comes to play, what would you predict to be the Narthani's next act?"

Yozef starred into space for several minutes. Finally, he refocused on Culich. "Obviously, the Narthani will move out from the three provinces they now control. There's no other possibility. The questions are when and how. I see two issues. One is their next target. They might simply invade a neighboring province with their army. You don't seem to know the exact number of Narthani troops on Caedellium, but there are undoubtedly more than any clan, or several clans, can hope to repel. Your best chance is if all the clans unite."

"An unlikely possibility, given the intransigence of too many of the hetmen in recognizing the Narthani as a threat to *them*, especially those clans farthest away from Preddi. If they attacked Keelan and Gwillamer, our Tri-Clan Alliance would respond together, plus I believe two or three of the other clans would join."

"Then it's hard to predict whether they'll go after one clan at a time or alliances. One argument would be that five or six clans joining to resist might make them go elsewhere first, but it could also be an argument to break the most dangerous coalition of clans, feeling that the others would be easy once Keelan and allies are defeated.

"They might go after one clan at a time. Stent, for example. I've studied maps of Caedellium in the abbey library. Sen Maera told me Stent is a strong clan but without reliable allied neighboring clans. The Narthani navy could be used to control the coasts and jump troops behind Stent forces. However, taking Stent doesn't help subdue the other clans.

"Yet Moreland would also be an attractive target, since it's more centrally located. In fact, an invasion with Orosz as the real goal would be more likely. It would have the advantages of taking control of a major portion of the center of the island and cutting Caedellium in half, thus making clan cooperation more difficult. Then there would be the psychological effect of taking the Conclave site."

Culich let the additional new word, *psychological*, pass without comment. He suspected he would learn what it meant soon enough and didn't want to interrupt what was apparently the free-flow thinking of Kolsko. Culich had learned from his lifelong friend Sistian Beynom that it was sometimes best to wait for scholastics to finish their thinking without interruptions and delve into meaning later. What he *was* interested in was Kolsko's recitation of Narthani options.

"Of course, they can always use their navy to land troops anywhere on Caedellium," Yozef continued.

"So you're saying the Narthani could do just about anything," Culich said gruffly.

Yozef mentally shook himself. "Sorry. I was just listing options."

"There are always options. What are they most likely to do, in *your* opinion?"

"Moreland, and on to Orosz," said Yozef, with overstated confidence.

"Why that option over the others?"

"It may be the quickest. If Moreland and Orosz fell, other clans may feel forced to seek accommodation with the Narthani, as did the Selfcellese and the Eywellese. Of course, that would be an illusion, as I said before. But it brings up a second thing you need to worry about in addition to an invasion."

"More to worry about?" Culich said dryly. "An invasion isn't enough?"

"Oh . . . it is, but this other thing may already be happening. Let me tell you a bit of history. There was a realm called Britain and the people, Britains. They wanted to conquer a wealthy and much larger land, one named India and made up of many separate realms. This India was far away, and Britain didn't want to expend too much coin and too many men. In the end, Britain conquered India with little effort, though it took many years."

Culich scrunched his forehead. "How did they do that?"

"The Britains bribed some rulers and others they helped against traditional local enemies. Each part of India was weakened, as the Britains grew stronger. The Indians failed to realize the real conflict was between all of them and the Britains. Almost until the end, the remaining independent Indians could have joined and thrown out the Britains, but they never agreed to cooperate."

"And you're suggesting the Narthani might do the same here?"

"I would if I was them. Why waste resources in conquering a people, if you can get them to help?"

"Hmmm . . . I've assumed the Narthani controlling Selfcell and Eywell was a consequence of their taking Preddi, but you say it might be an example of the Narthani instigating such a strategy: to use clans against one another. I need to consider this and make the other clans aware the Narthani might implement such a strategy."

"What if they've already implemented it?" Yozef asked softly.

Culich's eyes widened. Even when Yozef told his anecdote, Culich still had not connected it directly to ongoing events on Caedellium. "They might already be doing it!" he blurted. "We know there're rumors of Narthani influence among the clans, but I hadn't considered it part of a coordinated plan."

"Again, I'd have been doing it right from the start, if I was them. You know the other clans and their leaders, I don't. Are there cases where clans you thought would be willing to join against the Narthani have been strangely reluctant to do so? Or cases where clans who got along well enough are becoming more hostile to each other? Such cases might be just coincidences, but they deserve a closer look for Narthani influence."

A somber Hetman Keelan shook his head. "The Farkesh and Skouks clans have had serious skirmishes the last few months, as had the Nyvacks and the Pawell. I've been dismayed that they could revert to old patterns of behavior at a time like this, but now I wonder if the Narthani are behind it, as you theorize."

Their conversation went on for another hour until just before mid-day meal, when Norlin came to retrieve Yozef.

"I'm glad I met with you myself, Ser Kolsko. You've certainly had a difficult time, but I can see you're adjusting to your circumstances and contributing to Clan Keelan. You've also given me much to ponder, much of it not possibilities I *like* to hear, but that I *need* to hear. We'll talk again while you're here."

## Culich Keelan Evaluates Yozef

The hetman's eyes followed Kolsko, as Norlin led him out of the office. He studied his physique, as the man walked away, confirming last night's impressions: average height and girth, brown hair with odd lighter streaks. Then there were the eyes. That light blue, sometimes seeming to change to gray as light changed, very unusual and unsettling.

Kolsko gave the impression of being . . . *gentle* was the closest word. Culich had met such men. Rhaedri Brison came to mind, a theophist from Orosz and a man many believed closest to God of any Caedelli. Culich failed to imagine Brison holding a spear and stabbing a Buldorian.

When the meeting was over, they had clasped hands, a traditional acknowledgment gesture among Keelan men, though forearms were also used in Keelan and more often in other clans. Culich had found the man's grip firm. He had read with curiosity the report from Denes Vegga about this Kolsko's regular running and use of weights to gain strength. Vegga had passed on Kolsko's reasons for these activities, and, while it sounded odd, there was rationality to it. Still, *odd* seemed to be a common word when thinking about Kolsko.

As for the man himself, Culich wasn't sure. He considered himself gifted by God for his quick ability to evaluate men and formed a reliable opinion within minutes of meeting someone. But this Kolsko . . .?

He still mulled over the meeting while at midday meal with Breda and Maera. His wife had suggested they arrange their individual plans to eat together that day and let Culich give his fresh first impressions of Kolsko.

They were nearly finished eating, having made only light and intermittent conversation, when Breda asked, "Now that you've met with Ser Kolsko, my dear, any thoughts or impressions of him?"

"Impressions. Thoughts. Yes, many of both. What it comes down to is, I don't know what to think."

"The meeting didn't go well?" asked Maera.

Culich missed the edge of concern in her voice. "No, in fact, it went quite well. Ser Kolsko answered any question I asked." Culich laid down the fork stirring the food on his plate as he spoke and drummed his fingers on the tabletop. "Yes, he answered the questions, but I don't believe he's telling all of the truth when he answers."

Breda stiffened. "You believe he's lying about who he is and where he comes from or about something else?"

"There's a difference between lying and not telling everything. The answers he gave to many of the questions were often so similar to answers he gave last night and that he's given to others, as reported to me by Sistian and Vegga, that it makes me suspect he's rehearsed them."

"Father," countered Maera, "some of those questions he must have been asked so many times, it wouldn't be surprising that the answers became automatic and only *seemed* rehearsed. After all, how many different ways can you say, 'I come from a realm called America'?"

Culich nodded. "I know, and I try to take that into consideration, but the impression remains that it's more than giving the same answers to the same questions so many times. I'm not saying he's lying, only that there could be more to the answers than we realize. The problem is we don't know what more there is, so we can't be sure what other questions to ask. Be that as it may, I don't perceive him as particularly duplicitous, simply careful about what he tells about himself. I should ask Diera and Sistian whether they have any similar feelings about the medicant knowledge he's given them.

"No, he's not naturally deceitful. In fact, if anything, he possesses a strange naiveté. I know he's not from Caedellium, and there are so many aspects of language and culture he wouldn't be familiar with, but it's somehow more than that."

Culich paused, stroking his beard alternately with each hand, a well-known habit he was unaware of. Whenever he was gathering his thoughts, leading up to saying something, the hands signaled to all who knew him to be patient. This particular episode stretched into several minutes. Breda started to prompt him when whatever was being formulated came together.

"All of that is only part of what I'm trying to fit together into a more complete picture. He's beyond doubt *very* smart, an obvious assumption, based on his successful enterprises, his story of still being a scholastic in training, and the reports on him. It's better to sense it in person. Yes, he's intelligent. So much so that I wonder, if he wanted to deceive us, could I detect it? However,

I hope I'm correct that he's not deceiving us in any way harmful to Keelan. If he is, it may be to protect himself, though why, I have no idea.

"More than just being intelligent, he knows he is but doesn't pretend he knows everything."

Breda missed her husband's meaning, though Maera understood. "Yes," she said emphatically, "he listens to others and doesn't feel threatened if they disagree or if they have ideas better than his own. He also quotes his people's sayings that caution humility. I remember him once quoting that *'A wise man knows what he doesn't know, while a fool knows what isn't true.'* Another time he referenced a famous scholastic being lauded for his work, who said, *'If I've seen farther, it's because I stood on the shoulders of giants.'"*

"Well, he's no fool," asserted Culich. "Although there's something else I haven't mentioned. We talked at some length about the Narthani. New to the island he may be, and he claims he's only recently learned details about the Narthani from you, Maera, and Sistian. Nevertheless, I suspect he has a better understanding of the threat they represent than most hetmen do, and I might even include myself in that suspicion. He suggested several points to consider, based on his knowledge of the history of his and other peoples. Histories and names of realms and peoples I've never heard of, such as the India and Britain. Have you heard of these, Maera?"

She shook her head. "Never."

"He told me a disturbing story about how this Britain had conquered India, a realm many times larger, by tricking the people of India to fight one another or be bribed by Britain. Yozef suggested the Narthani may already be doing something similar here on Caedellium."

"He never told *me* any such stories," snipped Maera. Breda patted her daughter's leg under the table.

*Calmly, my dear, calmly.*

"I doubt he deliberately hid anything from you, Maera. Possibly you didn't ask the right questions, and I did without realizing it. That would go along with my impression there's more underneath than he lets us see. The answers may be there, but you may have to ask the right questions at the right time."

Her father's words mollified Maera only somewhat. Her father knew her well enough to see what was going on under that long brown hair.

"Don't beat yourself up for not getting more out of him." Culich paused and looked at his eldest daughter. "In fact, Ser Kolsko believes you are one of the smarter persons he's ever met, possibly *the* smartest. He also told me you're smarter than he is."

Maera was thunderstruck. *Yozef said what?!*

Breda sat smugly, eyeing her daughter.

Culich eyes were also on Maera, but as if seeing something in a different light for the first time. "Kolsko also said I was fortunate to have such an intelligent daughter helping me rule the clan."

*Oh, no.* Breda cringed within. *As good a hetman as Culich is, and as much as I know he listens to Maera and me, he's still a Caedellium hetman, and telling him he needs help from a daughter isn't the wisest comment to make.*

"He's right," continued Culich. "I may not have said it before or not as clearly as I should. Maera, I *do* appreciate not only your help but also your advice. While I may not acknowledge it as much as I should, the way our customs are, I want you to know it."

Both women teared up, Breda because she was happy for a daughter who rarely felt she fit into customary roles, and Maera because it was the strongest expression of respect her father had ever given her.

*My, my, Yozef,* thought Breda. *You* do *seem to bring changes wherever you go, don't you?*

Culich was not unaware of the response to his words and cleared his throat, returning to Kolsko.

"I originally planned to meet this Kolsko fellow once or twice to get a good evaluation. Now I think it'll take longer—both to get a better reading on him personally and to continue discussions on the Narthani. I called him here for a sixday, but, since I expected to be finished with him in no more than two days, I committed traveling to meet with the Hewell and Adris hetmen. The meeting in Hewell is more a formality. Hewell is ready to join the Tri-Clan Alliance, or whatever we rename it once the number of members increases past three. Lordum Hewell is still young enough and new enough at being hetman that he wisely is being careful to get the support of his boyermen for this alliance. Adris is another matter. Hetman Adris wants the alliance, though he has several boyerman who are strongly opposed, evidently believing all the Narthani problems are remote from Adris, and why should they get involved and invite trouble? Stupid, I know, though we still have to try to convince them.

"Another issue they bring up is that Adris doesn't have an adjoining border to any of the alliance members, including Hewell. In reality, Orosz is functionally, if not officially, also a member. They can't join because of the custom that Orosz stays neutral in clan disputes. While the Narthani are an external threat, Hetman Orosz and I agree that for now Orosz should remain outside the alliance.

"All of this means I'll need to be gone a full sixday or more and won't be able to speak enough with Kolsko until I return. I'll tell him to stay longer, two or three more sixdays."

"Father, he's busy with all of his shops and projects," cautioned Maera.

"They'll have to wait until I've finished speaking with him," responded Culich, automatically assuming the man would suborn other activities, if the hetman had different plans.

"Remember, Father, he's not from Keelan or anywhere else on Caedellium. He's not a member of the Keelan Clan, so he owes no specific allegiance to either you or the clan."

Maera was right. By custom or law, even a Keelander was free to acquiesce or not to a Keelan hetman's request, although, in practice, few resisted. Kolsko was not even a Keelander. Culich considered his daughter's words. As early as it was in his evaluation of Kolsko, Culich's intuition nagged that Kolsko would be important in Keelan's future. If Kolsko had no formal ties to Keelan, they needed to think about ways to remedy that lack.

"In that case, let's keep him occupied here until I return. He might like to take advantage of St. Tomo's library to learn more about the Narthani and Caedellium. Maybe he can find clues to where his homeland is or at least narrow down the possibilities. Maera, he thought you had been a good source of such knowledge while you were at St. Sidryn's. You could show him the library and see if he can find anything of interest to him and useful for us. You can also introduce him to the scholastics at St. Tomo's. From Sistian's letters, I'd imagine there are some mutual interests. He can look into expanding his enterprises to Caernford, as long as he's here. Plus, there must be local sights of interest to show him. I also think Vortig and Petr need to spend some time with him. I'll speak with them both and leave the rest to you to find ways to keep him interested until I return."

Maera nodded respectfully, careful not to smile. *Yes. I'll find ways to spend time with Yozef. And we shall see what happens.*

"All right. I think we have a plan for the next sixdays. I'll speak with the man who drove Kolsko's carriage here, Puvey something, and see if he has anything useful to add."

## Carnigan and the Hetman

A Keelan retainer tracked down Carnigan Puvey in Caernford, in time for the big man to get to the hetman's manor before Culich left for Hewell. Culich had glimpsed the man and knew from that momentary distant view that Puvey was big. But *this* big? Culich thought of himself as a good-sized man, though he was aware of starting the shrinkage that came with age. Still, there were few men much bigger than the Keelan hetman, and this was his first experience of being in the presence of a man who made him feel truly small. Puvey might only have an inch or two in height advantage, but his width and solidness were intimidating.

"Hetman," Puvey stated in a voice Culich suspected meant, "Okay, here I am. What is it you want?"

"Ser Puvey, I understand you've been at St. Sidryn's for three years and that you came originally from Swavebroke Province. You're not a brother at St. Sidryn's, are you?"

"You'll have to ask Abbot Beynom about that."

Culich almost grumbled at the man to answer but restrained himself. He would ask Sistian, and the purpose of this meeting was Yozef Kolsko.

"All right. Ser Kolsko has made quite a name for himself in so short a time. You've interacted with him since he arrived in Caedellium. I've spoken with him and will want to speak with him again when I return from travel. However, I want to hear any impressions or information you might have about Ser Kolsko."

"What kind of information?"

"I'm not sure myself. Perhaps we can discuss a few of your experiences with him, and I'll see if anything useful occurs during the discussion. For example, did you see him during the courtyard fight at St. Sidryn's?"

"He fought beside me."

"Would you say he's an experienced fighter?"

Carnigan laughed. "Hah! It might have been the first time in his life he ever held a weapon."

"You mean a musket or a sword?"

"I mean anything. Even a real knife. I gave him a spear and told him not to stick me with it."

"Did he actually use the spear?"

"He may have saved my life. I was fighting two Buldorians when another got to my side. I couldn't turn to face him, and Yozef stuck him before he did me."

Culich probed for another hour, learning little except the protective nature of Puvey's regard for Kolsko. Later that evening Culich related his meeting with Puvey to Breda.

"Once again, this Kolsko gives conflicting impressions. Puvey says Kolsko was totally inexperienced with any kind of weapon, yet he stood with the others when the time came. I think Puvey admires him because he was scared and didn't let that prevent him from doing what he could. I also think Puvey considers Kolsko a friend and perhaps something more. I'm not sure what. I guess I would call it a . . . commitment to Kolsko, although I don't know exactly what that entails."

They continued their meal, Culich missing the coy smile that played along the corners of his wife's mouth and eyes.

# CHAPTER 14

# LINGERING

Yozef's third morning at Keelan Manor started like the first: being awakened by knocking at the cottage door. Once again, Norlin waited with a basket. The difference this morning was that Yozef's head didn't throb from too much wine. He'd eaten the last two nights' meals with Carnigan at the Galloping Horse Inn, whose beer left no aftereffects.

"Good morning, Ser Kolsko," chirped Norlin, who never seemed to be in a bad mood.

*Which could eventually get annoying*, thought Yozef. *There are some times when not being in a good mood is normal.* Then he smiled at himself. *My, aren't you in a good mood? No need to take it out on poor Norlin just because you think it's time to head back to Abersford.*

Yozef and Maera had hardly spoken, except at the first evening's dinner, and then only a few perfunctory words. She toured him around the Keelan Manor grounds after his first meeting with her father, and her youngest sister persisted in accompanying them, oblivious to Maera's attempts to shed her sibling. Then her father had called on her to aid in correspondence. That was the last time he'd seen her that day.

Only by his disappointment at how the visit had so far gone did he realize how much he'd looked forward to seeing her again. The day of the picnic, away from Abersford, kept rising in his consciousness. He'd enjoyed being with her that day, and the kiss had been spontaneous. He thought she responded, then . . . what? She'd cut him cold on the way back to the abbey, although her later letters from Caernford hinted of overtures that things were okay between them, though maybe only in the formalities, not the personal. If true, did that bother him? He shrugged mentally. It was worth the trip to meet the hetman and to settle whatever existed between him and Maera.

*And what did I suppose there might be? For Christ's sake, she's a hetman's daughter, their version of royalty. Did I imagine an affair or a fairytale ending was plausible?*

Then there was the hetman. They'd met twice the second day, when Culich announced he'd be away a sixday and informed Yozef he'd being staying longer than initially planned to meet with other clan leaders, and then the hetman would meet with Yozef again when he returned. Yozef was *not* pleased.

He was ready to return to Abersford. He appreciated the opportunity to meet the hetman, and his evaluation of the clan's leader was positive. Culich Keelan fit Yozef's image of a beloved but stern Scottish laird. What he didn't discern was a sense of the hetman's personality, except for the inattentive assumption that Yozef would remain at the hetman's convenience. Satisfied when Yozef reluctantly agreed to linger, Culich ended their meeting, and Yozef had returned to his room and continued working on his thermodynamics notes.

"And good morning to you, Norlin. And how are you this day?"

"Just fine, Ser Kolsko. Just fine."

"What about our agreement when we're alone?"

Norlin grinned. "Well, I wasn't sure you were serious . . . Yozef."

"That's more like it. And your scholasticum work? How's that going?" Yozef had learned from Norlin that the fourteen-year-old was attending the St. Tomo's scholasticum, with an eye to become a medicant. To meet the "inventor" of ether had, by the boy's own statement, been one of the most exciting things in his life.

*Poor kid.*

"All fine there, too," Norlin said cheerfully. "I have examinations in herbs and surgery this afternoon."

*Jesus! He's even in a good mood with tests coming up.*

Norlin set a basket on the table and started laying out the morning meal. First the jug of kava and bowl of fruit, then something novel. Norlin set a folded cloth on the table.

For a moment, Yozef didn't register what the cloth must be for. *A napkin?* Caedelli were not quite stereotypic medieval diners, eating with fingers and throwing bones to the dogs, but hands were the norm for wiping food from lips. When necessary, the ubiquitous "handkerchiefs" that all men and women kept with them were used, the same cloths used for wiping sweat and blowing noses.

Further surprises came when Norlin removed the covers from two ceramic plates.

*As I live and breathe!*

Sitting in front of Yozef were what appeared to be an omelet and a stack of butter-lathered toast. A momentary feeling of disorientation washed over him, as his mind flashed back to Earth and his previous life. Omelets, napkins, toast, cars, television, Julie, Berkeley, 49ers, Giants, squabbling Democrats and Republicans, and a hundred other images kaleidoscoped as they were recalled and faded. His chest ached with a pang such as he had not felt in many months. He swallowed hard.

"Are you all right, Yozef?"

He looked up at a worried Norlin.

"Is there something wrong? The cook was unsure whether everything was done properly, since she had never prepared such food. Sen Maera told her what to do and said it was foods common to your people."

*Maera? She would have given the instructions to the cook.* She, along with the Faughns, among others, had recoiled at eating eggs any way except boiled or scrambled—and forget poached and fried with runny yolks. He had explained and demonstrated French toast and omelets more than a year ago. The former had taken off, but not omelets.

"No, no, Norlin," he reassured quickly, "just surprised to see the omelet and toast."

"Oh. Is that what they're called? Which one is the omelet and which one toast?"

Norlin, once apprised of the correct nomenclatures, excused himself with the message that Sen Maera expected him at the manor house after eating, to discuss his schedule for the next sixday.

*Schedule?*

Now that sounded like Maera. Always wanting to organize.

He took a bite of toast. Not bad. Just about the degree of toasting he liked. As for the omelet, he assumed the eggs were from ducks the Caedelli raised. He had never eaten a duck egg before coming to Anyar and had gotten used to the difference in taste. The cheese inside the omelet was too pungent, and inside were flecks of a chopped green and pieces of smoked meat he suspected was coney, the rabbit-sized indigenous mammals grown for meat. An omelet from Earth it wasn't. Somehow he didn't mind. While he tried not to read too much into the actions of others, he wondered whether this was a gesture from Maera. He found his mood markedly improved.

An hour later, Norlin returned and informed him that Maera was expecting him at the manor house. She met him in the large parlor, where chairs and tables provided several sitting areas. She sat in one of three armchairs surrounding what on Earth would have been a coffee table. Breda Keelan sat thirty feet away at the other end of the room in another furniture cluster, knitting. The mother smiled and greeted Yozef, as Norlin dropped him off and indicated the waiting Maera.

*Is the mother chaperoning?*

When he walked over to where the hetman's daughter sat, she put down a book and rose to greet him. She wore a long form-fitting dark green dress that hung to the floor. Slipper-like shoes peeked out from folds of the fabric. The neckline was deep enough to more than suggest the swell of her chest and exposed a goodly stretch of skin. She wore no jewelry, and her hair was held out of her face by a silver clip on the side opposite the part. Her arms were bare to near her shoulders.

*You know, she* is *quite fetching,* rose by its own volition in Yozef's mind.

Maera's attire and presentation were carefully designed. Her mother had long ago advised that different shades of green were her best colors, matching her skin tone and greenish eyes. The two women picked the dress as both appropriate for a hetman's daughter and to remind any male of her feminine form. From his glances, Maera assumed the dress had succeeded, and she, in turn, noted his appearance.

He was dressing better since he'd arrived here, more so than she'd seen in Abersford. She again saw an average-sized man of his middle twenties. His brown hair and beard were neatly trimmed. There were no standard styles for either with Caedellium men, and she was pleased that Yozef favored shorter cuts. She remembered the tingling of his beard surrounding his lips.

She rose to greet him. "Thank you for coming, Ser Kolsko."

Yozef smiled. "Do you think you and I could once again use our first names?"

She smiled back, almost shyly. "Yes, let's do that . . . Yozef."

"Great . . . Maera. So, what has the hetman planned for me to do while he's away?"

She didn't miss the sarcastic tone. "Oh, Yozef, he's really quite a warm person and not . . . what was the word you and Carnigan called me that day at the beach? Stuffy?"

"Are you saying that your father is never stuffy?"

Maera laughed, loudly enough that her mother looked up from the other end of the large room.

"Yes, yes, I'll concede that he can seem that way. When you know him better, you'll find you won't notice it as much."

"I won't notice it, or he won't be stuffy?"

"Perhaps both." Maera smiled again, then picked up a piece of paper. Even upside-down, Yozef could see the neat script and bullet points running down the paper.

"Father's requested you to meet with Vortig Luwis and Pedr Kennrick. They're both advisors, Pedr more on internal clan affairs and Vortig on what you call military matters. Father would like them to meet with you and discuss some of the same issues you and he have already discussed and questions they might have. He also requested that they meet with you separately, so he can get independent reports from them. Pedr will be here in about an hour, and we'll see Vortig at the Caernford armory after midday meal."

She indicated the rest of the list. "All of these others are my thoughts on what you might find interesting."

Her forefinger moved down the page, as she read off the suggestions.

"I assumed you would want to spend time in the St. Tomo's abbey library. It's about the same size as the one at St. Sidryn's, although it has different collections, especially on the histories of both Keelan Clan and the mainland Anyar realms. I know you read Caedelli, but some of the better histories are in other Anyar languages. I can describe the books' topics, and with those you find interesting, I can read selected parts to you and work to give you translations for a few of the most interesting."

"You can read the other languages?"

"Not all. Only High Landolin, Fuomi, Frangelese, and Narthani well, plus I can manage in some of the Iraquinik and other Landolin dialects."

"That's all?" said Yozef, smiling. "I'm curious, Maera. My impression is that few people on Caedellium know other languages. I suppose some were spoken in Preddi before the Narthani came, since it was the main trading center, but the rest of Caedellium hasn't had the need, with so little outside contact. How is it you know so many languages?"

"Some are necessary to read books from other parts of Anyar. High Landolin is the most recognized scholastic language, plus Fuomi and Frangelese, to a lesser extent. Also, important books in other languages often have translations into those three. Being the hetman's daughter doesn't give me that much to do, especially when Father's away, and I enjoy learning. I found studying history and languages often more enjoyable than interacting with other children and later with most adults."

When Maera finished talking, her face took on a stubborn look, perhaps defensive at her last words.

"Of course, I don't speak any of the languages well, since there's been little opportunity to use them. I used to practice when traders went through Keelan or with an occasional scholastic, though there's been minimal opportunity the last years."

"Still, it's impressive you have both the ability to teach yourself and the determination to do so."

Maera's defensive look evaporated, and her face relaxed, a slight flush coloring her cheeks. She knew and regretted that her studies were often a refuge and contributed to her reputation for being reserved. She had always been ambivalent toward the occasional praise for her learning. Somehow Yozef's regard meant more than that of other persons.

*So it's true. Yozef thinks I'm smart, and it doesn't bother him. In fact, he seems appreciative. He said it that day at the picnic, and Father said Yozef said the same to him.*

*I know it's true, but when others say it, I always wonder whether they're being honest or, if honest, are uneasy about it since I'm "only" a woman. Yet Yozef is different. When he says it, I believe him, and it feels better than when others say the words. It makes me feel . . . what? What's going on with me?*

She hadn't responded to Yozef's last comment, lost in her thoughts, twirling a strand of hair with her left hand. Then her eyes went from the paper back to him, looking at her expectantly.

Maera started to say . . . something, but her tongue caught. *Am I flustered?*

Yozef rescued her with a question. "What else is on the list?"

Maera cleared her throat. "There are many more tradesmen in Caernford than in either Abersford or Clengoth, and I thought you might like to visit with them and see if there are any crafts or methods of interest. Also, you mentioned the concept of 'franchising,' I think you called it, where you agree to let others use your methods for a percentage of the profits. I know you have agreements with some tradesmen in Clengoth to produce some of your products and I wonder if the shops you've established in Abersford and the Clengoth franchises are sufficient or if you might want to consider similar arrangements here in Caernford?"

Yozef scrunched his mouth sideways, as he ran his tongue over his teeth—a habit she'd noticed when he was contemplating an idea. "Now that you mention it, Cadwulf and Filtin told me the orders for lanterns and paper products were increasing so steadily, they predict we wouldn't be able to fill all orders within a few more months. We're already adding soap and kerosene production to other provinces. So, yes, I like your suggestion. Let's plan on my talking with some of the local tradesmen while I'm here."

Maera looked pleased, again. "Oh, and besides visiting the abbey library, did you want to meet with any of the scholastics at St. Tomo's? You'll find many of them not as open-minded as those at St. Sidryn's but there are exceptions, and Abbot Beynom has written Abbot Walkot at St. Tomo's about you. I'm sure Abbot Beynom also asked you to pass on his greetings."

Yozef grimaced. "The abbot did make such a request, and I'd forgotten until you mentioned it. Thank you, Maera. I need a pocket planner or a secretary."

Maera ignored the new words. If they were important, she'd hear them again from Yozef and ask about them then. She pushed the page in front of her to one side but kept looking at it with a turned head. "Those are the major items I thought to discuss with you. Is there anything else you can think of?"

"Since I've never been to Caernford, I'd like to see the city and some of the surrounding countryside. Are there any favorite places of *yours*?"

She wondered whether the question was deliberate. Yozef had taken her to one of his favorite places near Abersford, with the jacaranda trees and the day's outing that ended abruptly when he kissed her. She kept looking at the paper and said noncommittally, "There are a few such places nearby. I'll be happy to show them to you."

Yozef wrote to Cadwulf that he'd be staying longer in Caernford and to pass on the information to Filtin and the other lead workers. The next sixday passed quicker than Yozef expected. The single planned meetings with Luwis and Kennrick extended into two additional sessions, this time with both men. Luwis, a naturally dour man, had been borderline hostile at first, then had listened and become more interested in Yozef's comments once he'd thought them over. Kennrick was reserved but pleasant from the beginning. Only by the last meeting did Yozef fully appreciate Kennrick's acumen and Luwis's forthrightness.

During one meeting, Luwis commented on increased patrols and preparation for feared Narthani moves on other clans. At Yozef's request, Luwis took him to a field where fifty men on horseback were training. Yozef's first impression was that the men were engaged in demonstrating chaos.

"What exactly are the men doing, Ser Luwis?" Yozef was afraid of the answer but had to ask.

"Being sure the men can ride, fire their muskets and pistols, then go to lance and sword. Some men are accomplished riders but can't handle the horse and weapons at the same time. Others are skilled with firearms or blades but aren't good horsemen. This group is mainly shop workers who need work on controlling their horses."

"Maybe they would do better fighting on foot." *The Caedelli don't know about infantry?*

"Then how would they either escape from the enemy's horsemen," said Luwis, "or chase the enemy if they retreated?"

"So all the fighting is done from horseback?" *Please tell me no.*

"Of course, unless an enemy is hiding in buildings or heavy vegetation, or in cases like the raid on St. Sidryn's, where the citizens defended the abbey."

Yozef was discouraged. "Ser Luwis, I'm wondering what's the biggest battle or fight Keelan men have engaged in the last tens of years?"

"About fifteen years ago, there was a dispute with the Eywellese stealing cattle. We took two hundred men to catch the Eywellese, who numbered about eighty."

"Two hundred? Eighty? Nothing larger? Numbers in the thousands?"

"Thousands, no. Not in my lifetime, though there are records from past generations where fighting involved two or three thousand men."

"What if the Narthani attack in great numbers, and the clans need many thousands of men to stop them? How will you or the hetmen control the fighting? I see here that only fifty men have difficulty working together. What will happen if instead of fifty men, it's thousands?"

"That's a problem," deadpanned Luwis.

Yozef flinched. *No shit! That's it? "It's a problem?"*

Yozef remembered watching Carnigan ride off with men for a routine patrol and thought at the time they looked like a posse—a mass of riders with no organization. Now he cringed at the thought of that posse numbering in the thousands and facing a disciplined army. It wasn't an image to engender confidence.

The other planned meetings around Caernford were scheduled during visits to St. Tomo's abbey. While Yozef was accustomed to divisions in attitude toward himself by the brothers and the sisters at St. Sidryn's, at St. Tomo's the gap more resembled a chasm. Maera served as guide and clued him in on the abbey's internal workings. Several of the scholastics were eager to meet with him, though not all.

"Sorry, Yozef," said Maera. "Several of the St. Tomo's scholastics have stubbornly refused to meet with you. A few say they want to meet, though I suspect it will be to refute anything out of your mouth. I'm afraid there are feelings you're a threat to long-held beliefs and resentment that their expertise is belittled, if elsewhere on Anyar there're scholastics far in advance of themselves."

"Not to worry. Things aren't that much different in America. God knows, I've met and seen many a person who was threatened by novel ideas or any suggestion that their understanding wasn't the ultimate word."

Maera's caution came true, that Yozef should be prepared for difficult sessions with some scholastics from St. Tomo's. She witnessed one such meeting, this with a sister specializing in astronomy who had left the meeting in a huff.

"Gravity? Some unseen force holding people on the round planet? Obviously, it's simply God's will. Stars being how far away? Nonsense. My calculations proved them to be only a few hundreds or thousands of miles distant." Phht!! Huff, huff. Stomp, stomp.

As the irate sister left, Yozef smiled, to Maera's curiosity.

"Why are you smiling, Yozef? The sister essentially called you both a charlatan and the Evil One's agent."

"Oh, Maera, there're so many people with closed minds. If we let ourselves become upset every time someone won't listen to new ideas, we wouldn't have time to do anything else. I have sympathy for them. I'm seen as a threat to who they are and their professions. People also resist changes that threaten long-held beliefs. I expect many of the more honest ones will go away and think about what I've said, then come back later to learn more, if not from me, then from other scholastics or from their own thinking. Even if not, there will still be some here at St. Tomo's who *do* listen.

"Arguing with the others once you see how entrenched are their positions is unlikely to convince them at the time and may have the opposite effect of having them reject *anything* you say. All you can do is encourage them to reconsider their ideas in the future."

Maera listened and felt chagrined. She could recollect many of her past discussions, in which she was scathing when other people disagreed with her. She remembered only a few times when a person had later come around to her position. Being honest with herself, she wondered how many times Yozef was right, and all that she'd achieved was exactly the opposite effect, by pushing them into shutting out her ideas entirely. Part of her still liked telling people what fools they were; the other part admitted that Yozef's attitude likely achieved better results.

"I'm afraid I'm not as patient as you, Yozef. I find myself wanting to be *right* in any argument. It's not that way with you, is it? You want to get the right *answer*, not *be* right. Yet you seem to know so much more in certain areas. Doesn't it give you pleasure to be smarter than most others?"

"God, no! I may have more facts than others here, but having facts is not the same as having intelligence. I hope I haven't given the impression that what I've been introducing here on Caedellium are my ideas."

They had exited the scholastic hall at St. Tomo's while speaking and stood under a vine-covered arbor.

"I need to thank you again, Maera, for arranging these meetings. The ones with Brother Nywin and Sister Yesifa about the history of your people coming to Caedellium gives me more background into Caedellium clan interactions and history. Also, I'm glad I met the two brothers interested in the mixing of specific substances to generate new compounds, similar to what I studied—chemistry. Although we didn't have time to talk in detail, I believe they and I will have interesting correspondence. I may even invite them to come to Abersford to personally see our shops. I believe I know more of the basic science, but these two have practical experience I lack, and both seem open to new ideas."

"Science," echoed Maera. "You explained it to me in Abersford, but I'm still not clear what it means beyond studying the world. Is that not what scholastics do?"

"Science is a type of thinking. Considering all possibilities and being willing to change your ideas if there are shown to be better ones. In practical terms, in my shops, Filtin tries to make more efficient distillation apparatuses.

He may want stronger glass, but how does he get that stronger glass if he doesn't know how to make it? The answer is that he 'experiments.' He keeps trying different additions to the glass until he comes up with a solution. He then remembers the procedure and tells others. They, in turn, use his procedure until they or someone else comes up with a better one. They then tell Filtin, and he adopts their new procedure in an endless cycle. Once the question or the problem is identified, science would say there are no final answers, only temporary ones."

"What about the theophists? Their answers aren't temporary."

Yozef was slow to answer, as if carefully choosing his words. They hadn't spoken in depth about theological matters, so she wasn't sure exactly what he believed.

"That's one difference between your people and mine. We distinguish between science and theology. Theology deals with faith, while science says nothing can be taken on faith. That's a gross simplification and a difference that many great scholastics have argued doesn't necessarily exist. I tend to agree with the distinction."

Maera's looked thoughtful. "I need to think about this. However, I advise you to be careful in telling this to the brothers and the sisters. I'm not sure how many of them would react to the difference between what *must* be questioned and what *cannot*."

"I agree, and I try to be careful."

# CHAPTER 15

# UNEXPECTED

## Surprise

Yozef's Caernford routine changed on the fourth night after the hetman left. The second and third nights, Yozef had eaten with Carnigan at the Galloping Horse Inn. He had continued the morning meals in his guest quarters, along with working on getting Norlin to be less formal. On the morning following the fourth night, Maera passed on from her mother an invitation to eat again at the manor house the evening before Godsday. It was a small soiree, with a dozen other people in attendance, including Luwis and Kennrick, along with wives, a couple of the scholastics more receptive to Yozef, and several others whose names he managed to keep straight but whose roles in Keelan society he was unsure of.

Yozef sat opposite Maera and next to her mother, who was at the head of the table in the hetman's spot. They retired to the parlor after dinner to be entertained by the four Keelan daughters, singing and playing a variety of stringed instruments. Maera's looked and sounded something like a skinny cello, and he could pick out her voice from her sisters'. The quartet wasn't always on key, but the melodies were distinct, and guest sing-along was obviously part of the custom. Various guests contributed songs before Mared grabbed Yozef's hand and pulled him from his seat.

"Ser Kolsko, you must know songs from your homeland. Sing one for us. Please, please."

He became everyone's focus of attention, including Mared's pleading voice and Maera's eyes. Yozef reluctantly stood by his chair. His first frivolous thought was the English version "I've Got Friends in Low Places," but Maera's frown warned she was worried about the same. She'd heard the Caedelli version at the Snarling Graeko. He settled on something safe, where he knew several verses.

"This song is about the love of my people for their country," and he proceeded with a credible version of "American the Beautiful." The audience listened, not understanding the English words but sensing the essence of the song. Finished, he sat to respectful tapping of feet and verbal appreciations.

The entertainment session was followed by serving one of Yozef's new distilled whiskeys and biscotti-like sweets. The drink was not to his taste, and the other guests' opinions differed. Still, he received multiple congratulations and thanks for the new libation. Although everyone was polite, he was conscious of curious stares during the evening.

As the gathering ended, Yozef was taking his leave from the hostess when she changed his routine.

"Ser Kolsko, may I call you Yozef, if it's not impolite among your people?"

"Not at all. Our customs are that first names are reciprocated. Would it be allowed to call the hetman's wife by her first name?"

"It is if *she* says it is. There. It's settled. You're Yozef, and I'm Breda. That's better. Now that we're friendlier, I see no reason you should eat your meals either alone in the cottage or at the inn in Caernford, unless you prefer it. Please consider this an invitation to eat morning and evening meals with us here in the manor house."

For the next three days, he ate with the Keelan women twice a day. He noticed the younger daughters acting conspiratorially at the first morning meal, and Mared later told him her parents normally ate that meal alone, as their personal time together.

Ceinwyn, the next oldest daughter, remained initially aloof, then suddenly thawed the second morning and thereafter. The two younger daughters, Anid and Mared, took it upon themselves to further educate Yozef in Caedelli customs and idioms. They provided many a laugh, as they explained local idioms, and he in turn explained a few of those from America. While neither "happy as a clam" or "blast from the past" translated, "foot in the door," "if you can't stand the heat, get out of the kitchen," and "smoke and mirrors" were favorably received. In contrast, he didn't understand why "putting the horse on the roof" was so funny and had to wait for Carnigan to explain why "cold soup and sausage," mentioned by Anid, brought on a reprimand from Breda and a blush from Maera.

Yozef's last three days before Culich's return were filled with more scholastics meetings, a final trip to the St. Tomo's library to prioritize readings to be translated, and excursions to Caernford and the surroundings. A common thread those days was the ever-present Maera. On the second to last day before the hetman returned, they walked from St. Tomo's library across the cobblestone courtyard to their waiting carriage, when Maera offered to show him a panoramic view of Caernford from a ridgeline to the east.

"It's one of my favorite places, and I haven't been there for many months."

"Sounds nice," Yozef said. "When would be the best time of day for the view?"

"Mid-day is best, or early afternoon is when the sun gives the best light." Maera looked away, and he caught a change in the tone of her voice. "We might also take a basket and have one of your 'picnics' while we're there."

Yozef stumbled, his foot catching on the edge of a cobblestone, as his attention diverted to her words. It was the first time she'd mentioned that day. He'd intended to bring up the subject several times, yet always hesitated.

"Why . . . yes. That would be nice," was all he managed to say.

They met the next mid-morning in front of the manor, and she drove a small dray pulled by a gentle gray gelding up a winding road to the hilltop about three switchbacking miles from the manor. As promised, the view was panoramic. Although only fifteen hundred feet above the valley floor, there were no obscuring hills or trees. They could see ten miles north and south and four miles straight across to the western hills. They stopped several times for views and Maera's verbal travelogue but didn't linger, since she cautioned the weather was changeable at the top, which proved prescient. When they arrived at an open overlook near mid-day, a wind came over a higher ridgeline to the east, picking up the still air. They pulled up behind a screen of trees, shielded from the rising wind, yet still having a clear view down the valley.

Maera was tense. She had chewed over all thoughts, feelings, advantages, and disadvantages for several sixdays before Yozef came to Caernford and even more so after his arrival, and she'd talked with her mother. She argued endlessly with herself and finally had to console herself that she wasn't certain, though what in life was? She could spend eternity debating with herself all the reasons marrying Yozef was a good idea and all of the reasons it wasn't.

She finally decided this was the day, if she was to go forward. They had received a semaphore message that her father would be home the next day, and Yozef was certain to leave a day or two later.

"As I told you, Yozef, the weather up here can change quickly. I know it's not quite time for mid-day meal, but perhaps we should eat, in case the weather forces an early return to the manor."

"Sounds fine. We can set everything out and then eat at leisure. If the weather worsens, we can pack up and still have eaten."

He started to get the basket from the wagon. Maera beat him to it, moved quickly to a flat area, and pulled out a cloth to eat on. There was still time to change her mind and say nothing. Focusing on the basket contents gave her more moments to dither.

"Here, let me help you."

Maera found herself irritated at him for offering to help, since she was into delaying.

*You ninny*, she chastised herself. *Here he is making an offer to help and you're annoyed.*

She ignored how cold her hands were as they set out the meal. Yozef noticed when their hands casually touched while exchanging a woven basket holding bread.

"Are you cold, Maera? Do you need something warmer from the dray?"

*Oh, God. I'm nervous. No, more than nervous. Afraid. That he might say no. Afraid he might say yes. Am I going to back out now and say nothing?*

He waited, concerned when she didn't answer immediately. It was the expression on his face that brought back to mind all the reasons to go forward.

"Yozef, do you still think of your home and family?"

"Of course. I always will."

"If you had the opportunity, would you leave Caedellium and go back?"

"That's a difficult question. Although America *was* my home, I've been making a different life here for two years. I suppose it's a sign of how much I feel the ties I have here that it would be a difficult decision. However, I don't believe there will ever be a choice, since I see no possibility I'll return to America. I'm here on Caedellium, and this is where any future I have will be lived."

She heard a trace of regret in his voice and resignation.

"What do you see as your future life here? You have all your enterprises, but what else? Are those enough? Will you stay in Keelan or someday move to a different province? Have a family at some point?"

Yozef sat back and regarded her. Her manner and questions made it clear there was a serious conversation underway; he just didn't know what the topic was yet.

"As for keeping busy, yes, there's enough here to keep me busy for the rest of my life." There was a wryness to the statement, as if there was more to the answer than explicit in the words.

"Moving from Keelan? I doubt it. I'm established in Abersford. I know the people, have friends, and expect to be spending the rest of my life there."

"And someday having a wife and children?"

He didn't answer right away, busying himself with laying out the basket contents.

*Did that question bother him? I wonder if he's aware everyone knows he's the father of Bronwyn's child?*

It was information she'd learned by the end of her first sixday at St. Sidryn's.

"I suppose so," Yozef said. "When I think of all these questions, I wonder about the Narthani and what will happen. Bringing children into an uncertain future is always something to carefully consider."

"Isn't that *always* the case? Children are a commitment to *create* a future," Maera said, looking serene and assured for the first time that day.

"Yes," said Yozef, "although for a thoughtful person, one who recognizes the uncertainties I'm afraid Caedellium faces, it takes a brave person to commit to that future."

She agreed with his answer, but she knew she was only delaying. More preliminary questions arrayed themselves in her mind, though none that needed to be asked or answered.

*This is it. Time to quit asking questions, or, as Filtin says is one of Yozef's favorite expressions, "Shit or get off the pot."*

She took a deep breath, her pulse racing. Her hands were cold, her throat dry. She swallowed. Twice.

"Yozef, I like you, and I believe you like me. I know I'm more comfortable around you than anyone else in my life, except for Mother and Anarynd. Being the hetman's eldest daughter, and of a hetman with no sons, brings expectations and responsibilities. One of the most important is to produce heirs for the family and clan. Yozef . . . I would be interested in marrying you and having those heirs."

*Oh, Merciful God,* she thought, cringing, *if that wasn't the most pathetic offer of marriage in the history of Caedellium, I hate to think what the worst was! Like I was explaining a logical reason for choosing wine or beer to go with evening meal!*

Yozef stared at her, his face blank. Seconds passed.

*He's not interested. He's thinking of a way to tell me politely!*

"Well," he said finally. "*That* was unexpected."

More seconds passed.

*Well, what's your answer?!* part of her wanted to yell. Once having blurted out the proposal, she wanted it settled—yes or no.


Yozef was truthful when he said her offer of marriage was unexpected. Not that the thought hadn't occurred to him in passing, but the uncertainties, given her status, his status, and how either of them felt about the other had all weighed against his giving it serious consideration. Everything now changed, and his mind raced through implications and complications and delved quickly into how he felt about her.

Did he want to be married to her? She was attractive enough, though not a beauty. Smart as a whip, maybe more so than himself, even with whatever the Watchers did to him. She'd said she was comfortable around him. While that was not a dying declaration of love, maybe it was at least as important.

Did he love her? He couldn't say he could utter the words and honestly know he meant them. But he liked her and was as comfortable with her as she evidently was with him—or as comfortable as he was liable to be when he couldn't tell all of the truth about who he really was and how he'd gotten to Anyar.

There were the practical advantages. Being married to the hetman's daughter would solidify his status here even more than all of his innovations. He would be accepted as a Caedelli, even if a naturalized one. He wanted to introduce as much knowledge as he could and as the civilization here could absorb, and to be part of a hetman's family would provide blowback protection from people or institutions that might not like what he was doing.

*And she's right. If I don't live in the here and now, then I give up the future.*

His attention focused back on Maera, sitting on the cloth, legs folded under her, hands clenched in her lap, a pale face and wide eyes staring at him.

*Once again, to be honest and objective, am I likely to get a better option for a wife?* was his last chiding thought.

Her patience, never one of her sterling qualities, capitulated. "If you don't want to marry me, I'll understand," she squeezed out. "Forgive me for surprising you with such an unseemly proposal." Her mind had already begun processing that he was going to refuse, wondering how she would tell her mother, and dreading how she might feel after having committed herself.

"Sorry for being quiet, Maera, but you must admit your proposal was both a surprise and something that doesn't warrant or deserve a quick response."

*So, what's the answer?!* she wanted to scream.

He paused, ran a hand down his pant leg, and tugged at his beard. His eyes roamed from her face down her body, then stared off toward the valley below. Yozef's first reaction had been surprise, the second was that he should take time to consider before making any commitment. How did he feel about her? How did he feel about marriage? And in this world, that meant children, plural.

*Why do I need more time? To say no? What about her father? She hasn't indicated that he knows anything about this. Maybe he'll shitcan the whole idea. In this culture, if the father says no, then that'd be it. How would I feel then? Look at her. She looks nervous, afraid to be disappointed, and angry I haven't already answered.*

*Poor Maera. Someone that smart trying to fit into the pre-made molds of this society. In many ways, I may well be the best match she would ever find on the island.*

*The same could be said for me. I'm never going to share everything with anyone here, not even a wife. Maera may be the closest I could come. She's smart and inquisitive. She would be a help in anything I try to introduce. And I'm attracted to her. The kiss on the picnic was spontaneous, and the time we've spent the last sixday has only reinforced that attraction. Didn't she just solve for me my indecision on how to follow up?*

*Hell, sometimes you just gotta go with a gut feeling.*

He turned his focus back to her. Her jaw was clamped, her breath deep and halting, fingers rhythmically clenching and relaxing.

"Yes, Maera. I would very much like to marry you."

She went limp where she sat. Unbidden tears came to her eyes, whether from joy at the answer or relief at *having* any answer, she didn't know. She swallowed, started to respond and felt a croak coming, stopped, and swallowed again.

"That's . . . good . . . I'm pleased." *Well, God! What else am I supposed to say!?*

Yozef, bless him, once more came to her rescue. "What's your father going to say?"

Given a concrete problem to focus on, Maera regained her composure.

"I'll take care of Father. If necessary, Mother will help."

"There are, of course, many things to talk about," said Yozef. "When would the marriage take place? That is, how long before the formalities are taken care of, once we have your father's approval?"

Maera was in her element, planning details. "I think three to four sixdays from now, assuming Father gives permission when he returns."

"That soon?" Yozef chuckled. "And not even a shotgun wedding or the bride in trouble."

"Shotgun? And why would I have trouble?"

"Never mind, just some expressions from English. They don't translate well into Caedelli."

A sudden gust of wind took the lid off one of the food baskets. It sailed off downslope and disappeared into a clump of brush, as they took first notice of the changing weather—their having been engaged in becoming engaged. Cloud cover obscured the sun, and the wind whipped the tree branches.

"Perhaps we should eat and start back to the manor."

And they did eat . . . quietly. Maera passed morsels they had laid out to Yozef, who took them from her hand. Several times he held her hand momentarily. The first time she flinched, then held back in return. No words were said. They ate faster, as the air chilled and the sky darkened with thickening clouds rising over the ridgeline. Finished, they had repacked the remnants of the meal, folded up the cloth, and put everything back in the dray when she was about to climb up into the seat. He put a hand on her arm and turned her toward him.

"The day I kissed you at Abersford, I was afraid I'd done something terribly inappropriate, and you were mad at me. Especially when you wouldn't talk to me afterward."

"I was confused," said Maera, "and unsure of what I both *should* say or *wanted* to say."

He looked down to her from his six-inch advantage. At the moment, she seemed smaller than he remembered.

*Or maybe it's just her personality that makes her seem bigger.*

"Now that we've agreed to marry, I think another kiss is appropriate."

Her irises widened, and she leaned closer. "Yes, a reasonable suggestion."

This second kiss was longer than the first. This time, she didn't break off suddenly, but it ended on its own, as she lowered her head against his chest. He kept both arms around her and held her body to his, gently but firmly. Even with their heavy clothing, he could feel the mounds of her breasts. He ended the embrace with his hands stroking her back and arms. She was flushed and breathing heavily.

"There," he said. "Let's consider that the first sign of our coming marriage."

She nodded without words, and they returned quickly to the manor, arriving just as the threatening weather turned into reality and a driving rain covered the valley. A man sped over to hold the horse, as Yozef gave Maera a hand from the dray, and they ran to the veranda's shelter. There, he held and drew her to him. She put a hand on his chest.

"It's best if we don't give ourselves away until we talk to Mother and Father. It's only proper for a hetman's daughter."

He smiled. "No problem, Maera. I can wait for tomorrow before the next kiss."

She blushed and squeezed his hand. "I'll take the basket in and see you at evening meal."

Neither of them talked to anyone else the rest of the afternoon, each within a private world of thoughts, wondering whether they'd made the right decision, each not knowing but still anticipatory.

Evening meal was *interesting*. When the family members gathered in their usual places at the table, only the two middle sisters were oblivious that something had changed. Breda knew, because she and Maera had already talked about broaching Yozef that day, and Maera's awkward flush and sideways looks to Yozef told her all that she needed. Mared, the youngest daughter, was probably as sharp as Maera and had several days ago discerned what was going on between her sister and the strange but nice man from Abersford. Ceinwyn and Anid were clueless about events, yet couldn't help but notice Maera's mood. Ceinwyn actually became concerned that Maera was ill when one of her catty remarks was sloughed off with a wan smile.

After the meal, the three younger daughters were excused by Breda, to their protestations, because even Ceinwyn finally realized something was up.

When the protesters had exited, and their mother checked the door for dallying ears, Maera broke the news.

"Mother, Yozef and I have decided to be married."

"That's nice, dear."

Red flags hoisted in Yozef's mind at the equanimity of Breda's response.

*That's nice? Your daughter, the eldest child of the clan's hetman, announces she's marrying someone not even from the island, and that's all you say? Something tells me this isn't news to her.*

"Now we'll have to see what your father says," Breda added, smiling.

*That confirms it. It's a conspiracy. I was the first target, and now it's the father's turn. He may be hetman of all the Keelanders, but I suspect he's overmatched.*

Despite this thought, Yozef still wondered exactly what Culich Keelan's response would be and whether he should alert Carnigan to have himself and the carriage ready for a quick departure.

## The Hetman Returns

Yozef advocated that he should talk to the father first but was relieved when the female component of what was now a tri-partite conspiracy vetoed this noble gesture. Meara and Breda would go first, together at Breda's insistence and over the objections of Maera, who thought she should brace the father alone. Yozef was told not to appear for evening meal, and he walked into Caernford to eat with Carnigan, who wondered at his friend's distraction.

Hetman Keelan's carriage drove into the manor yard, along with several of his men, near dusk the next day. His mood was not the cheeriest. The meetings with the Hewell and the Adris had gone well enough. Hewell confirmed the desire to join the Tri-Clan Alliance, and only a formal meeting and acceptance with the alliance's three hetmen remained, scheduled for the next month. As for Adris, its new hetman had gathered all of his boyermen to meet with Culich, and by a nine to two advisory vote had supported making it a Five-Clan Alliance. Hetman Adris had not technically needed the vote, but Culich approved of the way he had gathered boyermen backing and then put it to a vote, once he had counted how the vote would go.

Less successful was the meeting with the Bevans and Pawell hetmen together, near their borders with Adris. Bevans reckoned themselves too remote from the danger, while Pawell was more concerned with the neighboring Skouks and Nyvacks clans and long-standing border disputes and ancient animosities. Culich's evaluation of the two hetmen was "Stupid heads up their asses, idiot bird brains."

It was the former success with Adris and Hewell that Breda kept bringing up at the evening meal's conversation, to keep her husband as upbeat as possible. Culich, as shrewd a leader as he was known to be, was oblivious to the moods running through the female contingent of his family, meaning everyone else at the table. Maera backed her mother in keeping the conversation light and positive, and the three younger Keelan females were under dire threat from their mother to behave and keep their mouths shut.

Thus, after Breda dismissed the three younger daughters, who left quietly, as forewarned, Hetman Keelan, leader of the sixty-thousand-member Keelan Clan, was relaxing after the family meal when Breda brought the conversation to the main topic of the evening.

Maera and her parents sat sipping glasses of one of the latest liqueurs to come from Abersford's booming distillation industry.

"How do you like this latest drink from one of Yozef Kolsko's enterprises, dear? Maera says it's called 'Amaretto,' for some reason. The flavor is from balco nuts."

Culich took another sip. "Perhaps a little strong on the balco flavor, but it certainly is smoother than the whiskey we've had before. I'm still more a beer man myself. I can appreciate this Amaretto, though, and maybe it'll grow on me. It certainly makes one glow inside."

Breda smiled at Maera. "It seems to be getting popular, along with all those other new products Kolsko is introducing. He is becoming quite a wealthy young man."

"Wealthy, yes. In fact, it wouldn't surprise me if in a few years he'll be the wealthiest man on all of Caedellium, just with what he has introduced so far. Only the Merciful God knows what else he'll come up with."

"And such a nice and respectable man, too, don't you agree?"

"Nice? I suppose. Respectful also, but in a way that always suggests he's not impressed by anything. Of course, as you and Maera have pointed out, that could just be differences in his people's customs."

"You've found your discussions with him about the Narthani and other matters of value, haven't you?" Maera chimed in for the first time.

Although Culich was not the most perceptive Caedelli male when dealing with family females, neither was he the worst, and his skill at reading and handling men had crossover. He narrowed his eyes suspiciously at the last run of comments.

"Why do I sense I'm being led somewhere?"

Breda ignored the question, thus by implication confirming her husband's suspicion. "Maera has something she wants to discuss with you, dear. Something important."

Culich's head tracked over to his eldest daughter, who, now that he thought about it, had been unusually demure during the meal.

Maera looked steadfastly at him, but . . . wait, *was she pale?*

"Maera?" he prompted.

"Father, I appreciate you haven't pushed me into marrying. I know my responsibilities to the clan, and I accept those responsibilities. It's been difficult for both you and me to find a suitable husband who would benefit the clan and whom I'm willing to marry. However, I believe I've found a satisfactory candidate."

Culich stared at his daughter, as he processed what she had just told him. He looked at his wife and then back to Maera. He might have been initially slow in detecting undercurrents since he returned, but his innate skill at reading men and dealing with such currents now came into full play. He looked back and forth again.

"Yozef Kolsko," he stated. "This man you propose to marry is Yozef Kolsko?"

"Yes, Father."

"I assume this means *you* wish to marry *him*. What from his side? Is he interested in you in that way?"

"He is. I spoke to him yesterday about it."

Culich took a larger sip of his drink. He looked at Breda. She looked back serenely.

The hetman grunted. *I take it from her demeanor that she approves.*

He turned back to Maera. "And the advantages to the clan and family to marry someone not even from the island and without formal clan affiliation?"

"Where he's from and his present clan status are irrelevant. Once married into Clan Keelan, he would be a clan member. As for advantages, they are many—projected wealth, likely even more innovations than he's already produced, which would enhance the clan status, and availability for advice on many matters, something I suspect you're coming to appreciate."

Father and daughter spent the next twenty minutes going over how Yozef Kolsko would be an asset to the clan and its hetman. It was all very logical and very annoying to Breda, even if she understood both the necessity of these considerations and the dance going on between her husband and daughter.

The advantage discussion exhausted, Maera switched gears. "In addition, Father, I don't see major disadvantages. I know it's mainly my fault, but there aren't many suitors eager to come calling. Not for the last year. I'm not what is . . . *expected*. We all know with time the choices were becoming more limited."

"As for what those suitors *expected*," growled Culich, "they're idiots." Then, softly, "I want you to know that I've *never* been disappointed in you, Maera. Only disappointed that you felt you hadn't found your place in the world and I didn't seem able to help."

"Thank you, Father," she said in a small voice with a catch in it.

"Harrumph. Now. As for this Yozef Kolsko. We've talked about the advantages and disadvantages. What about *you*? Is this what you truly want yourself?"

Whatever her internal doubts, she looked straight into her father's eyes and said firmly, "Yes."

Culich looked at his wife. "Can I assume correctly that you approve?" he asked with a sarcastic lilt.

"Yes, Culich, I *do* approve. I believe he'll be an asset to the clan, but more important is that I think he and Maera can have a good marriage."

"Why did this Kolsko not come to me directly, instead of sending the women?"

"He proposed to do that," Maera responded. "I convinced him that given all the circumstances, it would be better if I spoke to you first."

"And I agreed," added Breda.

"To prime me so I didn't throw him immediately out of the house for such temerity?"

"Something like that," said Maera honestly, with a twitch of a smile at the corner of her mouth.

"Hmmm . . . not an unreasonable strategy," said a mollified Culich.

He leaned forward in his chair. "All right. I won't say I give my approval. I need to talk more with Kolsko from a different viewpoint. Have him see me first thing tomorrow morning."

"Thank you, Father." Maera rose, planted a kiss on Culich's cheek, gave her mother a relieved smile, and went to leave Yozef a note.

Culich looked at his wife with an affectionate smile. "I assume I've been handled," he stated simply.

"Yes, dear," answered his wife, equally simply.

# CHAPTER 16

# CROSSHAIRS

### Narthani Headquarters, Preddi City

Okan Akuyun walked from his office to the staff meeting room. All the others were already present. Brigadier Aivacs Zulfa sat at the head of the table, the silver crossed swords on his epaulets freshly sewn on, his promotion from colonel having arrived in the last dispatches from Narthon.

Under most circumstances, the head chair would have been Akuyun's, but today Zulfa would lead the meeting as field commander and go over the final plans for invading Moreland Province. Akuyun had already approved the broad outline of the plan and took the empty chair at the other end of the rectangular table. Seated along one side were Zulfa's three sub-commanders, Colonels Erdelin, Ketin, and Metan. On the other side were Admiral Kalcan, Assessor Hizer, and, unfortunately, Mamduk Balcan, the senior Narth religious official on Caedellium. Generally, Akuyun tried to exclude Balcan whenever he could, but this was one instance where it was advisable to invite him and hope, probably fruitlessly, that Balcan kept his mouth shut.

Akuyun sat and nodded to Zulfa. "Brigadier Zulfa, please proceed."

Zulfa stood. "Thank you, General Akuyun." His eyes swept across the other men. "You've all had a part in developing the operational plan for the first major move outside our three-province enclave. Today we'll be going over the final details to ensure we all know our roles and give the opportunity for any last comments. Hopefully, nothing will require substantive changes, although, if necessary, we'll make adjustments."

Zulfa turned to the wall behind him and pulled aside a cloth that had been covering a six- foot by six-foot map of Caedellium. While individual clans might have more detailed maps of their own province and potentially the adjacent provinces, no clan had global island maps of such overall detail. The maps had been meticulously constructed during the last few years by combining observations from Narthani ships surveying the coasts, notes taken by supposed Narthani "traders" in the first years after the Narthani arrived in Preddi, and information from agents still operating within clan provinces, along with bribing Caedelli for copies of clan maps.

Zulfa drew his sword and pointed to a red arrow drawn from Preddi City to Moreland Province and a second arrow on to Orosz City. "The plan has two interrelated objectives. One is to capture Orosz City, the closest to a capital the island has, given the dispersed clan structure, and then subjugate the entire Orosz Province. By achieving this objective, we'll threaten to split the island in half, with the clans to the north and south being less able to come directly to each other's assistance. We estimate that when combined with the psychological impact of having lost their conclave site and the political center of the island, many of the clans will sue for terms and end the possibility of major united resistance."

"Major resistance, yes, but it may take time and effort to fully pacify the entire island, especially those clans that can withdraw into the mountains," said Metan, overseer of the Selfcell Province.

"Yes, we've discussed this at length," replied Zulfa. "The problem would be more with the northern provinces, because of the rugged mountains and their natural fractiousness. But by that time, we'd use men from the clans that surrendered to root out the holdouts. Even the more stubborn clans will eventually see the futility. If they don't, they'll be hunted down and exterminated."

Zulfa's sword point moved to Moreland City. "To get at Orosz City, we'll first go through Moreland Province and take their capital, Moreland City. It's to our benefit that the Moreland Clan leaders, especially the hetman's family, are widely considered hotheads prone to rash decisions. Hetman Moreland is also detested by the other hetmen, which makes it unclear whether the other clans will come to his aid. Even if they do, there's unlikely to be a coordinated effort against us. Whether other clans help Moreland or not, both scenarios will work for us, as I'll summarize in a moment.

"The second objective is to tempt the Caedelli into a major field battle or battles. No single clan can act alone and stop our advance. However, if other clans come to the aid of Moreland and Orosz, that presents the opportunity to gain a decisive victory. Killing enough of them should only hasten the clans falling to us, one after the other."

"Latest intelligence still finds no evidence they have artillery or infantry tactics," said Ketin, overseer of the Preddi Province.

"None," asserted Zulfa flatly, "as continue to be reported by Assessor Hizer's agents. What few cannon there are on the island are found in harbor fortifications. Even those few are relatively primitive and too large to be of practical use in field maneuvers. As for infantry tactics, there is still no sign they have any such concepts. Oh, they'll fight on foot in the right circumstances, but when facing our army, we expect masses of horsemen. Our best estimates are that we'll face a maximum of ten to twelve thousand, but even more couldn't prevail against our disciplined troops and the limited clan coordination."

Metan frowned. "I know I've brought this up before, but I'm still not comfortable with that many light cavalry potentially on our rear and cutting off supply and communication lines."

Zulfa's brow wrinkled, irritated that his subordinate still harped on something they had gone over numerous times. Akuyun thought for a moment he might have to step in. Zulfa was a gifted leader, but even under Akuyun's tutelage Zulfa still needed to work on handling senior subordinates. In this case, Metan was a valuable officer. Not the most brilliant or innovative, but solid. Akuyun was about to speak when Zulfa's expression smoothed from annoyance, as he addressed the group.

"I share Colonel Metan's basic concern. However, it's unlikely the Caedelli will be organized enough to threaten our rear, particularly after losing a battle. In their state of disorganization, we expect them to expend whatever forces they present to us in efforts to stop the advance. However, we have included in the operational plan two contingencies. One, we'll take a larger than normal supply train with us, so we can remain out of contact with Preddi for two sixdays without resupply. Plus, enough forces remain in our occupied areas to reopen supply lines or even come to our aid, if necessary."

"Come to our aid?" Erdelin said dismissively. "I hardly think that'll be necessary."

"Nor do I," said Zulfa. "But good operational plans try to consider even the unlikely scenarios." His tone and eyes also implied "good commanders."

Erdelin harrumphed, though didn't say more.

"It's my hope we can draw them into a major field engagement," Zulfa continued. "To encourage this error, our route will maximize the number of villages and towns we destroy on the way. Ravaging Moreland Province will convince them we'll do the same with Moreland City, which is where we predict the Morelanders will make a stand, if they haven't before. Once we near Moreland City, we'll slow our advance to give them time to finish gathering all their men and time for a few clans to come to Moreland's aid, if they're going to."

Zulfa paused and looked around at the other men, some of whom were gazing pensively at the map, others at him. "Are there any *new* general questions or comments?" The implication was implicit not to bring up anything they had already argued about in previous meetings.

To Akuyun's discomfiture, throat grumbling came from Balcan. The familiar series of sounds announced the prelate was about to say something, usually something Akuyun didn't want to hear.

"To be clear, although the objectives are to take both the Moreland and Orosz provinces, I heard nothing in the plan to include my priests in the invasion. For example, as soon as Moreland City is ours, it's imperative we destroy all vestiges of worshipping false gods and we convert their places of worship to Narth, whom we all know is the only *true* God. My inquisitors will also need to root out their theophists and any other religious leaders."

The other men at the meeting automatically turned their heads to the foot of the table, waiting for Akuyun to answer diplomatically, which he did in place of the response he would have preferred. He was the only one of them able to exert direct authority over the prelate. None of the commanders were true believers in Narth, but propriety was required.

"You're correct, Prelate. Although we believe the campaign will go well, there's no reason to risk yourself or your people if the unexpected occurs. I assure you that as soon as we believe it safe, we'll send back word, and you'll be escorted to Moreland City to begin what's necessary."

*And maybe you'll fall into a river on the way and drown,* Akuyun wished to himself.

Balcan drummed the fingers of both hands on the tabletop, as he considered Akuyun's words. "All right. I can understand the reasoning, just as long as my people can get into Moreland City as soon as possible."

"Naturally, Prelate. You have my assurances. Now, moving back to Brigadier Zulfa's request for comments about the campaign plan. Any other questions so far?"

When there were none, Akuyun gestured for Zulfa to continue.

"There are no detailed operational plans past Moreland City, because the results of our advance to that point will dictate what comes next. If our victory over Moreland doesn't convince other clans to capitulate, and they try to stop us again and precipitate more battles, we'll move on to Orosz City and beyond, splitting the island in half and disrupting the clans' ability to communicate and coordinate.

"The timetable for attacking Moreland is four months from now. In the meantime, we'll be giving the Caedelli reasons for keeping their men in their own provinces and discouraging a grand alliance of all the clans. It's a balancing act. While we'd like to face them several at a time to speed things up, for caution's sake we'd prefer not to fight them *all* at once.

"Admiral Kalcan will also see that our ships are constantly sighted all along the Caedellium coasts and will carry out enough raids to force them to keep men near likely targets, so they can't be sent elsewhere.

"At the same time, we'll increase pressure on two major potential allies of Moreland—the Stent Clan and the so-called Tri-Clan Alliance. Colonel Metan will use Selfcellese to carry out minor raids into Stent Province. Similarly, Colonel Erdelin will use Eywellese and our cavalry to threaten the coastal and inland portions of Keelan adjacent to Eywell territory and to make them wonder if Gwillamer is a target.

"Again, the goal is not to seize and hold territory, but to appear threatening, to force Keelan and Gwillamer to maintain forces along those borders, ones well distant from Moreland City. This prevents them from sending all their fighting men to Moreland's aid and delays those they send until it's too late for effective coordination.

"Colonel Erdelin will also see that the Eywellese posture and carry out incursions into Moreland to match what we're doing with Stent, Keelan, and Gwillamer. We don't want to make it too obvious where our thrust will be and give the Caedelli any reason to mass men into Moreland too early, until we've concentrated our forces and are well into the drive toward Moreland City. At that point, we prefer a few clans come to Moreland's aid, but at the last moment and without time to organize."

Zulfa looked at the men around the table. "Questions?"

Metan indicated by hand motion that he had something. "Perhaps an update from Assessor Hizer on suborning other clans would be in order."

Zulfa turned to the assessor, who opened a folder in front of himself. "Not as much success as we would like, though I believe we've neutralized several clans, and several others will be hesitant to commit themselves. Whether they eventually *do* commit is not as important as delaying any such action until it's too late." Hizer rose and went to the map.

"I agree with Brigadier Zulfa's plan to split the island. The two parts of the island will have only four clans in the south, but these are the three clans of the Tri-Clan Alliance and the Hewell Clan, which our reports indicated is close to joining the alliance. These four clans are also among the richest in resources and with better leadership. In contrast, the twelve clans in the north are fractious, with simmering long-term feuds and suspicions of other clans that we've tried to encourage. They also have no formal history of close alliances, and several have leadership that rivals Moreland in lack of brains and self-control.

"In addition, our agents in clan territory will continue reporting to us and be available should any sufficiently important target of opportunity occur, such as removing leadership."

Approving nods met the last statement, assassination being an accepted tactic in Narthani warfare.

"Thank you, Assessor," said Zulfa. "One scenario is that we continue on to Orosz City and farther to Adris Province. Once the island is split, we will see which clans perceive the inevitable. I'd be surprised if there's a general capitulation at that point, so I expect we'll still have to move either north or south, where we'll link up with Admiral Kalcan's ships at the first opportunity.

"We'll reward clans coming over to us with lands and spoils, but we need to move quickly to finish the remaining major resistance. Whether we go after the northern or southern clans next would be decided at the time, though I believe the southerners are the biggest threat, and knocking them out would almost certainly bring a quick resolution to the entire mission."

Zulfa uncovered a diagram of troops units. "When we move on Moreland, the force will consist of five thousand infantry in ten standard five-hundred-man blocks—each block composed of two hundred pikes and three hundred muskets. Such an emphasis on pikes wouldn't be advisable in a mainland campaign, since pike formations have become obsolete and are being deemphasized in favor of increased muskets. If our units were back in Narthon, they would have converted by now. In our case, the High Command believes the expected opposition here on Caedellium will be mainly horsemen with minimal to nonexistent infantry and artillery support. Since the pikes are the traditional solution to holding cavalry at bay while muskets and cannon fire work on the enemy, we don't foresee a problem.

"The force will have twelve 12-pounder batteries of five cannon each—a total of sixty cannon. The troop blocks and cannon batteries will be the main instruments to break the Caedelli. Light cavalry will scout and screen during force movements, and when we bring the Caedelli to a field engagement, the cavalry will protect both flanks and the supply train to the rear. We've planned on three thousand cavalry in two groups, one composed of fifteen hundred Eywellese and the second of a thousand Selfcellese, plus five hundred of our own heavy cavalry. If the situation warrants, the heavy cavalry will be available to break up Caedelli light cavalry groupings, in addition to stiffening the Selfcellese. The three thousand cavalry will also be available to encircle or ride down remnants of any islander forces, if proper conditions exist."

"Meaning, the Selfcellese still can't be trusted," groused Erdelin, ever ready to claim unspoken and unearned credit for the Eywellese he oversaw as being more reliable than the Selfcellese overseen by Metan, whom he considered a plodder.

Metan flushed and was about to snap back when Akuyun jumped in. "The Eywellese have always been more enthusiastic about the alliance than the Selfcellese—or, should I say, more gullible? Colonel Erdelin has done a good job in controlling and using them. The Selfcellese have been a more difficult challenge, but I have full confidence that Colonel Metan is bringing them along as well as possible until our position here is more settled."

Metan relaxed with an appreciative nod to Akuyun and a studied ignoring of Erdelin.

"True," said Zulfa, who returned to his seat, closed one folder, and opened another. "We believe any potential problems with the Selfcellese will be stabilized by having our own cavalry acting with them. Anyway, that's the rationale for composition of the two divisions of cavalry in the force structure.

"Moving on from the general action plan, now let's review preparation issues, and by this I mainly mean the infantry. This is an area I tasked Colonel Ketin to keep a close eye on. Colonel?"

Thus prompted, Ketin opened a folder of his own. "We have two interrelated issues regarding infantry readiness. First is the quality of these troops. As you know, we were assigned a mixture of experienced and raw troops. We can be honest with ourselves that neither of these is among the best quality for a campaign against a significant enemy. The experienced troops are not quite the dregs of other commands, but neither did commanders make any effort to give up their better people when levied to fill out our rosters. Many of the rest of the lower-grade troops are from various peoples the Narthon Empire has conquered in the last decades and have either little to no experience or have experience other than in the Narthon army. General Akuyun procured a good cadre of lower-level squad and platoon leaders, but I wouldn't want to use the bottom ranks against a Fuomi or Iraquinik army. The situation has improved markedly in the last two years, as the men have been integrated, trained, and, in the worst cases, disciplined severely enough that I believe the troop blocks are of acceptable quality for the foe we face here. Naturally, nothing is certain until their first real battle, but with the better men dispersed among the blocks, I believe they are as ready as they will be without coming under fire.

"The second issue is the lack of maneuver experience. The needs of our situation here on Caedellium have necessitated that much of the time the infantry had been relatively dispersed as garrisons, putting down minor revolts, building fortifications, and assisting the settlers brought in. Whatever training has gone on has focused on the smaller units, squads and platoons, with only minimal time working in complete five-hundred-man blocks and no training experience at all in multi-block movements.

"This needs to be rectified as soon as possible. The total force we will move out with will be eleven thousand—five thousand infantry, five hundred of our own heavy cavalry, a thousand artillerymen and engineers, two thousand support personnel accompanying the combatants and trailing back into Eywell, and twenty-five hundred total Eywell and Selfcell light cavalry. When we gather the force together, and before we seriously engage the Caedelli, we need intensive training to achieve an acceptable level of unit coordination. Since it is impossible to assemble the entire force for joint exercises full time, I have suggested to Brigadier Zulfa that we start immediately with exercises involving smaller numbers, something like two or three infantry blocks, plus a few artillery batteries and some cavalry. Then, as the date to initiate the move on Moreland approaches, we can consider larger assemblies, leading up to the full gathering in the last sixdays."

Ketin finished his presentation and looked at Zulfa, who said, "I agree with most details of Colonel Ketin's assessment, and we will implement these actions as he has outlined. He and my staff will send more details on training schedules in the next day or two. As for when to start assembling the force for large-unit training, I think we can wait and see how the training with fewer units is progressing after, shall we say, the first two months? Normally, I would prefer more maneuver training as a total force, especially with relatively untried units, so let's press the training vigorously.

"One final topic I wanted to address before we finish," asserted Zulfa. "You know or have heard rumors that three of our men were executed on Colonel Erdelin's orders. This incident relates to general discipline. I have endorsed the colonel's actions and will ask him to summarize what led to this. Colonel Erdelin?"

Erdelin looked unperturbed. "Three men under my command, all three among the newer recruits, raped an Eywellese woman at a horse ranch, while their squad was patrolling a forested region near the Moreland border. She was alone at the time, her husband providing local guide services to another squad. Based on testimony from other members of the squad and the woman's husband, I determined there was no doubt to this breach of discipline. The three men were hanged in front on their infantry block and the squad leader given ten lashes and demoted for losing control of his men."

"Again," said Zulfa, "I concurred with Colonel Erdelin's action, as did General Akuyun. The woman herself is of no consequence, but the loss of discipline can't be tolerated. The men had been warned to leave local women alone. That's what the brothels are for."

"As Brigadier Zulfa said," Akuyun took over, "I endorsed the executions as necessary. Not only was it a breach of discipline, but one inducement for clans to come over to us is the promise of better treatment than if they are conquered by force. The contrast between what happened to the Preddi and the current status of the Selfcell and Eywell clans is a lesson we want the other clans to take to heart. That contrast is lost if, as in this case, we promised a clan their women will be left alone by our men and then something like this happens. It's the same if we tell a Selfcellese farmer he will keep his land, and then we turn around and take it away. What incentives do they have *not* to revolt? While we can always destroy a people, if necessary, we prefer they're willingly integrated into the Narthon Empire.

"However, while I agree with the action, in looking into the matter I found something that may have created the climate where this discipline breach occurred. I have spoken with Brigadier Zulfa and Colonel Erdelin about it, and the colonel acknowledges that staff changes are needed."

Erdelin looked as if he had just bitten into a sour fruit and was slightly flushed but didn't comment.

"The number of functional women in the brothel serving the executed men's unit had declined to where the number of visits per man was down to once a sixday or even less. I also had one of my staff check elsewhere, and it seems a similar situation is developing at other sites. This is one of those minor details that have to be attended to. I realize no commander can be aware of everything affecting his command, but that's what staffs are for. In this case, a member of Colonel Erdelin's staff failed to recognize the problem properly and bring it to the colonel's attention."

By the time Akuyun had finished speaking, all present knew that one of Erdelin's staff was thrown under the wagon to save Erdelin's face, and the other two troop colonels and Admiral Kalcan would later that day be ensuring that their staffs also checked into the issue.

"As for the problem of staffing the brothels," continued Akuyun, "this is something all of us, including my staff, should have seen coming, because it has been a year since the last major batch of women was added. We need to be alert to such details. In this case, the problem should be solved as the incursions into clan territories take captives and we move on Moreland."

Sadek Hizer observed approvingly from his seat. Part of his role as assessor for the High Command was evaluating the command structure for performance. Akuyun had publicly rebuked one of his sub-commanders in front of his colleagues, then pointed out the same problem could be happening under their commands and emphasized a joint responsibility, including himself. Erdelin might resent the public rebuke but would accept it more gracefully than otherwise. Hizer had seen commanders who humiliated subordinates so often there was little loyalty returned. Erdelin and his staff had been negligent but had acted decisively in the executions, and he would be sure his staff was more attentive to the little details, as would Akuyun's other subordinates.

*Very well done, Akuyun.*

## Preddi City, Akuyun Villa

Akuyun drew deep breaths, his heart rate slowing after he'd spent himself. He and Rabia were still joined, her legs and arms around him. He stroked the top of her head with one hand, then raised his head from beside hers to look into her face and kiss her. She smiled. It was a well-practiced routine for them.

Whenever there was action about to take place, his libido was more active. She thanked Narth that the times when he personally headed off to fight were over. In those days, their coupling wasn't just to satisfy his desires before leaving, but also to allay her fears for his return and the possibility it would be their last night together. Over the years, it evolved into one of their rituals. Whenever he sent men out to do what he didn't do anymore or when a major plan was finalized, they kept this routine.

That he still desired her after twenty-eight years of marriage and four children and had never shown an interest in other women were gifts she didn't take for granted. They lay together for a few more minutes, then he rolled off to his side, holding her in one arm as she turned to him.

"So, you're satisfied that everything is ready to begin the next phase?"

To begin talking "business" right after sex might seem indifferent to some, but they had been married long enough and well enough that any tender murmurings afterward were by now assumed without being repeated.

"As satisfied as I'm likely to be," he answered. "It will be the first time for a major Eywell operation. I think Erdelin can handle the details. They've taken well to integration, but their hetman is a hothead and not the brightest light in the sky, though I don't think he's dumb enough to cause Erdelin any problems. The son is another story. We may have to eventually do something about him, since I don't see him becoming hetman."

Rabia stroked his face. "That's something for another day. Best not think about more tonight."

He held her tighter, and they drifted off to sleep.

# CHAPTER 17

# YOU WANT TO WHAT?

Yozef hadn't eaten with the Keelan family the evening of Culich's return. When Breda Keelan recommended the prospective groom not be present when her husband learned of Maera's desire to marry, Yozef made halfhearted objections, then gratefully made himself scarce in St. Tomo's library and ate evening meal with Carnigan at the Galloping Horse Inn.

"You're quieter than usual, Yozef. Do you feel all right?" queried Carnigan between two prodigious quaffs of beer.

"Oh, just things on my mind."

"Things? Like what?"

Yozef was stumped for a second. He didn't want to get into a discussion about the possibility of marrying the hetman's daughter, yet he needed to say something to distract his friend from probing harder.

"Well, for one thing, I'm remembering a story."

"Hah! About time! I haven't heard one of your stories for sixdays. Hope it's a new one."

Yozef had garnered a reputation in Abersford for telling amusing stories no one had heard before. He hadn't seen reason for the pub patrons in Abersford to know he cribbed them from Earth and they weren't Yozef Kolsko originals.

"It happened in a pub in Orosz City during a clan conclave. Three Morelanders are drinking their beers and spot a Keelander. One of the Morelanders walks over to the Keelander, taps him on the shoulder, and says, 'Hey, I hear your hetman is a drunken lout.'

"'Oh, really, hmm, didn't know that,' the Keelander says. Puzzled, the first Morelander walks back to his friends. 'I told him Hetman Keelan was a drunken lout, and he didn't seem to care.' The second Morelander says, 'You just don't know how to make him mad. Watch and . . ."

Yozef worked through the story, but at the punch line Carnigan wasn't impressed. His craggy brow scrunched as he went over the joke. "The first one . . . then the second . . . then . . . ah! I get it! A good one, Yozef. Though not one of your better ones. I had to think about it for a moment before I got it."

The rest of the evening, Yozef worked at diverting his thoughts from whatever was happening at Keelan Manor. Later, he walked the two miles back to his visitor's quarters on the manor grounds to find a note from Maera slipped under the door. He was to meet with her father the next morning.

A restless night later, the meeting in the hetman's study started off much as Yozef predicted. The hetman sat behind his expansive desk, not bothering to invite Yozef to sit.

"So you think you're a suitable person to marry the daughter of a hetman, are you?" were the first words out of Culich's mouth.

*So that's how it's going to be.*

Yozef didn't know whether Maera's father was mad or playing a role. Either way, he gauged that backing down wouldn't impress the hetman.

"Frankly, Hetman, not only do I not *care* if she's your daughter, that's a good reason *not* to marry her and avoid the complications of a hetman's family. I want to marry Maera *despite* the fact that she's your daughter." As Yozef said the words, for the first time he recognized that they were true. He was surprised when the events had percolated for a day, and the idea of marrying Maera made him smile. He liked her and assumed she liked him enough to propose marriage. She was smart and attractive, and he remembered the curves pressed against his body as they kissed. The advantages to marrying into the hetman's family faded to secondary considerations.

Culich's tone softened. "You realize she has obligations to the clan?"

"I know she feels responsibilities, and I'd do nothing to discourage those feelings. My main concern would be for her wellbeing, as well as that of any children we have. I understand there is an expectation that one or more of her sons might be a candidate to be the next hetman. I believe we can agree that having a broad education and being raised to be responsible would both satisfy my hopes for the children and be an appropriate basis for whatever other training you might deem necessary."

"I want you to realize that by marrying Maera, you would be accepting some responsibilities to the clan."

"I don't see that as a major problem. Keelan is my home, and here I'll do my work, live the rest of my life, and have a family. I could hardly want anything but the best possible for the clan. I'd strive to be aware of formal obligations, as long as it doesn't interfere too much with projects I believe are important to Keelan and all of Caedellium."

"Then maybe we have a basis for further discussion," said Culich, motioning for Yozef to sit in a chair facing the desk.

For the next half hour, Culich grilled Yozef on his background, covering the same questions as in previous meetings but pressing harder for details. Only once did Yozef take refuge in claiming his memory wasn't perfect after his ordeal of arriving on Caedellium.

## Interrupted

Culich Keelan's return home from the hetmen meetings had gone differently than anticipated. The announcement of his daughter's desire to marry a man her father had never met until a sixday ago, a man not even from Caedellium, and a man with no political connection to advantage the clan, all conspired to surprise Culich enough to need time to consider the implications for both the clan and his daughter. Not that he believed he would refuse permission. Maera's assertion that she wanted to marry Kolsko, Breda's support of the idea, Culich's worry for Maera's happiness, and the need for Keelan heirs all weighed toward his blessing.

What he didn't convey even to Breda was, aside from all other considerations, his relief that Maera would still be part of the clan. He had dreaded that she would marry the son of another hetman and move permanently away from Keelan, potentially to a clan far enough distant they would see her only yearly, if that often.

He had planned on meeting and assessing Kolsko because of the man's role in the defense of St. Sidryn's and all the innovations he was introducing. He hadn't imagined evaluating him as a prospective husband for Maera. Now that he had, the man had made a favorable impression. Culich accepted all the logical arguments presented by Maera and Breda, and either Kolsko was a skilled dissimulator or he honestly cared for Maera. Plus, he had a spine, something not apparent from earlier meetings.

Not that Culich was completely satisfied—although, as he considered the man sitting resolute, staring straight at the leader of the Keelan Clan and trying not to appear nervous, Culich was reassured. He would ask further questions, probe deeper into the man's background and opinions, and gather more impressions of his reliability.

Culich was pondering what he should ask Kolsko next, when a staccato knock on his study door interrupted them.

"Come in," he called out, irritated. He had given instructions not to be disturbed.

It was Breda. "Sorry, dear, for interrupting. A rider just came with what he says is an urgent message."

The hetman's irritation was replaced by foreboding. "Send him in."

Quickly ushered in by Breda was a man in his late twenties, half-soaked from the intermittent showers still passing through from the system that caused Yozef and Maera's abbreviated picnic. He wore riding gloves he removed as he strode into the study. With a short bow to the hetman, he opened a satchel at his side, withdrew a leather cylinder, and undid a flap at one end. He pulled out a rolled paper and handed it to Culich.

"A message from Boyerman Sarnin."

Culich took the paper, scanned it quickly, then read more carefully. His face tightened. "Did you come direct from Dornfeld?"

"Yes, Hetman. I left Dornfeld with the message from Boyerman Sarnin. I changed horses six times to get here as quickly as possible."

"I'll have an answer ready within an hour," said Culich. Looking at the man, he said, "You're in no shape to take it. I'll send another man." He turned to his wife, who was watching anxiously, wondering about the message's contents. "Breda, please send Norlin to summon Vortig and Pedr here immediately. Also, arrange quarters and food for this man."

As curious as she was, she didn't hesitate and hurried from the room.

"Do you know what's in the message?" Culich asked the messenger. "Herwold's your family, isn't it?"

"Yes, Hetman. I'm Jaekel Herwold. And yes. He read it to me as he wrote."

The man's tired frame straightened on being recognized by the hetman whom he had only met once briefly ten years earlier. Such a remembrance of people and places was one of Culich's skills.

"I'm sure there were more details than what is in the message. What can you tell me?"

"We see more and more Eywellese riders near the border; even a few times they crossed over in places near farms or roads. Boyerman Sarnin's worried they're testing the terrain in preparation for a major incursion such as happened in Moreland and Stent, as you warned about last month at the boyermen council."

Most of the clanspeople in the sparsely populated Dornfeld district were concentrated on the narrow coastal plan north of the town of Dornfeld on the Gwillamer border. Duwid Sarnin served both as Dornfeld's mayor and as Boyerman Dornfeld.

Herwold went to the Keelan map on the wall and placed a finger on the westernmost part of Keelan that poked through a mountain range to the Bay of Witlow. When Culich moved to the map, Yozef followed, standing behind the two men. Keelan land included no more than twenty miles of coast, and Dornfeld was the only settlement indicated on the map. The province and the clan of Eywell lay to the north.

"These sightings were along most of the coastal border to Eywell. Boyerman Sarnin sent men into the mountains north of the Dillagon Pass and found signs of encampments on Keelan land where men could observe the pass. At least once, they saw a group of four or five men moving north toward Eywell territory. Boyerman Sarnin also sent a group of men several times under darkness short distances into Eywell territory at places along the border where there had been several of these incursions. They found signs of many horsemen and went farther and found a major encampment, estimated at about five hundred Eywellese and the same number of Narthani not three miles from the border. The boyerman's worried, Hetman."

"As well he should be, Herwold," said Culich. "A thousand men? That close to the border? And who knows if there might be other encampments nearby?"

Culich was pleased with Sarnin. It had taken initiative to send men across the border and risk incitements, if it turned out nothing serious was underway.

*Good man*, he thought.

"If I remember correctly, Sarnin should be able to muster about three hundred men."

"More like three hundred and twenty, Hetman."

Culich looked at the map for several minutes, his finger tracing roads and features and at other moments stroking his beard. Breda and Maera returned, interrupting his thinking.

"Summons are off to Vortig and Pedr," said Breda. "They should be here within half an hour."

"We also summoned the Caernford semaphore station manager and Vortig's son Mulron, as commander of the Caernford garrison," Maera added.

*Good girl*, Culich thought. He'd need to send messages to the other clans about his worries and let them know he'd be going personally to assess what was happening near Dornfeld. Getting Mulron Luwis to the manor would save time from Vortig having to send for his son himself.

Culich noticed Maera rocking on both feet, rubbing her hands together, and casting furtive glances at Kolsko.

*She's likely wondering how my meeting with her potential husband went.*

Thinking of Kolsko drew his attention to the man standing to one side, listening. Culich still wanted to talk to Kolsko some more, although he doubted that he wouldn't give permission for the marriage.

Culich glanced at Kolsko again. *Abbot Sistian wrote that the man had interesting comments about the Narthani intentions. I wonder—*

"I suppose you'll be going to Dornfeld," Breda said, her voice breaking into his train of thought.

"Yes, yes, yes. I need to talk directly with Sarnin and see for myself what's happening."

"You'll be needing a carriage again. It's three hundred miles there and back by road, and you just got home from an even longer ride. I hate to think what this is going to do to your joints. I could hear them complaining at morning meal. I'll see to extra cushioning on the carriage benches."

His wife was right. His trip north had also been by carriage to meet the Adris and Hewell hetmen and later to the Pawell/Bevens meeting. His back, legs, and butt still complained vociferously and now would have to endure another trip.

For the next few minutes, Culich questioned Herwold further and studied the map until those summoned arrived. When all four were present, and Culich had input from his main advisors, he was decisive.

"Vortig, you'll accompany me to Dornfeld. Bring thirty men from the Caernford garrison as escort. Mulron will be in charge here while we're gone. We'll call on the Shamir and Nylamir districts to gather a hundred men each and get them moving to Dornfeld. They should be there by the time we arrive. We'll also alert the same districts, along with all the others, to be prepared to send more men, if necessary. I assume Sarnin will have all capable Dornfeld district men mustered."

Culich turned to the red-haired Kennrick. "Pedr, I leave you in charge here in Caernford for clan affairs. Hopefully, it won't be necessary, but if this is something major happening, you'll be responsible for mobilizing whatever's needed from here."

Kennrick nodded.

Culich looked around. Maera and the semaphore manager leaned over a table, composing semaphore messages to the other clans and Keelan boyermen close to semaphore lines. They wrote messages to boyermen out of semaphore range and drafted a response to Boyerman Sarnin in Dornfeld. Things were in motion. Culich's eyes lit again on Kolsko, who had edged up to the map on the wall, as the others drifted away.

"Yozef," Culich spoke up.

Only Maera and Breda noticed it was the first time Culich used his first name.

"I want you to come, too. You'll ride with me, and we can continue our discussions while you get to see more of Keelan. Plus, I'd like to hear your views on what we find at Dornfeld."

Maera started to say something, but her mother stopped her with a hand to her daughter's shoulder and a slight shake of the head.

For Yozef, it was a matter of "Now what?" He'd come to Caernford for a short visit at the veiled order of the hetman, got "engaged" to his daughter, and now the old fart wanted to drag him off to who knew what?!

He was tempted to beg off, but a look from the women stopped him. He sighed. He was stuck. Oh, well. It would give him a chance to let the hetman become more comfortable with him marrying Maera, assuming he didn't screw up by saying something wrong. Culich was right that Yozef would see more of Keelan, plus he should learn more about the inner workings of the clan just by observing the hetman. However, why Culich wanted Yozef's input on whatever was happening at Dornfeld was beyond him.

The next few hours were a whirlwind of activity, with Yozef on the outskirts. His only responsibility was to get himself ready, which wasn't hard, since he hadn't brought much from Abersford.

Whatever help he needed was provided by Maera. A pair of fur-lined gloves and a parka appeared. "You'll be going through the Dillagon Pass, and it gets cold at that altitude." She handed him a pouch of dry sausage, hard cheese, and crackers. "You'll be fed on the way, but you might get hungry."

*She sounds like my mother.*

The final items Maera pressed on Yozef were a brace of flintlock pistols and a wicked-looking knife. "You didn't bring any weapons with you. The other men will likely take care of any danger, but you can never be sure."

The biggest item of all, and one that wouldn't fit into the carriage, was Carnigan. Yozef first saw him talking to Maera. The big man shrugged, nodded to her, and came over to Yozef.

"I've been asked to come along as a second driver to the hetman's carriage." The big man laughed. "And to look after you, so you don't fall off the carriage or drown in a foot-deep creek on the way."

The party gathered, ate a mid-day meal on the veranda, and was ready. Yozef was about to climb into the carriage when Maera called his name, came up to him, and gave him a quick kiss, then turned and went back inside the manor. Stunned silence from the gathering was followed by whispers, as word passed to those not looking in the right direction. Something big was going on with this man, who was a stranger to most of the Caernford men. Not only had Maera, of *all* people, kissed the man, but right in front of the hetman, who hadn't reacted.

Into the carriage climbed Culich, the elder Luwis, and Yozef, with the driver and Carnigan on top, and they were off: carriage, thirty horsemen, eight pack horses, and eight spare horses. Breda's estimate of the road distance to Dornfeld meant that even pushing the pace, it would take the rest of that day and every daylight hour during the next to reach their destination.

The roads were mainly dirt, with occasional gravel sections. Even with their well-maintained condition, the jouncing of the carriage was continuous. They changed horses five times, stopping once to sleep four hours. Yozef found the trip to Dornfeld interesting. He talked more with Culich and Luwis, mainly rehashing previous conversations with Luwis and Kennrick. Yozef thought he hadn't contradicted himself any more than in any normally repeated interchange and managed to cover any inconsistencies. Not that they spent the entire time talking. Most of the time they looked at the land they were passing through.

Yozef also spent hours on top with Carnigan, who, on the second day, told him that Maera had volunteered him for the trip to take care of the prospective bridegroom.

"You devil." Carnigan chortled. "I leave you alone for a couple of days, and you cozy up to the hetman's daughter. And to Maera! People will start to wonder if you're an archangel come to Anyar or a complete idiot. Not that I don't like Maera Keelan," Carnigan hastened to add, seeing Yozef's face start to darken, "but you must admit she'd be a handful for anyone."

Yozef relaxed. "If she has a problem with people, it's only because of them and not her."

"That may be true, Yozef," he said seriously, "but then it's only more to your credit, and people will come to see that. Since you kissed her in the hetman's presence, does this mean there might be a wedding coming?"

"It's not settled. Hetman Keelan still has to give consent."

"Do you think you'd even still be within Keelan or that he'd ask you to come on this trip, if he wasn't going to approve? I also wouldn't want to be the one arguing with Sen Maera once she makes up her mind."

The image of Carnigan being intimidated by Maera brought forth the image of a Chihuahua confronting a mastiff, until he substituted Maera and Carnigan in place of the dogs. Then it didn't seem so preposterous.

"There's something else. I never told Maera about Bronwyn or the child. I guess I didn't know exactly what to say or how she'd react."

"All that was before you married, so I don't see a problem. In fact, I wouldn't be surprised if Maera already knows all about it. Remember who you're marrying."

Carnigan had a point.

Early the second day, they came within sight of the Dillagon Mountain foothills. The road's grade gradually increased, as the air cooled and valley vegetation gave way to a succession of forests.

An hour had passed without Yozef and Carnigan talking, when Yozef lay a hand on the big shoulder in front of him. "Carnigan, it's the custom with my people for what we call a 'best man' to present the man at a marriage. It's usually a brother, a cousin, or a close friend. If a marriage happens between Maera and me, would you be my best man?"

There was no speaking for more than a minute. Then an enormous hand was laid on top of Yozef's, still on Carnigan's shoulder. "I'd be honored, Yozef," the big man said in a strangled voice.

As warned by Maera, the half-day passing through the Dillagon Mountains proved the value of gloves and parka. The temperature fell near freezing at the top of the pass. Fortunately, once they reached the high point, they dropped steeply toward Dornfeld. The tiny stream they had followed down the western side of the pass merged with other streams and grew into a river with cataracts and falls. They continued along the last miles, Yozef mesmerized by the scenery and the lengthening mountain shadows that reached out to a town perched on ocean cliffs.

# CHAPTER 18

# DORNFELD

They rode into Dornfeld at last light. Kerosene lanterns and torches lit a square where awaited a cluster of men, two of whom clasped forearms with Culich.

"Cadoc Gwillamer's the tall one," mumbled Carnigan, "hetman of the Gwillamer Clan. The shorter, round one is Duwid Sarnin, the Dornfeld boyerman."

The three men talked, then went into a building. A rough-hewed man led the rest of the Keelan party to an inn to be served a meal and be directed to prepared baths and rooms to rest sore bones and bottoms.

Yozef woke the next morning to the smell of brisk ocean air through an open window in the room he shared with Carnigan. They'd also shared a bed, with Yozef relegated to one edge. He'd woken several times to stop from rolling off, as Carnigan shifted his mass during dreams.

A knock on the door was accompanied by an announcement that a meal awaited, and the meeting would start in one hour. Yozef threw back the bedcovers and dressed quickly.

Dornfeld sat astride the Keelan-Gwillamer border and was an oddity: a joint town of the two provinces and only possible because of long-standing good relations between the two clans. The town had a single mayor, Duwid Sarnin, a Keelander, and also the district boyerman, whose wife was from Gwillamer.

After a quick meal, Yozef walked the quarter mile to an overlook where a waterfall plunged directly into the surf. North of the waterfall, sticking into the sea, was a shelf of land whose southern edge provided a protected harbor for fishing boats. He looked west and wasn't sure but thought he could just see the hills of Preddi Province across the gulf.

So close, and so ominous.

He walked back and arrived just as the meeting began. The two delegations met in a room overlooking the bridge connecting the two halves of Dornfeld. The span loomed a hundred feet across a deep ravine, with the river cascading two hundred feet below. Yozef envisioned that once the river had descended quickly from the nearby mountains and eroded the upper strata of harder rock, it had worn through the underlying softer layers and kept eating down to its present depth.

There were eleven men in the room. Although most of the men knew one another, quick introductions were made. Cadoc Gwillamer led the Gwillamer delegation, accompanied by his eldest son, Cirwyn; what may have been a younger son or another male relative (Yozef missed the name); two rough-looking men Yozef interpreted as military types; and two other men introduced as advisors. For Keelan, it was Culich, Vortig Luwis, Duwid Sarnin, the local magistrate, and Yozef. Carnigan waited outside, by preference.

Yozef looked around the room and wondered why he was here. From the curious looks, the Gwillamese wondered the same.

"Hetman Gwillamer and I shared information and agree we believe the Narthani may be about to launch a move into this region," Culich said. "Since the Dillagon Pass is the immediate route into Keelan Province, I've ordered the garrison in the pass reinforced with another fifty men. Given the bottleneck at the fort in the pass, it'd be almost impossible to force the pass by anything short of an extended assault that would give time for more reinforcements to get there. What *is* vulnerable is the Keelan territory running from here north to the Eywell border. Hetman Gwillamer also reaffirms the Tri-Clan Alliance and Gwillamer's help in protecting Keelan territory, if necessary."

Cadoc nodded. "I also appreciate Keelan reaffirming its pledge of alliance. Not that I doubted, but it's always comforting to get confirmation. The question is, what do we do?"

"What do we do?" questioned Cadoc's son Cirwyn incredulously. "We defend our provinces and destroy any invaders."

Cadoc cast an annoyed eye at his heir. "That's our *wish*, but how do we *do* it?"

Cirwyn flushed at the implied reprimand.

"So far, we've no indication how many of them would be coming, when it would happen, or even if it will," Cadoc said, addressing Culich. "Is there any news farther east with the rest of your border with Eywell?"

Culich gestured to Luwis for an answer.

"Nothing definite, Hetman," he replied. "Only that there are movements of men in southern Eywell and that whatever happens will most certainly include both Narthani and Eywellese."

"So," said Culich, "our immediate problem is we don't know how serious this is going to be. It isn't likely Keelan is the target on this side of the Dillagon Pass. Are they going to try to push through Keelan territory and into Gwillamer, maybe even try to take the whole province?"

The Gwillamese looked grim.

"Father," said a previously chastised Cirwyn, "if they come with major forces, we need to gather everything we can as quickly as possible if we're going to stop them at the Keelan-Eywell border."

That border was twenty miles north across the narrow, flat plain and into rolling hills rising quickly to the mountains. The intervening land included half a dozen villages and scattered farms and ranches. The land was neither the most productive nor a densely settled part of Keelan Province.

"There are two questions," Luwis proposed. "How many are coming, and how do we defend?"

"Yozef," Culich said, "come look at the map and tell us what you think."

The Gwillamese looked up at Yozef with surprise. Only his name had been mentioned in the introductions, not his status or role at the meeting.

Yozef hesitantly scanned the room, then edged up to the table holding the map. "Sorry, Hetman, what is it you want me to do?"

"You've been listening to us. The Narthani might be coming this way. If they do, we have to decide where to try and stop them and with what forces. Are there many options or just one?"

"I'm not a military person, Hetman. I've no experience in such decisions."

"As you've said. Please look at the map and ask questions if you need to," pressed Culich.

The others looked curiously at Culich.

Yozef looked down at the map for a few moments. He was nervous and unsure what he was supposed to do. Nevertheless, he studied the map. It showed an area perhaps a hundred miles across, including the borders of Gwillamer, Keelan, Eywell, and Moreland. Tokens of different shapes and colors had been placed on several positions. His eyes turned to the map's edge where Moreland abutted Keelan and Eywell. Something tugged at his subconscious.

"Is there a map of all of Caedellium?"

Culich looked at Cadoc with a raised eyebrow.

"Cirwyn," Cadoc said to his son, "in the map case. Pull out the Caedellium map."

Cirwyn produced the map and spread it on the table, covering the first map after sweeping aside the tokens.

By now, Yozef had forgotten his nervousness and the others watching him. He focused on the provinces for a full minute. He didn't notice men glancing at one another, puzzled. "What would I do if I were the Narthani and wanted to take the entire island?" he said musingly, not specifically to anyone and more to himself. "What if I had a secure base in Preddi, Eywell, and Selfcell? What would be my next major move? Maybe Gwillamer?" He picked up a large token, a red horse, and placed it on Gwillamer. "No." He picked up the token and moved it east. "Moreland would be the prime target and then on to Orosz, as we've discussed. Everything else would be diversions and dependent on how they helped me take Moreland."

"Why Moreland?" prompted Culich.

"Because it's the center of the island and a rich province. If they take Moreland, it threatens the other provinces, cuts the semaphore lines connecting some provinces north and south, and makes it harder for the provinces to coordinate resistance."

"If Moreland is their main target, why threaten Gwillamer?" asked Cadoc.

"A diversion," said Yozef. "or a reconnaissance in force."

"A what?" said Luwis. Yozef had used the English word.

"What's this 'reconnaissance'?" said Culich.

"A military move to find out information, not necessarily to hold objectives," Yozef explained. "A big enough force to brush aside weak opposition and move as deep as possible into enemy territory before running up against forces large enough to be a threat. Then withdraw with the information gathered."

"The Narthani already know we're here. They must know the general lay of the land from the Eywellese," said Cadoc.

"If invasion is the goal, yes, but not if they have other intentions."

"Not to invade Dornfeld district or Gwillamer, only to threaten?" queried Culich. "If we move men here, we reduce our ability to respond elsewhere."

"Like Moreland," said Luwis, picking up the thread.

Cadoc still looked puzzled. "I don't understand what you're talking about."

Yozef responded, still focused on the maps, "If Keelan moves major forces here, it's limited in what can be done to help Moreland if *they* are invaded. On the other hand, if Keelan *doesn't* move men here, the reconnaissance in force will find this out, since the Narthani will see they face only Gwillamese. The reconnaissance could then be reinforced and attempt to roll down the Gwillamer coastal plain."

"*Forcing* us to send major help to Gwillamer," said Culich, "and, again, limiting our help to Moreland."

Yozef pulled the local map back to the top and pointed to several markers in the mountains between Gwillamer and Keelan. "Are these passes through the mountains?"

Cirwyn had followed Yozef's finger. "Yes. There are a series of passes and valleys that run through the mountains until you reach the southern part of Gwillamer. It turns into hills and more open land along our southern border with Keelan."

"What would happen if the Narthani pushed down past several of these passes and valleys?"

Culich grimaced. "Besides aiding Gwillamer, we'd have to reinforce every possible invasion point to Keelan. Whereas the Dillagon Pass is so narrow a relatively small force could hold it forever, as you go farther south, the passes get wider. By the fourth one, it's a valley two miles wide at its narrowest. At some point, there'd be no way we could help Moreland. All of our attention would have to be on how to push the Narthani out of Gwillamer and protect Keelan."

Vortig and the Gwillamese were shaking their heads.

"But surely the Narthani commanders would know that the farther they pushed into Gwillamer," said one of the Gwillamese, "the more danger there would be of Keelan cutting in behind them and isolating them from their supply line and being caught between two clans."

"So what?" said Cadoc, now seeing it all. "Once that happens, they simply embark their men on ships and move them elsewhere."

"And their goal is achieved even more, putting us even further away from helping Moreland," said Culich.

"Devious, and without much danger to them," said Vortig Luwis, looking questioningly at Yozef. "So where does this leave us? To stop them at our border with Eywell will take a large portion of our men, even with support from Gwillamer, limiting our ability to help Moreland."

"Only if we try to stop them at the Eywell/Keelan border," said Culich.

Yozef agreed. "If you're willing to give up Keelan land between your border with Eywell and here, they can be stopped at the Keelan/Gwillamer border. Here at Dornfeld. The river and its canyon are a formidable barrier. Why not use it? From where the river comes out of the mountains to here is only a few miles. Any place the Narthani tried to cross would be difficult and would give us time to gather forces to repel them."

"Give up Keelan land?" protested Luwis.

"Yes," said Yozef, never looking up from the maps. "Land is just land. It isn't going anywhere. Land is forever and uncaring. It's the people and the beliefs that are important. Land given or lost can be retaken. People killed or clans lost are lost forever." With that, Yozef looked up to see everyone in the room looking at him. His nervousness returned, and he stepped back slightly, looking confused.

Culich listened to Yozef and observed how he became engrossed with his thinking, as if listening to his own mind.

*I wonder if he even remembers anything he said the last few minutes*, Culich thought.

"Pardon me, Hetman, what was it you wanted me to do?"

*No, I don't think he does remember.*

"That's fine, Yozef. You've helped."

Culich turned back to the maps and the others. "All right. Do we all see the dilemma we face and the poor choices?"

They all nodded.

"So if the defense is to be here," Duwid Sarnin spoke up, "where *exactly* will the defense be? Half of Dornfeld is on the Keelan side."

"I'm sorry," said Vortig, "but the Keelan half will have to be abandoned. If we're going to cede the land from the border to here, it has to include the Keelan half of Dornfeld. All defenses will have to be on the Gwillamer side."

"Abandon half of Dornfeld to the Narthani?" said the distressed boyerman.

"If they do come, I'm afraid so, and we'll have to burn the Keelan half to prevent the Narthani from hiding in it and blocking our fields of fire."

Culich put a hand on Sarnin's shoulder. "Don't worry, Duwid, you have my word that when all this is over, we'll rebuild Dornfeld better than before."

Although not happy, Sarnin was reassured.

A cough from behind caught Culich's attention, and he turned to see Yozef looking at him. "You have another thought, Yozef?"

"Well . . . why not take the town apart and move it to this side of the border? Same with the other villages. If you start immediately, there should be time to move every building and animal, every piece of furnishing, and other possessions into Gwillamer. Take anything of any value and burn the rest. Leave nothing behind for the Narthani to use."

"If we cede land up to Dornfeld, then we'll have to evacuate all of our people, either through the pass into Keelan proper or into Gwillamer," Luwis said, "and we should start immediately."

"We'll take them," stated Cadoc. "It's the least we can do if you're willing to give up your land."

"Actually," said Culich grimly, "we're not *giving up* our land, we're just *renting* it to the Narthani."

"Renting?" questioned Cirwyn.

Luwis's mouth curved into a grin, but his tone was anything but amused. "I think Hetman Keelan means that the Narthani may occupy Keelan land for a time, but will find the coin they have to pay made it a bad contract."

Cadoc's expression matched Luwis's. "We'll start making arrangements for your people immediately. I don't think my people will have any hesitation in taking them in, considering yours are giving up their homes for a time and will stand with us if the Narthani come. We'll start what Ser Kolsko suggests and take down every building on the Keelan side and put it back together on Gwillamer land.

"We'll also need to improve the defenses from here to the mountains. At this point, it's only two miles before you reach so many cataracts and falls that only a few dozen men could prevent hundreds from crossing. If we're planning on stopping them at the Gwillamer-Keelan border, then we need to make those two miles even more defendable."

One Gwillamese looked confused. "Hetman, I agree that we can improve the defenses here, but if we're going to hold against a major invasion, do we have enough men for that purpose and to still defend against seaborne raids, in addition to helping Moreland?"

"We must do what we must," answered Cadoc, the Gwillamer hetman, looking at Culich. "If your man's reasoning is correct, at some point the Narthani are going to move on Moreland, who can't hold their province by themselves. I assume that the Tri-Clan Alliance intends on supporting Moreland. I think I agree that if Moreland falls, all of Caedellium may eventually fall. Perhaps it might take years, but it will happen. They have to be stopped at Moreland. Gwillamer will commit as many forces as we can to help, consistent with holding this position at Dornfeld and protecting our coastal cities against raids."

"And Keelan will hold the Dillagon Pass," affirmed Culich, "and send another two hundred men here to Dornfeld. That's all Keelan dare send at this time. If we hurry with the defenses, the Narthani and the Eywell will run up against a wall not easily breached, and that gives us time to send more help before the situation here becomes dire."

The details of the defense and evacuation of the Dornfeld district were left to Boyerman Sarnin and Hetman Gwillamer. Culich and Cadoc clasped forearms, and the Keelan party was on the road back toward the Dillagon Pass within the hour.

# CHAPTER 19

# PREPARATIONS

**Approval**

The return trip to Caernford was uneventful. Culich spoke little to Yozef, who wondered whether the hetman's opinion of him had changed. Was Culich pissed at him? Had he said too much at the hetman meeting? For that matter, what exactly *did* he say?

There were none of the probing questions about Yozef's past or his opinions about anything. Yozef spent most of the trip riding on top with Carnigan and the driver. The pace was as fast as on the way to Dornfeld, stopping only to luxuriate in a meal and six hours of sleep at the border of the Nylamir and Wycoff districts.

The next day they rolled into Caernford with Yozef praying never again to ride in a carriage as long as he lived. Three hundred miles over dirt and rock roads were punishment enough for whatever transgression he had committed. The weather had deepened the last few hours, and a steady rain turned roads to slush and seeped into their clothing. They were tired, damp, and exhausted, yet their triumphal arrival was met by . . . no one. No word of their imminent return had reached the manor. All of the hetman's family members were elsewhere.

Culich and Luwis went into the manor. Yozef, not being invited to join them, retired to the guest cottage, kicked off his boots, pulled a blanket up to his chin, and promptly fell asleep. Four hours later, he awoke to the ubiquitous knocking of Norlin, who informed him that evening meal at the manor would be in one hour, and did Yozef want to bathe before the meal? Yozef decided on the bath, compared to the alternative of sharing the accumulated aromas of the trip with the Keelan females. He suspected his acquiescence was merely a formality, since a tub of hot water waited in the cottage's attached bathing room.

Yozef's first sight of Maera was when Mared ushered him into the dining room. The last of the Keelans was sitting down, including Maera, wearing a form-fitting green gown again, this time a lighter shade of green and with a green ribbon of the same material tying back her hair. In addition, she wore a questioning look, and Yozef interpreted a slight twitch of her shoulders as, *"Well, what happened on the trip and is the marriage on?"*

Yozef twitched back with shoulder and hands, trying to reply, *"I have no fucking clue."*

The meal started with the traditional thanks and then on to courses, this evening a hearty meat and barley soup, a beef roast with red carrot-like sections, beets, and the ubiquitous heavy, dark bread and butter. Cold steins of beer also appeared.

*How* do *they do that?*

Yozef had often asked himself that question since the first time with Carnigan at the abbey and still had no answer.

Culich was in a cheerful mood. He deflected talk of the trip to Dornfeld and queried the three younger daughters on their activities, then engaged in more talk about what had transpired in Caernford the last few days: the weather, Mared getting into a fight at the scholasticum, Ceinwyn hinting about a new dress for a coming festival, and a major topic—a litter from one of the Keelan dogs. Half of the meal passed before Breda stopped Culich from torturing Maera and Yozef.

"Now that we've gotten all the important items out of the way, Hetman Keelan has some other news," Breda said dryly.

Conversation stopped. Everyone rotated toward the head of the table.

Culich smiled amusedly. "Oh yes, that other matter. Maera, Yozef, after carefully considering the possibility of your marriage, I've decided it's both acceptable and appropriate for the two of you. Therefore, I give my permission and blessing."

"Yes!" Mared shouted, closely followed by an exclamation from Anid and even positive sounds from Ceinwyn, possibly because she saw her chances of marriage improved with the older sister out of the way.

"Congratulations, my dears," said a smiling Breda. "I predict it'll be a good marriage."

"Thank you, Father," said Maera, her voice catching on the words.

*My God! I'm committed now*, roared through her mind in panic.

The moment faded quickly, as her natural inclination to plan and be orderly set in. When to schedule the wedding? How big? Who to invite or, moreover, who *not* to invite?

Yozef had a similar moment of panic.

*My God! I'm committed now!*

That thought also faded when he saw Maera giving him sideways glances with a smile at the corners of her mouth.

"Yes, thank you, Hetman Keelan. I promise to try my best to be a good husband to a wonderful woman."

"I certainly hope you appreciate how lucky you'll be with a smart and beautiful wife," Culich said sternly. "She takes after her mother."

"Yes, Hetman," said Yozef, for the moment forgetting to be respectful, "she *is* lucky that's who she takes after."

*Whoops*, thought Yozef.

*Uh-oh*, thought Breda and three daughters.

*Damn it, Yozef—things were going so well!* thought Maera.

Culich looked at Yozef with one raised eyebrow, then roared with laughter. "By Merciful God, Yozef, I know you're from another land, but I somehow think things will be more refreshing with you around."

More laughter followed exhalations of relief from the Keelan females.

"And as for calling 'Hetman,' if you're going to be a family member, you may call me Culich and Maera's mother Breda, with her permission."

"Granted easily," answered Breda, not bothering to mention she and Yozef were already on a first-name basis.

Yozef was oblivious to the rest of the meal and the conversation, looking forward to getting Maera alone and practicing kissing and feeling her body against him. He was to be disappointed. As the family rose from the table, Culich escorted Yozef out the front door, wishing him a restful sleep and warning him the women would be into planning mode the next morning.

## Maera and Bronwyn

On the return trip from Dornfeld, Yozef had struggled with how to tell Maera about Bronwyn. The next morning, Maera allayed his concern.

"Uh, Maera, there's something I need to tell you. Before I met you, there was a woman from a farm north of Abersford. We . . . uh . . . we, that is . . ."

"You mean Bronwyn Merton? I met her when she was visiting the medicants at St. Sidryn's. She and the baby were developing well, and she was hoping for a boy, which I understand it was. That was good news."

"Er . . . yes, that *was* good news."

*Now what do I say?*

"It'll be appropriate for us to pay respects when the baby is named. If we're in Abersford at the time, I'll suggest to Bronwyn that she and her entire family come to a Godsday service Naming Day as soon as the child is three months."

"Naming Day?"

"Well, yes. You don't know that a child isn't given a name until it's three months old? So many die before then, but Bronwyn's new baby is reported healthy, so on Naming Day it'll be given its name and can be blessed. That's the best time for you to publicly recognize you're the father."

"Maera, I, uh, hadn't said anything about Bronwyn before, which I should have, but I wasn't sure how you'd react."

She looked at him quizzically. "How did you think I'd react?"

"I didn't know. Angry for me having a child with another woman. Angry at me for not telling you about it. Hell, I don't know. Just angry, I guess, for whatever reason."

Maera took Yozef's words sedately, accustomed by now to his still not understanding the ways of his adopted home.

"There's nothing to be angry about. You bedded with her before we met. It has nothing to do with us. I'd mind if it had happened *after* we agreed to wed. Bronwyn told me you said you'd recognize the child and provide for it as necessary, which I naturally expected from you."

"Bronwyn . . . told you . . .?" Yozef managed in a strangled voice.

"Yes, while I was at St. Sidryn's. I had a pleasant talk with her after a Godsday service. They seem like a solid family, and the child will flourish with them."

"And it doesn't matter that I had a child with Bronwyn before you and I do?"

"Why should it? Bronwyn's child has no claim on the Keelan family. I'm sure you'll be interested in her child, since you fathered him, and that's appropriate. But one of *our* sons will be the next Keelan hetman."

Her words were spoken as if from a Delphic Oracle: a fact not to be questioned.

## Planning

Culich was correct. With approval for the wedding secured, planning by the women came to the fore, and the men faded into the background. Long engagements were not expected on Caedellium. After careful consideration and once a marriage was decided, the Caedelli saw no reason for unnecessary delay. Yozef had assumed it would be some months off, an assumption that evaporated when he was told three sixdays were all that was necessary to make preparations and give those guests not in Caernford time to make travel plans.

The next few days Yozef saw little of Maera. She recognized his initial consternation, but planning with Breda took all of her time. Their few minutes a day together focused on the "who, what, when, where" of the wedding day. After two days, Yozef told Maera he saw no obvious reason for him to be in Caernford for at least a sixday. He proposed he return to Abersford to check on his various enterprises and arrange for an enlargement of his house, since now there would be two of them living there.

The statement caught Maera by surprise. Not at the idea of his disappearing for a sixday, but the reality she would be leaving her family in Caernford for a different life in Abersford. In her focus on the marriage possibility, she had ignored what came afterward. She had lived her whole life at Keelan Manor, in the same set of rooms since she'd moved out of the nursery; had helped raise her three younger sisters; knew every inch of the manor grounds and most of the surrounding town and countryside; and knew by name hundreds of citizens in the area. Though she was not a stranger to Abersford, her experiences there were fleeting, with the expectations she would return home. Now, *home* would be with Yozef in Abersford. It took until the next day for her to fully process her thinking. She still wasn't comfortable with the move but accepted it as part of becoming her own woman, wife, and eventual mother, away from the security of her Caernford family.

## Word Gets Out

When Yozef and Carnigan arrived back in Abersford, although only four days had passed since Culich gave permission for the marriage, the news had reached Abersford and St. Sidryn's three days previously and was the only topic of conversation.

The Keelans gave Yozef letters for the Beynoms—Culich to Sistian, Breda to Diera, Maera to them both. Since the carriage passed the abbey on the way to Yozef's house, they stopped to deliver the correspondence and found themselves caught in a Caedelli version of a surprise party. Word of their coming had reached the abbey the previous day, and somehow the organizers of the festivities estimated to within fifteen minutes when they would arrive. Instead of the quick mail drop and going on home, Yozef found himself the center of an ongoing celebration, apparently attended by all of the abbey complex's staff.

The first warning sign came as they rolled into the abbey courtyard. A hundred people or more waited, headed by Sistian and Diera. Yozef groaned. He saw his bed receding into the near future.

"Yozef!" exclaimed Diera, as he stepped off the carriage. "We've heard the news! Congratulations, and may you and Maera be happy together." She hugged him and kissed him on his cheek.

"Yes, congratulations indeed," added a benevolently smiling Abbot Sistian, with a clap on the shoulder and a shake of his head. "Who but Merciful God would have thought the wretched creature washed up on our beach two years ago would marry the hetman's daughter? Just shows us God has plans for us all, even if we don't know it."

Diera locked arms with Yozef and pulled him toward the dining hall. "You must be tired from the all-day trip back, but we've arranged a little celebration."

He was tired and dusty, his joints ached from the carriage ride, and he was stuck for the next three hours being congratulated and having food and steins constantly forced on him.

He only vaguely remembered Carnigan pouring him into bed later that night and knew nothing more until he awoke at noon the next day. His first impulse was to anticipate a headache from the bottomless steins of the previous night. His first clear thought was, *Where's the hangover?* Nestled under the covers, he futilely felt around for that expected consequence. He lay there reviewing memories since his Anyar arrival. While he wasn't a particularly heavy drinker, there had been a few occasions, particularly with Carnigan, when he had over-imbibed. He also remembered the morning after the first meal at Keelan Manor and the wine. The headaches then or on other mornings weren't severe enough to rate as serious hangovers. He had enough examples from his previous life to know that, for him, too much alcohol had regretful repercussions. But not here on Anyar? Was this one of the side effects of whatever the Watchers did to him? If it was, bless their little green hearts, if they had hearts.

The next thing he noticed was that he still wore his traveling clothes, had transferred dust to his bedding, and stunk. He padded barefoot out of the bedroom, only to find the Faughns waiting for him. Elian did a respectful curtsey, and Brak bowed with a board up his ass.

*Oh, Christ! Am I now supposed to be royalty or something?*

"Master Kolsko, we've heard the news. Congratulations and God's blessing on your coming marriage," said Elian, curtseying again, and Brak bowed once more, after an elbow in the ribs from his wife.

Yozef was irritated. "Thank you for the good wishes, but unless I suddenly got transformed into someone else by the Tooth Fairy or Gandalf the White, I'm the same person who left several sixdays ago."

Blank looks conveyed that the references weren't connecting.

"Don't treat me any different than before, which means none of this bowing nonsense," he said.

Brak grunted, gave his wife an "I told you so" look and left the room.

Yozef chuckled to himself. *That man can communicate more by nuances of grunt that many can with whole speeches.*

Elian wasn't reassured. "Will this mean you wish us to stay in your service?"

Yozef stared. It hadn't occurred to him they might assume the hetman's daughter would bring her own staff or would want to choose a new one.

*Well, for all I know she might . . . but the Faughns are staying*, he told himself firmly.

The reaction of the Faughns clued him in to what followed. In various forms, he went through the same rigmarole six times the first day back. In fairness, he tried to understand that many believed a change in his status had occurred. Instead of the strange, friendly, smart, and well-paying "Yozef," he was now "Yozef the Important," a member of the hetman's family, holding some as yet unknown influence on their lives, and the husband of the infamous Maera Keelan. He suspected the latter was the most impressive, at least to those who knew Maera.

The day ended by the process being repeated at the Snarling Graeko with Carnigan. The big man laughed at Yozef's discomfiture when they walked in. All noise died, half of the crowd rose from their chairs, and a few hesitant bows made Yozef groan aloud. It took two rounds for the house and two stories before the noise level returned to his pre-entrance state, but he couldn't fail to notice there wasn't quite the level of camaraderie toward him that had developed over the previous months.

*It'll just take a little time until everyone realizes nothing has changed*, he told himself. It would be many months before he realized the feeling of belonging to the community would never again be exactly the same. Not necessarily worse, only different.

Fortunately for Yozef's state of mind, the next sixday was filled with reviewing all of his enterprises, providing suggestions, settling arguments, making decisions, and meeting with Filtin's father. Since the elder Fuller had directed building Yozef's getaway cottage west of Abersford and organized guano gathering at Birdshit Bay, Yozef never wondered whom to go to for expanding the house. Dyfeld Fuller assured Yozef that several of the envisioned new rooms could be added by the time of the wedding: a larger kitchen area, a new master bedroom, a workroom for Maera, and an extra room in case a child came along. The barn was also too small, and Dyfeld said it was easier to build a new one than expand the existing one.

It took Dyfeld two days to show Yozef written plans for the constructions. Yozef was about to approve them when Filtin asked the critical question.

"Are you sure you want to make changes before your new wife arrives? I don't know about hetmen's daughters, but for most women I'd bet anything you do to the house won't be quite the way she would have done it. Unless you want to be reminded of this forever, I'd be inclined to wait until she's here. Even if she's not the nagging type, it'd please her having her opinions taken into account."

Yozef considered Filtin's advice. He didn't see Maera as the nagging type, but she'd definitely give her opinions. He decided there was no rush, then alerted Dyfeld Filtin to be ready to build once Maera arrived. Since he had told Maera he would look into expanding the house, he wrote her that he had decided to wait for her input. He didn't mention Filtin's warning.

No sooner had the house decision been postponed than a new issue arose. To Yozef's dismay, formal intentions to celebrate the marriage and Maera's return to Abersford proliferated beyond his tolerance. Despite his objection, he seemed to have no say in an elaborate reception and festival the Abersford mayor was planning. Then there was the special Godsday service at the abbey. The final straw was word that the district boyerman, Longnor Vorwich, would come to Abersford as a "social" call on the newlyweds and for the locals to arrange various dinners and receptions.

*Damn! What else? Marching bands, dancing bears, fireworks? Every time I turn around, there's more plans coming out of the woodwork!*

Yozef wrote to all parties that he and his new wife, Maera Kolsko-Keelan, would be unavailable for two sixdays following their arrival from Caernford, due to following a custom of Yozef's people called a "honeymoon." No one knew what the English words *honey* and *moon* meant, but the word pronounced "huh-nee-moon" was a period of seclusion for a newly married couple to allow them time together to start their marriage. Yozef found that his attempt to forestall the planned events only postponed them with a reprieve until after the honeymoon.

The honeymoon custom seemed strange to all, though was readily accepted, because it came from Yozef, who redefined *strange*. Upstanding and friendly, yes. Still, strange.

Although he had put his foot down in Abersford, two issues remained. Since Maera was unaware of the honeymoon plans, he procrastinated about informing her. As for where to go, the only viable option was his retreat cottage down the coast. However, *his* going to the cottage for a few days was a different proposition than taking Maera there for two sixdays. Naturally, Elian was aghast at the idea, Cadwulf thought him crazy, Carnigan shrugged as if to say, "What do you expect from Yozef?" and Sistian was dubious at best. In a distinct minority was Diera, who volunteered herself, Cadwulf, and the Faughns to reassure Yozef they would take care of everything and the cottage would be ready. It was a testament to Yozef's faith in Diera, or his distracted state of mind, that he took her word and promptly put the entire issue in the "over and done" category.

In a sixday, Yozef caught up with his workers and left in capable hands plans to receive the newly married couple. Yozef and Carnigan returned to Caernford.

# CHAPTER 20

# WEDDING

The last sixday before the marriage Yozef spent as a gofer. Go to a Caernford shop to deliver an order. Go back to Caernford to pick up the order. Go with Maera to visit aunts and uncles. Go with Culich to a meeting with several boyermen. Go back to Caernford to pick up what had been forgotten on the last trip. Go, go, go. As little as he physically did, every evening he fell into bed exhausted and marveled at Maera and Breda, who both seemed indefatigable.

What frustrated Yozef was spending so little time alone with Maera. Not that she avoided him, only that she was constantly busy. Seldom in the sixday were they alone long enough for a serious talk. They found seconds for a furtive kiss or deeper, lingering ones when briefly alone. On too few occasions, there were minutes with embraces and, for Yozef, opportunities for tentative wandering hands. Maera caught her breath and stiffened the first time a hand moved from her back to below her waist. By the third occasion, she tightened her embrace, and he imagined a sigh. That was as far as she allowed his hands. Wandering to her breasts brought entreaties for patience until they wed.

Four days before the wedding, he also experienced a facet of Maera he'd heard of but never witnessed—anger. He sat on the manor's front veranda, waiting for his next assignment, when an angry woman's voice was audible coming from inside the manor, despite its thick walls. The voice got louder, overlaid with a placating second one, when Yozef recognized Maera and Breda.

Suddenly, the manor's double front doors flung open, and Maera flew out and stood at the top of the steps, her arms stiff at her sides, one hand holding a piece of paper. "Damn Brym Moreland to eternal flames! That piece of shit defiles the very ground he walks on! Forgive me, God, but please let him choke to death on the next bite he takes!"

She turned and stomped to the other end of the veranda, spewing a stream of invectives. Yozef had heard versions of most. It was impressive, especially when he no longer understood Caedelli words and assumed she'd switched to other languages. At the corner, she stopped walking and yelling, staring upward. Yozef shifted in his seat, tempted to go to her, but not certain he wanted to get in the path of whatever had riled his prospective bride. Finally, she turned back, walking normally, arms crossed in front, the paper crumpled in one hand. She was halfway back to the manor door when she saw him watching. She froze and clamped one hand over her mouth and pressed the one with the paper against her throat.

Maera walked toward him as he rose, then halted just out of arm's reach. "Oh, Yozef. You shouldn't have seen me in this state, though I suppose it's only fair you realize I have a temper. It's just—"

She choked on the next words, and Yozef went to her and pulled her into an embrace.

"What is it, Maera?"

"It's Ana. My best friend. Her father's refused permission for her to come to our wedding! She was packed and ready to leave when that sh—" She choked again, trying to regain control.

She slowly relaxed in his arms. "I'm sorry, Maera, I know how much Ana means to you. Isn't there anything we can do? What about your father making a hetman-to-hetman request to Hetman Moreland? Ana's father is a cousin or something, and maybe he'd relent if their hetman got involved."

Maera pulled back to look up at Yozef, sad-faced with moist eyes. "Father'd be mortified to ask anything of Gynfor Moreland, although he'd do it if I asked. But it's too late. If Father made the request, it'd have to be a formal letter and not a semaphore message. Father would have to write, get it to Gynfor Moreland, who might not agree, and even if he did, the Moreland hetman would have to order Brym to let Ana come. By now, there's no time for all this and her to get here in time."

Maera sat in a veranda chair, hands clasped in her lap, and shook her head. "It never occurred to me that Ana wouldn't be here. We've always talked about being at each other's weddings, and now ..."

Yozef knelt by the chair and put a hand on Maera's hands. "I wish there was something I could do."

Maera's anger had subsided, replaced by resignation. "There's nothing you *can* do. I'm sorry you had to see me like this. I don't usually lose control."

"Nonsense. Everyone gets mad occasionally. We wouldn't be human otherwise. And in this case, I certainly understand." Yozef paused as an idea occurred. "What about this? If Ana can't come to the wedding, what if we plan to visit her in Moreland? It may not be for a few months, but then there's time to arrange the trip and figure out how to get around Ana's father, even if we have to get the hetmen involved."

Maera perked up, her eyes flashing, and she grabbed his forearm with both hands. "Oh, Yozef. Yes, let's do that. Or better yet, work to arrange her coming here for an extended visit. As much as he'd hate to ask it, I'm sure Father would help."

It was the longest exchange Yozef and Maera had had in several days or from then until the wedding. The last three days Yozef didn't see Maera at all, according to Caedellium ancient custom, until the moment of the ceremony.

Maera was ravishing in a shimmering gown of multiple shades of green, the traditional bride color to signify fertility, with her long brown hair gathered within a fine netting embellished with pearls. A garland of white flowers encircled her head. She looked pale and flushed at the same time or perhaps at alternate moments.

Yozef wore a plain jacket and pants of dark olive green, the jacket buttoned to his neck. He obsessively trimmed his beard until Carnigan took away the scissors, made a final snip of his hair, and then refused to give back the scissors. "For God's sake, Yozef, you look fine! I swear, you're more nervous than a bride."

The service began at noon, with the sun straight up in the blue Anyar sky, a deeper robin's egg blue than on Earth. The formal vows took place in a grove of trees on the hetman's manor grounds. Sistian and Diera had traveled from St. Sidryn's, and he presided at the traditional ceremony.

Culich presented the bride and Carnigan the groom, both of them asserting to the good character of whom they represented. When the moment came for Sistian to ask if anyone objected to the marriage, the only sounds were leaves rustling in the trees and a distant dog bark, as if anyone dared object after the clan hetman and a scowling mountain had vouched for the couple.

The ceremony itself lasted only fifteen minutes, more than compensated for by the following festivities, which included the reception for hundreds of guests from throughout the province. Then, a procession of family and guests moved to tables set up under more trees, followed by endless food and drink, musicians, and speeches.

*God, do Caedelli love to give speeches.*

Yozef remembered reading how, before mass media, American political rallies could last hours per speaker. Here, individual presentations were shorter, but all of them combined seemed to go on forever: Culich Keelan welcomed guests, Breda Keelan welcomed guests and enjoined them to drink responsibly, and the mayor of Caernford, the abbot of St. Tomo's abbey, and men and women of whose identity Yozef had no idea gave speeches. Abbot Sistian gave a sanitized version of how Yozef came to Caedellium. Anid Keelan extolled her older sister's virtues and shared a humorous anecdote about her. Maera summarized her life and meeting Yozef. Then finally . . . *thank God, he thought* . . . it was his turn.

He had a sheet of paper with notes on both sides. Culich, Breda, Sistian, and, most important, Cadwulf and Maera, all had emphasized to him what the guests expected him to say—something about his life and where he had originated. The "History of Yozef" notes were copied from the script he kept for any occasion to maintain a consistent story.

Yozef and Maera sat on a raised platform, flanked by her parents and an obviously uncomfortable Carnigan, who relaxed only after his fifth or sixth stein of beer. Yozef ate sparingly of each course, while Maera ate next to nothing. Yozef downed one stein of beer rapidly, and, when offered a second, Maera declined for him, to the merriment of nearby guests.

"Surrender now, Yozef. Your days of making decisions are over."

"That's Maera. Being sure Yozef can do his duty."

"Not too much and falling asleep, Yozef. Maera has something for you to do later tonight."

At last, two hours past sundown, the mistress of ceremonies, an elderly sister of Culich, announced the time for the newly wedded couple to withdraw to consummate their marriage. By now, Yozef thought he was accustomed to the ribald nature of many Caedelli but was still taken aback. The aunt was reasonably decorous, but as the couple walked out, side by side, relatives voiced advice. Maera's fourteen-year-old sister, Anid, hugged her, and Yozef heard her say, "Everyone says, *Oh, Maera won't let out a peep the first time*, so I've gotten good odds and have bet you will. Be a good sister and don't let me down." To which Maera blushed and shook her head at the young sister, who gave Maera another hug and kiss on the cheek. Then a female cousin called out, "Remember, lie on your back and spread your legs." To which Maera responded, "Oh, thank you, Ioneid, I appreciate advice from someone who's had so much practice."

Maera's riposte garnered loud laughs from all within hearing range, including Ioneid.

Not that Yozef went unscathed. One of the male cousins called out to him as they passed, "You remember, too, Yozef. In, out, repeat if necessary." Another unnamed voice, "Let us know if you have trouble catching her!" To which another followed up, "If you do catch her and need directions, I've sure Maera will give you detailed instructions."

They finally made it to a two-story cottage decorated with flowers and colorful banners, the structure located behind the main house. He held Maera's hand as they crossed over the threshold, and Maera whispered, "Wave, Yozef." He followed her lead, they turned together, waved at the hundred or more who had followed them from the main festive area, then went into the room lit by candles, and Yozef shut the door. They could still hear the people outside offering suggestions, talking to one another, and keeping up a continuous patter. Maera climbed the narrow stairs, and he followed to a second-floor bedroom with a balcony. A score of freshly lit candles gave a yellowish cast to the room. The clamor outside picked up with banging pots and several drums.

"How long are they going to keep this up?"

Maera smiled wanly. "Some will go back to the festivities. Most of the younger ones will stay to wait for proof."

"Proof? What kind of proof?"

Even in the candlelight, he could tell her face reddened. She continued looking around the room . . . not looking at Yozef.

"Proof that we have consummated the marriage," she said in a small voice—one Yozef hadn't heard before from Maera.

"I have a feeling I'll regret asking, but what exactly's the proof they're waiting for?"

Maera didn't respond for a few moments, which made Yozef more nervous. Then, "First would be to hear me scream. The first time is known to be painful for the woman. As her husband penetrates her, a scream is expected to show she's a virgin."

Yozef swallowed. "And this is customarily expected from the bride?"

Maera nodded, finally looking at Yozef. He had wondered. As strong-willed as Maera was and from a different lifestyle and responsibilities than most Caedellium women, he wouldn't have been surprised if she had had affairs in the past, certainly discreetly. Evidently not . . . she was a virgin.

"It doesn't necessarily have to hurt that much. We can take our time, and I'll be careful as I can be." He wanted to reach out to hold her, though now he was also nervous.

"We can't take too much time. Those outside will wait for their proof, and I've seen them get pretty aggressive if it doesn't come fairly soon."

"What if the bride doesn't scream? And are all Caedellium brides virgins?"

Maera laughed ruefully. "Hardly, but the custom is what it is. Even if there is no pain, the bride will pretend there is and yell out to satisfy those waiting to hear. They'll then cheer and wait again for the last proof."

"Now I *know* I don't want to ask . . . what's the last proof?"

Maera motioned with her right hand to the bed festooned in colorful ribbons on the four posts at the bed corners and the simple white cloth covering the bed. "Blood of the bride will show she was virgin. If she wasn't, they'll draw enough blood to put on the cloth, which is hung from a window or a balcony as soon as consummation is complete."

Yozef was silent. He didn't know how he was supposed to feel. "I see . . . ," was all he could manage. Finally, "And this is the custom for all Caedellium marriages?"

"With some variation in different clans and position in society, yes. It's not always followed with the lower classes." Her tone changed from expositing on something embarrassing to a firmer one implying duty. "*I'm* the daughter of the Keelan hetman. The custom is more important here, since I'm part of the primary family of Keelan. Father and Mother have no sons, so a son of their daughters will be the next hetman. Since I'm the oldest, and, let's be honest, because of my reputation in the Keelan Clan, most people expect me to produce strong sons worthy of being a hetman. All the Keelan daughters are expected to be untouched at marriage to ensure claims to succession and prevent conspiracies when Father dies."

"Is that likely? My impression is your family's well regarded by the people."

"They are, and conflicts are unlikely, but who can say once the time comes? To be sure, my sisters and I were taught our duty from the earliest age.

"I should tell you we're fortunate only this part of the custom has remained. In older times, the consummation of a hetman's daughter's marriage would have multiple witnesses to attest to the bride's virginity."

Yozef tried and failed to envision himself performing on the wedding bed with an audience. He stayed silent for a minute, while he shifted through pieces of Caedellium culture.

"Maera . . . wife . . . ," he said softly. "You know the customs of my people are different. However, I'm here, and I know we must follow your customs. I have to say that all of this makes me uneasy. Since you're a virgin, I want to be careful, especially this first night, both not to hurt you and because I care for you. This is a little too 'formal.'"

Maera smiled resignedly. "I'm afraid tonight it *is* formal, as you say. I know you're a gentle man. I would never have proposed the marriage otherwise. You're also a thoughtful man, more so than anyone I've ever met, except possibly a few medicants or theophists or perhaps my great-grandfather, who died when I was ten. I think our marriage will be good, and I expect to see that gentleness from you in the future. That's not today, though. Today we must do our duty."

He sighed. "So what do we do?"

Maera walked to the bed, stepped out of her embroidered slipper-like shoes, and set the flower garland on her head on the table next to the bed. She removed pins from her hair and pulled away the pearl-and-thread netting to let her hair fall down her back. With her back to him, she slipped off the shoulders of her wedding dress and let the cloth fall to her feet.

As much as Yozef wanted this night to be good for Maera, he hadn't been with a woman for many months. When it came time to start the procession to the wedding cottage, stirrings in his groin had begun, and he had had to force his attention into innocuous paths to avoid a premature erection. Now, seeing her naked form standing beside the bed, that restraint was nigh impossible. She was slender, with a definite feminine form, long dark brown hair flowing two-thirds down her bare back, her narrow waist flaring out to firm hips, lower legs with downy hairs, and bare feet.

She turned to face him, her expression calm, nervous, determined, and warm to him, all at the same time. "Come, husband. This is only our first night. Let us do what's necessary. I believe our real marriage will come after today. Today is for duty to my clan and family."

She smiled as her eyes moved down from his face. "I see that we won't have to worry about your being able to perform *your* duty."

His efforts to restrain his physiology had lapsed, and an erection pushed against his trousers.

Maera lay on the bed, her head on a single pillow, and motioned for him to come to her.

Emotions rolled over Yozef: anticipation of this moment with his new wife, reluctance at the cold calculations of the event, aversion to the thought of simply and quickly mounting her, and . . . lust. The battle over emotions raged briefly, and he later cringed as the last emotion triumphed. It took seconds to shed his clothes, his manhood standing before him.

Maera took him all in, especially the proof of his readiness to consummate the marriage. She swallowed at the sight and, with a firm set to her lips, held out her arms, drew her knees up, and opened her legs. "Come, husband. I'm your wife, and it's time we prove it to the world." She looked away from him, pointing to a bowl on a stand next to the bed. "Mother says it may be easier if you use the scented olive oil."

He had smelled flowers, though there were none in the room. He dipped two fingers into the bowl and applied the oil.

Yozef would later question himself about the next few minutes, not that Maera ever did. He might criticize himself, while also recognizing that given the customs of where he was, his actions were appropriate. It sometimes helped.

He climbed onto the bed and moved between her legs. When his hand first touched her leg, she twitched at first, her eyes never leaving his face.

"Tell me when you are about to . . . do it. I need good lungs full of air for those outside to hear me."

*This is about the strangest wedding night I could imagine*, thought Yozef, fighting to maintain minimal restraint. He knew she was nervous and apprehensive. About what? For herself at what he was about to do? Or that she might not put on the appropriate show for the outside audience? This wasn't how he imagined a first experience with any woman and definitely not a wife. Yet somehow it fit Maera. No matter how she felt inside, she would think things out and plan how to fulfill her role.

Despite his unease, nature was nature, and the evidence of his readiness to fulfill his role was evident before both of them. There was no foreplay. He guided himself to her. Her eyes widened at the first touch and probe. Her breathing quickened and she tensed, as he eased into position against her. By now, his breaths were heavy with anticipation, and his blood throbbed.

"Ready, Maera," he stated, full-throated. "Here we go."

She closed her eyes for the first time and took a deep breath. As she finished inhaling, he thrust. Her eyes flared open and her scream almost knocked him off her. Even though he expected a yell, it was still a jolt.

"Sorry, Maera!"

She swallowed and took several deep breaths. "It's all right, husband. I'm all right," she said in a strangled voice. "Are you all the way in?"

"No."

"Then do so."

He thrust a second time and then a third before he was fully inside her. The second and third screams were progressively less, but he found himself idly wondering how far the sounds reached. Now that he was fully inserted, his concern returned. They touched the full length of their bodies, with most of his weight supported by arms and knees.

"Maera, are you all right?"

She managed a small smile. "Only the first one hurt that much. I think my yell was sufficient for custom. The other two were for you."

"For me?" he repeated, astounded.

"I know my reputation as a cold bitch. Now they will think more highly of you, since you dominated me."

It was one of the weirdest conversations Yozef had ever had. "Somehow I don't see anyone dominating you."

"As long as *you* realize that, husband, then I can live with whatever the others think."

Yozef felt Maera's hands on his back, as she embraced him and clasped her legs onto the backs of his thighs. "Let us complete the consummation. It'll enhance your reputation more if they can hear *you* at the end."

With those instructions, Yozef slowly withdrew partway, then pushed back. She winced a little the first time, less with each successive thrust as the pace quickened. It didn't take long for him to come with a final firm thrust and an exclamation he didn't have to fake.

Yozef relaxed, breathing heavily, his face buried for the moment in the nape of her neck. She stroked his back and whispered, "Now we're husband and wife. May our marriage bring both of us satisfaction and children."

He rose slightly to look her in the face. "I think it will."

"I know," she said. "You're a good man. Not like Caedelli men, but I think our marriage will be good for both of us."

It wasn't an expression of love. Maera didn't express feelings easily, and neither of them had said the word yet to the other. It would have to do for now. The marriage was based on respect and advantages. While neither spoke of love, both hoped to themselves that love would come.

He withdrew and could see blood on the cloth and a little on them both. Maera rose from the bed and went to a washbasin and cloth towels on a table nearby. She wet two towels and used one to clean herself. Yozef was, once again, startled when she came to the bed where he still lay and, instead of handing him the other towel, she proceeded to matter-of-factly also clean him. When finished, she donned one of the two robes hanging on the wall and handed him the other.

"Now we need to display the wedding bed cloth for the final confirmation of my virginity and consummation of our marriage."

Yozef pulled on his robe, and Maera handed him one end of the wedding cloth she had pulled from the bed. "We're to go outside and hang it over the railing for all to see."

Yozef simply went along, as he had since the proposal. They opened the twin doors to the second-floor balcony and stepped into the evening air. Though the sun had set over two hours ago, there was more than enough light from a bonfire blazing thirty feet from the house and a dozen kerosene lanterns lit and hanging from trees. A cheer went up when the balcony doors opened. As they draped the cloth over the railing, more appreciative calls rang out, along with a few Yozef would have considered in extraordinarily bad taste back on Earth. But here, as before, Maera took it all in stride, clasped his hand, and raised both of their hands high in a sign of triumph. Another, even louder, cheer rang out, and they went back inside.

Once the doors were closed, the voices outside vanished for the first time since they had arrived at the cottage. She noticed him listening, and when he raised a questioning eyebrow, she explained, "Custom is that once the consummation is confirmed, the guests and the family leave the married couple alone for the rest of the evening. They will now go back to the festivities and let the men finish getting drunk."

She smiled. "Speaking of drink, I wouldn't mind one right now. Could you pour me one?" She pointed to another table across the room at a glass decanter of reddish liquid and two ornate glasses. "The glasses are ours to keep as a remembrance of this night." She spoke as if reading from a text, and Yozef recognized a ritual.

"A remembrance of this night. The two glasses represent that now we are a pair. The clearness of the glass represents that everything we are and do should be open between us, with no lies or deceptions. The red wine represents the wedding bed blood and my virginity on this night. The sturdy flagon represents your strength for your wife and children. The intricate design on the glasses represents my providing care for our children and my husband."

She took the glass he offered her. When she started to raise it to her mouth, his hand without a glass stopped her. "Here are some of the customs of my land." He positioned her hand and glass at her eye level, gently clicked the two glasses together, and then crossed their arms, so each could drink from his or her own glass with arms crossed.

"To life!" he exclaimed and brought his glass to his mouth for a swallow.

Maera did the same and then laughed. "So, do we do this *every* time we drink?"

Yozef chuckled. "No. The glass touching could be for any occasion; the arms crossed is only for special times."

There was no other furniture in the cottage, except the bed and two tables. The newly married couple sat on the bed and talked of inconsequential things for the next hour, accompanied by several more glasses of wine. As usual, it was too sweet for Yozef's taste, although the flavor itself was rich and aromatic. When Maera finally started dozing off or passing out—he wasn't sure he could tell the difference at the time himself—he took her glass from her. She simply slumped down on the bed and was asleep. He covered her with another of the cloths folded on the table and followed her within seconds.

Maera awoke first the next morning. The sun was up and coming through the lace curtains that were another remembrance they would hang somewhere in their house. She turned in the bed to face her . . . husband. It was an odd feeling, and she wasn't sure how she felt about her new state. Traditionally, the Caedelli man was the master of the family, with the wife obeying, though in real life it depended on each couple. Sometimes the woman was lucky, and the man was considerate. In other marriages she knew of, the husband controlled everything about their lives. She even knew a few cases where the couple had equal authority in the family, and it was rarer still when the wife ruled.

Maera couldn't conceive of being totally controlled by anyone. Even her father, the hetman of the entire Keelan clan, recognized limitations. Although the family head, he always listened to her mother, who knew that even when

Culich made a decision his wife didn't approve of, he took Breda's wishes and opinions into consideration. All within limits, of course.

Maera had made it a plan by the time she was twelve that she wouldn't marry anyone she didn't agree to. She might agree out of duty if necessary, being whose daughter she was and cognizant of the political realities of her station and family, but it would ultimately be her decision.

Her father had unwittingly fostered her independence. If she had had brothers, maybe things would have been different, and she would have slid into more traditional women's roles. However, Hetman Keelan had no sons to train to take his place when the day came to move on from Anyar and meet God. When it became apparent that she was unusually bright, her father provided an education far beyond what even sons would have had, and Maera quickly exhausted the initial tutor her family provided. Her further education was by her own efforts and interactions with scholastics, with whom she could carry on complicated discussions by her eighth year.

She had joked last night that many thought her a bitch. She spoke her mind and didn't acquiesce to others if she didn't agree, especially to pompous men or men who thought women should be seen and not heard. It also didn't help that she was far smarter than most men and more educated than all but the senior scholastics. Even in those cases, while she might not know as much in their specific fields, her breadth of knowledge was wide-ranging, especially about the history of the Caedellium clans. By the time she had passed puberty, her father found her keen observations of people, general knowledge, and analytic ability invaluable assets to him.

Now, lying in bed next to her new husband, she wondered, how would her life change as a wife and when she became a mother? To be tied down with children for the next few decades of her life was not something she eagerly anticipated. She knew she would love her children, and she knew that there would be help from staff hired by her family or Yozef. But she would never again have the level of freedom to study or to be part of running the Keelan Clan the way she had been. How would the pluses and minuses balance out? She didn't know.

She looked again at Yozef as he slept. *The sleep of the dead*, she thought. Her mother always complained that men seemed able to sleep anywhere, as if the world didn't exist. Yozef looked that way now, his face relaxed, his breathing deep and regular, his chest and abdomen rising and falling. Last night had been . . . different. She knew that wasn't the word she wanted but didn't know of a better one. He had been considerate, as she knew he'd be. Still, the first time had been more painful than she'd expected, and she hadn't had to pretend what came out of her mouth. Regardless of what she'd told Yozef, the second and third screams weren't totally faked. She was sore now. Everyone said it faded quickly and that only the first time was like this.

She'd known what to expect. Women talked freely among themselves, and her mother had spared no details. Neither had Anarynd. She and Ana whispered speculations about what men and women did together when they were younger, and then Ana went into great detail on the few occasions she experimented with this thing called sex. Ana's experience was limited, and she was circumspect on those occasions, but she relayed every detail to Maera, including that while the first time might not be pleasant, Ana's few later experiences encouraged anticipating marriage.

Yozef turned. He'd be waking up soon. It was time for the last part of the ritual, the new couple's morning meal with the family. Maera sighed and stretched. Only God knew the future, so she needed to remember to focus on today. She remembered the *Word* saying, *"If you concern yourself with today, the future will take care of itself."* She sat up on the edge of the bed, holding the cloth to her chest, and bounced a little to see if Yozef would waken. Nothing. Stronger bounces elicited stirrings, and a third time led to an eye opening.

"Ah, you're awake," she said slyly.

"Did I have a choice?" he groaned. "Isn't it too early? We didn't get to sleep until late."

"My, my. Don't tell me I exhausted you already?"

He opened one eye and saw her smiling. He opened both eyes, blinked several times, then rubbed at the corners. "As I remember, we're due to a Keelan family breakfast this morning. Am I to take it this is my alert to get ready?"

Maera frowned. "This is important. Last night was the wedding, and today you formally become a member of the Keelan family and myself as Maera Kolsko-Keelan for the first time."

"Kolsko-Keelan? You'll have a compound last name?"

"It's the custom for hetmen and boyermen's daughters, though not always other clan members. The compound name reminds everyone of the important linkages, particularly in interclan marriages."

He still had not moved from under the cloth, so she pulled it off him and wrapped it around herself.

"Okay, I'm getting up." Yozef sat up, then swung off the bed and onto his feet in a single motion.

*How do men do that?* Maera thought. *Go so quickly from deep sleep to activity. Maybe it's just because they're men and need to be ready to act quickly in case of danger? Then why not women? Oh, well, another of those mysteries.*

Maera went to the cottage door, opened it, and poked her head out. A young boy of about nine was sitting on the front step and sprang to his feet when he heard the door. "We'll be there in ten minutes," Maera said, and he dashed up the path to the main house. She closed the door again.

"Come. They'll be ready for us, so we need to dress."

She went to a wall from which a series of racks held two piles of clothing and shoes. For Yozef, she put his attire on the bed: a pair of brown trousers, a plain white shirt, and shoes. Next to her sat a pile with a white shift, a long green plain dress, and slipper shoes.

There was an awkward moment—one she hadn't anticipated. Where would she dress?

Yozef read her mind. Softly, he said, "Wife, there's nothing I didn't see last night." He rose and dressed.

After hesitating, Maera shed her robe and pulled the shift and the dress over her head and shoulders. Yozef made no pretense of not watching, and although she overtly ignored him, the rise in color made it plain she was aware of his scrutiny.

When dressed, she looked at him almost defiantly. "Are we ready?"

"One custom of my people is that married couples sometimes hold hands while they walk together."

Maera was unsure until Yozef added, "It's a sign of affection and indicates the two are side by side and not one ahead of the other."

With that explanation, Maera took his hand, and they walked to the manor house. The main parlor had been turned into a dining hall. Waiting for them were two long tables along the length of the room and a small cross table at the head with four places set—two already occupied by Maera's parents.

Yozef chuckled. *I guess it doesn't take rocket science to figure out where we're supposed to sit.*

They sat looking at forty to fifty faces staring back at them, Maera's family and prominent clan members attending the wedding. Yozef had been resigned to hearing more crude comments, but everyone was a model of decorum. Culich Keelan rose and raised a glass.

"Today we welcome into our family and clan a new member and the husband of my daughter, Maera Keelan, who is now Maera Kolsko-Keelan." With that, he downed the contents, followed by a unison "Welcome," and thud, as the roomful of glass bottoms hit the tables.

Maera had cued Yozef on what was coming, so he joined her in rising and raising their glasses and, with a "To Clan Keelan, may it prosper in God's grace," downed the contents. Applause and offerings of congratulations concluded the formal custom.

For the next two hours, courses were brought in, and Yozef ate until he thought he would explode. He was thankful that the toast was the only alcohol. Kava, the coffee substitute, cleared his head, and he kept eating at a steady pace, as seemingly everyone in the room came to personally congratulate them and converse for a few minutes. By the end, he lost track of who was who or what they were saying. What he did grasp was his acceptance into the family and clan, perhaps a semi-honorary member, since he married in, although *in* nevertheless.

At mid-morning, the wedding breakfast finally came to an end. Culich rose, this time to thank the guests and send them on their way. Some would be heading home immediately and others spending the night before a longer homeward trip the next day. A few of the family's closest relatives would stay various lengths of time at the main house, in cottages on the grounds, or elsewhere. The final part of the wedding was sending off the married couple to the bride's new home. Since there was no Caedellium custom similar to a "honeymoon," Yozef had had to explain it to Maera and her mother. She had run interference for them with Culich, who still had not quite accepted that they wouldn't be living in Caernford. Culich's initial proposal had been that he would provide a house for them near the manor. Yozef had politely but firmly declined, saying that his working shops were in Abersford, and it would be more efficient to live there. There had been a mildly heated discussion following this, resulting in a compromise that they would live at Abersford until Maera became great enough with their first child, and then they would revisit moving to the capital. Yozef had no intention of moving. Maera thought she could eventually convince Yozef but sided with her father that the first child be born at the clan's center.

It took another two hours for Yozef and Maera to extricate themselves from well-wishes and tearful goodbyes from her mother and sisters. Even Culich had damp eyes by the time Carnigan drove the carriage from the manor, accompanied by two wagons of Maera's possessions and wedding gifts, eight outriders, and two matched riding horses gifted by an uncle.

# CHAPTER 21

# SETTLING IN

**Honeymoon, West of Abersford**

He didn't know why he woke up. They had gone to sleep early, both Maera and the covers providing him with warmth against the night chill. He remembered drifting off, then he was awake, lifting his head to find the digital clock that didn't exist. One more thing he'd never experience again, but habits remained.

He lay in the darkness, listening to Maera's breathing, faint under the sound of the wind and the rain that had moved in before dusk, accompanied by intense bands of lightning. Sometimes steady drops hit the window, and at other times the sound was a heavy drum, as an overladen cloud emptied its cargo. The wind ebbed and flowed like a heartbeat, whistling through cracks in the walls.

Yozef had always loved wind and rain. He remembered the stormier winters in Berkeley and nights like this, where he awoke next to Julie. What was her life like now? He hoped she'd moved on after the shock of his "death." Was she married? Children? Child? They'd discovered her pregnancy before he left for the trip to the chemistry conference in Chicago. Did she keep the baby? Was it a boy or a girl? He'd missed her terribly the first months, then time slowly moved on, and the wound turned to a scar, a remembrance of what had been.

Maera shifting in the bed brought his mind back to her. Without a light and with the storm covering the stars and the moons, the room was black, but he could imagine her. Bright, inquisitive, more attractive than she recognized, fiercely loyal to her family and, he hoped, to him.

He folded away part of the covers, letting in some of the cold, moist air that came with the storm, careful not to wake Maera. The cold was good, too. Then, just about when the cold got uncomfortable, he folded back the cover and drifted off, warmed up again, lulled by the rhythm of wind, rain, heartbeats, and two breaths.

When his breathing was regular, with a slight snore, Maera opened her eyes. She hadn't been asleep. The storm wasn't comforting for her as for him, one of the many things to learn about her husband. Things that rarely seemed understandable. Like now. She found heavy storms threatening. No storm ever shook her family's manor, where outside sounds were faint, even in the worst conditions.

And why *would* she have such experiences? Weren't they something to avoid? To endure but not seek out? Yet Yozef did more than endure, he sought them out. That evening he'd stood on the porch, protected from the worst of the rain but exposed to the wind and the cold, the thunder shaking the overhang. He came back inside exhilarated. Did he feel a kinship with such elements? When she asked about it, he said, *Feeling the forces of nature is like getting a glimpse of the power of God*. She hadn't thought of him as a devout man. He attended abbey services and was respectful but didn't talk about the beliefs of his people, another of the many topics he skirted around when pressed.

She had been dubious about the "honeymoon." She understood making time for a new husband and wife to know each other better, but why isolate themselves in this one-room cottage? And with no servants? They hadn't seen another soul for more than a sixday, and they'd be here another three days. The first few days she'd felt ill at ease with only the two of them. They'd talked more than in all of their time together since she'd left Abersford, with enough details and anecdotes about families that Maera felt she "knew" his family, even though they'd never meet. She also knew more about his studies, his aspirations to help the people of Keelan, his worries about the Narthani, and his fear during the raid on St. Sidryn's.

At first, hearing the latter made her uneasy. Few Caedelli men, especially those close to a hetman's family, would ever admit fear. Yozef had. Flashing unbidden through her mind was the question of whether her husband was a coward. No, both Carnigan and Denes Vegga spoke not only of his insight on how to save the abbey, but also of how he took part in the fight. She didn't believe Carnigan and Vegga would think highly of a coward.

Yozef simply made honest assessments of the way things were. Maera didn't doubt most Caedelli men were afraid during a fight, although they'd never admit it as easily as Yozef did. He took it for granted that one should be afraid.

*So, who's braver?* she thought. *The man who's afraid and won't admit it, or the man who's afraid, admits it, and still fights?*

Another example to caution herself when making judgments about her husband.

She snuggled up next to him. The covers were warm enough, but his body next to hers was beginning to be . . . safe? No, not just safe, something else. Drifting off to sleep, she smiled when she remembered the first couple of days. They found the cottage well stocked with food, kerosene, bedding, and everything Diera could think of for their two sixdays, though no one to prepare the food for them. At home, her mother had insisted on occasionally preparing meals, and her daughters would join in, except for Maera, who would always be too busy. Maera never understood her mother's interest in cooking.

This was different. They prepared the meals themselves, and although Maera initially proved virtually useless, Yozef was more than competent. It was only one more item to hang on the confusing tree of Yozef's being. To her surprise, by the third day she found herself relaxed and even enjoyed working with him to ready the food they ate. She mainly assisted under his direction, but she learned fast.

More striking was that she found that when they made the meal and ate together, it was almost . . . sensual. While she knew the food they prepared wasn't extraordinary, somehow fresh bread she kneaded herself tasted better than any she had ever experienced. Logically, she knew it wasn't true, but there it was, anyway.

Sharing a bed with a man would also take time to adjust to. Sleeping occasionally with younger sisters was one thing. A *man* seemed wrong at first, though less so each night. She needed even more adjusting to a man touching her everywhere. Not that it didn't feel good at times, and she was determined to do her duty to her husband. He hadn't pushed his rights the first night after they'd arrived in Abersford or the second night at the cottage. He said it was out of concern for her to recover from their first night together. She had been relieved, disappointed, and confused. Her brief wondering whether he might not find her appealing was assuaged the next night, most nights thereafter, and, for the first time, yesterday morning. Her *duty* wasn't as bad as her misgivings, and she wondered if, as other women had whispered to her, she would come to enjoy it as much as her husband obviously did. Time would tell.

Their days were "planned doing nothing," as Yozef paradoxically termed it. Not that they did nothing. They walked along the beach every day. Maera ran in the surf as they had that day at Abersford and with more abandon than since childhood. They swam in the little cove below the cottage. The water was calm and not too cold, once you immersed. Yozef swam like a fish, but for her swimming had been in quiet ponds, not ocean surf. While initially she was hesitant to get into water over her head, he was solicitous and hovered nearby until she became more confident.

They played—silly games in the water, while walking, and in the cottage. Who could count the most seagulls, the loser doing the meal cleanup. Not that it made any difference, because they did everything together. They taught each other songs. She didn't understand what "doing the hokey pokey" meant, but the lilt of the tune, the word cadence, and the silly dance were addictive.

She didn't want to live this way forever, although she began to see why Yozef was attracted to *getting away*. It surprised her during last night's meal when a hint of regret seeped into her thoughts about them leaving in three days. What might seem a frivolity to most people, she now wondered if brief times away might be healthy and might make the person more effective when he returned to the real world. She wondered whether her father could use such time and knew he would only look at her askance if she suggested it.

*Strange. I understand even better than before why people use the word for Yozef. I should know, because they've often thought that of me. Now that I'm married to Yozef, will I take on some of his strangeness? It's odd that the thought doesn't bother me.* She smiled again before drifting off. *Maybe being married to Yozef will make me appear to others as less odd?*

## A New House

Their arrival back in Abersford revived the events the honeymoon had only delayed—a special Godsday service, a formal reception attended by several hundred, individual invitations for dinner with prominent citizens of Abersford, and endless stops for congratulations wherever they went. It took most of a month before the attention abated, and they settled into their new routine.

As expected, a new house was one of Maera's first major impacts when they returned from the honeymoon. Yozef had been satisfied with his small house. As long as he had a place to eat and sleep and enough room to write, he was content. Adding Maera didn't translate into merely adding more rooms. As Filtin Fuller had cautioned, Maera had ideas. Yozef could easily afford to build whatever Maera wanted, although her father insisted the Keelan hetman had to be generous with the newly married couple. Yozef wisely didn't argue, particularly when Maera and her father presented a united front. The house of Yozef Kolsko, wealthy entrepreneur and mysterious man of new knowledge, and Maera Kolsko-Keelan, wife of Yozef and eldest daughter of Hetman Keelan, required a substantial home. Not as grand as her parents' manor, but well beyond Yozef's cottage.

At first, Maera planned to import designers and workers from Caernford, but at Yozef's urging, she met with Dyfeld Fuller and she agreed he was competent enough for the task. Her first few ideas about the design of house were grandiose. During one session, as she leaned over a diagram of her latest idea, Dyfeld looked at Yozef and rolled his eyes. Yozef suppressed a laugh and shook a warning at the elder craftsman. Over time, Dyfeld understood best what Maera wanted, and the final design was an elegant, good-sized house, comfortable rooms, high ceilings, and many double-paned windows, a suggestion of Yozef's that Dyfeld had grasped the advantages of and improved on.

At first, Maera assumed the original house would serve for guests; then Yozef declared they would build separate guest quarters, with the original house reserved for the Faughns. Maera was dubious about giving such a nice house to servants, and Brak was his usual gruff self, ever suspicious of charity. Yozef told the Faughns his intent was a logical step, because, as their employer moved up to a grandeur house, the most important servants also must have better quarters. Maera's doubts disappeared when Elian broke into tears, and Brak's objections were silenced with a stern look from Yozef and a nod to Elian's response. The old man looked at his wife, and his visage softened. Yozef wasn't sure he didn't see a trace of moisture, and, with a bow and thanks to their employer, the Faughns promised ever more diligent service to justify such fine housing.

The new house would sit just downslope from the cottage and likewise face the sea. A large veranda allowed sitting and viewing on three sides, with a screen of transplanted eight-foot trees providing privacy from the Faughns' new home. Inside, a dining room separated a generous parlor from the kitchen, three bedrooms provided for themselves and guests, and each of them had a workroom. Yozef was constantly griping about his work areas being crowded, so was pleased to find his new workroom would be the size of the old cottage, with windows on two sides, built-in bookcases, and lockable cabinets covering two walls.

## Maera Finds Her Place

Yozef wasn't surprised by Maera's usurpation of planning the new house. While he knew she could be assertive, it was his first time on the receiving end, and he was happy to let her free him from involvement. Moreover, once the house was completed, he acknowledged to himself and to Maera, and to anyone who asked, that she had a better eye for their requirements than he did.

However, the house was only a preamble for Maera, the inveterate organizer. Once they settled the major issues of the house, she shifted focus to target number two—Yozef's daily schedules. As his enterprises grew, he went from one urgent issue to another. Between working with the various craftsmen, going to meetings, and doing his writing, no day was without too many tasks. Maera brought a sense of order similar to how she functioned for her father. Yozef at first chafed but quickly came to appreciate having an "assistant." First, more got done. She kept track of progress and interleaved times better than Yozef's seat-of-his-pants scheduling, and it pleased his workers to have his regular attention, instead of waiting for a crisis.

Second, he had someone to blame when he preferred to avoid a meeting or a person. "Sorry, Ser Businessman, but my schedule is full today. Please see Maera Kolsko-Keelan to arrange a time." Maera then judged whether the event was important enough for his time, scheduled it efficiently if it was, and intimidated those whose meeting rationale was mainly self-interest.

A third advantage was that Maera scheduled daily time for him to write. She didn't understand the significance of his writings but recognized their importance to him and fit in an hour most days. It was his explanation that raised her suspicions: that he needed to write down his daily thoughts in English, because his written Caedelli wasn't good enough.

As soon as the words left his mouth, Yozef recognized she didn't believe him. He tried to recover by adding that he also worked on science notes to discuss with Cadwulf and the scholastics. He had already transmitted to Cadwulf all he remembered of mathematics, and the Beynoms' son had moved beyond Yozef's level on his own and was in active correspondence with several mathematics scholastics elsewhere on Caedellium. Yozef foresaw the irregular communications turning into a more formal mathematical periodical, if enough practitioners developed—if not on Caedellium, then eventually elsewhere on Anyar.

He filled the one set of journals with everything he remembered about science, which the Caedelli were not yet ready to assimilate. The second set recounted how he came to Anyar and as much as he recollected of the history and the cultures of Earth. A key to both sets was the English-Caedelli dictionary he'd started when first learning Caedelli, along with a grammar supplement. These were the most carefully secreted journals, because he didn't want anyone, particularly Maera, to read them and think him mad.

She pestered him at first on teaching her English but quit when she realized it was one place he wouldn't accommodate her. He couldn't risk that she would read the secret journals, either by accident or in her inability to contain her curiosity.

Maera kept up a steady, voluminous correspondence with her father. He partly filled her place as the hetman's aide with a young scholastic from St. Tomo's abbey in Caernford. However, Culich Keelan still valued his daughter's insights and skill with words. Though now separated by distance and time, she continued summarizing and editing, albeit at a slower pace, as she and her father passed papers back and forth.

Still, her change in status awakened a need to establish a position uniquely her own. An opportunity emerged from a casual remark made to her by Diera Beynom, as the two women walked together one afternoon.

"Maera, do me a favor and ask Yozef how his planning for the university is coming along."

"University? What's that? Another of Yozef's projects? I've never heard the word."

"Never . . . ? You mean he hasn't told you his idea to expand the number of scholastics at St. Sidryn's and house them in new buildings? I thought Culich told me months ago he was going to discuss the idea with you when you first visited. He must have forgotten, what with everything else going on. Anyway, Yozef calls his idea a 'university.' You say Yozef hasn't mentioned it to you?"

A chagrinned Maera shook her head. "No, and that's not the only thing he doesn't talk about."

"Oh, dear, I hope the two of you aren't having problems already."

Maera sighed. "Not really. He's . . . you know, Yozef. He treats me well, is considerate, and is the most interesting person I've ever met. Still, there's always the underlying sense there so much more he isn't telling me."

"Yes, that's Yozef. I think most of us who've known him longer accept it as part of his idiosyncrasy. It may be one thing you have to come to terms with on your own, unless you want to make it a serious issue with him, which I'd caution against doing."

Maera looked with surprise at the older woman. "Why? What do you think might happen?"

"While Yozef may seem mild mannered, which has been my experience with him, my instincts are that he can be immovable. He accommodates to a point and then shuts down. I wouldn't recommend that in a new marriage."

"I don't know, Diera. It's bothering me more and more, even though part of me knows our marriage is going well. No, better than well. I was resigned to a marriage to benefit the clan, possibly to a man I didn't even like. Instead, I find myself with a husband I truly enjoy being with and whom I respect. Am I just being silly?"

"Silly? No. It's normal to want to know everything about the person you marry and with whom you share a bed. A difficult truth is that we never know anyone completely. Even Sistian, after all our years together, still surprises me occasionally with something new. That little sense of mystery adds continuing spice to a marriage."

Maera laughed. "In that case, I may be the most seasoned woman on Caedellium! All right, Diera, I'll try to listen to your advice and focus on what's going so well. Now, what about this university?"

Yozef and Maera had barely begun to eat that evening when she queried him.

"Diera mentioned today your idea to expand the number of St. Sidryn's scholastics and gather them into what you call a university. Diera's enthused about the concept and asked me how plans were progressing. Naturally, I had no answer, since you've never mentioned it to *me*."

He ignored the implied rebuke. "It's an institution where I came from . . . America. We believe scholastics are better concentrated in larger numbers than here on Caedellium into a critical mass to generate new ideas."

"Critical mass?"

"Sorry. In numbers large enough that their interactions allow them to have new ideas and clarify their own thinking more easily than by themselves or in smaller groups. It's something I feel strongly about. I'd talked to Abbot Sistian about it, and we agreed to start by adding about twenty-five scholastics in three areas of study—mathematics, the study of the history and customs of different peoples and realms of Anyar, and the study of living creatures. The three to be organized in the departments of Mathematics, Nations, and Biology."

Maera asked questions about why those three areas, either quickly grasping their potential importance or willing to take Yozef's word. "I can see why you believe mathematics so important, Yozef, but I must warn you that most people will see it as merely intellectual puzzles with no application to their lives. I've listened to you and Cadwulf enough about how mathematics is applied, so why don't you call it the Department of Applied Mathematics and be sure to emphasize utility?"

Within an hour, they similarly changed the other names to the Department of Biology and Medicine, and the Department of History and Societies. Maera went beyond his broad-stroke ideas on each of the areas and had intuited some of the rationales Yozef hadn't mentioned to anyone else.

By the time they finished, they'd also added a Department of Apothecary and Chemistry. Yozef insisted the two were different, in that chemistry was dependent on rules and principles, while apothecary was little more than rote memorization of recipes.

"Yozef, no one on Caedellium, including myself, understands about your *chemistry*, but we all see what you've done with ether, kerosene, soap, and gunpowder, all of which you insist involves chemistry. I've heard you say that apothecary will eventually change into chemistry, so why not set up a department to speed it along? Doesn't some of what an apothecary does relate to chemistry?"

"Probably to some extent. St. Sidryn's library hasn't many apothecary books, and I haven't had the time or opportunity to look elsewhere. For all I know, there's more basis for chemistry than I'm aware of in books elsewhere on Caedellium."

"The answer is for you not to do the search yourself. We'll hire an apprentice from one of the abbeys training apothecaries, such as St. Alonso's Abbey in Hewell Province, a good place to start. He can scour libraries throughout Caedellium for everything known about apothecary and mixing substances. We'll collect it here, along with enticing additional apprentices who can form the basis of your Department of Apothecary and Chemistry. Then, as you think it possible, you can begin introducing more chemistry knowledge."

Yozef tugged on his lip, then chewed on his beard while thinking. "Yes, I hadn't thought of that strategy. You're right." He chewed more. "Yes. A core of young apothecaries not yet stuck in the rut of their profession is the perfect place to start. I can put them to work experimenting with distillation, differential precipitations and extractions, elementary thermodynamics . . ."

Yozef lost Maera, as he ruminated in what she assumed were English words.

*Well,* she thought, *looks like it'll definitely be four departments.*

Five minutes later, Yozef remembered Maera was in the room, and he realized another problem.

"All these ideas are wonderful, but there's a stumbling block. The number of new scholastics will need to be larger. The abbot and I talked about twenty-five as all we could support to begin. I now think the number may need to go higher, perhaps forty or more. I doubt the abbey can help more, and I'd have to check with Cadwulf on the conditions of my enterprises to see how much more I could do."

"That shouldn't be a problem," Maera said. "I'll write to Father and describe the university idea, offering reasons it would be advantageous for Keelan. You can write up a summary of your ideas, and we can get Abbot Sistian to write a supporting letter. I'm sure we can arrange for additional coin to reach the forty scholastics you believe is a better number to start with."

Yozef stared at his wife. "Maera, and this is meant as a compliment, having you around is like having more hours in the day or even a second me. Too often, I come up with ideas I don't have time to implement, and sometimes I'm simply bad at carrying through on plans. With you to help, I'm wondering if I've underestimated what's possible."

The rest of the meal and the evening, they were two colleagues planning a grand venture.

"Unfortunately, we won't have access to more knowledge outside of Caedellium," she rued.

"Damned Narthani again!" said Yozef. "Why do so many things have to keep coming back to them?"

"We all pray they'll be gone someday. Until then, we can only do what we can do. And what we can do now is establish your university."

Yozef sat back in his chair and scowled. "As good as all this sounds, someone needs to be in charge, a head of the project and the university itself. I don't have time to do what I'm already involved in, so someone else would need to lead this. I'll have to find someone to . . ." The solution was obvious before he finished the sentence. "Maera, is there any reason *you* couldn't lead the university project?"

"Me? I'm not even a scholastic."

"The leader of the university doesn't have to be a scholastic. Often they are, but it's not required. What's needed is someone to lead, plan, and keep everything organized. I can't imagine anyone better than you to get the project started. You're smart enough to talk to scholastics in different areas, even if you don't know details of their studies. Moreover, I've heard the abbot say you're almost a scholastic in your own right on Caedellium history and customs. You're the hetman's daughter and the wife of the man providing much of the coin. Who else would be better?"

Maera sat considering. As seconds passed, he could see her face slowly flush, her eyes dance, one hand stroking her chin faster and faster. "I can do it. Women are not usually in such leadership roles, although it's not unheard of. Think of Diera being the lead medicant at St. Sidryn's." She pounded a fist into the other palm, raised both hands shoulder high, and almost danced in her chair. "I *know* I can do it." She was talking to herself, her eyes focused on a distance. "I can hold my own with any scholastic. I'm the hetman's daughter and the wife of Yozef Kolsko, so by those alone I have to be taken seriously. And by Merciful God, it sounds exciting!"

She jumped from her chair and hopped into Yozef's lap, plopping a kiss on her surprised husband's lips. "Yes, yes, I can do this, and I *want* to do it! Oh, Yozef, what an opportunity! It's something important that can be *mine*. Even with you and Father supporting me, if it succeeds everyone will acknowledge Maera Kolsko-Keelan. Thank you, husband!"

Approval of additional funds came a sixday later from Hetman Keelan, and Maera formally became Chancellor of the planned University of Abersford. They agreed that the four planned departments each needed a leader. To begin, Cadwulf would lead Applied Mathematics, Diera Biology and Medicine, Maera History and Societies, and Yozef Apothecary and Chemistry. As the university staff grew, each could relinquish leadership once the department was established and a suitable candidate identified.

Yozef tempered Maera's enthusiasm to expand rapidly, cautioning they needed to recruit carefully. At the same time, he contracted for new structures to house the university. This time the workers came from Caernford, Dyfeld Filtin being too busy for a project this size. It would take many months to finish the buildings, and recruitment would take even longer, but establishing the first university on Caedellium had begun.

# CHAPTER 22

# SECRETS

### Children

Yozef wasn't completely comfortable that Maera's diligence in the bedroom often seemed too much a duty. When he had such reservations, he usually chided himself. The marriage was new, Maera had been inexperienced, and he knew she took "duties" seriously. While he didn't know if she felt pleased by their couplings, he perceived that she was relaxing more, and there were worse things than a wife willing to have sex every night. Given Maera's dedication to duty and the lack of birth control, the consequences were inevitable.

Yozef got the news one evening.

"I saw the Mertons today," Yozef said, after Elian had served the evening meal and left. "They stopped at the shops so I could see the baby and hold him for a while. I must confess, it feels a little strange for me to have a son and not see him regularly. I suppose that will change if we have a child."

"It's no longer an 'if,' husband," said Maera.

Her tone was composed, but he'd swear her eyes and mouth attempted to hide elation. He stared, his mind recognizing that she was telling him something.

"Uh . . . does that mean . . . ?"

"I believe so. I've missed my monthly bleeding and noticed my breasts are more tender. While it's too early to be positive, I'm confident I'm with child."

She took another bite of beef roast and, while chewing, broke off a piece of dark bread and lathered it with butter, only then sneaking a look at him.

*Well, I gave him the news. Is he going to be pleased? What will he say? Maybe he doesn't want children right now. Maybe I'm a total ninny!*

Other thoughts were going through Yozef's head.

*Well, I knew it was going to happen. She's certainly been dutiful enough to increase the odds of it. One child here and now another on the way. Good lord! How do I feel?*

*Ambivalent, for sure. Thinking about the possibility of children and the reality aren't the same.*

Maera's expression had become tense. He wasn't saying anything.

Yozef noticed. *Hell, no matter if I'm ambivalent, it's a fact, and Maera Kolsko-Keelan, Scourge of the Unwary or not, needs to be reassured.*

He pushed his chair back, went around the table to her, took her hand, and pulled her to her feet to envelop her in a tight embrace.

"What wonderful news, Maera. It was just so sudden to find not only that Bronwyn's child was here, but now the news you're pregnant." He kissed her deeply and held her against him.

She sighed and hugged back. Husband or not, more thoughtful than most Caedelli men or not, gently respectful and affectionate to her or not, there was always the tinge of uncertainty about what he would do or say next.

They resumed the meal, Maera talking about how they needed to further expand the house now that children were really on the way, getting word to her family, how the good news would be welcome throughout the province, how she would need some new clothes once she began to swell, and on and on.

Yozef responded when it seemed appropriate, although his thoughts were elsewhere: How could they bring children into this world with all of the uncertainties about what the future might hold for Caedellium? How would his life change now that he would be a father twice over? How would Maera adjust her life when there was an infant to care for? Did high-caste Keelan women have daycare or wet nurses? Did Caedelli custom not expect sexual relations during pregnancy? Of those five, the first was unknowable, the next two would only be answered with time, the fourth Maera would handle, and the fifth a pregnant wife would answer later that evening.

## Top Secrets

One troublesome issue hovered over the first months of their marriage: Maera's inveterate inquisitiveness. Keeping his background story straight for causal encounters or even friends not overly curious, such as Carnigan and Cadwulf, or those who chose not to pry was one thing. Keeping everything secret from a wife, especially one like Maera, proved something else. Inconsistencies that others might have passed off, she remembered and probed further.

He hadn't appreciated how hard it would be. The first few times, he tried covering his lapses as momentary slips of the tongue or the mind. A critical mistake was when he blamed her faulty memory. The set of her mouth and the toss of her head expressed her rejection of that possibility. For two sixdays, they danced around the issue. She quit hinting one day, as they walked home from Abersford. It was an hour before sunset. The onshore wind tugged at their clothing with a chill preceding dark clouds on the southern horizon.

The words came without preamble. "You're hiding too much, Yozef," she asserted.

He didn't know what to say. This moment had been anticipated, with no escape plan formulated. They walked several hundred more yards without speaking. At a loss about what to do, he opted to delay.

"Maera, there are things I need to say to you, but right now I need time to think. Can we talk about this later?"

"Of course, husband."

The last word was laced with insinuations of obligations.

No further word on the matter was mentioned again for several days. Their routine continued as before, until . . .

Yozef's gasps of pleasure accompanied several final thrusts, and he let his head sag next to Maera's on the bed, his weight supported by arms and knees, their bodies pressed together. His breathing and heart rate slowed, as he stroked the opposite side of her head, her arms under his and her hands firm on his shoulders. He started to withdraw, but her arms slipped around his back, and her legs clutched at the backs of his, pinning him to her. He raised his head to look into her impassive face.

"What?"

"I haven't pressed you these last few days, Yozef, but with a child coming, I think you've had time to think."

"Think?" he said in a futile attempt to feign ignorance.

"About what you're hiding from me."

*Christ! Talk about being ambushed. And not to mention the attempt to lay a guilt trip on me. Right after sex and knowing she's pregnant.*

She said nothing more but held him tight. He could have moved away, but, still connected as they were, his intuition told him this might be the best time, even if the position was unorthodox.

He kept stroking the side of her head and hair. "You're right. There are things that I've kept secret. Not because I wanted to, but because I thought it best."

"So you don't trust me enough."

He stared firmly into her eyes, their faces inches apart. "I trust you more than anyone I know, Maera. However, there are things I can't tell *anyone* right now, no matter how much I want to. Maybe someday, and if that day comes and there's only one person I can tell, it will be you. I know that's not the answers you wanted, and I wish more than you can know that it was different, but it's not. All I can ask is that you trust me."

She was silent for a minute, still clutching him, her eyes searching his face in the candlelight. Finally, she sighed, and her face softened. "You're right, it's not the answers I wanted, but God tells us in the *Word* not to expect answers to all our questions. While I won't pretend it doesn't bother me, it's something I believe I can live with." Her grip eased, her hands rubbed his back, and her heels ran along the backs of his thighs. "I don't pretend to understand you. Still, as different as you sometimes seem, I know you're honest and caring.

"You're still the mysterious Yozef Kolsko, even if people in Abersford and St. Sidryn's are accustomed to you. I suppose I have to accept there will always be things I don't understand. The *Word* also says a person is judged by his deeds, and you've given me no reason to judge you harshly."

Yozef sighed with relief. *I'm going to get away with it.*

"My people say, 'You know the tree by its fruit.'"

Maera laughed and gave him a playful tap on the cheek. "There you go again. Just when I'm being noble and understanding, you go and pull a phrase or a piece of knowledge out of the air."

"I'm sorry, I—"

She laughed again. "No! Don't apologize. It makes me feel like I've done something wrong and makes me wonder if I should have reacted differently."

"You react as comes naturally to you, Maera. All you have to do is be yourself. Maera Kolsko-Keelan is the only person I want you to be."

"Now you're trying to flatter me. It's working, but I'm afraid we'll have to uncouple. My legs are starting to cramp."

Yozef rolled to one side, keeping one arm under Maera. She stretched her legs, then turned to him, and they embraced, legs intertwined.

"I'll try to be patient, but this doesn't mean I'm not going to stay curious."
She poked him in the abdomen with a finger. "There isn't *anything* you can tell
me?"

"You don't find a contradiction in telling me you'll try to be patient and
then in the next breath asking a question?"

"Just this once?"

"All right, but I'm serious, Maera. This will be the last time until the day
comes when I believe I can tell you more."

She nodded eagerly.

"The secrets have to do with where my home was and how I got here.
They have nothing to do with any intentions for anything except the best for
Caedellium and its people. I know that doesn't tell you anything you didn't
already suspect, but that's the best I can do."

She hugged him tighter. "One thing to remember, Yozef, you *have* a home.
It's here with me, wherever we are, be it here in Abersford, in this house, in
bed with me, or wherever we're together."

# CHAPTER 23

# RAID

## Memas Erdelin

He pushed his horse up the inclined road, then reined in only momentarily before spurring again down into a wide valley. The twenty-man escort strove to keep up with their commander, who was a superb horseman and relished long, punishing rides. They would change exhausted horses in another six miles and continue to Hanslow, the Eywell Province capital. His men would have preferred making the sixty-mile trip from Preddi City in two days, but Erdelin wanted to get back to his headquarters as soon as possible. The Eywellese leaders had orders to meet with him in Hanslow at sundown.

As military commander of the Eywell Province, Colonel Memas Erdelin's main responsibility was maintaining Narthani control over the Eywellese Clan, the instrument of which were the three thousand troops under his command. In addition, he had the duty of training the Eywellese to serve as auxiliaries for the coming campaign against the other clans. The Eywellese would carry out large-scale, fast-moving raids and later act as light-cavalry screens and scouts for the main Narthani forces. Keeping control of the Eywellese was frustrating, because they had minimal concepts of coordinated actions in the field and chafed at following an operation plan's details. He thought perhaps half of their leaders, particularly the hetman, had some level of understanding; the other half were hopeless, including the hetman's eldest son.

The staff meeting in Preddi City had started before sunup and was the final session before the Eywellese carried out the first large-scale destructive raid into Moreland. He and Nuthrat Metan, his counterpart in the Selfcell Province, had been the main presenters at today's meeting. Metan's assignment was to feint at the Stentese north of Selfcell and carry out raids into the northern border with Moreland. Erdelin's assignment was to direct similar actions to the central and southern parts of their border with Moreland, plus feints toward Keelan and Gwillamer provinces in the south. The main action was also his responsibility, an aggressive 450-man raid on Moreland towns near the Eywell border.

After Erdelin and Metan gave their reports, the other Narthani leaders needed less time to summarize their parts in the operation: Colonel Erkan Ketin as the headquarters commander in charge of Preddi Province, plus supply and training issues concerning all of the 12,000 Narthani troops on Caedellium; Admiral Morefred Kalcan, who would keep the coastal clans' attention with sporadic coastal raids and repeated Narthani ship sightings all along the island's coasts; Assessor Sadek Hizer, on the latest intelligence on Moreland; and High Prelate Mamduk Balcan, reminding all of the others about the importance of converting the Caedelli to the worship of Narth. Although Erdelin thought the idea of any god was for deluded minds, Balcan had authority over religious matters, and even high-ranking military leaders had to be careful.

While General Akuyun commanded the mission on Caedellium, Brigadier Zulfa was the field commander and Erdelin's direct superior. Privately, Erdelin detested Zulfa and his perceived overweening pride at his descent from a higher caste tribe than Erdelin's. Even worse, Erdelin acknowledged that Zulfa was sufficiently competent to have Akuyun's approval. Thus, Erdelin tolerated Zulfa and strove to carry out his assignments in an exemplary manner. There was always the chance Zulfa would befall some misfortune and Erdelin could compete with Ketin and Metan for Zulfa's position. Such misfortunes were not uncommonly arranged by subordinates in the Narthani army, but the perpetrator had better be successful and clever. Erdelin wouldn't risk such a venture with Akuyun in overall command; the general wasn't a commander to be taken lightly.

How Commander Akuyun put up with coordinating the various demands on his role never ceased to amaze Erdelin. Somehow the meetings always ended with all parties thinking their input had been heard and acted on, even if it hadn't happened. Akuyun was a master at this, and Erdelin, if he had believed in Narth, would have given offerings in thanks for having Akuyun as the mission commander, especially after having served under far worse.

Still, listening to Zulfa, Balcan, and the others for too much of the three-hour meeting had put him on edge. He was grateful for the hard ride to get his mind ready for the meeting later with the Eywellese.

## Just Follow the Plan

Six hours later, Erdelin went over the Moreland raid plan with Brander Eywell, the Eywell hetman, his two sons, and several of his boyermen. They had reviewed the plan enough times to annoy the Eywellese, who assumed the Narthani didn't think them smart enough to remember the details, which was close to the truth. Erdelin was thankful the hetman himself would lead the raid, instead of the older son, an arrogant and stupid argument against oldest sons as automatic heirs to titles and responsibilities.

"Once again, Hetman," asserted Erdelin, "the raid needs to move fast and burn as much as possible. We want to test the Morelanders' speed of response to the raid without getting into any significant fights with them. Move through the countryside, burn as you move, and keep moving. The exceptions are the three towns of . . . ," Erdelin checked the map on the table they stood around, "Allenford, Lanwith, and Anglin. Don't spend more time at each town than necessary to burn it to the ground. Kill whomever you find, and be sure to keep scouts out to alert for any large Moreland forces.

"Those three towns are yours to loot. Take some of the younger women and smaller valuables, but only what time and speed of movement allow. Given the pace you've assured me you and your men can move, the entire raid should end by the evening of the second day. Are there any final questions?"

"No, Colonel Erdelin, I think we've gone over the plan enough times," said the Eywell hetman, with more than a little sarcasm in his heavily accented voice. Many of the Eywellese and the Selfcellese spoke passable Narthani after years of association, although most, including the hetman, had trouble forcing their native open and soft Caedelli into the guttural sounds of Narthani. The accent reminded Erdelin of Narthani children just learning to speak properly and reinforced the impression of the islanders' limited mental abilities.

"We don't believe the Morelanders will risk coming after you into your own territory, but just in case, I'm keeping a thousand of my men in Hanslow on alert to move toward the border, along with the five hundred men you have on standby."

After the Eywellese left to return to their staging encampment for the raid, Erdelin spoke with Captain Tunak, the Narthani officer assigned to accompany the Eywellese.

"Captain, your assignment on this raid doesn't include taking direct part in the action—unless absolutely necessary. You're to observe both the

Eywellese and the Morelanders as my eyes for a detailed account of the progress and results. You'll have fifty men with you, more for your protection than to be used against the Morelanders. The four hundred Eywellese should be more than enough for the raid, assuming they follow directions. Your other assignment is to remind the hetman what the objectives are and what they are not to do. You won't have overall command, as much as I wish you did, but try to keep the islanders from totally screwing up the plan."

Captain Tunak didn't look happy, nor did Erdelin blame him. The sooner they pacified the entire island, the sooner they could quit pretending any islander was an ally instead of the vassal they should be.

The raid was staged from Parthmal, a garrison town near the Moreland border, and they left an hour before dawn the next morning. Captain Tunak and his fifty men followed the Eywellese party.

## Crossing into Moreland

The raiding party crossed the border into Moreland Province as the sun first peeked from behind the western hills. The three targeted towns all lay within twelve to twenty miles of the border, and the raid would parallel that border and then duck back into Eywell territory after the third town.

A forward party of 300 horsemen pushed ahead over flat to rolling terrain to the outskirts of Allenford, twelve miles from the border. No scouts screened ahead to avoid alerting locals before the main body fell upon the town. Captain Tunak and 25 Narthani accompanied the main party. The remaining 100 Eywellese, 25 Narthani, 50 pack horses, and 5 wagons followed. Although this split the party, the roads and the terrain were clear enough that by the time the trailing group caught up, the sack of the town should be complete or nearly so. They would appropriate other wagons as needed and then move on to the next town. It was during the initial assault on Allenford when the plan started to unravel. A chance musket ball hit Brandor Eywell, a glancing strike along his side. While not immediately critical, it broke a rib, which threatened to puncture a lung. Brandor's two sons and Captain Tunak stood by when the medicants told the hetman he couldn't continue.

Brandor gasped from pain when two men helped him rise to a sitting position. "Biltin, the medicants say I can't continue, and I'm afraid I have to agree. Plus, there's the chance I might slow the rest of you down if I can't keep up. You'll have to continue without me."

Biltin Eywell smiled. *A chance to lead for most of the raid!* "Yes, Father. I can do it. Let the medicants take care of you."

"Remember the plan and stick to it. No changing anything. Listen to the senior men with you. They have experience and are along on the raid because of that. You must command but listen to them!"

Captain Tunak was anxious. This wasn't a contingency covered with him by Colonel Erdelin. He knew the colonel thought the father marginally reliable and didn't trust the sons. If this had happened before they reached Allensford, Tunak might have insisted they abort the raid. Now, they were committed . . . or were they? The Morelanders didn't know the original plan, so the Eywelleses could finish sacking Allenford and return, having partly completed the objectives. After weighing the factors and remembering Erdelin's reservations about the son, he made a decision and hoped his superior would later approve.

"Hetman Eywell, it would be best to finish here in Allensford and return to Eywell territory. The raid will have successfully shocked the Morelanders, so hitting the other two towns is not an absolute necessity."

Biltin Eywell flushed at the implied insult—that with the hetman incapacitated, he wasn't trusted to complete the raid. "Hetman Eywell's already decided," he bit off, scowling at the Narthani officer.

The hetman also scowled, at his son. He read into the Narthani's suggestion a lack of confidence in the son, one the hetman himself shared at times. What if Biltin showed himself incompetent? He didn't want the Narthani to lose confidence in the entire clan, due to actions of any one member, even if that person was his presumed heir. Yet this was their first major opportunity to strike at the hated Morelanders. For years, Brandor had pressed for stronger action against both Moreland and Keelan, but the Narthani had constrained them. He knew the Narthani didn't keep him fully informed of their plans, so who knew when another such opportunity would arise to pay back past indignities?

"No," he said finally, giving his son a stern look. "The raid will continue as planned."

Tunak had no further options. He didn't command the raid, and his fifty men couldn't force four hundred Eywellese to retire once their hetman decided to continue.

"As you wish, Hetman," Tunak said, "as long as the operation is carried out as ordered by Colonel Erdelin." The last words were accompanied by a look straight at the son.

Thus, when the sack of Allensford was completed, the raiding party continued under Biltin Eywell's command. Hetman Eywell returned to Hanslow in a wagon with a 25-man escort. In two hours, the Eywellese burned the entire town, killed more than 300 of its citizens, took 31 women prisoners, and filled 3 wagons with valuables. By mid-morning they were on the move again, this time toward Lanwith, the next target and twenty miles distant.

## Lanwith

It was a typical day for the 420 citizens of Lanwith, along with another 70 Morelanders living nearby or in town on various types of business. The earlier showers had passed, and clear skies to the southeast promised a sunny day.

Shopkeepers talked to customers, the abbey's only medicant tended a series of citizens with various complaints, and the abbey's school had been in session for more than three hours. A stern seventy-year-old Brother Skanston ruled the fifteen boys attending. Brother Skanston had tried in vain for decades to convince more of the boys' families to send their sons for education and attempted equally in vain to get permission for a few of the girls. Girls were a rarity in Moreland schools. He knew other clans, such as Keelan and Stent, paid more attention to education, but the Moreland Clan didn't value time spent away from farm, shop, and home.

As mayor of Lanwith, Dwelfin Camron spent entirely too much time dealing with minutiae—or so he told himself—ever since being appointed to the post by Hetman Moreland fourteen years ago. His wife knew better. Daily involvement in numerous community issues was her husband's greatest pleasure. Whether because he enjoyed the feeling of authority it gave, or because he truly was conscientious about the people of Lanwith, even his wife was never sure. Either way, he performed well enough that the position had remained Dwelfin's these many years. His tenure was about to end.

Twelve-year-old Mylin Naernwill brought water to his father and two older brothers working in their farm's wheat field. They were a mile from the edge of Lanwith and had been at work before sunrise. Although farming was constant hard work, it was the only life Mylin knew, and he couldn't imagine any other. Everyone in the family knew that one day Mylin would leave to start his own farm. The eldest brother would inherit the family farm, once the father died, and would be obligated to help Mylin and the middle brother in starting out on their own. His mother and two sisters, one older and one younger than Mylin, were at the farmhouse doing what women do while men did what men did. His older brother would never inherit the farm.

Tilda Purcells hadn't needed to come to Lanwith that day. The real purpose of the trip was to get her niece Anarynd Moreland out and about for a few hours. Tilda's oldest sister, Anarynd's mother, Gwenda, was far too timid, as far as Tilda was concerned. Tilda wished that Gwenda asserted herself more. Men might be ordained by God to be the head of the family, but that didn't mean women didn't have the right to respect and their opinions listened to. Of course, being fair to her sister, Tilda had to admit it was easy to give advice since she wasn't married to Brym Moreland and didn't have to deal with that ass every day. Tilda never forgot to give thanksgiving at Godsday services for her own husband. Of the four sisters in the family, Tilda considered herself the most fortunate in husbands, although her sister Glynas's husband, Balamus, compared well.

The current discord in Gwenda's family originated from Anarynd's refusal several months previously to be courted by the oldest son of an elderly boyerman, the son a widower with two daughters. While Brym thought the marriage would be advantageous to the family, Anarynd took one look at the squat, snaggle-toothed, balding man of forty-six years and walked out of the first meeting arranged by Brym, who had predictably exploded at Anarynd after making profuse apologies to the would-be suitor.

Relations between father and daughter had never been warm, and when Brym retaliated by refusing Anarynd permission to attend Maera's wedding, the ensuing screaming match between both parties reverberated throughout the family. Anarynd hadn't spoken to her father for several months and swore she never would again.

It had been Glynas who convinced Anarynd to meet the latest potential suitor in the vain hope of improving family relations. Surprising all, including Anarynd, was that the young man who visited was pleasant and earnest. Not the husband of her dreams, but she was tired to the bone of being shopped around by her father. Harwyn Moreland was a distant cousin, third or fourth removed, and the second son of a boyerman of an eastern Moreland district. The eldest son had been married to two women during a ten-year period, and neither marriage had produced a child. Thus, it was likely the second son or one of his sons would eventually become boyerman. The district was prosperous and Harwyn's family wealthy in lands and herds, so a marriage promised significant coin and animal stock to Brym Moreland.

Anarynd's ability to refuse numerous potential husbands was as far as she could go. She'd known she'd have to eventually accept one of them, and whether it was Harwyn himself who convinced her or her weariness of the process and family tension, even she wasn't sure. While nothing was official yet, Anarynd told Harwyn privately that she was favorably inclined. A visit to Harwyn's family was arranged, and, if it went well, Anarynd foresaw a marriage within a few months, one where she would be out of her father's control, and Maera would be there.

It had taken extensive persuasion for Brym to allow Anarynd to accompany her aunt to Lanwith. Tilda's argument was that keeping the girl cooped up wouldn't improve their relationship, and now that the girl seemed favorably inclined to a marriage, it would be smart of Brym to relax how sternly he treated her.

Anarynd had become surprisingly strong-willed the last few years, a development Brym blamed on the influence of that damned Keelan daughter. He'd never approved of the friendship between the two young girls. However, even with long-standing animosity between Moreland and Keelan, it hadn't been feasible to prevent their communications and yearly visits. After all, a hetman was still a hetman, even if from a despised clan.

Tilda and Anarynd arrived in Lanwith by carriage just before noon. They left the driver with the carriage and strolled through the town, browsing the shops and the stalls. Maybe Anarynd would find something Tilda could buy her to improve her mood. It was a kind and thoughtful invitation by a concerned aunt—but a fateful invitation.

The Naernwill farm was the closest to Lanwith and in the path of the Eywellese. The terrain between Allensford and Lanwith discouraged farming, and the Eywellese moved too fast for warnings to reach Lanwith. Mylin was the first to notice something out of the ordinary.

"Look, Father. What's that? A storm coming?"

The father looked up to see a dust cloud rising from behind a hill on the road that ran next to the farm. There was no wind. The four of them stared, as the cloud grew. Only when the first riders appeared over the crest of the hill a half-mile away did he recognize a large body of riders moving fast. He had a bad feeling and ordered his sons to run back to the farmhouse.

Mylin didn't understand what was happening, only that his father and his brothers were grim and his mother and sisters frightened. He protested at first when his father told him to take his six-year-old sister into the brush fifty yards behind the house, as a precaution. Mylin grabbed his crying sister, and they ran into the brush and lay down, with Mylin peeking back toward the house.

By now, an endless stream of riders poured over the hills. As the lead riders passed the edge of their land a hundred yards away, a dozen riders peeled off the main body and galloped toward the house. Mylin could hear his father yell.

Everyone ran for the woods east of the house. His father and brothers carried muskets. His father stopped and fired at the lead riders, one of whom pitched backward out of his saddle. His father was reloading when a rider passed him, swung a sword, and suddenly his father lay on the ground. None of the family reached the woods. Both brothers fell. His mother and his older sister were knocked off their feet. Men leaped from their horses to tie the hands of both. Several men talked for a moment, then one drew a knife and ran it over his mother's throat. His sister screamed and sagged. The men tied her feet, threw her on the back of another rider's saddle, and rode to the column of riders. Several other men came out of the house carrying family possessions, then the first flames followed.

Mylin kept still. His family had run *away* from where he and his sister hid, to draw the men away. His mind froze with what he'd witnessed. In less than three minutes his entire world had died, except for the little girl whose head he hugged against his body, so she hadn't seen what had transpired. The last he'd seen of his other sister was her being unceremoniously tossed from the saddle into a wagon at the column's end.

Dwelfin Camron's first hint of anything out of the ordinary was when he heard shouting in the street. He walked to the door of the mayor's office, a small room attached to his leather-making shop. He didn't immediately recognize the man shouting and pointing to the south end of Lanwith's main street. Others also shouted and ran.

*What? What's going on?* Then he thought he heard the word *Eywell. Eywell?*

"Dwelfin!" shouted one of his workers. "He says it's the Eywellese! Hundreds of them! Coming fast behind him!"

Camron stood shocked for several seconds. *Eywellese? Eywellese!! Oh, my Merciful God! Are they attacking here!* There had been unspecific reports from Moreland City to be on alert for any sightings of Eywellese or Narthani, but nothing like this! On occasion, he had thought perhaps the town should make some plans in case of serious threats, then something else always seemed more urgent than vague threats about something the likes of which hadn't happened in Moreland Province for generations.

The street turned into a chaotic churning of people, running from shops, running to shops, running to look for relatives, or running nowhere specific because they didn't know what else to do. Camron and his family—himself, his wife, and their last child—lived behind the shop. The others lived elsewhere in Lanwith or outside the town. Mayor or not, he thought first of his family and ran around the shop to their house. His wife had just come out the door, her look questioning the uproar, when he yelled, "Into the root cellar!" When she didn't immediately respond, he shoved her roughly back into the house. "It's the Eywellese! We have to hide!" They pulled a rug off the cover to the root cellar under the kitchen. His wife climbed down the ladder, then he handed her their seven-year-old daughter and followed down the steps. He draped the rug over the cellar cover, then lowered it, trying to arrange it so that when he finished lowering the cover, folds in the rug didn't give away their hiding place.

Brother Skanston moved from one cluster of boys to another. The boys within each cluster were at approximately the same stage in their education. With the boys' ages from six to eleven and years of classroom from their first to sixth, there were no common lessons except for readings and lessons from the *Word*. Within each group, an older boy helped the younger ones. The abbey lay too far from town to hear the chaos that erupted with the rider bringing the warning, yet although the town had not begun emergency preparations, the abbey had kept aware of ongoing events and cautions shared among abbeys over most of Caedellium. The few brothers and sisters in the Lanwith abbey had discussed the only two priorities they saw as important. One was to protect any patients or students within the abbey, and second, to save what they could of the abbey's library, especially the older and irreplaceable volumes.

By chance, a brother had started cleaning the abbey bell tower when he heard musket fire from the town. Heavy musket fire. From the hilltop where the abbey sat and higher yet from the bell tower, he saw a mass of horsemen flowing into the town from the south, with another group circling to the north end of the town. While his vision was becoming progressively worse with close objects, his distant vision was still intact. He saw people fleeing on horseback, in wagons, and on foot in all directions, some being ridden down by riders with lances and swords.

By pre-arrangement, he struck the single gong in the tower. No one knew why the abbey bell tower had a gong, the origin lost in the abbey's past. Since it was otherwise not used, it became the signal to implement the emergency plan. Discipline took over. The abbey staff and everyone within the building moved to assigned emergency tasks: taking books to the deep cellars under the abbey, where they would be safe even if the abbey burned to the ground; bringing wagons to load patients; and Brother Skanston taking any students out the side gate, past the vegetable garden, and into dense reeds along the nearby stream. Only the last effort proved fully successful, although, of the fifteen students, eleven would be orphans by sunset.

Tilda Purcells and Anarynd Moreland exchanged opinions on which scarves best matched Anarynd's dress of several blue shades she thought went well with her blonde hair and fair complexion. Tilda was in her late thirties, a mother of five, and as lively as her sister Gwenda was not. The two women had laughingly discussed which scarf would most annoy Anarynd's father, when suddenly shouting started. The shopkeeper went outside while they continued browsing, only to return moments later, screaming, "It's the Eywellese coming! Run!"

The shopkeeper ran out the back. Tilda grabbed Anarynd's hand and rushed outside to the street chaos and the first sounds of musket fire.

"Quick! To the carriage!" They ran the hundred yards to find their driver nowhere to be seen. "Get in!" Tilda shrieked. She pulled up her skirt and climbed into the driver's box. Anarynd had barely gotten into the passenger compartment when, with a yell and a crack of the whip, the carriage lurched forward. Anarynd fell onto the floor of the carriage, then righted herself as they raced in the opposite direction from musket fire. Tilda was experienced in driving horses, though not at the speed they were going, and she lost control of the horses.

They tore past buildings and had just cleared the town when a line of horsemen closed the road ahead. Tilda strained to rein in, but the horses couldn't be stopped until horsemen rode parallel to the carriage and grabbed their bridles. Eywellese men quickly pulled Tilda from the driver's box and Anarynd from the carriage. An animated conversation among the Eywellese lasted several seconds, interspersed with hands running over the women's bodies. After more exchanges, both women were tied hand and foot and thrown across horses, and all they could see from then on was the ground as they bounced on their stomachs. They heard continuing musket fire, screams, and shouts of Eywellese. The horses stopped. The women were dumped first onto the ground, then picked up by their feet and shoulders and tossed onto a wagon bed.

Anarynd jolted when her head hit wood. She was dazed for a moment, then could see a dozen or more women in the wagon, including Aunt Tilda. All were stoic, shocked, or crying.

# CHAPTER 24

# AWRY

**Lanwith, Moreland Province**

Captain Tunak worried after the hetman gave command of the raid to his son Biltin. The concern was assuaged by the speed at which the Eywellese finished with the first town by mid-morning and moved on to Lanwith.

En route, parties broke off to burn farms and a few villages, though the general advance kept pace with the schedule. Similarly, the assault on Lanwith seemed satisfying, until he saw Eywellese herding several score bound Morelanders toward the town square. Captain Tunak followed and cursed when he found thirty Eywellese guarding more than a hundred prisoners. Instead of limiting captives to a few younger women, the huddled prisoners included many children and older women. Also moving through the street were local wagons being piled with loot from businesses and homes.

He found Biltin Eywell lounging on a chair in front of what he assumed was the town's central authority building. Biltin drank from a leather flagon, and from the red stain around the hetman's son's mouth, Tunak knew he wasn't drinking water. The Eywell leader laughed with several younger Eywellese, while older leaders stood farther away, frowning and shaking their heads.

Biltin's good humor vanished with Tunak's approach. He said something in Caedelli to his companions and nodded in Tunak's direction. Whatever the son said elicited snickers from the group.

"Commander," Tunak said, addressing Biltin. The word wanted to catch in his throat, and he had to remind himself he needed to be as cordial as possible, even if he thought the hetman's son could hardly lead himself to an outhouse. "Why are your men taking time to loot and why so many prisoners? The plan is specifically to move fast. We should already be finishing up here and moving on to the final town."

Biltin discounted Tunak's questions with a dismissive hand wave. "Everything is going to plan. Even after Allensford, we completely surprised Lanwith, and we'll do the same to Anglin. I see no reason to burn what we can take back with us, and there are plenty of prisoners we can use as slaves ourselves or sell off-island. Why waste it all for no reason?"

"Delaying here gives the Morelanders time to alert Anglin and gather enough men to force a battle, something we've been directly ordered to avoid."

"I've seen no sign the Morelanders will do anything in time to stop us, and if they try it, my men will cut through them like a newly sharpened knife through soft cheese."

The bravado brought worried looks from the older and more senior Eywellese. They were neither as sure as Biltin of the Morelanders' response, nor as comfortable with not following Narthani orders.

His *men? My, hasn't he become full of himself?* Tunak pondered. *Now what do I do?* Tunak wasn't in charge, and he didn't have enough rank or men to order the Eywellese.

"I must strongly remind you of Colonel Erdelin's orders and your father's instructions to follow those orders."

Biltin flushed angrily. "*I'm* in command of this raid, and everything is proceeding fine. You worry like an old woman." With those words, Biltin turned away from Tunak, implicitly dismissing the Narthani officer.

Tunak grated his teeth, as he walked back to his horse and his men.

## Anger All Around

When Erdelin watched the Eywellese leave after the final meeting, he debated with himself where to be during the raid into Moreland: stay at his headquarters in Hanslow, the Eywell capital, or go with the Eywellese to the staging encampment near Parthmal, five miles from the Eywell-Moreland border? He had moderate confidence in Hetman Eywell, but one never knew what might go wrong. He finally stayed in Hanslow, leaving orders to keep him apprised of when the raiding party returned. The raid would commence the next morning and was scheduled to be completed by the evening of the next day, so he should hear word by the third morning at the latest.

By noon of the expected day, there had been no word, and he sensed something was wrong. He dispatched riders to Parthmal for an update. One rider returned that evening, having ridden the twenty miles and back in six hours. The raiding party hadn't yet returned, but several wagons of prisoners and loot had arrived late the day before, evidently from Lanwith, the second of the three target towns. The second piece of news was that Hetman Eywell had been wounded during the Allensford attack and had passed command to his son Biltin. Erdelin's insides tightened at these two pieces of news, sure they were closely related. Erdelin had to go forward to assess for himself what was happening and hoped a disaster wasn't underway.

By first light the next morning, Erdelin was riding hard with a hundred men for the launch encampment. They arrived at midmorning to still no news of the raiding party. Erdelin went immediately to confront Hetman Eywell, only to find him abed in considerable pain and only partly coherent, due to poppy extract given for the pain. Erdelin stomped out of the hetman's tent in a foul mood, with nowhere to vent.

What was going on across the border?

The sun hung a hand's breadth from the skyline that late afternoon, when a party of five Eywellese riders crossed the border with news that the main party was less than a half-hour behind. Brandor Eywell was more alert by then, though had no more news of what caused the delay than did Erdelin. The hetman was less arrogant than usual, also worried at the delay.

Erdelin stood watching to the east when Captain Tunak and forty-two riders, several with minor wounds, galloped into camp ahead of the Eywellese column. Erdelin's experienced eye automatically saw fewer Narthani troops than had started, and his lips tightened.

Tunak said something to two men riding beside him and left the group to head straight for Erdelin's banner. He reined in, dismounted, and gave his lathered horse to a trooper.

Erdelin noted that the captain's face indicated news would be bad, and the captain was nervous.

"Where's the rest of your men, Captain?"

"Sir, we have four dead and four more wounded in wagons coming up with the Eywellese."

"How many Eywellese casualties are there?" Erdelin asked, the sinking feeling increasing.

"I estimate forty dead and sixty wounded."

*Great Narth! That's a quarter of the raid's strength!*

"How did that happen, and why are you back in three days, instead of two at the latest as planned?"

Tunak looked as if he'd bitten into something unbelievably sour. "It was the hetman's son, Biltin. Once the hetman was wounded, I recommended terminating the raid. The first town had gone as planned, so the raid still would have achieved a partial success. The hetman decided to continue and appointed his son as the new commander."

"Can I assume you reminded both of them of the mission's objectives and details of the plan?"

"Yes, Colonel. *Several* times. We moved on to the second town, Lanwith, right on schedule. That is where it started falling apart. Biltin decided the Morelanders were caught so unaware that they needn't rush. They spent the rest of the day sacking Lanwith, filling wagons with everything from valuables to trivial trinkets, and getting drunk. They also took more prisoners than planned. Perhaps a hundred from Lanwith and nearby farms."

Tunak shook his head in disgust. "He wouldn't listen, the arrogant ass. We finally left Lanwith the next morning. By this time there were no surprises for the Morelanders. We didn't see a single islander until we approached Anglin. From a half-mile away we could see them throwing up barricades and people running everywhere. There was no way we could take the town without significant casualties and more time than I thought we had.

"Although I again advised we pull back into Eywell territory, Biltin was determined to sack all three towns, ignoring that there were other objectives, such as not getting into major fights. At first, he sent the men straight at the town with no real plan. That first attack took many casualties before pulling back out of musket range. Then he tried sending men into the town on foot at different places. They took more casualties, though did gain a foothold by late afternoon, until one of the few lookouts Biltin had thought to post spotted horsemen approaching from the east. It looked to me like sixty to eighty riders, and we had no idea if there were more on the way. I finally convinced Biltin to withdraw only by pointing out that if we got into a real fight, he'd have to abandon the wagons of booty and prisoners. That finally got through to him."

"What happened on the way back?"

"By the time we got back to the border, we had a hundred or more Morelanders sniping at us from all sides. There weren't enough to stop us, but a large mass of horsemen closed in on us at the end. I suspect a few more miles, and we could have found ourselves badly outnumbered."

Tunak stiffened and looked straight at Erdelin. "My apologies, Colonel. I failed to keep the Eywellese adhering to the plan."

Erdelin had been watching the bedraggled-looking Eywellese horse column passing by and the disgustingly long series of wagons that followed. At the captain's assumption of responsibility, Erdelin looked back at him. "No apologies needed, Captain. I doubt if there was anything anyone in your situation could have done different, including myself. See to your men."

Erdelin went looking for Biltin Eywell. He couldn't let this pass.

He found Biltin in his father's tent. The hetman was looking better than earlier, but with evident apprehension when Erdelin stormed through the tent flap.

"Colonel Erdelin, I—" Biltin started to say.

"What exactly in the *orders* did you not understand, Eywell?!" Erdelin barked out at the son. There was no pretense who was in charge and no use of titles. "This was to be a single quick raid into Moreland, destroy three towns, minimal looting, a few women prisoners, avoid battles if possible, and be back by the evening of the second day." Erdelin's voice rose as he talked, more accurately matching his temper.

"Instead, you take *three* days and come back with a quarter of your men casualties—including some of my Narthani troops—from having to fight the Morelanders once you gave them warning! That also meant you failed to destroy the third town! I see wagons full of loot and prisoners of all ages, again, contrary to *orders!*" Erdelin's voice was clearly audible by now to anyone within a hundred yards. He targeted the son to avoid forcing the hetman to say anything or take action to protect his own position among his clansmen. The Narthani needed the hetman and his family, for now, but needed them obeying orders.

Biltin's face was a deep red, whether from anger, embarrassment, or anything else Erdelin didn't know or care. Biltin started to yell back at Erdelin when his father said, "Shut up, you idiot!"

The hetman shifted his position on the bed, wincing from his wound. "You are correct, Colonel. My son ignored yours and my instructions on how this raid was to be carried out. I assure you that had I been able to lead the raid, there would have been no such deviations."

Erdelin forced his tone down to a more respectful level to address the hetman. "Hetman Eywell, of that I've no doubt. We've always worked well together. However, I must tell you that the evident inability of your men to keep discipline during the mission disturbs me, and I assure you that General

Akuyun and Assessor Hizer will also take note of this incident. I trust that there will be no repetition of such actions?"

"I assure you, Colonel Erdelin, I'll see to it."

Erdelin let himself appear somewhat appeased. "See that you do, Hetman. I'll expect a detailed written report from your son on his decisions and independent reports from your senior men on the raid. Captain Tunak will be doing the same. I expect the major details to agree, but I also want to see observations on the Morelanders' responses when surprised and after being alerted by your son. Also details on how the Morelanders performed in the fighting, their weapons, and anything else relevant. I'll prepare a consolidated report to send on to General Akuyun."

Without further formalities, Erdelin spun and started out of the tent. As he raised the flap to leave, he stopped, turned back again, and said casually, "Oh, and since the prisoners and loot were contrary to orders, naturally Eywell can't keep either. I'll take possession of them in the name of the Narthon Empire." Without waiting for a response, he walked out, letting the flap go.

"Father, I—" started Biltin, only to be cut off.

"As I said in Erdelin's presence, you're a complete idiot! All you had to do was follow orders. We'd finished sacking Allenford when I was hurt. You couldn't even follow orders for a few more hours?" The hetman's low growl kept those outside from hearing, but his tone was deadly and finally got through to Biltin that he could be in serious trouble. Brandor Eywell ruled his clan with an iron fist, and it was a brave or exceedingly foolish man who crossed him, son or not.

"The Narthani are going to take the entire island and absorb it into their empire. The only way our family and clan will survive is to prove useful to them. It's even possible that if we impress them enough, we could end up in charge of most, or even all, of Caedellium. But they have to believe they can rely on us. What you did on this raid jeopardizes those chances. I don't want to die knowing our family and clan will disappear. I certainly can't have an heir who risks the future of the clan by acting stupidly. If it's not you, remember I have another son and many nephews."

The implied threat chilled Biltin to the bone. He knew his father and had no doubt the threat was real.

## Hetman Moreland

Gynfor Moreland rode at the head of three hundred riders into Anglin. They had passed through the remains of Lanwith and forged on without stopping to help with the injured or put out fires still burning. The hetman hoped to catch the raiders before they destroyed Anglin or more of his province. They were late again but found the local countryside had enough warning and time to gather men at Anglin. After several attempts to force the town, the Eywellese had retired back toward the border.

Hetman Moreland seethed, as he led the Moreland pursuers to the Eywell-Moreland border, the dust of the raiders still hanging in the air. They crossed the border and less than a mile later ran into the first Eywellese sentries, who then retreated and obviously sent word of the Moreland pursuers. When they crested a hill three miles from the Parthmal, they could see what appeared to be many hundreds of Eywellese and as many Narthani riders, along with more on foot, forming up and facing them. Badly outnumbered and no longer on Moreland land, the Morelanders turned back, Gynfor Moreland swearing he would have his revenge on both the Eywellese and the Narthani.

## Anarynd

Erdelin gave orders to his subordinates, and the Narthani started the twenty-two-mile trip back to his headquarters in Hanslow. The wagons of loot from the raid he had no plans for; his staff would see it was portioned out to their troops in Eywell Province or sent on to Preddi City. For the prisoners, there were different fates. Senior officers would have first choice, then officials in charge of the Narthani troop brothels would choose enough of the women to bring staffing to recommended levels and a few extras. There were always those who never accepted their fates and fought to the death, committed suicide, or just died. The extras would ensure that staffing levels stayed acceptable for many months. By the time more women were needed, there might be supplies from other clan provinces. The rest of the slaves would be sent on to Preddi City to either be distributed where needed and useful within the Preddi civilian occupied areas or be shipped back to Narthon.

As soon as they arrived in Hanslow, soldiers pulled the captives from the wagons and herded them into a corral. Captain Tunak had underestimated.

There were more than two hundred Morelanders from the two sacked towns, villages, and farms, all women and children.

The sight of the Moreland captives reminded Erdelin that he needed a replacement woman. His latest slave had displeased him once too often with her sullen moods. Moreover, he'd had her for eight months, and she hadn't gotten pregnant, meaning he wouldn't have considered taking her with him when he rotated back to Narthon. A sixday previously he'd had her taken, sobbing, by one of his guards to a troop brothel. If she couldn't serve him adequately, let her see how it was to service fifteen to twenty men a day.

Erdelin strode quickly among the captives, ignoring children and older women. No one in particular caught his fancy. Two of his officers pulled out women. One of the officers was Captain Tunak. He was young for such a privilege, but he performed well, given the situation he found himself in, and Erdelin wanted Tunak and the other men to recognize his approval of the captain's performance.

Halfway around the corral, a woman caught Erdelin's eye. She was striking. Long blonde hair in disarray and hanging to her waist. He caught a glimpse of blue eyes that otherwise stayed downcast, as appropriate for a Narthani slave. The blonde color was found in the Caedelli, though rarely with the Narthani. Tear tracks streaked her face, but she wasn't crying or wailing like many of the others. Erdelin took that to indicate a sterner mettle. He pointed her out to the leader of the guards, who looped a noose over her head and handed her off to one of Erdelin's aides. He didn't see her again until reaching Hanslow and his villa. There, several staff members came running out. A Narthani soldier took his horse, and Erdelin's chief house slave led the blonde woman into the house.

Anarynd couldn't understand what the Narthani leader said to the middle-aged slave who held the rope around her neck. After an exchange, the slave led her into a room with basins, ewers, and cloths. The leader stood watching her, while the older man hustled away, then returned shortly with two slave women, one older with graying hair and the other younger. Both kept their eyes downcast. The leader gave obvious instructions to the women, and the men left, while the woman undressed Anarynd and cleaned her using warm water, bars of soap, and cloths. When they finished, they wrapped a white cloth around her and pulled her by her arms to a room where the leader sat at a desk, examining papers. The three of them stood in front of his desk while he worked. After a minute, he wrote something on a piece of paper, placed it to one side, and looked up. He spoke to the younger woman, who then translated to Anarynd.

"You no longer have a name. You'll be called 'Slave.' If you please your new master, he may someday give you a name. He commands me to tell you to do whatever you can to please him. Your previous life and name are gone forever. Your only purpose is to please him, in bed or any other way he wants."

The woman's voice softened. "Do it, girl. No matter what it is, it'll be far better than being condemned to the brothels. If you please him enough, he may even keep you when he goes back to Narthon. Forget about home. It's gone forever. Even if you escaped, would your family and clan take you back? They took me in Preddi three years ago. It hasn't been the life I wanted, but it *is* life. If you want to survive and stay sane, do as I say."

The woman squeezed Anarynd's arm, gave her a sympathetic smile, and then spoke to Erdelin. With a curt word, he dismissed the two women. The man rose and walked to her. She trembled when he pulled the cloth from her, then motioned her to the bed at the corner of the room. When she hesitated, he slapped her smartly across one cheek—not enough to knock her down, but enough to sting and obviously merely a warning. She put a hand to her face and walked toward the bed.

As she passed him, he stroked her buttocks, then followed with his hand on her back. She lay on the bed and tried to steel herself for what was to come. She wasn't a virgin, but her few experiences were furtive youth's experiments. Part of her wanted to scream and cry; another part wanted to fight; another wondered whether she should or could take her own life. However, the *Word* forbade suicide. Could she endure what was to come, as the sympathetic younger woman had advised?

What would Maera do? She would be strong, Anarynd knew. Maera would do what she had to survive and would look for a chance to escape. She imagined Maera hugging her and asking her to be brave.

She looked at the face of her new master, smiling with a confidence that conveyed dominance over her. He pulled his robe over his head and stood naked by the bed. His swarthy complexion and body hair gave him an animal-like look.

Anarynd would spend many years trying to forget that night. It wasn't just that he hurt her, it was his laughter while doing it. Never saying a word, just grunting and laughing as her face pressed against the hair on his chest. When he finished, he left her on the bed, curled into a ball but not crying, because she swore to herself she wouldn't give him the satisfaction.

## Word Reaches Maera

Maera was annoyed that Ana's latest letter was two sixdays overdue. Not that she blamed Ana. The delivery of letters wasn't on a reliable schedule. Plus, Ana on occasion forgot or delayed writing for a sixday—and on rarer occasions more than one. Maera knew her own punctual writing reflected her orderliness, which she didn't expect of others, or so she told herself. Still, Maera *so* looked forward to the letters. The recent exchanges had increasingly focused on Ana's possible marriage and plans for Maera to come early to help with the preparations and be with her friend. Fortunately, the wedding would be at the groom's family's house, so Brym Moreland couldn't stop Maera from attending.

By the third sixday without a letter, Maera alternated between irritation and concern. Her pregnancy only accentuated her worry. Her mother had warned her that mood changes would come and go instantly, especially in the early months. Maera's concern changed to alarm when a letter from her father mentioned a fast and hard-hitting Eywellese raid into Moreland Province. Especially hard hit were the towns of Allensford and Lanwith. Her heart skipped a beat as she read the locations. Ana's family lived not far to the east of both towns. Surely, the aftermath of the raid was interrupting letter movement, and Ana was fine . . . wasn't she?

That evening Maera explained her worry to Yozef.

"I'm sure she's fine. It's just the raid and letters stopping at the same time that worries me."

"Why not write to your father and have him inquire to the Moreland hetman?" suggested Yozef.

Maera winced. "Gynfor Moreland and Father have never been on good terms. Gynfor hates Father, and Father barely tolerates him at clan meetings. Father has so much to worry about I don't want to bother him, though he'd contact Gynfor if I asked."

"That's part of his role as a father. Don't worry. I'm writing a letter to him, so I'll just add concern about Anarynd and ask him myself. I also have several soap and paper franchises in Moreland. I'll write Factor Molin Gilmore, my agent in Moreland, and ask him for any information."

Maera breathed easier and gave her husband a wan smile. "Thank you, Yozef. I'm sure it's nothing, though I'll feel better having it confirmed."

As a result, Culich sent a semaphore message to Hetman Moreland, asking, as a favor, if he would confirm the status of his distant relative Anarynd Moreland. No answer came back for more than a sixday and then only a vague statement that he would look into it when he found the time away from all of his other pressing matters.

A sixday later Yozef received a semaphore message from his factor in Moreland City, the province's capital. The factor had personally gone to Anarynd's family. The news the factor summarized in the semaphore message was followed up with a detailed letter two days later. Yozef waited for the letter before talking with Maera.

After reading the letter, Yozef left the Bank of Abersford, where Cadwulf was giving him a monthly verbal report, and went straight home. He dreaded relaying the news, though he thought it best to let Maera know as soon as possible.

She was standing on the veranda when he walked up to the house.

"You're home early," she said questioningly. She had been working and resting at home that day.

"Let's go inside," he said grimly.

Maera's good mood vanished. He took her arm and guided her indoors. She looked at his face for a hint of what was happening. They sat on a wide sofa-like piece of furniture. He held her hands in his.

"I'm afraid it's not good news, Maera. I've heard from my factor in Moreland City. He went to Anarynd's family. Her father and others wouldn't talk to him, but a younger brother and an aunt confirmed that Anarynd had been in Lanwith when the Eywellese raided it."

Maera's grip on his hands tightened and she paled. "Is she . . . dead?"

"She's been missing since the raid. She was in the town with her aunt, a Tilda Purcells-Moreland, sister of her mother. They went to do some shopping, some of which was in preparation for Anarynd's wedding. Neither of them has been seen since, and their bodies weren't identified. One survivor believes he saw a young woman who looked like Anarynd being taken prisoner and put into a wagon."

Maera said nothing at first, then . . . , "Any possibility the reports are wrong?"

"It doesn't seem likely. The factor said Anarynd's family is convinced she was taken prisoner, and that from what he could find out in Lanwith, it makes it seem likely to be true."

Maera again was quiet for several minutes.

"Maera, I'm so sorry. I know how much Anarynd means to you."

She knew he was trying to be kind, but no . . . he didn't know what Ana meant to her. The only person she had ever truly felt she was just herself was with Anarynd . . . until Yozef came along. A prisoner of the Eywellese or the Narthani? No, not a prisoner. A *slave*, if all they'd heard was true. And for a young woman who looked like Ana, there was only one use they'd have for her.

*Oh, Merciful God! ARE you merciful? How could you let something like this happen to someone like Ana? To me!*

Maera rose and walked outside. Yozef held out a hand to her. She grasped it with one hand firmly, then patted it gently and pushed it away as she left the house. He took it to mean she wanted to be alone and granted her wish. She sat on the veranda for two hours. Yozef checked on her several times. Finally, she came inside and went straight to their bedroom. He waited a few minutes and then followed. She was in bed, under the covers. He undressed and lay next to her, not touching. After a few minutes, she turned to him, buried her face in his chest, and sobbed . . ., never saying a word. She finally stopped and fell asleep, still tight against him. He held her until he, too, fell asleep.

When Maera woke the next morning, there was a moment of confusion. She was awake, but there was something wrong. Then the news of the previous evening washed over her again. Tears came to her eyes; however, she didn't cry. Crying was over. Anarynd was gone. The thought was a hole in her chest, and there was nothing she could do. "Maera Kolsko-Keelan" was back in charge. She had responsibilities—her husband, the child on the way, duties to the clan and her new community. Life would be good, but it would never be the same.

# CHAPTER 25

# WHAT IF?

### Cannon and Ammunition

Yozef was sensitive to supporting Maera, as she dealt with the news about Anarynd. Neither of them mentioned her name, though he never doubted what was constantly on Maera's mind, especially when he found her staring off into the distance or clinging to him longer than before when they embraced. As sixdays passed, then a month, Yozef saw her slowly returning to her former self, at least outwardly.

Anarynd's fate reinvigorated Yozef's thinking about the Narthani, something that had seemed less urgent as he became absorbed with Maera, their marriage, the child-to-be, and all the adjustments that followed. Now the worries for the future came back with a vengeance, prompted by memories of the raid on St. Sidryn's, the Narthani, his talks with Culich, and the implications of the Moreland raid.

What if the Narthani attacked Keelan? Every intuition pointed to cataclysmic events to come. If the worst came, what could he do to help protect Maera, the child, himself, and all the Caedelli? The question and the search for answers felt overwhelming, and when he tried to focus on what was doable, his first thoughts returned to their failure with cannon. After months of effort, the foundry still hadn't succeeded casting a functional 6-pounder barrel.

*Christ, I wished I'd read more about early weapons technology so I could dredge up out of my new memory how to make a damn cannon barrel.*

Yozef and the foundry workers stared in disgust at the 6-pounder barrel that peeled back from the opening, the jagged bronze splayed like petals of an opening bud.

"Sorry, Yozef," said the foreman. "I thought this one would work. The barrel was as straight as we can make them, and the first five shots were successful. Obviously, we're missing something important in scaling up from the swivel guns to longer and thicker barrels."

"I know," said Yozef, "and we weren't even up to a full powder charge yet. I'm afraid I'm out of ideas. I'd hoped you and your men could figure out the problem by trial and error. I think we have to admit we're stymied for the moment and give up on the bigger cannon and stick to producing more of the swivels."

Their failure was both discouraging and ominous. An escaped Preddi slave described what to Yozef sounded like a Narthani field cannon in the 9- to 12-pounder size. He'd hoped they'd be smaller, since 12-pounder cannon had been the mainstay of armies on Earth from the Napoleonic era to the U.S. Civil War, a hundred years later than the approximately early 1700s he associated with Anyar technology.

He wondered whether the mainland wars here had gone on so long and been so intensive, it had accelerated military science. He remembered how the U.S. Civil War led to innovations that revolutionized warfare: ironclad warships, repeating rifles, the use of railways to move armies, military telegraph lines, ambulance corps, balloons for reconnaissance, and Gatling guns.

He stared longer at the ruined barrel. *Even if we make 6-pounders, the islanders will still be outgunned.*

The carriages with two or three swivel barrels would be useless against real cannon, but were better than nothing and would provide gun crew training if they ever solved the casting problem.

"All right, men. Let's put the bigger barrels aside for now and concentrate on producing another twenty swivel barrels. This time, only mount them two at a time, instead of three as with the first carriages. That'll give us three with three swivels and ten with two. Also, go ahead and mount a 6-pounder barrel."

"Why, Yozef? What's the point having a carriage with a barrel we don't dare fire?" asked the foreman.

"What if we figure it out? Even a non-functional 6-pounder will let the gun crews drill with a cannon, instead of the swivels. They won't fire it, but they'll have the motions memorized. Then, if we figure out the barrel problem, we'll have gun crews accustomed to the size of real cannon."

One positive outcome of developing the swivel carriages was working out canister rounds and powder sacks in predetermined weights. Yozef had hoped to extend the idea to muskets. The Caedelli method of loading muskets was still in the powder horn stage. To load, one had to remove the stopper at the end of a powder horn, pour into the barrel an estimated of amount of powder, ram a musket ball all the way down with a ramrod, rotate the musket ninety degrees and give a rap to let some of the powder into the firing vent, cock the hammer, and pull the trigger to let the hammer point strike a flint that ignited the powder in the vent into the barrel—then do it all again.

The problems included variations in the amount of powder affecting accuracy, firing downhill being plagued by the ball rolling down the barrel if it wasn't firmly seated, and having to manipulate both the powder horn and the bag of musket balls.

The same escaped Preddi who'd described Narthani cannon also witnessed Narthani ranks of muskets firing more rapidly than any Caedelli, and he had stolen a Narthani cartridge. It was a paper compartment containing a musket ball and a pre-measured amount of powder. The musket man pulled a cartridge out of a bag, held the ball with his fingers, and shook the paper so the powder fell to the bottom of the compartment. Then he bit off the end with the ball, poured powder into the barrel, took the ball and the paper out of his mouth, put the ball into the barrel, followed by the paper as a wad, and rammed both home.

The Caedelli had no history in which rapid mass musket firing was a critical advantage; that luxury was now gone. Convincing Denes and Maera of the problem came quickly after he described the Narthani cartridges.

"Imagine two groups of a hundred men firing muskets at each other. Now imagine that one group can reload and fire three times faster than the other. What do you think would happen?"

Denes shook his head. "The slower group would be all dead within minutes."

"The Narthani," Maera said. "You're saying the Narthani use these 'cartridges,' you call them, to fire faster than our people can. If three times faster, that's as if they had three times as many men as they do."

"If this is true," said Denes, "along with what we hear of how easily they destroyed the Preddi, what chances do the clans have against them?"

"Can we make these cartridges ourselves, Yozef?" Maera asked, ignoring Denes's pessimism.

"I think so. It would take some experimenting, but the principles are simple."

"Yozef, write down what you know about these cartridges and give us the one from the Preddi. Denes and I can work on this," offered Maera. "I'll check in Abersford tomorrow for women to start working on making cartridges, and Denes can have them tested."

Within a sixday, the first cartridges were found adequate. They took practice to use, and the user's face and hands ended with powder smears, but the cartridges worked, and the rate of fire more than doubled. The problem was in manufacturing enough cartridges to make a difference, because it had to be done by hand. Maera scoured Abersford for available workers, and within two sixdays the Abersford Cartridge Works was staffed by two men and eleven women, turning out two thousand cartridges a day. The problem was numbers.

"I know it's important to fire faster," said Denes. "Think of the numbers, though. At a minimum of a hundred cartridges each, supplying a complete muster of Keelan men would require four hundred thousand cartridges. It would take . . . ," Denes pursed his lips, doing the math, "most of a year at this rate of production."

"I know, and it isn't practical to increase production here, unless we recruit men and women already busy with jobs and families. I'll write Hetman Culich to see if production could start elsewhere in Keelan. What I suggest is that we arm small groups with the new cartridges and keep the men together, if fighting is necessary. In one month, we can arm three hundred men with a hundred cartridges each." Yozef didn't elaborate that those hundred cartridges per musket would only last one day's battle.

## Grenades

Yozef had shelved an earlier consideration of grenades for lack of fuses and safety concerns. He envisioned more damage inflicted on their own men through accidents and crude grenades than any damage they could do to the Narthani. He figured they'd eventually get to the fuses and safe protocols. The Moreland raid convinced him *eventually* was *now*, and he resurrected the effort.

The first thing he decided was to reduce the grenade to the essentials—a container of gunpowder, a source of shrapnel, and a cord fuse. His fuse problem puzzled Maera, because fireworks were part of each year's Caernford Harvest Festival, and Yozef had seen the fireworks during two Abersford festivals without it registering that they must use fuses. An embarrassed Yozef discovered the fireworks came from a single shop in Stent Province, and a letter from Culich to Hetman Stent succeeded in getting both the method of making paper gunpowder fuses and a supply of foot-long fuses.

Yozef settled on a tin container the size of a Campbell's Soup can. A mixture of gunpowder and any small pieces of metal available filled the inside, and the container was glued to a seven-inch wooden handle with the fuse cord attached to the opposite end. It was a crude version of the World War II potato masher grenade of the Germans and could be thrown farther than a round grenade, such as the American military had used variants of for a hundred years.

Lighting the fuse required carrying live coals in a small insulated box. Flints were too slow in getting a spark to the end of the fuse, and matches didn't yet exist among the Caedelli.

Yozef hurried to the shops one day in response to a message that the workers had a surprise for him. He arrived just as a projectile trailing sparks arced into the air, flew over the cartridge shop, hit a tree, and exploded, severing the tree trunk eight feet off the ground and sending pieces of wood and bark showering for thirty yards.

"What the fuck!" yelled a startled Yozef.

A red-faced worker explained he had stumbled while hurrying to aim the crossbow after lighting the fuse.

"Crossbow? Fuse?" queried Yozef. "What crossbow and what fuse?"

The worker showed him a large crossbow and longer-than-usual quarrels with grenade containers tied to the forward ends.

Yozef looked at the apparatus, then at the worker, then back to the crossbow. "You gotta be shittin' me."

"They're not very accurate, but if you're happy with getting the quarrel within twenty yards of a target two hundred yards away, they're okay."

"That's close enough," said Yozef, suppressing an insane giggle. "Let's do any future testing down by the beach. We can anchor targets offshore. And for lighting the fuse, let's make it a rule that the quarrel is in the crossbow already aimed before the fuse is lit by a second person."

## MASH

Successes with things that went bang prompted another "what if" thought by reminding Yozef of consequences when men tried to kill one another. If the Narthani invaded in force and the Caedelli tried to stop them, he cringed at imagining the number of casualties. During a visit to the abbey, Yozef shared his concern with the abbot and the abbess.

They met in Diera's office in the hospital building.

"Diera, what if the Narthani attack other clans? Have you thought about how medicants will treat injuries if large-scale fighting breaks out between the clans and the Narthani?"

"Large scale?" questioned Diera. "What do you mean by large scale?"

"During the Buldorian raid, you had how many casualties to care for?"

"Perhaps twenty serious injuries and another thirty treated and the people walked away."

"In that case, the medicants treated the injuries immediately. What if the injuries occurred fifty miles from any medicants? What if instead of twenty serious casualties, there were three hundred? Six hundred?"

"Six hundred!" exclaimed the shocked abbess. "Merciful God!" Diera stopped talking as she weighed his questions.

"This has also occurred to me, Diera," said Sistian, "though not with the numbers Yozef proposes. However, I've known Yozef long enough to realize he's not just asking a hypothetical question. Am I correct?"

Yozef nodded with a serious expression. "What if the Narthani send their army into the rest of Caedellium? It could be anywhere—Moreland, Stent, Gwillamer, Keelan—or even use their navy to land somewhere else on the island. If the clans resist, battles might involve tens of thousands of men and hundreds or even thousands of casualties. Given the severity of wounds to be expected, how will they be treated in time to save lives?

"I suggest that plans be made to have mobile hospitals to accompany any large groups of clansmen headed for a fight. The sooner the wounded get medicant attention, the better their chances of surviving or avoiding permanent injury."

Diera sighed deeply and looked at Sistian. "Part of me hates to even think about such things, but Yozef's right. We need to plan for it. Sistian, you should communicate with Culich about this, and I'll discuss it with the other medicants here and send messages to St. Tomo's and a few other Keelan abbeys to alert them and ask their opinions."

Thus was born the first Keelan mobile army surgical hospital. Yozef never explained why he called the mobile hospital a MASH, since the acronym in Caedelli was KLOP. Culich gave his support, leaving the details to the Keelan medicants, with Pedr Kennrick coordinating. The hetman also communicated the concept to other clans, with mixed responses.

## Spies and Assassins

An unpleasant thought occurred to Yozef, prompted by Maera at an evening meal. She glowed, the mild morning sickness having long ago eased, and she looked and claimed she'd never felt better. Even her chronic migraines hadn't occurred since they'd married and she started swelling with their child.

"I had a wonderful day, Yozef. Why I felt that way I don't know, it just *was*. After you left this morning, Elian and I spent two hours sewing clothes for the baby. My God, I never thought of myself as sitting and enjoying sewing and talking with a common woman.

"Then I worked at translating that history of the Landolin kingdoms you wanted to read. I hadn't refreshed my Landolin for ages and was surprised how much I remembered. It was like I was reading Caedelli. After lunch, I walked to the abbey by way of the beach and took off my shoes and stood in the water until my feet started to wrinkle." Maera laughed. "Then at the abbey I talked with Diera about the mobile hospitals idea, and I offered to help plan an organized effort for all of Keelan. I'll also write Father, suggesting he contact the other Alliance member clans to do the same. On the way home I—" She broke off and put a hand on his arm. "Oh, Yozef. Listen to me prattle on. I didn't ask how your day was."

He'd been listening, bemused. As much as he liked and respected his new wife, "cheerful" and "prattling" were not two words he'd normally associate with her. The news of Anarynd's disappearance by the Narthani still lingered, but her moods improved the further she got into her pregnancy.

"A busy day, Maera. I hardly sat down, except to eat. The foundry workers had an idea and wanted to try again to cast the 6-pounder barrels. After listening to them, I decided it wasn't a new enough idea to divert from the swivel guns. I also talked to Sister Diera. She wondered if I had any ideas about several patients, but I had nothing to contribute. I'm afraid she and others expect me to have too many answers. I hope they don't suspect I'm deliberately withholding from them.

"Then I had a fast mid-day meal while talking with Filtin about his latest idea for increasing kerosene distillation, hopefully without blowing up the facility and the staff. Most of the afternoon I spent composing queries and responses, handling written communications to and from Culich, and reading letters from other towns within and outside Keelan, inquiring about using some of the techniques I've introduced and the possibilities for franchises in other provinces. Then I did the exercise routine—weapons, running, and weights. I got the usual odd looks about the running."

"People've gotten used to seeing you running, though I admit even I still find it odd," Maera said.

"I'm sure it looks odd, and it's certainly something I don't enjoy. Every time I'm tempted to skip it, though, I remind myself how easily I could have died during the St. Sidryn's defense. Now there's you and the baby. I have to feel I'm better prepared to defend all of us, if it comes to that."

Yozef took a final bite of his meal. "This is about the only non-working time I'll have all day. Later I have an hour of writing to do, mostly what I remember about more chemistry now that we've decided to add a chemistry department to the university, Chancellor Kolsko-Keelan," he added at the end and was rewarded with a smile.

He didn't mention he was struggling with how to introduce the concepts of the periodic table and chemical bonds.

Maera sipped water as she listened to Yozef recount, then set the glass down. She finished her plate of food, pushed it aside, and leaned forward, arms crossed and on the table, staring thoughtfully at her husband.

"You know, Yozef, before moving to Abersford, I hadn't realized exactly how privileged and restricted my life had been, as far as contact with the common Keelanders. I told you about sewing and talking with Elian this morning. It felt awkward at first to be talking normally with *regular* folk, and I'm surprised at my growing attachment to Abersford and being a part of the community. But then the other news was a letter from Father, reminding us the baby is to be born in Caernford."

Yozef groaned. "Let me guess. He pressed again for us to move to Caernford permanently. It seems like a long time ago when I promised to consider the move. I can't say I'm any more enthused now than I was then. Oh, I can see the logic of moving my enterprises to Caernford, but so much effort has gone into setting things up here, plus, I *like* living here. And our house! We've only lived in it for a few months, and we'd have to leave it."

"Well, you've months to think about it before the baby comes, and we don't have to lose the house. It isn't that far from Caernford, so perhaps we could spend part of the year here. There's time to talk about it. For tonight, you need to get to your writing, and I need to write Mother and my sisters."

They both rose and were carrying dishes to the kitchen sink for Elian to clean in the morning when Maera stopped, holding plates in both hands.

"Oh, another thing, before I forget. While I was walking home, I reflected on how amazing it was that you all beat back the Buldorians when they attacked St. Sidryn's and how unfortunate it was that the raid happened when so many of the fighting men were away. It reminds us how much of life depends on good or bad luck."

Yozef had set his plates down and was returning for more when Maera finished speaking. He froze, and his eyes took on a distant focus, as his mind made odd connections.

"Yozef?" she prompted when he remained frozen for more than a few moments. "Yozef?" she said again, this time louder.

His eyes focused again. "Sorry. Just that I had a strange thought from what you were saying."

"What I was saying?"

"About it being bad luck for the raid to occur when so many men were away. Something just jumped into my head. What if it wasn't bad luck?"

Maera's face took on a look of concentration. She placed her plates in the sink, then twirled a strand of hair with her left hand, one of her subconscious "I'm thinking hard about something" habits. "If not bad luck, then you're saying it was planned? The raid happened when it did *because* the men were away? That would mean the Narthani knew. How?"

"They'd know if someone told them."

"It would have to be someone near Abersford," Maera said dubiously.

"That's right."

"You believe someone near here is communicating with the Narthani? How's that possible?"

"I don't know. It may be the raid happened when it did by accident. If it wasn't . . ."

"Then we have to find out!"

The next day Yozef and Maera corralled Denes in the Magistrate office. He listened blankly at first, then grew more interested and agitated as they explained the previous evening's discussion.

"This also might explain something puzzling," said Denes. "Those Narthani sloops that cruise offshore, Garel Kulwyn mentioned how curious it was that the sloops sometimes stay around for a day or more, instead of passing on. What if it's related to a spy passing information?"

"Wouldn't it have to be done at night?" said Maera. "Otherwise, they'd be seen during the day."

"Yes," agreed Denes, "they could row out at night, and since no one is looking for them, it's unlikely anyone would notice."

"Or do it by light signals," said Yozef. "As long as the information flow was only one way, from shore to ship, a covered lantern at a point of land where the light couldn't be seen except out at sea would work. The sloop would sit offshore at prearranged days of the month and wait for signals."

As Yozef had observed previously, ideas might not occur to Denes spontaneously, though once brought to his attention, he jumped on them.

"I'll set up a watch for the nights we know sloops are lurking offshore. There are only a few points where a lantern wouldn't be seen."

"Denes, you might consider having a small boat position itself offshore after dark so it could see a suspicious light," Maera suggested.

"And to see if anyone goes out to meet the sloop," added Yozef.

"I don't know if your worry is justified or not, but we'll assume it is for the next month or so," Denes stated decisively. "Whenever one of the Narthani sloops lingers off our shore, I'll arrange a couple of men to watch for suspicious persons near the coast on those nights and a man in a rowboat to sit a few hundred yards offshore. I'll also investigate possible suspects. I doubt it could be a long-time resident—more likely someone who's moved to Abersford recently or visits regularly and lives elsewhere."

It was a month before Yozef's suspicion was confirmed. On two of the three times a Narthani sloop lingered offshore, the Keelander manning a dinghy rowed back and reported seeing a long series of light flashes from a bluff jutting out from the east end of the Abersford beachfront.

In the previous month, Denes had identified three men as spy candidates. One was an escaped Preddi who worked in one of Abersford's three pubs. The second was a man of unknown origin who worked odd jobs around the town and had built himself a cabin north of town. The third was a Clengoth trader who spent an inordinate amount of time in Abersford. Each of the three was kept under surveillance. On the next night of the flashing lights, suspect #3 was in Clengoth, #2 drank beer in a pub well past time the flashes stopped, and suspect #1 was unaccounted for.

Probable cause for search warrants didn't exist on Caedellium. Denes and five men surprised the man at his home at first light the next day. While the man's frightened Keelan wife and year-old child waited outside the house, two burly men held the Preddi, and Denes and the others ransacked the house, an attached shed, and a barn. In the shed, they found a kerosene lantern with three of the four glass sides painted black and the fourth side with a leather flap that could be lifted and lowered. They also found a bundle of papers with Narthani writing and a code key.

*Like Morse Code*, thought Yozef, when he later saw the papers.

When confronted with the lantern and the papers, the man collapsed, confessed, and begged for mercy. He hadn't actually escaped Preddi. He had been sent by the Narthani to settle in Abersford and send reports of local happenings, including patrol schedules. Communication was all one-way, because the sloop never sent messages back. When pressed about why he was helping the Narthani, the man wept and said the Narthani had his Preddi wife and two children, plus two sisters and their families, as hostages to ensure his following orders. To convince him, they shot his father in front of the entire family. Denes and the others cursed the Narthani when they heard the story. They believed the man, who appeared broken now that he thought the Narthani would do the same to the rest of his Preddi family.

Later, they met after questioning the man further and confirming the consistency in his story. Among the papers found were previous messages. Most were innocuous, while others contained enough information for the Narthani to have known one of the town's Thirds of fighting men would be absent the day of the raid. Given that information, it was simple enough to fake the Gwillamer raid that drew off a second Third.

Yozef had wondered whether Denes would execute the man, because he could be held to blame for deaths and injuries during the raid. However, Denes surprised him.

"I don't know that I might not have done the same, given his circumstances. A problem now is that if we execute him or keep him captive and his messages stop, the Narthani might well carry out their threat and kill the rest of his family. I'd prefer to avoid that, if possible. Yozef, what if we send the messages ourselves? How would the Narthani know it was us and not their spy?"

"It's possible, but what if there's something that alerts the Narthani? It could be some detail in how the messages are transmitted, some signal or something, that we're unaware of. Also, what if there's more than one spy here, and a second one alerts the Narthani? I suggest you let him return to his routine, including sending the messages. The difference is that we'll write the messages so they contain nothing of consequence, unless we wanted to give the Narthani false information."

"Denes would have to keep a close watch," cautioned Maera.

"Tell him you'll look into getting his family out of Preddi," added Yozef.

"You mean lie to him," frowned Denes.

"No promises, only that you'll do what you can."

"All right. What about his Keelan wife? She has to act normal, too."

Yozef shrugged. "Just say it was a mistake and apologize."

They agreed and gave the Preddi the choice, not that he had options. All messages would be cleared with Denes and the man watched closely. Other than those measures, everything would continue as before.

"It might sound like I'm overly worrisome," Yozef added cautiously, "but once I thought about Narthani spies, something just as bad or even worse occurred to me. If the Narthani have spies, could there be Narthani agents in place to assassinate important clan leaders? The hetman being the obvious target, of course."

Denes's face turned red and Maera's white.

"Kill the hetman! Would Narthani do such a thing?" Denes spat out.

"I fear the Narthani would do anything they believed would make the conquest of Caedellium easier," Yozef said grimly.

"But–but," Maera stuttered, "how would they possibly attack Father?"

"From what I've seen, by just walking up to him, if the assassin didn't plan on escaping. Otherwise, a musket, poison, or anything you might imagine."

"I have to get a semaphore message to the hetman immediately," said Denes.

Maera was getting color in her face, as she thought of how her father would react. "I think we need to get the message to others besides Father. He may not believe the threat is real or may think that he can deal with it by himself. I'll send the warning to Mother. He won't be able to ignore *her*. Also, Denes, I suggest we alert Vortig Luwis and Pedr Kennrick. With the three of them, it will ensure Father takes this seriously. I'll write letters right now, and we can send a rider to Caernford, instead of using the semaphore. We might be overly worried, but for the moment let's not let this possibility be widely known. I know the semaphore messages are supposed to be kept inviolate by the operators, though with something like this . . ."

"I suggest warning Luwis and Kennrick to also watch out for themselves," added Yozef. "In fact, any Keelander with a leadership position should take care."

"Yozef's right," urged Maera. "Father, his advisors, and all the boyermen need to be careful. None of them should go anywhere without several guards accompanying them, and their homes and places of work should be guarded as well."

Maera looked sharply at Yozef. "That includes you, husband. If there are Narthani agents and they're looking to weaken Keelan by assassination, you may well be one of their main targets once you've gotten their attention, if you haven't already."

Yozef was momentarily taken aback. His thinking hadn't gone as far as himself, though now that Maera mentioned it, she was right. This might all just be his scaremongering, but if he were a Narthani, Yozef Kolsko would be number two on a Keelan hit list, right below the hetman.

A rider took the messages to Caernford. Maera later learned from her mother that Culich had been skeptical until word came over the semaphore days later of an attempt on the life of Welman Stent, hetman of the Stent Clan. The attempt failed, and the unidentified assailants escaped. Less fortunate was Lordum Hewell, the Hewell clan hetman. A stable worker from a neighboring estate killed both the hetman's younger brother and his wife. The couple was visiting and the husband looked similar enough to the hetman that it was assumed a case of mistaken identity. Although a massive search for the killer was underway, he'd disappeared into nearby mountains.

After these events, Culich sent warnings to all other clans to be wary of attacks on clan leaders and other targets such as weapon storehouses.

After he sent those warnings, Culich stared into the abyss he'd avoided.

*It's coming. God help us.*

# CHAPTER 26

# EPHEMERAL JOY

### Next Generation

One evening over their meal, Maera informed Yozef that the coming Godsday ceremony was also a Naming Day. The Melton family would be there. Yozef and Bronwyn's child would be given his name, and Yozef would acknowledge fatherhood.

Four days later, Yozef was ambivalent as he sat with Maera at one end of a front pew. The entire Melton family occupied the opposite end. After the main service, Culich rose again after the service's closing prayer.

"People of Abersford, before leaving today we have one more joyous event to celebrate. The arrival of new souls here on Anyar, by God's grace."

There were six little souls to welcome that day. Each family came forward, and the child was introduced by name, with the Merton family last. They walked to the rising where Sistian stood, Bronwyn carrying the baby, her sister, their husband, and their three other children. They all went to their knees, while the abbot recited a litany of duties in raising the child, to which the three adults affirmed. Then Sistian called on Yozef, as the child's father, to come forward. Maera had primed him on what to do, and he went through a similar series of affirmations. Although he felt awkward, no one else thought it odd to see a mother accompanied by another wife, a husband who was not the father, and the father who was sitting with his pregnant wife.

"People of Abersford, the new soul in our midst is now to be given a name. The mother, Bronwyn Merton, requests that the father, Yozef Kolsko, choose the first name of the child."

*What!! No one said anything about this!*

"Yozef Kolsko, what is the given name of this child?"

Yozef's mind froze. *Name? What name?*

He never comprehended what came out of his mouth. It may have been a shard of hysteria at being put in the situation without warning, but "Aragorn" was clearly heard throughout the cathedral.

*Oh, shit! I didn't really say that! Wait! Wait! Let me try another one—*

"Aragorn," repeated Sistian. "A new name for Caedellium, appropriate for the son of a father cast upon our shores and making himself a valuable member of our society."

*No! Wait!*

"People of Abersford," intoned Sistian, "meet Aragorn Merton-Kolsko."

"Oh, shit!" Yozef mumbled.

Maera jerked, as she wondered if she'd heard correctly, having witnessed the exclamation previously and been given the explanation of its meaning.

Yozef ignored her look and told himself it wasn't *that* bad a name.

The congregation broke into exclamations of welcome for a baby whose connection to Middle Earth would be forever lost to them.

*Well*, Yozef sighed. *At least the first thing out of my mouth wasn't Frodo. Or, for that matter—Gollum.*

Yozef was only half cognizant of the next hour, except that after the service he held Aragorn for several minutes, while Bronwyn and Maera congratulated each other for a child arrived and one on the way. When he handed the baby back to its mother, there was a moment of regret, followed by back slaps and more approving comments from friends and strangers. Cadwulf declined to hold Aragorn, but Carnigan commented on how tiny new babies were, while holding Aragorn in one hand. Maera took her turn, and Yozef had a surreal moment seeing Maera hold Aragorn against her own growing stomach. When they walked home, Yozef and Maera had their arms around each other's back, both thinking of their child to come.

## Preparing for War

Life in Abersford took on a sense of impending . . . something. New activities were added to the community routine. Eighty men in unison practiced on foot with the new musket cartridges. Denes decided that only one-third of Abersford's fighting men, called a Third, would be issued cartridges. On his suggestion, Hetman Keelan agreed that other groups would be trained in Clengoth, the district center, and in Caernford, the clan's capital. The rationale was to train cadres in multiple locations, who in turn would train other men once cartridge production increased. Denes spent several sixdays traveling among the three towns to oversee training five hundred men in using the cartridges and, at Yozef's insistence, the necessity of firing while on foot—he argued that this made it easier to use the cartridges and maximize the rate of fire. Yozef convinced Denes to call the men "dragoons," without explaining the Earth reference of men who rode horses to battle sites, then fought as infantry.

They hoped all of Keelan's fighting men would have minimal training within six months. Yet events would overtake the hope.

Yozef and Denes stood watching what passed for the entire Keelan operational artillery corps practice against hay bales. Although four swivel gun carriages with two barrels each were completed, Yozef waffled on which design was best. While the middle barrel of the original three-barreled carriages weren't reloaded when the crew wanted to fire the fastest, they still had the advantage of one extra barrel in the initial salvo. Unsure exactly which design was best, he settled on initially focusing on the three-barrel pieces, the three of them providing nine barrels for the first salvo and six thereafter.

New additions to the artillery corps were three smaller carriages, each mounting one of the large crossbows firing the explosive quarrels. While Yozef wasn't confident in their usefulness, his workers were so enthused he hesitated to discourage them.

The three swivel carriages were lined up twenty yards apart, facing a hundred straw bales standing on end. Paper covered the sides facing the Keelanders a hundred yards away, to allow counting holes from the canister. The bales simulated a block of Narthani infantry standing shoulder to shoulder, as the Preddi escapee had reported. The three crossbow carriages had a greater effective range and, if used in coordination with the swivels, should have been placed in the rear to fire over the swivel carriages. However, Yozef didn't trust the crossbow crews enough to fire their contraptions over the other crews, so they were placed behind, 50 yards to one side, 150 yards from the bales.

He supposed he shouldn't be so cynical about the crossbows. After all, the French had used something not so different during the trench warfare of World War I. Still, he wanted to be a little more confident.

"All ready, Yozef," said Denes. All eyes of six crews, plus extras and onlookers, focused on the two men.

"It's your show, Denes. Give the go."

Denes raised a hand holding a small white flag. All of the crews turned to their carriages, with only the crew captains watching Denes. Seeing he had all of the captains' attention, Denes slashed the flag to his side, the crew captains yelled, and the first swivel barrels fired, followed seconds later by all of the second and then third barrels, after realigning to the bales. When the third barrels fired, the crews swarmed to reload the outer two barrels, the third one now abandoned in an effort to keep up the fastest rate of fire possible.

From the first barrel to the third lasted nine seconds: fire one, realign from the recoil, fire two, realign from the recoil, fire three. Another fifteen seconds passed, as crews swarmed reloading and the two outer barrels fired again. As planned, after four rounds of reloading and firing, the crews stopped and viewed the results. Yozef had drilled into them that only the crew captains looked downrange. The crews' task was loading and firing, not evaluating and aiming.

The crossbows firing couldn't be heard, but their crews had launched four quarrels each before the swivels ceased firing. The quarrels' flights were silent, though the trail of sparks and smoke outlined their arced passages. One quarrel lost its gunpowder/shrapnel container shortly after firing. The explosion was only forty yards in from of the carriage, and Yozef winced. It would have landed within the swivels if the crossbows had been directly to the rear. Four quarrels passed over the bales, three impacted and exploded short, and four landed within the formation.

When firing ceased and the smoke cleared, the results were gratifying or nauseating, depending on the viewer's perspective and imagination. Of the one hundred bales, eleven stood unscathed. Twenty-one had single canister holes in their paper, twenty-nine had multiple holes, and thirty-nine bales were unidentifiable—either shredded by canister or shattered by quarrel charges.

Denes gathered the crews together and had to shout to silence the self-congratulations.

"It was a successful test. You all performed well, and I'm proud of you. Don't forget that your victory was against hay bales. No one was shooting back at you. If we have to face the Narthani, it will be different, and not all of us will return home to our families."

A more somber artillery corps packed up and returned the carriages to the storage buildings.

## Nights Out

The arrival of Maera Kolsko-Keelan in Abersford refashioned Yozef's social life, though not as much as expected. Most evenings they spent together, and although invitations from Abersford and the abbey came regularly, Maera limited them to one evening a week.

Yozef had been concerned about Maera finding a social circle of her own, but he needn't have worried. She dove into planning the university and found association with the abbey's scholastics fulfilling. To both his surprise and her own, friendships developed with several young mothers and mothers-to-be from different strata of Abersford society.

Maera insisted Yozef go with Carnigan and Filtin at least one night a week to the Snarling Graeko, with or without her. "I saw how much you enjoyed being with the other men. You need that occasional night of relaxation, and I'm not going to be a wife who expects her husband to stop what he enjoys to pamper her. Just try not to get too drunk too often."

She also enjoyed an occasional evening at the pub but had to forswear beer on Yozef's insistence.

"One thing, Maera. Now that you're with child, you'll have to stop drinking any spirits until the baby comes. American medicants know that spirits can affect growing babies. The worst consequences are when the woman drinks to excess, though even a little can have effects. It's safer for the baby if the mother abstains completely."

By now, Maera was accustomed to Yozef making assertions pulled as if haphazardly from a bag of his people's knowledge. Most of the time he was worth listening to, but it got annoying. This time, Maera went to Diera.

"My," said Diera, "he hasn't said anything like this to me. If what he says is true, then I wish he'd shared this before, but that's Yozef. I don't believe he does it deliberately; it's just something that doesn't occur to him until triggered. In this case, it's your child coming."

"Is it always like that? A trigger?"

"No," said Diera carefully and then with a quieter voice, as if saying something not quite to be shared, "then there're the rumors of his acting like the knowledge is being whispered to him. I know it sounds silly. With Yozef? Who knows?"

Maera smiled ruefully. "Merciful God, do I know. It's so frustrating at times. I try not to let it bother me."

"This spirits warning he mentioned," said Diera, "let me look at our records. I'll check for new babies with unusual problems and see if there's any connection with medicant notes about the mother."

Four days later, Diera came to Maera in the abbey library. "I suppose I shouldn't be surprised, but once again one of Yozef's droplets of knowledge seems to be true. I checked records for births the last five years, and too often to be coincidence we had new babies enfeebled or deformed from mothers known to drink spirits to excess. It's not connected in every case, but in enough that I've shown the other medicants at St. Sidryn's the evidence and we agreed to issue a general warning. I'm also writing to other Keelan abbeys for them to check their records for confirmation. If it comes, we'll expand the warning to the other provinces."

Maera still accompanied Yozef to the pub on occasion, but for a different purpose than beer, jokes, and loud camaraderie. One corner of the Snarling Graeko was the turf of Go players. It wasn't the same game as on Earth, but so similar that Yozef kept the name and wondered at some genetic predisposition in human brain wiring.

Maera had played the game by the time she was seven, usually with staff at St. Tomo's abbey when visiting with her mother. By twelve, no one she played could beat her, and she stopped playing as she grew older. It was a revelation to find a Go culture in the Snarling Graeko, but a humbling one after losing first to one of Cadwulf's bank clerks and then to Brother Wallington, the naturalist scholastic from St. Sidryn's. The pub's patrons weren't sure how to react when the hetman's daughter and the wife of Yozef Kolsko let loose a stream of curses after her loss to Wallington.

"Hah!" chortled Carnigan. "People think Maera's a cold fish. Maybe they're wrong. What do you say, Yozef? Are there times when she's . . . you know . . . warm?"

Yozef pretended he didn't know what Carnigan referred to and walked over to see what had incited his wife. By the time he arrived, she was apologizing to Wallington and challenged him to a second game. It was intense, and a crowd gathered around their table. She won. She never lost again, including the few times Yozef played her. That he was proud of her ability at Go, even admitting publicly he was out of her league at the game, meant more to her than winning.

## Narthani Mustering

Okan Akuyun sat on his horse next to Aivacs Zulfa and the other senior Narthani leaders, watching the expedition force start toward Moreland. The complete formation had been together the last two sixdays, drilling relentlessly from dawn to dusk to keep a semblance of order in the combined Narthani infantry, cavalry, and artillery, all coordinated with the Eywellese and Selfcellese horsemen.

Akuyun *supposed* they could call their islander allies *cavalry*, even if they *were* more like mobs of horsemen.

Their roles were to scout for the main advance and then serve as flanking screens, if and when they could entice the Caedelli into open field battles.

"I hope you don't mind my looking over your shoulder this once, Aivacs. There's no reason for me to be here, and I wouldn't want to give the impression I don't have complete confidence in you. However, for once I'll invoke the commander's right to do what he wants. There are times I just *have* to see things for myself, and sending our first large formation against the islanders is one of those."

"I understand, Okan. This is a major inflection point, removing all pretense that we're on the island for any reason short of complete subjugation and incorporation into the Empire. I don't envy your having to sit back and let someone else lead the way."

"It's the inevitable consequence of rising in rank and being stuck in headquarters, as I suspect you'll find out one day. You'd think I'd be accustomed to it by now, yet there are still times I miss being in the field."

Akuyun wiped his brow from the morning's heat. "Not just seeing you off is hard. Now I have to wait for dispatches on your progress. I'll have to be concentrating on everyday matters in Preddi and imagining what's happening in Moreland. How will the islanders respond and in what strength? Will you be able to entice them into mass horsemen charges to allow our infantry and cannon to chew them up?"

Zulfa didn't respond. He knew the questions were only rhetorical, Akuyun restating questions none of them knew the answers to. A crushing defeat would set the islanders back on their heels and prod some of the clans to rush to make accommodations with the invaders. If a decisive battle or battles weren't forthcoming, they would cut a swath to the opposite coast, destroying every town and city across Moreland and Orosz provinces. If necessary, they would then circumnavigate the island, supported by the navy, destroying provinces one by one. None of them thought that would be necessary, expecting a culmination to come quickly following the first battles, especially if several clans came to Moreland's aid and got crushed.

"The only unknown in my thinking," said Zulfa, "is how many clans join Moreland. We hope it's enough that a decisive defeat so weakens those clans that most of them come to terms, but you never know. We've looked at contingencies, but I continue to think it will all be decided at Moreland City. I can't imagine the Moreland Clan letting us burn their capital unopposed, and if they commit, then the other clans coming to help Moreland will be forced to do the same."

"Well, Aivacs, we'll know for sure in the next couple of sixdays."

The first infantry columns started after the Eywellese, followed by artillery, more infantry, more artillery, then Narthani cavalry last to keep the dust raised by the horses from being breathed by the infantry. Finally came wagons of supplies, medical units, and behind them more Eywellese and Selfcell horsemen, forming rear and flanking screens.

Having felt he'd satisfied his personal need to see, Akuyun addressed Zulfa. "I'll leave you to it, Aivacs," he said softly enough that the others didn't hear. Then, louder and more formally, "Good hunting, Brigadier Zulfa, and glory to the Narthon Empire!"

With that, Zulfa and the other leaders saluted the Caedellium mission commander, who wheeled his horse and, followed by immediate staff and escort, headed back to Preddi City. Akuyun stopped once to look back from a hilltop. The sight of the force stirred feelings he thought were in the past—the fleeting wish it was himself leading men to battle as he once had, and not Zulfa. It was only fleeting, because knowledge of battle's consequences tempered the memories.

# CHAPTER 27

# INVASION

### Call for Help

Culich and Breda sat finishing their meal under a pergola in the manor's rear garden. They had attended a Godsday ceremony at St. Tomo's Abbey in Caernford, then returned home, instead of eating mid-day meal with the abbot and select clansmen, as they often did. This evening's meal at Keelan Manor would host Breda's family, and the couple wanted time to themselves to relax before she focused on preparations and Culich sequestered himself in his study with endless paperwork. Only in Maera's absence did he fully appreciate how much he'd relied on her help and how integral she'd been to their everyday life. Yet, as much as they missed their eldest daughter, both parents thanked God that Maera's letters reflected she was happy, something they had feared might escape their precocious offspring.

"My letters from Maera are full of facts, as usual," said Culich, "but she doesn't dwell on herself. How about letters to her mother?"

"I suppose I read a lot between the lines, but I think the marriage is working better than we, and I suspect she, hoped. She misses her sisters and us, but the letters are filled with a sense of belonging and purpose. The only concern I detect is the coming child. She's worried how it will change her life, if she'll resent its constant needs, if she'll be a good mother, if . . . well, you know Maera."

"You think it'll be all right?"

"I do. Still, I'm looking forward to her coming here when her time nears and to holding our first grandchild. I know it's selfish of me, but I'm hoping you'll convince Yozef to move here."

Culich reached across the table and patted his wife's hand. "It'll happen. Yozef's enterprises are growing too large for Abersford. He'll eventually accept the practical reasons for moving to Caernford." He lowered his voice and grinned. "Don't tell Maera, but I'm confident enough to consider looking for a site to build them a home not too—"

Culich broke off when they heard a horse gallop to the front of the manor, then faint urgent voices.

Culich's meal no longer sat satisfied in his stomach. *What now?*

Moments later, a young man raced around the corner to where they sat. Culich's and Breda's thoughts were of urgent news and a list of possibilities they didn't want to hear.

The rider was a son of the semaphore station keeper at Caernford. He ran to Culich, gave a nod to Breda, and said, "Hetman. An urgent message from Moreland. Father said you needed to see it immediately."

He reached into the pouch carried across one shoulder and gave his hetman a folded and sealed sheet of paper.

```
To Hetman Keelan
From Hetman Moreland
Large Narthani force plus Selfcell and Eywell
clansmen crossed into Moreland yesterday.
Est 6000 Narthani 3000 clansmen. Cannons
and many wagons. Assume invasion.
Can you help?
```

Culich slammed the paper on the tabletop. "May God damn all Narthani to the hottest reaches of Hell!" he shouted in a tone angry and bitter.

Breda paled. "What's happened!?"

"What I've been expecting and afraid of. The Narthani are attacking Moreland and in enough force that it's not merely a raid. It's almost certainly an effort to take over the province and add to those they already control."

Culich smoldered for a moment. "Breda, please bring me quill and paper while I think."

She jumped to her feet and disappeared into the house.

Culich turned to the messenger. "I'll give you a semaphore reply to Hetman Moreland, plus others to Mittack and Gwillamer. There'll also be written messages to several of our people. Take the messages to the clan headquarters in Caernford, and they'll be dispatched to the appropriate persons from there."

Breda returned and placed the quill, ink, and papers in front of Culich. Without acknowledging her, he began writing. First, an answer to Moreland.

*To Hetman Moreland*
*From Hetman Keelan*
*Gathering Tri-Clan forces. Est arrival*
*Moreland City 4 days 2200 men. Will*
*semaphore when leave. Will follow*
*semaphore route, check for messages*
*every 4 hours.*

Then, semaphore messages to the other two clans of the Tri-Clan Alliance, invoking their agreed-on action in the event of a major Narthani move, and to Keelan boyermen near the semaphore lines. Finally, written messages to relevant clan leaders in Caernford and by horse to more distant boyermen without semaphore connections.

"The rest of today to alert all the boyermen," Culich thought aloud. "Give them a day to gather men and start them on the way here or position to meet us on the way to Moreland, then all of us two days to reach Moreland City. Yes, we should link up with other clans by end of the fourth day, if all goes well. Four days? Will we get there in time to make any difference? If the Narthani are already into Moreland territory, it may be over before we get there."

Culich shook his head. "There's nothing for it. We do what we can and pray."

The Tri-Clan Alliance had plans for this eventuality. All three clans had designated men ready to muster and depart on short notice. Gwillamer would send 400 men. They had a smaller population than Keelan and needed to secure the southwest border with Eywell. Mittack was also less populated but was under no immediate threat, so agreed on 600 men. Keelan would send 1,200 men, and all three clans kept enough men to defend against Narthani coastal raids. All 2,200 men would be under Culich's personal command, although Vortig Luwis, as Keelan's titular military advisor, would make the actual field decisions. Culich needed to be there to show support for Moreland and to prevent Tri-Clan forces from engaging in actions that might waste them to no good purpose.

Finished with messages to his boyermen and the other clans, Culich wrote one for Denes Vegga at Abersford to come with the Abersford dragoons and artillery, then, once at Caernford, to organize the dragoons from the other cities. He hesitated, then picked up one more sheet of paper and wrote:

To Yozef Kolsko
From Hetman Keelan
Moreland invaded by Narthani.
Tri-Clan forces to leave in 2 days.
Request you accompany.

He wanted to assume Yozef would accompany his artillery creations, but one was never sure of anything with his daughter's husband. The messenger took the last of the communiqués, secured them in his pouch, and was gone.

Breda had watched silently, one arm across her abdomen tightly, the other raised with a hand against her cheek. "How bad is it going to be, Culich?"

"I honestly don't know. It still could be just a large raid. I don't believe it, though. I think this is the next major move by the Narthani to take over all of Caedellium. I'm also taking Yozef with us."

Breda had been expecting this. "I'll pray for both you and all the clans. Poor Maera. She's seemed so content, with child, and now this. It'll be the first time she sends her husband off, not knowing whether he'll return."

Culich went to Breda and held her at arm's length. "Does it ever get any easier?" he asked gently.

"No, I'm afraid not."

"I've always come back to you."

"There's never been a danger as great as this one."

"I'm sorry, Breda. You know I wish I could make it easier for you."

"Of course, I know. Just as I acknowledge I knew what I was getting into when I agreed to marry you. Unfortunately, knowing doesn't make it easier. What can I do?"

"I'll be busy with the men the next couple of days. You can help the abbey staff and Pedr prepare the medicant units and double-check the supply preparation. Be sure I know immediately about any problems."

Culich didn't say it also gave her something to do for the next few days.

## Abersford Muster

Scarcely an hour later, a semaphore message arrived at the Abersford station over the spur line Yozef had had installed. Even though it was Godsday, Yozef was in a workshop, along with several of his workers. He figured if they were dedicated enough to be working on their rest day, the least he could do was show up to support them and see how it was going, though Maera made him promise he'd be home well before evening meal.

A worker was about to test the latest attempt at making a steam cylinder when a messenger rode up to where they stood outside the shop, behind a thick six-foot-high barricade, in case the trial run went bad, as had happened before and was the reason one corner of the main shop had been recently rebuilt.

He read the message once. Then again, and the third iteration was when it sunk in. Culich wanted him to accompany an army to help fight the Narthani? Not something high on Yozef's list of things he wanted to do. The one experience was more than enough for a lifetime. A combined flashback and flash forward rose unbidden, involving him standing in front of a Narthani horse charge, firing a musket at an infinite number of sword- and lance-bearing Narthani on huge horses breathing fire. Which would be the one to skewer him?

He thanked the messenger, who informed him the hetman expected a response. Yozef asked the messenger to follow him home. There, he went in the house and, without speaking, gave Maera the message.

*Maybe she'll tell me I don't have to go. Or that I'm more important here. Or anything not involving me turning into a shish kabob.*

He was disappointed.

"Naturally, Father expects you to help push back the Narthani."

Not the response Yozef hoped for, and not in her satisfied voice. She immediately focused on what he needed to take with him and started giving the Faughns orders. It somehow didn't seem the appropriate moment to tell his militant, pregnant wife that going to fight the Narthani was low on his wish list.

"Brak, saddle a horse."

*As if there are options. Seabiscuit's still the only nag I trust not to throw me first chance.*

"Elian, lay out several sets of clothes—rugged ones."

*What? Best for a battle? Something to deflect sharp objects? How about wearing a tank? Or body armor?*

"Weapons. I'll get them ready," Maera finished.

*I'm more likely to hurt myself than scare any Narthani.*

Maera acted energized. Within thirty minutes, she handed Brak a pack to tie behind Seabiscuit's saddle. "There are extra clothes, rain gear, a blanket, water, and dry sausage and crackers."

Maera accompanied Yozef to Abersford. The 160 men gathered in the town square consisted of Vegga's dragoons, Yozef's artillery crews, and three wagons, one of which held four medicants, including Diera Beynom. Carnigan was there. He seemed to take it all in stride and looked perversely happy at the prospect of killing Narthani. Maera surprised Yozef when she collared Carnigan and Wyfor Kales, Yozef's instructor on blade fighting, and in Yozef's presence told them in no uncertain terms to be sure her husband got back in one piece. It wasn't quite explicit but sounded to Yozef as if she got the message across to come back with him or not at all. Carnigan grinned and Kales grunted. Yozef felt reassured.

*Well, maybe she does care about me. Or doesn't want to bother with a replacement.*

Yozef didn't expect a demonstrative farewell from Maera. He wasn't disappointed.

"Take care of yourself, Yozef. Listen to Carnigan and Wyfor, and don't get yourself killed." With a hug and a quick kiss, she left, never looking back.

He was afraid, frustrated, and guilty: afraid of finding himself once more pulled into a battle; frustrated that as much as he wanted to bid the party good fortune and run home, he was trapped by expectations of how he should behave; and guilty at the thought of sending the artillery crews he'd organized and trained to fight without him.

When satisfied everything was ready, Denes asked Abbot Sistian to lead the hundreds of family and friends seeing them off in a prayer for their safe return. They left, keeping a steady pace without pushing the horses too hard, and reached Caernford well after midnight. Yozef made the ride, he and Seabiscuit bracketed by Carnigan's and Wyfor's horses, never noticing the aching rear buffered by adrenaline.

The next day, Yozef never spoke with Culich to get a hint about why he was there. He wondered if it was simply one of those "all hands on deck" things, and he was now one of the "hands" because he was part of the family. He caught only brief glimpses of Breda. Most of the time he waited with the other Abersford men, which included sleeping on the ground both nights—whether by intent for him to be among the men or because the Keelans forgot about him now being part of the family, he didn't know.

When they left Caernford, Yozef admitted it was an impressive sight. The road to Moreland only fit three horses abreast or one wagon, so the column stretched more than a mile. Yozef and his two caretakers were part of a group of about fifty attached to the hetman—personal guards, advisors, senior commanders, and both the head medicant and theophist from St. Tomo's.

As far as he could tell, the closest to organization of the men was that groups of 50 to 100 had a leader whom Yozef hoped knew what he was doing. Other than that, it resembled a mob. They took all day to reach the Moreland border. By then, they had met up with another 600 Keelanders, 400 Gwillamese, and 600 Mittackese. The 2,200 heavily armed horsemen, 500 extra mounts, and 90 to 100 wagons of supplies and support personnel, such as medicants and cooks, were out of an epic, one Yozef would have preferred to watch in a theater, rather than be a part of.

Carnigan didn't help by commenting that some of the wagons containing grain for the horses would carry the dead and the wounded back to Keelan once the wagons were empty.

## Moreland City

How far the complete force stretched was not apparent until, from one crest, Yozef looked back and could see the column disappear into the distance over another hill two miles away. When they bivouacked for the evening, the column divided itself into groups of about two hundred and set up temporary camps for staking the horses, eating, and sleeping on the ground or in tents, using the Caedellium version of ponchos made of water-repellant animal hide. The next morning, they were up at the first hint of light to be fed and on the road by the time Yozef could identify the face next to him.

As they crossed the Keelan/Moreland border, Yozef noticed piles of fresh horse dung already flattened by the first fifty horses. He suddenly had a feeling of wonder imagining what it must be like at the end of the column, where the accumulated shit of 3,000 horses carpeted the roadbed. He almost insanely giggled, hoping the local farmers took advantage of the unexpected plethora of fertilizer.

When they were within twenty miles of the Moreland capital, the land flattened and the column spread out into the adjacent fields. One advantage was that traffic in the other directions could use the flanking areas, instead of waiting for the Tri-Clan column to pass. That reverse traffic consisted of wagons loaded with belongings, Yozef assumed fleeing for some hoped-for safety elsewhere, and single riders on lathered horses—probably messengers going who knew where with whatever messages. Every hour or so, a messenger or a small group of riders would stop at the Keelan hetman's grouping and race back where they'd come from.

He knew they'd arrived when they came upon the first encampments of other clans. Carnigan and Denes explained which ones. First Hewell, then Adris and Orosz. Four riders, two of whom carried green flags with red Xs, stopped at the head of the column and spoke with Culich, who in turn spoke with aides. The flagmen directed them to a bivouac area set aside for the Tri-Clans, within sight of Moreland City's walls. It took an hour for the entire column to move into their area and most of another hour to set up an encampment in the same groupings as on the road. Horses were watered and fed on grain they'd brought from Keelan. Men were fed hot stew of some undetermined meat and loaves of the usual dark bread. Yozef was surprised at how fast cooking fires were set up and already-cooked stew heated to boiling. By then it was dark, and all were told to sleep, the implication being that tomorrow might see a battle. A few simple tents appeared, although most of the men would sleep again on the ground that night.

It was not quite light enough to read the next morning when Denes came and said Culich wanted Yozef to accompany them to a hetman conference being held in a large farmhouse a mile from the city and approximately in the middle of the encampments.

"Nine clans came," said Denes. "Hetman Keelan is surprised so many. I hope it's enough to turn back the Narthani."

Forty-eight men were crowded into the room: ten hetmen, plus other clan members. Yozef did a quick count, as he and Denes stood along a back wall. The hetmen sat in chairs around a rectangular table in the center of the room. One of the occupied chairs was larger than the other nine.

*Five'll get me ten he's the Moreland hetman. Denes had said he was a jerk.*

He looked it: arrogant eyes, a shorter-than-average trimmed beard that contrasted with a pompadour-like head of gray hair, and enough jewelry and embroidery on his cloak to remind Yozef of a strutting peacock.

Mr. Pompadour rose to his feet, surveyed the room as if he were doing an inspection, and spoke. "First of all, Moreland wishes to thank all of you for answering our invitation to help drive Narthani from Moreland lands."

*Now I know* he's a jerk. And stupid. It's like he's doing all the others a favor by allowing *them to fight for him.*

The hetmen whose faces Yozef could see remained expressionless. Yozef suspected they all knew the Moreland hetman and weren't surprised by the opening remark. They wasted the next half hour with the same meaningless blather Yozef had seen in meetings on Earth, each hetman introducing himself, although everyone obviously knew the others, thanking Moreland for its hospitality, swearing death to all Narthani, boasting about what they would do to these evil invaders, blah, blah, blah. Yozef wished he could leave and come back when they were through posturing.

It was Culich who got them down to business.

"Gynfor, please give us the current situation. Exactly where are the Narthani and what are they doing?"

The Moreland hetman frowned, and Yozef wondered whether it was because Culich used his first name or because he had more posturing to do before getting down to real business.

"They are encamped southwest of here." He motioned to another Morelander. "Caedem, open up the map." A dark-haired young man with a Van Dyke beard pulled a folded sheet of paper out of a satchel and opened it onto the table.

Denes whispered to Yozef, "That's Caedem Moreland, younger son of the hetman. Sitting next to him is Owain Moreland, the hetman's older son."

Yozef thought the younger son looked normal. The older brother had some of the same in-your-face arrogance of the father, although, instead of the big hairdo, his brown hair was lank and disorderly.

When the map was laid out, the Moreland hetman pointed with a finger to Moreland City. The map covered approximately twenty miles on all sides of the city. "Here's Moreland City, and the Narthani bastards are right now camped six miles southwest. We're right here . . ." He moved his finger to an arc between the city and the Narthani army, closer to the city.

"That close?" asked one of the younger hetmen, a sharp-eyed balding man with a trim beard. "How fast have they been moving? They could be on us early tomorrow morning!"

"That's Welman Stent, hetman of Clan Stent," Denes whispered.

Moreland hesitated, then leaned on the map with his right hand while answering Stent. "I think they are having second thoughts now that they see the clans coming to help us drive them back. They haven't moved the last two days."

"Haven't moved!" exclaimed the youngest of the hetman, a man of his early twenties.

"Lordum Hewell, Clan Hewell," Denes said quietly.

Moreland ignored Hewell, a slight not to be missed, which raised a flush on Hewell's face when Moreland continued.

"They reached their current position three days ago, encamped, and haven't moved since. I think our only decision is whether we give them more time to withdraw or attack them immediately. I offer the first alternative only to show I am open to discussion. My belief is we attack and destroy them. Now that most of their men are out in the open, it is our chance to end the Narthani threat, once and for all."

Yozef could see from the hetmen's expressions that none were as enthusiastic as Moreland for a battle with the Narthani.

One of the more elderly hetman, a short man in his late fifties or early sixties with an unkempt long gray beard and medium-length gray hair swept back, raised a hand to signal he wished to speak, which he did without waiting for Moreland to acknowledge him.

"I thought your first messages said that they crossed into Moreland five days ago. Have they been stopping like this other places?"

"No, they continued until their current location," replied Moreland.

"That means they were only traveling about six to eight miles a day, even before they stopped. That doesn't make sense. An invader would want to keep pushing to retain surprise and overwhelm Moreland before help from other clans arrived."

"Again," said Moreland, "they're afraid of getting too committed."

"Maybe," said a hefty hetman in his middle thirties with shoulder-length brown hair and a full, neatly trimmed beard, "but this feels bad. As if they have something planned."

"Even if they do," another hetman spoke up, "we still have to decide what we're going to do. I agree with caution, but if Hetman Moreland is correct, this may be, as he says, our best chance to rid Caedellium of them."

A tall, lean hetman with salt-and-pepper hair spoke for the first time. "Hetman Moreland, I've heard rumors that most of their men are on foot. Is this true?"

"Teresz Bultecki," Denes murmured. "One of the northern clans. He's one of the more reasonable hetmen from the north. Some of the others have been as much trouble as the Narthani, though not for some years, since the conclaves have stopped most raids and fighting between clans."

A chorus of exclamations and sighs swept through the room: "On foot!"

"Are they insane? We'll ride them down!"

"Is that true?"

"No horses at all?"

"We should attack at once!"

Moreland finally called them all to settle down with a snide expression. "That is one reason I'm so confident. And yes, there's some truth to the rumor, although it's not completely accurate. As far as we can estimate, they have two to three thousand horsemen and another five to six thousand on foot."

"That would explain how slow they've been," said Stent.

"Not completely," cautioned Hewell. "Even on foot, they should have covered more than six miles a day. And that certainly doesn't explain sitting where they are the last two days."

Yozef leaned into Denes's ear. "Good infantry can cover twenty-five miles a day, even over broken country."

Denes whispered back, "What's *infantry*?"

Yozef had unconsciously used the English word. He couldn't think of a comparable Caedellium one.

"Men fighting on foot. Like our dragoons, except without horses at all."

"I can see fighting on foot with towns or forts and, of course, where horses can't go. Why are the Narthani not mounted? Could they not have enough horses?"

Yozef shook his head, while thinking, *Oh shit. I keep forgetting the Caedelli have no history of army maneuvering or the capabilities of infantry.*

Stent voiced Denes's question to Yozef. "Maybe they don't have enough horses to mount all their men?"

"Unlikely," said Culich. "Within the three provinces they control, there are more than enough horses. No, this is deliberate and agrees with reports we've gotten from escaped slaves. The Narthani have many of their fighters on foot and clustered together in groups of hundreds."

Yozef was mumbling and cursing to himself—at least, he thought it was to himself.

Denes nudged him. "What is it, Yozef? What're you thinking?"

Denes didn't wait for an answer and made his way to Culich's chair, leaned over, and whispered in an ear.

Culich's expression didn't change, nor did he look in Yozef's direction, but he spoke over the general hubbub. "Hetman Moreland, the Narthani horsemen we've seen were armed with muskets, swords, and lances, and I understand the Narthani coastal raiders are armed in the same, except for shorter spears. Can you tell us if these Narthani on foot are armed in the same fashion?"

"Some of the footmen have muskets. The odd thing is that others have spears much longer than we've seen before. There's no way they can throw such long spears any distance or fight with them, so it's a puzzle."

*Mixed muskets and pikes*, thought Yozef. *And probably formed in blocks like smaller versions of the Spanish tercios that evolved as musket and cannon fire developed on Earth. Each block can defend in all directions and provide support for adjacent blocks.*

Culich listened to the answer, then said, "Can we take a few minutes to let us all gather our thoughts before continuing? I would also like to consult with my advisors." The session had been going for only an hour, and Moreland looked surprised at the need to break the discussion so soon. With a sour look, he agreed to begin again at the top of the next hour.

Culich rose and walked out the door, followed by Lewis, Kennrick, and Denes, who came back to Yozef, still standing against the rear wall and wondering what was next.

"Come," said Denes, "you need to tell Culich what you told me." Denes gripped his left elbow and forced-marched him out of the still crowded room. The Keelan group was standing under a large shade tree about forty feet from the house.

When Yozef and Denes reached them, Culich looked at Yozef, who wondered whether Culich was angry at being interrupted. However, Culich's face was neutral, and he simply said, "Denes tells me you have thoughts on what's been discussed inside."

"Well . . . I guess two things seem important to me. One is that your people don't seem to understand the importance of 'infantry'—men fighting on foot. I'm guessing, but I wonder if the largest battles in Caedellium history were a few thousand on each side, all on horseback."

Yozef looked expectantly to Culich, who nodded. "In my lifetime, perhaps one thousand total on both sides, though in the histories, and before the conclave was established, there were some that supposedly involved three or four thousand."

"All on horseback?"

"Yes."

"Never on foot?"

"Only when raiding towns, a few less-than-successful attempts to besiege major towns or fortresses, or during battles when many men became unhorsed. That was long ago."

Yozef shook his head. "What you have here is something totally different. The Narthani cavalry is mainly to protect the infantry from your cavalry getting behind them or attacking their flanks. They figure on winning any battle with you with their infantry and cannons."

Although Culich was dubious, Yozef saw that the hetman was trying to comprehend what he was saying. Yozef continued, this time with more energy, forgetting he was no military tactician and simply took his understanding from reading, movies, books, and video games.

"Hetman, consider that the infantry is armed with muskets and pikes. That's what those long spears are called. They are meant to present a wall of spear points far enough in front of the men so that enemies with only swords, lances, or shorter spears can't reach them. Only another wall of pikes has any chance of defeating when it's hand to hand. The pikes serve two other purposes. They protect the men with the muskets. The pikes hold off the enemy, while the muskets shoot them. The other main purpose against your men will be to stop your riders. Horses will not charge into a wall of pike heads. They'll either stop or look for a way around, no matter what the rider tries to make the horse do."

Yozef sweated as he spoke, not knowing whether he was telling them what they needed to hear or if he should say anything at all. He could make things worse, because he was hardly a military tactician, but every fiber of his being told him he had to say what he thought.

"Then all we'd have to do is not charge them," said Culich, "and wait for them to retreat, since they can't catch our men and force a battle."

"Eventually, they *will* force a battle. What if they advance on Moreland City to burn it to the ground? Will the clans stand aside and watch it happen?"

"No. The Morelanders would fight even if alone, and the rest of the clans would have to join in, because destruction of Moreland would put all other clans in worse danger."

"There you have it. A battle is inevitable. Something else to remember. The Narthani don't care about Moreland City. They only use it as a lure. Their goal is to kill so many Caedellium fighting men that the clans are forced to surrender. With forces of this size, seizing land, crops, gold, women, or whatever is not the objective. Destruction of enemy forces is the objective, and all else follows from that."

Culich seemed to be understanding more and not liking it.

"And then there's the Narthani cannon," Yozef added.

"Why are cannon important here?" Kennrick asked. "Oh, I see their importance in protecting harbors and forts, but in open field combat, while being hit by a cannonball is fatal for whoever it hits, they can't possibly kill enough to be decisive."

"Canister," said Yozef, to a look of incomprehension from Kennrick. Only Denes, Culich, and Luwis understood. Denes had personally seen the effects of Yozef's carriage-mounted swivel guns during test firings, and while Culich and Luwis had read reports, Kennrick had not.

"Imagine that instead of firing a single cannonball, the cannon fired hundreds of musket balls at the enemy. The balls would spread out farther from the cannon. Imagine these hundreds of musket balls hitting a charge of clan horsemen. Then imagine scores of cannon firing all at the same time."

"Like the loads we sometimes use to shoot birds," added Denes.

"If the bird is flying, a single musket ball has very little chance of hitting the bird. But birdshot, with hundreds of pellets, always hits the bird," Kennrick said, catching on.

"Now, imagine you fire a single musket ball into a flock of birds so thick you can hardly see the sky behind them," Yozef continued. "How many birds might that musket ball kill?"

"It might go through several birds. Say, two to four birds," answered Kennrick.

"How many birds would you hit in that dense flock with birdshot?"

"It could be a dozen, if the birds are that thick."

"Now imagine that each of those birdshot pellets was the size of a musket ball."

The grim visages of most of the men evidenced the message had gotten through. Luwis spoke slowly, as if framing his words carefully and reluctantly. "So, if we charge, the pikes will prevent us from closing with their infantry, the muskets will fire at us from behind the pikes, the cannon will fire canister into our ranks, and their cavalry will keep us from attacking their rear or flanks before their infantry can make countermoves. Plus, if we don't attack, they'll move on Moreland City and force the battle in the open, or we'd have to fight them within the city, which will almost certainly lead to as much destruction as if the city weren't defended at all. That's the unpalatable scenario you're telling us?"

"I'm afraid so, Ser Luwis."

There was silence among the Keelanders until Vortig Luwis spoke. "If we can't attack and can't wait them out, then what *do* we do?"

"What I've told you are lessons from the history of my people. Not necessarily my people experiencing all of this themselves, but having written histories of other nations and peoples over long periods of time. What I've said is what I remember reading or hearing about. I can't know for sure whether the Narthani fight battles the same way or not. Maybe I'm wrong, and they've left themselves open to being destroyed, as Hetman Moreland believes. Yet when the fate of your people is at risk, isn't it best to plan for the worst?"

"As the *Word* says," recited Culich, "the faithful pray to God but must work for their own salvation." He then looked again directly at Yozef. "So what is it we *can* do?"

"What I would definitely *not* do is charge directly into the Narthani until you can see how they plan to fight the battle. Musket and pike fighting usually means they'll form into blocks, probably longer sides facing you, with rows of men. The first few rows will hold the pikes and present a front of pike heads, while the rear rows will have the muskets, who either will step through the pike rows, fire, and then return to the rear to reload, or the pike men might kneel or lie on the ground, while the musket men fire over them. If you pretend you're ready for battle and perhaps even start a charge, then whatever formations the Narthani assume would tell you exactly what you'll face."

Culich nodded thoughtfully. "I see the wisdom. We'll see their intentions and can withdraw and reconsider our next move. There's no reason to rush to get so many killed."

Culich turned to the other Keelanders, and they discussed what they'd heard and what they should propose to the other hetmen. They asked a couple of short clarification questions of Yozef; otherwise, he wasn't part of the rest of the discussion. A bell rang, calling the meeting back into session, and they joined the other clans in filing back into the room. Yozef resumed his place standing behind the hetman.

Moreland looked at Culich with a raised eyebrow. Was he ready to proceed? Culich nodded. It took two hours of discussion and argument before most the hetmen agreed to Culich's proposal that the clans demonstrate in front of the Narthani by mid-day to test the invader's reaction. Moreland wasn't pleased that the clans wouldn't attack immediately.

# CHAPTER 28

# MORELAND CITY

**First Day**

The sun was two hours past mid-day before the clans were arrayed, facing their enemies. The Narthani were in their final positions two hours before the masquerading clan army. Yozef winced far too many times while the clans sorted themselves out, as the Narthani commanders allowed their men to sit in place and watch the entertainment.

Confusion reigned. Hetman Moreland tried insisting he command the entire mass, but Culich and the other hetmen demurred, and the final organization was for three groups. The clan center was composed of Moreland, Stent, Adris, and Hewell, with Hetman Moreland as the lead. Hetman Orosz led the right wing, including Bultecki and Pewitt. The latter had answered the call for help, to everyone's surprise.

Culich Keelan led the Tri-Clans of Keelan, Gwillamer, and Mittack on the left. Culich, with Yozef's urging, had convinced the other hetmen not to bunch their men but to present the Narthani with an even distribution across the entire front and not give them information on intention or organization. What the Narthani saw was a mile-and-a-half solid line of Caedelli horsemen six deep.

Yozef and his two caretakers didn't join the Keelan men, much to Carnigan's and Wyfor's annoyance. Yozef wanted to get a clear view of the potential battlefield. The Narthani had obviously picked this spot for some reason, and he wanted to know why. He and the others stood under trees behind the arrayed clan horsemen on a hillock twenty feet above the surroundings, the only elevated feature in an otherwise flat plain two miles across. On their right (the Narthani left), a ridge spine rose sharply from the plain. The spine started just before the Narthani position and ran to the southwest, cutting off any easy route around the Narthani left flank. To the Caedelli left (the Narthani right) appeared an area of low hills covered in trees.

Beyond the trees ran a creek bed and more brush and trees, with reduced fields of fire and difficult terrain for horses to move fast and maintain any semblance of order. Beyond lay a forested lower ridgeline.

Yozef needed to get higher, so Carnigan threw a rope over a sturdy-looking limb forty feet up a tree and pulled the other end of the rope down. They rigged a rope saddle, and the two men hoisted Yozef up into the tree. From the limb, he was able to climb another thirty feet, and there, seventy feet above the plain, he had a panorama as the two foes finished positioning. The Narthani were so organized and precise in their movements, Yozef wondered if they were laughing at the chaos on the Caedelli side.

*Well, overconfidence on their part can only help. If only that overconfidence wasn't justified!*

Yozef had all of the information he was going to get long before the clans were in position. Thanks to the discipline of the Narthani troops, it didn't take him long to draw out their positions and make notes. Initially, it was depressingly informative and puzzling at the same time. The Narthani infantry was organized into five-hundred-men blocks. Yozef saw enough detail with the latest telescope from one of his shops. The lenses weren't perfect, so there was distortion, but the magnification was better than expected, and after some experience his brain adjusted to the view.

Each Narthani square was composed of five rows of about a hundred men each. The first two rows carried pikes; the last three, muskets. There were ten such squares. The forward positions were symmetrical, starting from one end, a square, then artillery, two more squares with a third square positioned behind them, a surprisingly big gap before a single centrally located square, then another gap and a mirror image of the other wing.

To the rear of the Narthani center was a group that, if the flags were an indication, included the Narthani commander. Several smaller groups were scattered behind the squares that Yozef thought were likely auxiliaries, such as medical units waiting for the expected casualties. A tenth square was just to the right of the command group, serving either as security or as a reserve unit to plug breakthroughs. On both flanks were masses of horsemen, somewhere between one and two thousand on each wing. Yozef hadn't noticed him appear but found Denes next to him on top of the tree. Denes identified the flanking horsemen—Eywellese on the Caedellium left, and both Narthani and Selfcell on their right. Yozef had no trouble distinguishing their identities: the Narthani cavalry were orderly.

Yozef wrinkled his brow, as he studied the Narthani deployment: two strong points on each wing and a thin line in front of the command group.

*What are they thinking? What if I'm the Narthani commander? I have a disciplined army facing a totally unorganized mass of cavalry. How do I get them to do exactly what I want and kill as many of them as I can?*

He wrestled with the possible answers before one jumped out.

*They WANT the clans to attack at the center! The apparent vulnerability of the Narthani command station is the lure.*

He looked closer at the two wings.

*The clans may think they can break the Narthani line in half and destroy the command structure by launching an all-out attack on the Narthani center.*

He noticed the end units were more advanced, and the two artillery positions slanted slightly inward instead of straight ahead. He envisioned the Narthani might let the central block move back and the two rear-positioned blocks move into gaps next to the central block. All of the infantry and two battery positions could form a 145-degree arc with muskets and canister producing crossing fields of fire. Whatever clan horsemen entered the arc would be slaughtered. If the clan riders then broke and tried to retreat, the lack of central command, uncertainty over who was doing what, and the shock of the slaughter would be ready made for the three thousand cavalry in the Narthani flanks to sweep around the retreating clans in a classic double envelopment. Yozef's memory pulled up histories and sketches, such as the Carthaginians crushing a Roman army at Cannae in 216 BC, and the pincer movements of the Germans in World War II. It could be repeated right before his eyes on the planet Anyar. Such a crushing defeat would be a death knell for the clans.

*I wonder if the Narthani need a chemist.*

He tried to shake the thought, but his mind refused to ignore that he might be seeing the end of whatever life he'd built on Caedellium. If the clans lost, he might survive if he could convince the Narthani of his value and save Maera and their unborn child, though that might be iffy, because she was of the hetman's family. Others he knew, such as Carnigan and Denes, if they didn't die in battle, they'd probably be executed as potential fomenters of resistance.

*Well, shit! Let's see if there's anything I can do to avoid this outcome. First, I have to convince Culich that a center attack would be a disaster.*

The clans *had* to attack. By threatening Moreland City, the Narthani negated the islanders' mobility advantage. All the Narthani had to do was wait.

There was only so long the different clans could leave this many men in front of Moreland City. In a sixday, two at the most, clans would start leaving. Culich had brought fodder and feed for the Tri-Clan horses, enough for perhaps two sixdays when supplemented with grazing. Sixteen thousand horses from individuals and wagons would consume a lot of grazing, especially since it was late in the summer and the grass was brown, with limited nutrient value.

Yozef used the telescope to look at the two flanks. If a center attack was out, that left the flanks and the rear. Getting behind the Narthani was unlikely to be successfully coordinated by the islander mob, plus it would leave Moreland City open for occupation and destruction, something to which the Morelanders wouldn't agree. It would have to be the flanks. Another quick look at the right flank confirmed it couldn't be attacked. The spiny ridge provided an impossible barrier for the Caedelli horsemen. He kept coming back to the Caedelli left flank. From his current perch, he could see low tree-covered hills but no details and nothing in depth. He needed to get higher.

He handed the telescope to Denes. "I need to examine the land on the left side and see what it's like."

Denes took the telescope, put it to his right eye, and swung it back and forth over the area. "Okay. We should be able to get onto the lower ridgeline, but we'll send out men to push back any Narthani."

"We don't want to seem too interested and alert the Narthani," cautioned Yozef.

"We'll do the best we can, but my orders are strict that you not be put in any more danger than absolutely necessary."

They climbed and slid down the tree on the ropes, and they and ten escorts circled behind the arrayed clans to a rocky point atop the lower ridgeline south. It took half an hour to get to a position where they could see the entire potential battlefield, this time from the side. The Narthani squares, the flanking cavalry, and the auxiliary units of the Narthani arrayed north to south were clearly visible, even without the telescope.

Yozef compared his notes from their view on top of the tree, facing the middle of the Narthani positions, and made a few changes and additions to his earlier sketches. He focused on the terrain directly below them. To the Eywellese left was the Narthani infantry square, to their right the low hills and trees, except for a hundred-yard-wide lane running south away from the Eywellese. Three hundred yards down the lane was a streambed where the lane widened to a ford in the stream. The ground sloped, so that a horse could gallop down one side, cross the stream, and continue up the other bank whose top was covered with chest-high brush. He looked again, envisioning the scene and possible movements, starting from the Narthani lines and coming back to the streambed. Then again—he looked farther southwest for the terrain circling back behind the Narthani.

*This might be it. Or, at least the only chance I can see.*

By now, the two armies had faced each other for nearly two hours. As planned, the clans began moving back toward Moreland City, making it seem they were uncoordinated, which didn't take much effort.

"Denes, please find Hetman Keelan and see if he can come here."

Denes took another look around their position. "Is it wise to risk bringing the hetman here?"

Yozef looked surprised, as if he hadn't considered that problem. He scanned the surroundings. "The Narthani are likely to fall back into their encampment once they're convinced the clans are pulling back toward the city. I think you should be able to push enough men forward from here into the trees to secure this position and still not be detected by the Narthani."

Denes walked away, shaking his head doubtfully. Twenty minutes later, he returned with fifty riders, whom he directed to fan out in between them and farther along both sides of the ridgeline. Following shortly were Culich and fifty more riders, who stopped short of Yozef's position, while Culich and Vortig Luwis came forward to his observation point.

"What do you see, Yozef?"

Yozef knew the hetman's question asked both what they could see from this position and whether Yozef had an idea, an inspiration, or a vision.

"Thank you for coming, Hetman." Without further preliminaries, Yozef started explaining. He pointed out the Narthani positions and the terrain details, both as they could see them and on the map. They then worked their way down to the creek Yozef had noted on the map and knelt under a spreading tree, where Yozef laid the map on the ground and drew a similar map in the dirt.

He pointed out the Narthani positions. "When one looks at their deployment, one might think the center is weak and subject to attack."

"Yes," said Luwis impatiently, "we can all see this. If this is their normal arrangement of men, it gives us the chance to break their middle and split their army in two. Perhaps even kill their leaders, if we're fortunate."

"That's likely what they *want* you to believe," said Yozef. "This is an experienced Narthani army and leaders who have likely commanded in many battles before. Don't you think it strange that they would arrange their men in such a vulnerable manner?"

Luwis frowned, scratching his beard as he looked at the map. "I have to say that thought occurred to me. I took it as overconfidence or stupidity on their part. But you're right to point out it may be deliberate."

"If this formation is somehow to fool us, what do you think are their intentions?" asked Culich.

"Of course, I *can't* know their true intentions, though I'll point out one possibility." With a hand, Yozef smoothed over the positions in the dirt of Narthani formations and redrew them with the stick, showing movements. "What if you charge the center, and the Narthani move their men this way . . . ?" He drew the development of crossing fires.

He was only halfway through the explanation when Luwis saw it all. "Great God on high! With their muskets firing from three sides and the cannon canister, they'd slaughter our men!"

"That might only be the beginning. Once the main charge was destroyed, the rest of your riders would be trying to retreat and would run into more riders coming behind them. Those in the back might not be able to see how bad it was in front until they were in range themselves, or they'd be so confused you'd lose any control of your men. The Narthani cavalry on both flanks could encircle your riders, while the Narthani infantry moved forward. Such a maneuver is called a 'double envelopment.' There's too many of you for them to kill you all, but you could easily lose half of your men before withdrawing. The Narthani would then occupy Moreland City, and the conquest of Clan Moreland would be essentially complete. The number of men lost and the memory might make if difficult, or even impossible, to rally the clans in the future."

Culich was thoughtful. "If they want us to attack in the center, have they left weaknesses? If we stay away from their crossing fields of fire, what about their right flank and the Eywellese horsemen? If we attack there, will the Narthani simply adjust their infantry formations, and we'll be back to having no place to attack?"

"What if there were no Eywellese cavalry?" asked Luwis, looking at Yozef.

Yozef was encouraged that Luwis was thinking tactically. "If the Eywellese cavalry was not there, then there might be an opportunity to attack the last square on that side. It would have to be a fast and overwhelming attack before the artillery position turned their cannon and the other Narthani infantry blocks moved to face you. Even better would be if you could overrun the artillery position and turn the guns on the next Narthani infantry block; then the entire Narthani flank might collapse. I doubt you could completely defeat them, but they might have to withdraw out of Moreland."

Culich stood, a more determined look on his face than minutes earlier. "I think we understand enough to finish talking about this back in a safer position. We need also bring the rest of the clans into the planning of what to do next."

They mounted and returned to the main Keelan force that was already heading back to their bivouac site.

The hetmen argued long into the night over the next day's action. The Moreland hetman was unconvinced by Yozef's arguments, as laid out by Culich. In the end, most of the hetmen backed Culich, either because they had some inkling of the arguments or because they settled on a plan not requiring their clans to launch an assault on the Narthani positions. The final plan was more an exploration of whether the Eywellese could be lured into abandoning their screening position. Even if that happened, Yozef doubted the clans could take advantage of the opportunity.

Yozef was alternately excited and scared—thrilled to participate in planning an actual battle and terrified that he had no idea what he was doing.

## Second Day

The sun rose on a clear day and moderate northerly winds. The same sun that prompted Yozef to raise a hand to block its rays also warmed Breda Keelan's left cheek, as she sat on the veranda and looked north toward Moreland; the same sun that shone through Maera Kolsko-Keelan's bedroom window, as she lay imagining what was happening 160 miles north; and the same sun that shone through St. Sidryn's windows to rest on a kneeling abbot.

The clans deployed into three adjacent groupings. The center and right groups had the simplest and least risky assignments. All three groups would pretend to launch direct charges on the Narthani. However, as soon as they came within estimated musket and canister range, they would stop and mill about as if undecided how to continue. Only the left group, the Tri-Alliance clans, would continue on, veering with a feint directly at the Eywellese on the Narthani flank.

The plan was simple in conception but dependent on the Eywellese doing something stupid, such as leave their position guarding the Narthani right flank. It was Culich who suggested the most likely way to achieve this. Culich and his household banner would lead the charge, then pretend to break away to the south, in the hope Eywell would be unable to resist pursuing. To help, the Keelan banner would fly over an upside-down Eywell banner—a traditional symbol of domination or, in the case of inimical sides, "fuck you," as Yozef interpreted.

The three Tri-Clan hetmen, the senior clan leaders, and Yozef stood around a map laid out on the ground in front of the massed clans' horsemen.

Culich summarized. "As Yozef Kolsko suggests, let's go over the plan one final time. Of the twenty-two hundred Tri-Clan men answering Moreland's call, we've left two hundred to guard our encampment and support people. The other two thousand are divided into four groups. Two groups of six hundred men each will be under me and Hetman Gwillamer. We will charge directly at the Eywellese. When my flagman signals, Vortig will lead four hundred men in an apparent retreat, while Hetman Gwillamer's group will mill and shift left and parallel to the Eywellese and Narthani positions. The other two hundred men will follow me and the Keelan banners to the south, where we hope to tempt the Eywellese to give chase.

"If Hetman Eywell follows me, four hundred Keelan dragoons under Denes Vegga await, hiding in the brush across the creek bed at the end of the alley in the trees and low hillocks. Yozef Kolsko will be with Vegga to oversee the swivel gun and crossbow carriages."

"Pardon, Culich," interrupted Hetman Mittack. "None of my people have experience with this artillery, as it's being called, and we only know of them in a few Caedellium port defenses. I know you say they are important, but how much of this plan depends on them?"

"I've seen them in test exercises, and they're impressive," said Denes, "though I'm not counting on them today. The muskets in the ambush should fell the most forward Eywellese horsemen who follow Hetman Keelan. Those Eywellese farther behind will run onto a tangle of downed men and horses, and it should be chaotic enough for us to pick off most of the rest. If the swivel carriages work, it will go even worse for the Eywellese."

*I hope he's right*, Yozef prayed. *We've practiced enough, but drills and battles aren't the same.*

"The plan is of three parts," continued Culich," all dependent on tricking the Eywellese into abandoning their primary role—protecting the Narthani infantry flank. *If* the Eywellese follow our feigned rout, the two hundred men under me will lure the Eywellese into the ambush. If needed, we'll wheel and support the four hundred men forming the ambush. Plus, Hetman Mittack waits farther behind the ambush with our final four hundred men. If the ambush is successful enough, my two hundred plus Mittack's four hundred will circle north to attack the rear of the Eywellese. Vortig Luwis and Hetman Gwillamer will rally their thousand to cut off the retreat of the Eywellese in the ambush and, if possible, assault the remaining Eywellese screening the Narthani infantry block. Once the ambush is cleared, the dragoons and the artillery will remount and move toward the last Narthani infantry block. Yozef assures us that smoke from the Narthani guns will already be obscuring views, and that will be enhanced by Luwis's men dragging burning straw bales along the Narthani flank, setting the grass afire."

Culich stood up from the map, as did all the men. "Remember, this is a multi-step plan and is to be aborted at any point, if necessary. If the Eywellese don't fall for our trick, we simply withdraw back to the current positions. Same thing if the ambush doesn't succeed as well as we believe or takes too long and the Narthani adjust their positions. If we proceed to attack the Narthani flank, we will press on only as long as we have the advantage. Kolsko warns us, and I agree, not to try to engage the Narthani under any conditions where we don't have advantages. Any final thoughts or questions?"

The grim men glanced at one another. None spoke.

"Then, men of Mittack, Gwillamer, and Keelan, may God be with us this day. I pray to see you all this evening."

# CHAPTER 29

# COMMITTED

Aivacs Zulfa's horse sensed its rider's tension and skidded to one side, bumping against Nuthrat Metan's mount. Other horses reacted, and the Narthani command staff settled each of their horses and resumed a semi-circle, facing east toward Moreland City. Zulfa had carefully selected their army's position, a mainly flat plain with clear fields of fire for muskets and cannon and limited room for the clans to use their horsemen to threaten the Narthani rear.

Metan commanded their left wing, including the Narthani heavy cavalry and the Selfcell horsemen. The ridgeline farther left obviated any clan attack on that flank and freed their cavalry to exploit openings. If all went according to plan, the Caedelli mass horse charge would be broken up by artillery and crossing fields of fire, and Zulfa would signal for their heavy cavalry to use the weight of their larger horses and armor to ride down the disordered and disheartened islanders or to lead the Selfcellese on the left wing of a double envelopment.

Erkan Ketin directed the middle of the Narthani line, which included maneuvering the infantry and the artillery into the killing arc. He was the oldest of Zulfa's subordinates, and Zulfa doubted Ketin would rise further in rank, but he was solid and dependable—the right man to orchestrate this maneuver.

The right wing of the deployment was under Memas Erdelin, a member of a prominent family with significant influence in Narthani society and imbued with excessive self-confidence. Zulfa didn't like the man, but, despite reservations about his ability, Erdelin hadn't yet given Zulfa sufficient reason to approach General Akuyun to replace him. Zulfa suspected the relative unreliability of the Eywellese was somehow related to Erdelin, though he didn't know how. Not that there was any doubt about either Erdelin's or the Eywellese's willingness to fight. Rather, Zulfa's concern was their not thinking clearly and acting more aggressively than warranted. For today, Erdelin and the

Eywellese had an easy task: hold the right flank and be prepared to join a general pursuit or envelopment.

Zulfa surveyed the Caedelli arraying a mile away in three separate masses of horsemen, separated by gaps. Banners identified nine clans besides Moreland.

"A few more of them than we expected from Assessor Hizer's briefings," noted Ketin quietly, as he swept down the Caedelli deployment with his telescope. "The middle group is larger and aimed directly at our center. Those two flanking groups are smaller and won't come completely into the killing zone. I think our last blocks and the cavalry can hold them off while we deal with the main group."

"The more of them the better," appraised Erdelin, lowering his own telescope. "If we kill enough today, the sooner the clans submit and we can get back to Narthon."

"Well, we're ready, and they're here," Zulfa said loud enough for this three immediate subordinates and all of their staffs to hear over the horses and the background noises of the army. "If they don't attack today, we'll move forward to Moreland City tomorrow and force their hand."

"It'll be today," said Metan. "I can feel it."

"We'll see," said Zulfa, looking down at a diagram of their deployment.

An aide spoke urgently, "Brigadier, they're moving."

Zulfa looked up sharply and saw all three masses of Caedelli horsemen in motion. At first, it appeared as a rippling; then, when he used the telescope attached to his saddle, he could see the Caedelli horses moving forward at a walk. It was at times like this when he felt helpless. All his sub-commanders knew their roles, and he could only watch and trust them to carry out their instructions. Only if things went badly would he issue new orders in the next few minutes.

"This may be it," he said more calmly than he felt. "Colonels, to your positions."

Ketin, Metan, and Erdelin galloped to their stations, their staffs following.

Denes Vegga halted the ambush force behind a forest patch a quarter-mile south of the dense brush covering the western bank of the creek bed where they hoped to ambush the Eywellese. The men sat or stood holding their horses' reins, the swivel gun and crossbow artillery crews huddled to one side. The carriage limbers carried premeasured bags of powder, shot bags, explosive quarrels, and powder horns to charge the swivel initiation chambers. Six horses pulled the swivel carriages, plus their limbers. Although four horses could manage, six provided more speed and a safety margin if one or two horses were injured, either in battle or through accidents. The lighter crossbow carriages and limbers needed only four horses.

The effective range of the three-barreled swivel pieces was not much more than 150 yards, better than nothing. However, Yozef wasn't confident about the quarrel launchers and ordered the crews not to take part in the ambush.

Each carriage had a crew of eight men, more than needed, but it took into account possible casualties, so extra men would allow the guns to continue firing. It also provided extra men for a hoped-for use, along with another thirty men with muskets waiting nearby. All the men had experience with the swivel and dry runs with inert mock 6-pounders. They all could man the tri-swivel carriages, but as important was the possibility that the islanders would capture the southern Narthani artillery position and turn the guns on their owners.

Yozef was dubious about their plan. It all sounded plausible when talking and diagramming on the ground and later on paper, but too many parts had to work, and once set in motion the opportunity to adjust would be limited. He had argued vociferously against the hetman exposing himself to the forefront of the feigned attack on the Eywellese but begrudgingly understood the best chance of enticing Hetman Eywell out of his position was to offer a prize Eywell couldn't resist.

Gynfor Moreland and his two sons, Owain and Caedem, led the Moreland contingent forward. First at a walk, then quickening the pace to a trot, as the entire mass of horsemen flowed forward. Behind him were three thousand Moreland riders, the best fighting men of his clan. To his left and his right were another two thousand riders from the Adris and Hewell, and the Stent and Pewitt clans, respectively. A sense of exhilaration flooded through him, followed by frustration. As an adolescent, he'd dreamed of leading such a charge as recounted in legends, but this was only to be a feint. He could see the two wings of the Narthani deployment and the sparsely occupied center. With the men at his back, how hard could it be to burst through the Narthani line, split their force in two, and annihilate them?

Welman Stent urged his horse into a trot. He had reiterated to his major subordinates that their clan's role was a ruse, reminding them so often, they sickened of his nagging. Beside him at the head of his clansmen were flagmen pointing their flag staves forward. On his orders, they would raise the flags, the signal for Stent and Pewitt men to wheel ninety degrees and sweep to the right across the Narthani front. The Hewell and Adris contingents to the Moreland left had similar instructions from their hetmen.

Culich led the Tri-Clan Alliance advance. Their instructions were more intricate. They aimed at the junction between the last Narthani infantry block and the Eywellese cavalry screening their flank. The twelve hundred Alliance horsemen would only feign an attack. Most would pretend to retreat or would slide slowly right in front of the Narthani. Only two hundred riders would follow Culich in tempting an Eywell pursuit into the ambush. Although they hoped to stay out of effective musket range and out of alignment with the Narthani artillery position, they would still take casualties—a price Culich understood had to be paid.

Erkan Ketin sat on his horse a hundred yards behind the central infantry block, along with his staff and signalmen carrying the flags that would direct the planned force movements. So far, the Caedelli were cooperating in taking the bait to attack what they saw as the weak Narthani center. The two smaller groups of clansmen might not enter the trap, but the large central group, now at a canter, was aimed directly at him. He smiled. There were enough islander horsemen to deal them a crushing blow.

Hetman Brandor Eywell watched from the head of his fifteen hundred men, his oldest son, Biltin, next to him, tried to control his black stallion from biting other horses. For his youngest son, Demian, who was only seventeen, this was his first major fight, and his father thought it time. The boy was eager enough, though not experienced in leading older men.

Brandor could see the Tri-Alliance horsemen approaching his position. He had feared they would attack the Narthani directly and not give him a chance to pay back his clan's traditional enemy, the hated and arrogant Keelanders.

Major Patmir Tullok stood left of his command, the rightmost Narthani infantry block of five hundred pike and musket men. It was his first battle as a major, and his block's primary task was protecting the flank of the artillery batteries containing half of the army's cannon. They also formed one end of the arc of the trap. To his right were the Eywellese riders and the sounds of their horses shuffling hooves in place, neighing and snorting, and the voices of their riders made it necessary for his subordinates to raise their voices to be heard. It would worsen, because the rumbling of the Caedelli horses moving into a gallop was just rising above the Eywellese noise. Once the artillery and his muskets opened fire, it would be impossible to hear anything from the man next to him without shouting in his ear.

Denes and the four men commanding a hundred each watched to the east, where three men stood on a hilltop a half-mile away. Those three men could see the battlefield hidden from Denes's view. There were three men to ensure the correct signal was given. They each had two flags lying on the ground in front of them. A raised red flag meant the plan was called off, and Denes was to withdraw back to the original Tri-Alliance position. A white flag meant the clans had moved to a full gallop and Denes's group was to move into ambush position. He didn't know which flag he hoped for most.

His wondering ended when a man next to him shouted, "The white flags!"

Denes jerked his head to the northwest, and there they were—three waving white flags. "You're off, Wainrin," he ordered to his cousin, who was leading the hundred men in their vanguard. Wainrin acknowledged with a touch to his hat and rode off to his men, some of whom had also seen the flags and were mounted by the time he got to them. They rode hard toward their intended position, followed by the next two hundred, the eighty men of the artillery group, including Yozef and his bodyguards, and the final hundred. Four hundred Mittackese waited farther back and would follow Denes's group to await the outcome of the ambush.

Not from his own choosing, Yozef found himself leading the pathetic excuse for Keelan artillery. He had no sooner sat in the saddle than Seabiscuit followed Carnigan's and Wyfor's mounts to the front of the carriages and crews. He shifted uneasy in the saddle, knowing he was no leader. By the time they moved a half-mile, he realized his mood had shifted almost to anticipation before he jerked himself back to reality. He knew from reading and experience with gaming that a martial spirit was addictive, but this wasn't a game. Men would soon be dying, even possibly himself.

*Christ, I hope they understood enough to break off if any part goes wrong.*

He also prayed that having *any* plan was a good idea.

Aivacs Zulfa stood at his command position on an eight-foot-high platform rising from a slightly higher portion of the flat plain. From there, he had partial views of his army's deployment and the Caedelli. So far, so good. If they kept coming, the middle group would be entirely within the killing zone. They'd moved from a trot to a canter. Soon they'd have to be at a full gallop. He knew even the inexperienced Caedelli must realize the need to close the distance in the shortest time once they were in musket and cannon range. Where they erred was expecting to survive to close with his troops. Their mistake would be fatal and the beginning of the end of clan resistance.

The drumming of his own horse's hoofs striking the ground was felt but not heard by Culich Keelan: the thunder of thousands of hooves drowned out any other sound. He and the accompanying riders carrying Keelan Clan banners were thirty yards behind the leading riders. His men had insisted he have a screen in front of him for when they came within Narthani and Eywell shot range. It rankled him to know his men offered themselves as living shields, for he still felt the pull of the traditional Caedellium code of leading from the front. Another part of him was ashamed that he couldn't hide from himself some measure of relief for his own safety.

"Now!" exclaimed Zulfa into the air, as he watched the central clan mass of horsemen approaching the edge of shot range. As if Ketin had read his mind, Zulfa saw signalmen hoisting colored banners on poles. Within moments, there was a shift in the Narthani block positions, the single isolated central block moving back, the side blocks turning slightly inward, and the two side reserve blocks trotting forward to fill the gaps alongside the central block. The entire change took less than a minute to form an arc with the main clan mass charging straight to the arc's focal point.

Hetman Gynfor Moreland was eight hundred yards from the Narthani central block when he saw them raise their ranked pikes, turn, and run to their rear. A quick glance to the neighboring blocks also revealed movement.

*They're breaking!* Gynfor exulted to himself. *I told those timid fools at the conclave the Narthani footmen would break when they saw us bearing down on them—no men on foot can stand up against a horse charge!*

All thoughts of the agreed-on plan evaporated. He had a fleeing enemy in front of him, and he led an irresistible wave of riders. He would ride them down, crush the Narthani, and show the other clans who not to trifle with! They roared past the stopping point. Several of his leaders looked at him, waiting for the signal to turn. He held his sword high, then pointed straight at the Narthani and urged his horse on ever faster. Three thousand Moreland riders—two hundred across and fifteen deep—followed his vision of glory.

Welman Stent had waited for Hetman Moreland's signal to halt the charge. At first, he stared dumbfounded when, instead of flags signaling to break off the charge, Moreland swung his sword in a circle, pointed straight at the Narthani, and continued the charge. It took Stent ten seconds to process what was happening. By then, they had closed the distance to the Narthani by another hundred yards.

*The idiot is carrying through the charge, instead of holding up! God damn all idiots!*

Stent pulled up his horse, which still took him another thirty yards deeper into the now-formed Narthani arc, albeit just at the right portion of the arc. The Stent riders behind and beside him also reined in, but almost fifty men were too far in front and didn't see they were now the only Stentese still charging. Stent pointed to their right, and they moved parallel to the Narthani. Several riders had been pulling bales of hay, which were now lit and the burning bales dragged along the ground behind the main Stent body, setting some of the partially dry grass on fire.

To the Moreland left, a similar shock was going through hetmen Lordum Hewell and Klyngo Adris. Hewell hesitated longer than Stent, costing the Hewellese another fifty yards, but Adris stopped at the agreed position and wheeled left.

Culich saw the coming disaster the moment the Moreland hetman committed his men. Unlike the other hetmen, he instantly understood what was happening. He also recognized that the Moreland action made no difference to his role and that as bad as the disastrous move was for Moreland, it helped his own part by focusing Narthani attention to the center.

They continued their charge until within two hundred yards of the Eywellese. Culich could easily identify Brandor Eywell sitting on his horse amidst Eywell banners.

He nodded to his flagmen, and they signaled Luwis and the Gwillamese to lead their men in a simulated retreat. The remaining two hundred riders followed Culich another fifty yards and then turned south and feigned retreating away from the battle scene and down the open alley toward the stream, the waiting dragoons, and their pitiful Keelan artillery.

From his vantage point, Zulfa watched the central cavalry mass flow into the Narthani cul-de-sac. The apparently isolated central infantry block was joined on both sides by blocks previously held to the rear. There were now nine blocks plus the two artillery groups forming an arc two-thirds of a mile across. He regretted the two flanking masses had stopped their charges.

*No matter*, he thought. This way, even more Narthani firepower would focus on the central group, while still holding off any new charges on the flanks.

As more and more clan horsemen flowed into their trap, Zulfa gauged when it was time to spring. Just as he was about to say to himself, *Now, Ketin, now's the time*, Ketin seemed to read his mind again, and a rocket shot up from Ketin's observation position. Within seconds, the Narthani arc erupted in flame and smoke. Sixty cannon firing canisters and twenty-seven hundred muskets fired within three seconds. The Moreland charge hit a wall.

Gynfor Moreland saw the smoke and seconds later heard the thunder. The Narthani line vanished behind white smoke. Then most of the riders in Gynfor Moreland's view crashed to earth, as horses and riders were hit by musket and canister balls, some of the leaders hit several times. Clouds of blood exploded in Moreland's vision, horses collided with those down, and screams of men and animals rose over hoof beats. Whereas an instant earlier Moreland had ridden behind a thin screen of riders and had masses of more riders in his peripheral vision, he suddenly rode alone. Glancing to his rear, he could see mounds of downed riders and horses with more coming behind them crashing into their fallen brethren. Those Morelanders still ahorse snaked their ways around the chaos and kept coming. Among those missing were his two sons, Owain and Caedem.

*They must have fallen*, rose to his stunned mind.

Perhaps only their horses had been hit, and they had jumped from their saddles before crashing with their mounts. Both were such good riders and had been since they were eager children first learning to ride from their father. The incongruousness of the scene flashed through Gynfor Moreland's mind at that moment and was lost forever when a second volley of muskets ended his universe.

Welman Stent's heart was stout, but it froze when the Narthani fired. He could see some of his men and their horses fall, mainly those who had been in front and failed to see his signal to stop. Of those fifty, perhaps half went down. Those few remaining looked around and saw their isolation and reined in. Stent waved at them to get back. Ten of them made it. The Narthani firing continued, and with each volley a few of his men fell. Even outside of the presumed effective range, a few balls found human and horse flesh. By the fourth volley, the smoke from the Narthani line and the smoldering grass fires being set by clansmen spread a cloak over the battlefield, and the Narthani were firing at where the islanders had been, instead of where they could be seen. Stent pulled his group farther back and the bulk of the Stent, the Hewell, and the far too few surviving Morelander horsemen used the smoke to withdraw back to their original positions and let the Narthani waste ammunition firing through smoke. By the time the remnants of the Moreland debacle escaped the trap, the plain was carpeted with dead, dying, and wounded men and horses. The cries and screams of both reached ears two miles away.

From Zulfa's elevated position, he could see the main islander charge disintegrate, as hundreds of clan riders and their horses went down. It had not worked as well as hoped, but then what battle plan ever did? Not all of the middle group of Caedelli had entered the trap, and the two flanking groups withdrew or stayed out of range. He regretted that not more of the clansmen had fallen, but the bodies littering the battlefield gave evidence that the central group had suffered catastrophic losses.

Not all Moreland horsemen either fell to the volleys or retreated. Despite the storm of lead, enough horsemen survived and kept moving forward that not even the disciplined Narthani ranks had been able to hit them all. A hundred riders reached the Narthani infantry blocks, only to find, as Yozef predicted, that the wall of pikes was too much even for their shocked horses. Those temporarily spared flowed between the infantry blocks. Once to the rear, they found no succor. They were too few, scattered, and too unled to have any noticeable effect on the infantry blocks. The Narthani musket men turned their muskets to the rear and picked off individuals. None that penetrated the Narthani line survived more than two minutes.

Zulfa saw all of this. Erkan Ketin, his initial task complete once he signaled for the trap to be sprung, fell back to Zulfa's position with his staff and guards. Zulfa would use him as a reserve commander, if needed and if a major change in plan was warranted. Having a senior commander deliver changes was more likely to be obeyed immediately.

Most of Zulfa's attention was on the center of the Caedelli charge, and the devastation was gratifying. It was too bad about the flanks. They'd wanted more of the clansmen in the kill zone.

What should be the next move? The two flanking masses of islanders were intact, as were the parts of the central group that pulled up before entering the kill zone, so sending in his cavalry and island auxiliaries in an envelopment wasn't automatic. He strained to see through the smoke. The battlefield obscurity wasn't as bad as some battles he had been in. Only his own men had fired significant powder; few Caedelli got off shots. From his position, he could still see more than in other battles he'd been in, where, after the first few volleys, neither side could see more than a hundred yards, and it became a game of intimate contact orchestrated by imperfect information on dispositions. The islanders setting the grass afire was unexpected. Now that firing had slackened, the smoke should begin to clear.

# CHAPTER 30

# AMBUSH

The results of the Moreland charge were unknown to Culich. Although he saw the Morelanders continue toward the Narthani position and heard and witnessed the Narthani fire, his focus had narrowed to the Eywellese. He stayed in the vanguard of his clansmen, even though endangering himself. For their plan to work, the Eywellese must see him and his banners and follow them as he "fled." The Keelan banners couldn't fall. If any bannerman fell, others would pick up the banner. His men also had instructions that if their hetman were killed, they would tie his body upright in his saddle and lead his horse. Neither Culich's wife nor Maera knew his saddle had braces at his back for such a task and not to help him stay on his horse, as he'd told them. If his horse fell, his body and saddle would be transferred to another mount.

The pounding of his horse's hooves reverberated up his backbone and jolted his bad knee. He heard cannon and musket firing, but he and his clansmen weren't the main targets, although he did see a few of his men and horses fall.

By the time they were two hundred yards from the Eywellese, Luwis led the feigned retreat, leaving Culich and two hundred riders.

For Brandor Eywell, the battle was frustrating in both planning and execution, because the Narthani had relegated his people to doing nothing, which was what he considered protecting the Narthani right flank. He watched, as the other clans deployed into three points of attack, and he understood the logic behind Zulfa's plan. He reassured himself that he and his clan would be on the winning side in this battle; the other clans were clueless what they were up against. Still, the traditional feuds and histories chafed that he wouldn't have an opportunity to strike at old enemies. Then God smiled on him. He recognized the Keelan, Gwillamer, and Mittack banners facing his side of the

Narthani deployment. Maybe there was a chance to pay Keelan back for past indignities, after all.

He also identified the banners of the Moreland-led group. Too bad the Adris and Hewell clans had stopped. He smiled to himself at the same time that he winced when the Morelanders rode oblivious to their deaths. Once the firing started, he lost sight of anything except what was directly to his front. His eyes fixated on the cluster of Keelan banners, where Culich Keelan himself would be. His face turned first to stone and then red with fury when he saw his own banner inverted under Keelan's.

*That arrogant bastard even now can't refrain from insults—and this . . .?*

Wait. His eyes narrowed.

When the charge in front him seemed to falter and most of the riders retreated or wheeled left, he cursed in disappointment until he realized that the riders to the far right were still coming. There couldn't be more than a few hundred of them, including Keelan himself.

*What's the arrogant prick thinking? That Eywell would run just at the sight!*

The thought fueled his anger. Was this his chance? An opportunity to pay back the hated Keelanders? Killing Culich Keelan and many of his best men would cripple the Tri-Alliance and solidify the Eywell position in a Narthani-dominated future.

The Keelanders suddenly reined in.

*Finally*, thought Brandor. *Culich has realized how exposed he is and is about to pull back. If I'm going to act, it has to be now.*

"Demian!" he shouted out to his younger son by his side. "Ride back to the last five hundred and tell their commanders to hold position to defend this flank. I leave you here in charge. I take the rest of our men to ride down Culich Keelan."

"But, Father," protested the seventeen-year-old, "our orders are to hold this position."

"Do as you're told," Brandor snarled. "This is a chance to crush the Keelanders, and I mean to take it."

With those orders, Brandor turned from his son to listening subordinates.

"Forward to destroy Keelan!"

Culich's eyes focused on the Eywell leaders. Would Eywell take the bait? Brandor would be stupid to do so. Then again, they were dealing with Brandor Eywell, so stupid wasn't out of the question.

On cue, the Keelanders milled for perhaps a minute, before Culich pointed south and the Keelanders rode toward the alley at the end of which awaited Denes Vegga. The Eywellese must have seen both his banners and the upside-down Eywell flag, for suddenly the front of the Eywellese horsemen surged forward, a hetman's banners in the lead.

Despite his low opinion of the Eywell hetman, Culich was still surprised. *Stupid wins again.*

By the time the leading Eywellese trailed only fifty yards behind the last Keelan rider, both groups were racing toward Denes and the ambush.

"Run, you dogs!" yelled Brandor Eywell. He outnumbered them four or five to one. If he caught them against a barrier, even if only slowing them down, Culich Keelan would die.

The lead men in his pursuit were within twenty yards of the trailing Keelanders. Occasionally, one fell from a pistol fired by his lead men, shots from horseback finding a Keelan more by accident than skill. One of his men carrying a lance and on a fast horse caught a Keelan rider and pierced him in the back to fall from his horse and be trampled by pursuers.

Two hundred Keelanders raced through the open alley about a hundred yards wide between low hillocks with scattered trees. Ahead, Brandor saw an approaching line of brush and a hundred yards farther a twenty-foot escarpment the horses couldn't climb. Would the brush slow the Keelanders? Maybe this was where they would pen them. Then . . . no . . . the front of the fleers dipped down and then back up in sight. A creek bed. Once they crossed the creek, the Keelanders would be pinned against the escarpment!

When Denes arrived at the creek, the first hundred of his men had already deployed. One man in four held the reins of four horses behind the screen of shrubs and small trees on top of the north section of the west embankment. The other men finished positioning for clear firing lanes and room to reload. South of the break in the brush, the swivel artillery and the rest of the musket men moved into place. Nine swivel barrels and three hundred muskets waited to see if the Eywellese obliged.

The three crossbow carriages were set up fifty yards behind the swivels, with orders from Yozef not to engage the Eywellese. He didn't want to worry about quarrels landing short.

All of their positions were exposed, both the men with muskets and the swivel carriages. In the expected chaos, they hoped the mounted Eywellese couldn't return effective fire. Nor could they directly assault the ambushers, since a six- to eight-foot vertical embankment fronted the men and the guns. The only way for the Eywellese to attack the ambush was from behind, after following Culich's men down the far shallow embankment, across the creek, and back up a similar opening on their side. To prevent this, once the horsemen led by Culich passed between the two lines of ambushers, they would wheel to face any Eywellese riders reaching the Keelan side of the stream. When it was clear no significant number of Eywellese would survive to reach the ambush's rear, the two hundred Keelan bait horsemen would join with Hetman Mittack's four hundred riders and circle behind the remaining Eywellese horsemen protecting the Narthani flank.

Yozef crouched behind a rock next to the three makeshift artillery pieces. He rested one elbow on a rock and pretended to steady the telescope he held in both hands with a death grip. This was not what he had planned for his future on Anyar. What else could he do? He had made a place among these people, better than he could have hoped for. For this society, he was wealthy and provided with such luxuries as were available. He found the work in developing products and slowly introducing knowledge to the Caedelli more engrossing than he'd expected. The local hetman thought highly of him, and he had a wife who was bright and evidently dedicated to the marriage. He had one child already and another on the way. His memory flashed briefly to Maera, her belly just swelling, kissing him briefly and walking away, as he rode to join the Keelan contingent headed for Moreland.

So why was he here, waiting for a thousand screaming lunatics on horseback to gut him with sword or lance? The obvious answer was he had no choice, especially after he had suggested the very tactic they were attempting, after he had designed and overseen these abortions of artillery pieces, and after his wife expected that he would *want* to be part of this.

*I wonder if it ever occurred to Maera I'd be scared shitless and wish I was back in our house, waiting for news of the battle.*

He quit pretending to study the approach to their position, hunched down even lower behind the rock, took several deep breaths, and looked around. Denes alternately watched the alley and swung his gaze along their line, checking for any exposure that might warn the Eywellese.

*Brave, honorable Denes.*

Yozef remembered Denes's family, a wife and three children. Would they have a husband and a father at sundown today? Carnigan. Hulking, sour-looking, gruff, and a heart bigger than the rest of him. Yozef wondered whether anyone but him realized this about Carnigan. And secrets. Why did Carnigan seem tied to the abbey? Some dark secret? Yozef had probed a few times with Carnigan and the abbot and gotten nowhere. Carnigan was the first person Yozef had connected with after he came to Anyar. Who'd held him that day in the garden, then taken him for food and cold beer. Would Carnigan be alive tomorrow? Would the men manning the cannon pieces? None were "friends," except for Filtin, but several were his workers and had trained hard at handling the carriages. He knew all their names, and if any of them died, he'd feel the loss. How many of them would survive the day and how many widows and orphans would there be by sundown?

Yozef returned to observing the alley, this time not pretending to look through the telescope, though he stayed crouched behind the rock. They heard the thunder of cannon and muskets and the cries of thousands of men and horses. What was happening back at the main battlefield? He hadn't expected so much fire from a feigned charge.

Next to the farthest carriage from Yozef, a man crouched behind another of Yozef's contraptions: a bladder two feet in diameter, fixed to a narrowing funnel with a fluted end, lay on the ground. At Denes's signal, the man would lie hard on the bladder, forcing air into the end to emit a piercing shriek. They didn't have signaling rockets yet, but even if they had, the bladder–horn was quicker and more reliable, albeit of shorter range. Everyone who needed to hear was within a hundred yards.

Yozef felt the earth shaking from thousands of hooves. The men crouching behind the brush also heard the thunder approaching, looked at one another, and gripped their muskets in silence. Even the hundreds of horses held only fifty yards behind the position were silent, as if they, too, anticipated.

Dust clouds rose from the north, and the first Keelan riders appeared in the alley, a few at first, then the cluster of banners within which Yozef hoped was Culich Keelan, then a solid mass of riders, stirrup to stirrup across the alley. They raced toward their waiting fellow clansmen and covered the two hundred yards from where they first appeared in seconds that seemed like minutes. Down the far slope they raced, splashing across the foot-deep water, hard up the near slope, through the opening in the brush, and past their clansmen, the

Eywellese hard on their heels. As Yozef watched, pursuers cut two of the slower Keelanders from their horses. Then, the last Keelan rider cleared the brush opening, and Denes tapped the bladder-horn man's shoulder. The man jumped to his feet and let his full weight fall on the bladder.

A shriek pierced even the cacophony of horses and men, followed seconds later by the first swivel barrels, the muskets, then the second barrel on each swivel carriage, and finally the third barrel. Six seconds passed from the shriek to the third barrel firing. The first swivel barrels and muskets swept the creek and the opposite slope of riders and horses and turned them into a jumble of dead and dying. The closeness of the ambush meant many of the balls hit the most exposed targets many times, shredding those nearest and partly shielding those deeper into the Eywellese formation, who were only briefly spared.

As the horses in front of them went down, those following at full gallop had no time or room to react, and their horses collided with the fallen, adding to the tangled mass. As many Eywellese were crushed under the weight of horses or felled by thrashing legs as were struck by lead balls. The Eywellese not hit in the first salvo couldn't see the extent of the devastation until too late. When still mounted Eywellese tried to rein in, the momentum of riders behind pressed them on. The second and third barrels of the three artillery pieces swept more riders and horses away. A hundred and fifty Eywellese fell from the Keelan fire in those first seconds. Another two hundred piled into the tangle of dead and wounded horses and men before the rest of the horsemen could stop.

Yozef heard nothing recognizable. The musket and cannon fire, overlaid on top of hundreds of men yelling and screaming and the wounded horses, saturated either his ears' or his brain's ability to process a wall of sound.

Twenty seconds after the first salvo, hundreds of Keelan muskets and three swivel carriages began independent fire, as the men reloaded as fast as possible. They had no cover themselves, especially once they rose from or stepped out from concealment, for which there was no need. Most of the Eywellese firearms were dropped in the chaos or fired from panicked horses. Meanwhile, Keelan men reloaded and fired directly into the Eywellese mass. Scores of unhorsed Eywellese ran toward the woods, often having lost their weapons, in no frame of mind to be a threat and who could be ridden down at leisure.

By the time the remaining Eywellese horsemen tried to retreat down the alley, Vortig Luwis closed the trap, as he led four hundred Keelan men back from their feigned retreat to block the alley's entrance. The four hundred Eywellese riders still on their horses had no order or goal except escape. They scattered, every man for himself. For some unfathomable reason, a few turned back down the alley, only to face Denes's muskets again. A few flung themselves at the blocking Keelan horsemen, perhaps in a fatalistic move to go down fighting. Of the thousand Eywellese who had left their positions to pursue Culich, less than two hundred escaped in all directions and ceased to be relevant.

As Culich and his men passed the ambush opening, they wheeled to support Denes and face any Eywellese who got through the ambush. It wasn't necessary. Eleven Eywellese survived the hail of lead and the tangle of dead and dying, to find themselves surrounded by Keelanders on horseback and on foot. Brandor Eywell was one of the eleven but escaped only for seconds before a musket ball severed his aorta. Culich noted the body on the ground, as he forced his horse back through the milling mass to assess the ambush results. He thought himself prepared until he saw the creek clogged with bodies of men and horses, the downstream water flowing red, and the alley an abattoir.

Although the island had been relatively peaceful compared to the earlier generations, Culich had seen his portion of conflicts: criminals, bandits, family or clan vendettas, and a few more serious skirmishes, particularly with the Eywellese. He knew, intellectually, that the Narthani brought a new level of conflict to Caedellium, but this was the first time he saw the result for himself.

"Merciful Creator! My God! What have we come to?!"

The swivel cannon and crews stood silent after firing five times. Only sporadic Keelan muskets continued, as men thought they had a living target. Denes yelled, the muskets quieted, and Culich cringed, as men ran into the carnage to finish wounded Eywellese and horses.

*What kind of world are we in? Is this the real world of Anyar, and we've been living a deluded fantasy?*

Culich turned away to assess his clansmen. So few of his people had fallen, compared to what they did to the Eywellese.

*I thank you, God, for that mercy.*

Denes and Yozef likewise stood, eyes on the slaughter, although with different thoughts than Culich. They had seen it all happen—every second, every volley—the Eywellese horses and men swept down by the merciless Keelan fire.

For Denes, it was grim satisfaction that the ambush had worked so well.

Yozef hadn't pissed himself, as he had during the abbey raid, although he again tasted bile. Wyfor had given him a musket, still unfired. Part of him wanted to keep himself separate from the fighting, as if keeping himself, or his soul, clean.

*I did this. I know I didn't kill anyone myself, and lord knows I didn't want to be here, but I can't avoid it was my suggestions that led to this.*

He knew the fate planned by the Narthani and the Eywellese for his adopted people and Maera, and he knew they had no choice. Any help he gave was justified, but he also knew his hands were covered in blood that would never quite wash clean.

Despite his nausea, Yozef was the first of the three men whose thoughts moved on.

# CHAPTER 31

# TURN THE TABLES

Yozef ran to Vegga. "Denes! We need to move."

Denes didn't acknowledge Yozef.

"Denes!" Yozef shouted again. No response. Yozef reached out, grasped Denes's right arm, and swung him around. "Denes! Wake up! We need to move *NOW*, before the Narthani realize what happened! If we wait too long, all this'll have been for nothing."

Denes's eyes cleared and he focused on Yozef. They stood staring at each other for several seconds, then as if a switch flipped, Denes whirled and ran fifty yards to where Culich sat frozen on his horse. Yozef couldn't make out the words, but Culich shouted, horns sounded, and a score of men on foot or horse raced to their hetman.

Yozef roused the artillery crews to secure their pieces. The horse teams were brought forward with their limbers and the carriages attached. By the time Denes returned, their three artillery pieces, crews, cannon-experienced men, and the crossbow carriages were ready to move.

When Denes reached Culich, he brought the hetman back to the moment, similar to the way Yozef did him, except Denes grabbed the hetman's horse's bridle and swung the mount around to break Culich's fixed gaze on the result of the ambush.

"Hetman! Hetman!" Denes yelled until Culich focused on him. "We must move quickly to take advantage of this!"

Culich shook himself, glanced once more at the abattoir of the creek bed and alley, and started yelling. Horns sounded for leader assembly, and within minutes, men raced off with their orders. Riders went to Luwis to initiate the smokescreens, as had been done for the frontal demonstration against the Narthani line, and then to use his own judgment to decide the right moment for his men and those of Hetman Gwillamer to attack the remaining Eywellese protecting the Narthani right flank. Hetman Mittack joined his men to the Keelanders Culich had led as bait and moved north to come in behind the Eywellese on the Narthani right flank. Culich's part was over. The hetman would remain to the rear and maintain *command-and-control*, as Yozef called it. Yozef didn't tell Culich there was little the hetman could do except stay out of the way and be safe.

Denes's dragoons remounted and moved up the northern side of the alley, which was more devoid of bodies. On the way, a few men finished sweeping the nightmare in the alley to dispatch wounded horses and men. There would be no prisoners. Any medical care would be reserved for their own wounded. If the allied clans took wounded prisoners, what would they do with these enemies? They couldn't be returned to fight again and kill Keelanders, and there was no will or resources to hold them prisoners. The men moved swiftly through the piles, pausing only to use knives and swords.

The casualness reminded Yozef that this was a different world. That however "civilized" Caedelli such as the Beynoms seemed, they were part of a harder worldview than he knew on Earth. He understood all of the reasons for what he could see being done and reminded himself not to judge too harshly. There were still places and situations on Earth where it would have been the same.

Yozef deliberately quit looking at the Keelanders "cleaning up" and focused on getting himself and the artillery down the alley toward the Narthani line.

Patmir Tullok alternated scanning his front for threats to his command, watching his subordinate commanders to see if they were doing their jobs or looking to him with irritation because he missed something, and occasionally glancing to his right, where the Eywellese horsemen screened his block's flank. He noted fewer of their clan allies than before. He had seen some of the Eywellese go charging at the clan riders who had retreated out of sight to the south.

Aivacs Zulfa sat satisfied. Not that the plan had gone according to their most optimistic forecast, but nothing obviously bad had happened, and they had clearly dealt a major blow to the Caedelli clans. For three-quarters of a mile wide and a half-mile deep, the alcove formed by their redeployment, he saw the ground littered with dead and wounded men and horses. His experienced eye estimated more than a thousand clansmen down. That part of the action had been successful enough. Now he waited to see what the islanders would do next. After this debacle, might they pull back and wait for his next move? Would they concede Moreland City and watch it burn? Would the battle dishearten enough of the clans that their tenuous coalition broke apart and let his people conquer them one at a time?

An aide interrupted Zulfa's thinking. "Brigadier! A message from Colonel Erdelin."

Zulfa snatched the sealed sheet from the aide's hand, broke it open, and read,

To: Brigadier Zulfa
From: Colonel Erdelin
Estimate 2/3 to 3/4 of Eywellese left positions
to pursue clan group withdrawing to the south.
No immediate threat, but possible cannon and musket
fire to the south. Request permission to shift one
block to support flank.

"Narth damn the Eywellese!" Zulfa's staff members' heads jerked toward their commander.

Zulfa looked to his right. He could see no obvious threat through the smoke from the Narthani cannon and muskets and the smoldering grass set afire by the islanders, and he saw no reason not to agree to the repositioning. He turned to his scribe. "Message to Colonel Erdelin. Permission granted to redeploy block. Stretch other block spacing to cover gap. Keep me informed of any change."

The scribe wrote two copies on paper and handed the sheets on a support to Zulfa, who signed both. The scribe placed one inside the shoulder bag he carried and gave the other to the aide, who ran to pass it to a rider to gallop back to Erdelin.

Denes halted their advance behind a screen of trees just out of sight of the remaining Eywellese, who were still unaware of the disaster befallen their clansmen. Through foliage he saw Eywell banners at a cluster of riders to their front, probably whoever was in charge when Brandor Eywell went off to the afterlife. He estimated three hundred yards of open ground between himself and the edge of the Eywell horsemen and perhaps four hundred yards to the end of the Narthani infantry line. Not that he could see either the Narthani or all the Eywellese through the smoke. His role now was to wait until Luwis and Gwillamer attacked from the east and Mittack from the west. He looked behind at his 471 men. They'd suffered only 9 casualties during the ambush. Denes decided on his own initiative that once they got within firing range of the Narthani, they would stake out their horses and leave only one man in eight to tend them. He figured if things went wrong, he would need every musket to extricate his men.

Demian Eywell was simultaneously proud that his father had left him in charge of five hundred men to protect the Narthani line, angry he couldn't take part in riding down the Keelan hetman, and hoping his father returned before he had to make any major decisions. That hope vanished when he saw a mass of Keelan and Gwillaer clansmen galloping straight at his position.

He was smart enough not to go charging directly at the attackers and lose supporting fire from the Narthani block to his left, but suddenly shouts came from behind him. He stood in his saddle to look to the rear and froze for several moments, as his mind took in riders led by Mittack and Keelan banners. Uncertain what to do, he sat on his saddle as the seconds ticked off, his mind a whirlpool of conflicting and confused options. Thus, he did the worst thing possible. Nothing.

Subcommanders screamed at him for orders, and when none came, they acted independently, with some charging the Keelanders to their front, others wheeling to face the new threat, and a hundred or more still milling around, waiting for Demian's orders. Outnumbered badly on all fronts, they were overwhelmed. The Eywellese fought bravely but failed in their primary mission. In less than seven minutes the Eywell screen was eliminated, and the Narthani flank was completely exposed.

Patmir Tullok intuited the problem as soon as he saw the melee of horsemen to his right. In response, he ordered one rank of pikes and one of muskets to face right, even though he couldn't identify what was happening through the smoke and chaos. One islander looked like any other to him, and all he saw was unidentified horsemen. He also did the right thing by sending a message to the right wing commander, Colonel Memas Erdelin, that his flank was threatened. He did everything right, not that it ultimately saved him or his men.

Erdelin got the messages from Tullok and Zulfa within seconds of each other. He immediately sent orders for the former reserve block to move from their position as part of the arc of the Narthani trap back and to the south to support the right flank.

The remaining Eywellese screening the Narthani right were pushed west and away from the now exposed flank. Denes gave the order committing his men to move toward the Narthani infantry block. Their mounted clansmen either pursued the Eywellese or moved aside, following orders not to attempt a direct horse assault on the Narthani infantry. Denes's dragoons weren't as disciplined as the Narthani infantry, but in four groups, each under a leader who tried to maintain a degree of order, they moved quickly toward where the Narthani block was supposed to be. It was a chaotic order of battle but the best they could do. The groups moved abreast forward with the three artillery pieces following in a central position, and the extra men with cannon experience followed the artillery. There was no reserve. This was an all-or-nothing throw of the dice.

They trotted 200 yards before making out the first vague figures through the smoke. Occasional Eywellese riders retreating from either the north or the south engagements sporadically appeared. Many rode on, ignoring the Keelanders on foot. Some Eywellese stopped and attacked, to be cut down by musket fire. Other Eywellese saw Denes's dragoons, recognized who they were, and rode off, whether to warn or escape was unknown.

At one hundred yards from the Narthani, Denes signaled to dismount, the horses were led to the rear, and the dragoons and the artillery formed up to face the flank of the Narthani infantry block and moved forward.

Patmir Tullok was alerted to something happening by the sporadic musket fire to their right and then the first outlines of men on foot through the smoke. Since there weren't supposed to be any Narthani infantry to his right, he hesitated for another minute until the figures became more distinct and then ordered the rank of musket men to open fire and start bringing the other ranks to face the new threat.

Eleven Keelanders fell to the first Narthani musket volley. That it wasn't more was due to smoke-obscured vision, the distance being at the limit of effective musket range, and disorder in the Narthani ranks. The Keelanders kept moving, and each man began firing independently. If it didn't have the shock impact of coordinated volleys, the number of muskets compensated. Almost four hundred Caedelli muskets fired into the compact Narthani formation. More than eighty Narthani were hit, inflicting moderate wounds to fatalities. The solid ranks of pike and musket men facing the Keelanders suddenly had gaps, with standing men separated by dead and the wounded who lay still or writhing, silent or screaming.

While the surviving Narthani musket men reloaded and the other ranks attempted to swing into position to fire, the three Keelan artillery pieces rolled into line, all pointing to the center of the Narthani formation. As soon as each piece was ready, it began firing its three barrels. It took twenty seconds to fire all nine barrels, resulting in hundreds more musket balls scything into the Narthani. Many balls impacted the ground before reaching the Narthani or went over their heads. A quarter of the clansmen's balls found human flesh and Yozef saw sprays of blood.

He had followed his carriage crews, offering no advice or leadership. They'd been drilled enough not to need his help. He also wasn't eager to be at the forefront but was startled when he thought rockets arced over toward the Narthani infantry. As his eye followed one trail of smoke, he realized they were crossbow quarrels. The three crews were fifty yards behind and began firing as soon as they set up their carriages. He hadn't expected they would get this far, so he hadn't given the crossbow crews instructions on what to do after the ambush.

Two quarrels flew over the Narthani, but one landed within the block, scattering bodies. The Keelanders stopped and poured independent fire into the Narthani, the swivel carriages firing as fast as the outer two barrels were reloaded, and quarrels impacting in and around the disintegrating Narthani block. By the time the swivels fired for the third time, there were barely 150 of the original 500 Narthani still standing. Not among them was Patmir Tullok, who, despite his inexperience, had done everything right but now lay lifeless after any one of four Keelan balls killed him.

Of the surviving Narthani, only 50 carried muskets. The pike men had knelt or lain flat to allow their musket men to fire over them and had thus escaped most of the Keelan fire. Now 100 Narthani pike men stood helpless or tried to flee, as they were shot down piecemeal. In less than five minutes, a 500-man Narthani infantry block ceased to exist.

# CHAPTER 32

# FORWARD

*What in Evil's name is happening?!*

Lieutenant Narfak Salel commanded the rightmost 12-pounder battery of cannon in the right Narthani artillery position. His senior noncommissioned officer stood beside him, as they watched the frantic movements of the last infantry block. He had no word of any threat, so why was the block repositioning? They'd heard firearms and shouts beyond the block, but residual gunpowder smoke and smoldering grass lit by the islanders obscured details of the action.

Salel watched for only a few more moments, then cursed and ordered two of his cannon to face ninety degrees, while he sent a runner off to Major Urtek, commanding the entire artillery position. Lacking orders, he hesitated to reposition all of five of his pieces without approval.

*What in Evil's name is going on!* Zulfa raged to himself. As the firing died down toward the islander horsemen milling just out of canister range, he could hear sounds of fighting toward his right flank. Suddenly, an Eywellese rider galloped up to this staff area, the horse lathered and the rider with a superficial slash on his cheek and blood on one shoulder. Zulfa's guards stopped him twenty yards away, took his sword, and led him to Zulfa's platform. The man did a quick bow in the saddle and blurted, "General! The clans are on our rear!"

Zulfa didn't question the man's veracity. His appearance, the uncertainty about events on their right flank, and Zulfa's instincts combined to elicit decisive actions after a moment's reflection.

*If they're on the rear of the Eywellese, then the entire flank might be in danger.*

He quickly wrote out orders for Colonel Metan on the left to send all the Narthani heavy cavalry to Zulfa's position, along with half of his artillery, and a second message to Colonel Erdelin warning of clan horseman possibly threatening their rear. It took two minutes to write the messages, six minutes to get it in the hands of the recipients, two minutes to issue orders to subordinates, three minutes to organize the units chosen to respond, and six minutes to bring the five hundred heavy cavalry to Zulfa's position. In those nineteen minutes, the Narthani right collapsed.

When they rushed forward to the first Narthani infantry block, Denes told Yozef to accompany their three artillery pieces and the extra men. Yozef had planned on staying as far back from the point of conflict as possible and that he could get away with. This left him little choice. Yozef knew Culich had instructed Denes to keep him well back of the front, but in the furious action of the moment, Denes either forgot his instructions or figured that despite such orders, he needed Yozef's advice as far forward as possible. Yozef swallowed hard and followed to the rear of the artillery group.

From where he stood, Yozef could sporadically see the Narthani infantry, although most of the time the smoke continued to obscure. He wasn't sure what was happening until the Keelanders opened up with musket fire and their cobbled-together field pieces. Any visibility vanished as their gunpowder smoke added to that of the Narthani and the smoldering grass. All he saw were the backs of Denes's dragoons and the swivel crews firing and reloading.

Suddenly, the firing subsided, and the men pushed forward again, then stopped at Denes's shout. From the corner of his right eye, Yozef detected movement. He turned in time to see outlines of horsemen, swords held high, lances leveled, pound past the dragoons toward where the Narthani infantry lay shredded. Hundreds of Keelan and Mittack horsemen. He heard shouts, Narthani cannon fire, pistols, and a few muskets. Two or three minutes later, some of the riders galloped back the way they'd come, and a group of four rode up to Denes, said something, and followed the others. Denes shouted, and the dragoons and the artillerymen surged forward again. Yozef followed to avoid being left standing alone.

The dragoons hadn't gotten off unscathed. As Yozef hustled past the position the Keelanders just left, he saw Keelanders lying on the ground, perhaps thirty either dead or wounded, a couple screaming from wounds. Medicants came forward, several running past Yozef to the injured. Yozef passed one man he thought he recognized, though he couldn't recall from where. The man lay staring at the sky and arguing to "someone" about a dog.

*In shock*, Yozef thought, as a medicant tied a tourniquet above where the man's arm used to extend. Another man was beyond the medicants' help with a musket ball hole in his forehead and a surprised look on his face. Yozef hurried forward to catch up with the advancing Keelanders.

Then, the scene of Keelan wounded and dead became a relative refuge, as they reached the ground where the Narthani infantry block had stood and died. The men in front of him made no efforts to avoid walking on dead or wounded Narthani. The dead didn't care, and Yozef could see the wounded being reassigned to the first category, as Keelanders moved over them, using musket butts and knives. The men pulling artillery pieces and limbers also made no effort to avoid bodies and pulled carriages over whatever was in the way.

Finally, Yozef found himself past the carpet of Narthani bodies, still following Denes's men. More Keelan horsemen flowed to their right and left, their departure revealing their target—the Narthani artillery position. In the hundred yards between the original Narthani infantry block and artillery positions were scores of downed clan riders and horses, medicants rushing aid to the wounded, and dragoons giving mercy to the animals. Beyond, he could see 12-pounder carriages and limbers interspersed with Narthani bodies.

*Well, kiss my ass*, Yozef thought in wonderment, as they moved into the artillery position, the dragoons moving on past. Half of the 12-pounders still faced the Moreland charge, while the others had obviously been turning to face the clan horsemen when they were overrun. Narthani bodies lay still, twitching, or screaming.

*Luwis and Mittack! They surprised the Narthani artillery once the infantry block was gone. When I suggested taking the artillery positions, I didn't actually believe it. It was just a remote possibility.*

Yozef's wonderings came to an abrupt halt when musket fire erupted to their front, and musket balls whizzed nearby. Several Keelan men fell, and Denes and other leaders tried to get their men to form lines. The next Narthani blocks had realized what was happening and were responding.

For Memas Erdelin, the textbook battle plan turned to disaster. As soon as he realized his end block was under serious attack and the Eywellese no longer protected his flank, he asked for and received permission to move the reserve block for support. By the time they started moving into position, the artillery battery was already being overrun. Not the most capable of commanders, he still recognized the severity of the danger, and, even to his own surprise and without Zulfa's permission, he ordered the next two blocks to face right and move to support the artillery position, a saving correct move if it had occurred ten minutes earlier.

Aivacs Zulfa stood even farther behind events happening to his right flank but was experienced and decisive enough to act, based on what he knew and what he didn't know. With firing to his front having stopped minutes previously and a slight pickup in wind clearing visibility, he knew their front was secure, but from his position, he could see something major happening with Erdelin's wing of the formation, although he couldn't pick out details.

He heard continuous musket fire interspersed with what sounded like light cannon firing. He knew for certain from the distinctive sound that it wasn't Narthani field cannon, so had to be from the Caedelli.

*Where did they get field artillery? They weren't supposed to have any.*

Even if lighter than his own cannon, such unexpected capabilities of the islanders could wreak havoc with his packed infantry blocks. His heavier cannon could easily handle what he assumed were these smaller-caliber cannon, but since he wasn't hearing the heavier guns firing, he assumed the islanders hit his flank and his artillery hadn't yet turned to suppress the lighter guns.

As yet, Zulfa had no thought that his right flank might be in serious danger, but he left nothing to chance. His left flank was reasonably secure from direct attack by the ridgeline only if he didn't leave a gap between the leftmost infantry block and the rising ground, thus preventing islander cavalry from using the gap to attack or get to his rear.

"Ketin!" he barked out to his subordinate, who had initiated the trap maneuver and then rejoined him at the headquarters position. Ketin stood looking at the map of the battlefield and dispositions. "Get forward and reposition blocks four, five, and six to form a line facing south."

The order didn't surprise Ketin. He knew of the messages coming to Zulfa and could hear and interpret that something was happening to their right. "You think we're in danger from an islander flank attack?"

"There's no immediate danger from the clan horsemen to our front, so prudence dictates we reposition until it's clear what is happening on our right flank. Get down there and assume it will be necessary for our right flank to retire to your position and repel a flanking attack. I have the rest of our cavalry here to provide a flanking screen, in case our entire line has to redirect. Leave room for artillery also. I've already ordered half of the left batteries here, and I'll now order them to your new position."

Without further questioning, Ketin saluted, leaped off the platform, and mounted his horse. He and his aides raced off. Zulfa quickly wrote an order to Nuthrat Metan, commander of the left flank.

To: Colonel Nuthrat Metan
From: Brigadier Aivacs Zulfa
Major Caedelli attack on our right flank of unknown severity.
Army is to prepare to reposition to defensive stance.
Your artillery to move west and southwest
to approx position block 5. Block 6 detached
from your command to Erkan Ketin. Stretch your 7, 8,
and 9 blocks to cover gaps.

Denes stopped his men facing the next Narthani block only eighty yards away. They fired as fast as they could reload, while the Narthani musket men finished their maneuver to face the islanders and answered in return. For three minutes it was a worst-case scenario—a duel with guns at eighty yards. Only the disorganization of both sides saved them from mutual suicide. More Narthani fell, then Denes saw another Narthani block coming at them from their oblique left. Denes redirected his leftmost men at the new threat, which lessened their suppression of the forward block.

Thus far, the Narthani pike men had only served as targets for the islander fire. That was about to change, as the two Narthani blocks moved into position facing Denes's men. Yozef had warned them what might be coming. The Narthani musket men would fire a volley, followed by a charge by the pike men. Even with losses, the number of pike men was more than sufficient to overrun his men trying to reload their muskets or defend themselves using muskets against twelve-foot pikes.

*Where are our artillery pieces?*

Denes looked around just in time to see two of the three pieces pulled into firing positions, the ropes pulling them dropped, and the crews straining to turn the barrels toward the advancing Narthani. The third piece had overturned in the haste to move it forward, and its crew frantically tried to get it back upright.

Yozef trailed the advancing Keelanders and was behind the overturned carriage and limber. He saw that only six men had been pulling the piece, four on one side and two on the other. Where the missing two men were, Yozef didn't know, but likely they had fallen somewhere farther back. In their haste to get the gun forward, the unbalanced effort upended the carriage. Yozef recognized that the gun chief, a carpenter who had sailed on merchant ships in his younger years, was among the missing. Yozef assumed the serious, reliable man must lay dead or wounded somewhere behind them. The six remaining crewmembers argued about whose fault it was the piece had upended, while musket balls hissed around them.

While Yozef watched, one crewmember spun clockwise as a round struck him in the back, and he fell to the ground without uttering a sound. The other five stopped their pointless argument and looked down at the one who had been standing with them seconds earlier.

*They're about to abandon the piece!* Yozef thought. *Denes needs this piece with the other two!*

Without it, their firepower was reduced by a third, and who knew if it could be decisive?

Later Yozef couldn't remember making a decision, only that he suddenly ran to the five men, yelling and directing them to get the piece upright. Carnigan had been a large presence shadowing Yozef and now pitched in, along with Wyfor and two medicants. The nine men got the piece upright, ropes untangled, and the seven of them got the piece moving again, with Carnigan providing the strength of two and the two medicants going back to their primary task.

As they pulled up beside the first two carriages, Yozef could see both pieces firing barrels alternately. As before, they reloaded only the two outer barrels. Several of the men were down, hit by musket fire. He saw one man fall, to be immediately pulled aside and another take his place. Their smaller-barreled pieces were having an effect, but with only six swivel barrels firing and crewmembers falling and being replaced, the loss of crew cohesion dramatically slowed the reload and accuracy rate.

Other men were trying, unsuccessfully, to get some of the Narthani pieces into action. A knot of Keelanders had turned a loaded Narthani 12-pounder at the next infantry block but had the elevation high, and the already loaded canister passed over the Narthani.

*We have to get more guns firing faster!* Yozef thought frantically.

Despite the dummy practice Yozef had put these men through, handling Narthani 12-pounders under fire was a different world.

He ran to where a crew tried to get another Narthani gun into action. They worked hard but were uncoordinated. With Yozef yelling and Carnigan forcing men into their proper positions, they got the gun turned and properly elevated. This crew wasn't sure what to do next, because the Narthani shot components looked different from the ones they had practiced with. The powder bags were black cloth; their own practice ones were white. Their own canister rounds were simple thick cloth bags holding the rounds, while Yozef recognized the Narthani rounds as wooden cylinders. One was lying to its side, split open and the balls visible.

Yozef put a powder bag in the muzzle. A man with a rammer was by his side immediately and rammed it down the barrel. Yozef grabbed the nearest canister round and slid it into the muzzle, and the same man rammed it home. Normally, a wad of something—cloth, rope, or whatever was handy—would follow to hold the powder and the shot in place. Since the gun already pointed in the right direction and elevation, Yozef skipped the wad. Another man roused himself and found a powder horn draped over the shoulder of a dead Narthani and remembered what to do next. He tapped powder into the firing hole of the cannon, pulled out a smoldering piece of rope from a leather bag at his side, and touched the glowing end to the hole's opening.

The cannon, to Yozef's surprise, fired, didn't explode in their faces, and had an immediate effect on the Narthani block. A whole section of line flattened, as if a giant fly swatter had swept through. The men in the crew whooped and scrambled to reload.

Yozef left them and went to the next crew. There were six men when he started toward them. A Narthani musket ball hit one crewmember before Yozef got to them. They had watched enough of Yozef helping the other crew that he only stood by for a few seconds, as they finished loading and fired, before he moved on. Another crew figured it all out themselves, and Yozef ran to the next cannon, this one with ten men getting in one another's way. Two of the men went down simultaneously, and Yozef quickly got the others to remember their crew positions, and he helped load.

While they fired and started the reloading cycle, Yozef looked back down their line at how the other guns fared. As far as he could see, their three light pieces and four Narthani 12-pounders fired with only seconds passing between firings. Added to the fire were explosive quarrels from two of the crossbow carriages. A wheel on the third carriage broke while running over a wounded Narthani, and the metal rim twisted and broke the bow stock.

Suddenly, Yozef noticed that the buzzing of Narthani musket balls seemed to have slackened, and for the first time since the initial firing of a 12-pounder, he looked at the Narthani position. The original block was decimated. Fewer than a hundred of the original five hundred men still stood, without a cohesive formation—the chance survivors of dragoon muskets and the bites each round of canister had taken from among them.

The second block, the one that came to support the first, had been preparing a pike charge. That plan was no longer tenable with half of their men down, most of whom were the pike men in their front ranks who had taken the brunt of the Keelan musket and canister fire. The remaining pike men were in no position or had no inclination to charge and were falling back to allow their musket men a clearer field of fire—in theory. In less than a minute, the remaining men dropped their pikes and ran to the rear. The remnants of the first block tried to follow suit, but the merciless Keelan fire felled all but a score before the survivors reached the next Narthani line.

Yozef found himself twenty yards to the left of Denes, who surveyed the scene and was obviously trying to decide what to do next. They had captured half of the Narthani guns, destroyed two blocks of infantry, and savaged a third block. Now the Narthani were redeploying the center of their line, and about two hundred yards away they faced three unscathed blocks with cannon setting up between blocks. Until now, they had had the advantage of both surprise and numbers. No longer. The new Narthani line facing them would outgun them with experienced artillery and match them in muskets. Denes could see this, but Yozef was afraid their unexpected level of success might tempt him to keep going. That they shouldn't do.

Yozef ran to Denes. "Time to go, Denes!"

Denes just looked at him.

"Time to go," Yozef repeated. "We accomplished all we can and need to pull back and regroup. We can't attack a Narthani line that's ready for us."

Denes looked again at the Narthani line, then licked his lips and his eyes widened, as he looked at the next Narthani block.

*Shit! He's tempted to keep going!*

"No, NO!" exclaimed Yozef. "We're too close and in range of their canister. They'll rake us with massed muskets and artillery as soon as they set up, which is going to be soon. We have to *GO!*"

This time, there was no hesitation from Denes. He grasped what Yozef was saying and ordered a withdrawal, taking their wounded and the guns with them. Their swivel carriages still had the ropes used to pull them this far, and men quickly had those three well on their way, this time avoiding the carnage of the first Narthani block they had annihilated by heading straight for their original position at the end of the clan alignment. The Narthani guns and limbers were something else. Yozef yelled to forget the limbers, just get the guns. They could always make more limbers, but the guns were priceless, because who knew when they could cast such pieces themselves, if at all. Lacking ropes, men pulled and pushed at the larger pieces, and some men turned the wheel spokes, a slow process.

Yozef filled his lungs to yell at one cluster of men to get ropes on a 12-pounder when a carriage crosspiece shattered, sending wood fragments in all directions. Knocked flat, Yozef stared at clouds. "Wha . . ." he croaked.

Wyfor's face filled Yozef's vision. "Nothing serious. It's just bleeding a lot. Head wounds do that."

"Head wound?" Yozef asked, before realizing something warm and wet covered the right side of his head. He sat up, dizzy, and put a hand to his ear. It came away covered in blood. "Oh, shit."

"Not to worry," a deep voice growled. Carnigan knelt next to him and wrapped a cloth around his head. "Probably will need stitches, but it's not deep. A cannon ball got lucky and hit the crosspiece of the 12-pounder. Must have been from a Narthani cannon too far away to use canister or grapeshot."

Yozef's two wardens helped him to his feet. His first instinct was to sit back down, as vertigo washed over him, then abated.

"Let's get him out of here," said Wyfor. The two men supported and half-dragged him, as they joined the retreating Keelanders who were still the target of Narthani cannon fire.

A shallow depression gave temporary cover, but by the time they were again visible, the Narthani field pieces had switched to grapeshot. The deeper drone of two-inch iron balls passing overhead spurred them on. At another hundred yards, one piece was hit by a ball, shattering the carriage and killing one man. Another ball missed the gun but tore through three men on one side of the carriage. Other men immediately replaced the dead, and the gun hardly slowed.

By now, Luwis had had horses brought up. Every rider carried a length of rope, and all artillery pieces were pulled by several horses. In many cases, no attempt was made to roll the carriage. Ropes were tied to barrels, and the cannon dragged along the ground.

At 900 yards, the Narthani switched to solid shot. One last carriage was destroyed and five more men wounded before all firing ceased at 1,200 yards. When they reached their original encampment, Denes and the medicants made a fast count of his men. Of the original 480, 406 men had survived, including 92 wounded. They had 74 known dead lying somewhere on the battlefield. Of the 80 men in the artillery group, they had 17 dead and 12 wounded. The mounted clansmen would take another two hours to be accounted for, but the clans' total losses were mild compared to their enemy's.

Besides the decimated Eywellese, an estimated 1,000 Narthani infantry and artillerymen were killed or critically wounded. The clansmen had captured seventeen 12-pounder field cannon and picked up hundreds of muskets, pistols, and swords from dead Narthani and Eywellese. By any rational measure, it had been a smashing victory, though of little consolation to families of the dead.

Zulfa left the command platform for his horse, to allow more mobility. Firing had died to an occasional musket shot, likely from someone either firing out of range, due to frustration, or accidental discharge. With the cessation of firing, the powder smoke cleared, and only a smattering of smoldering grass generated scattered risings of smoke. These, along with a slight increase in wind, cleared the battlefield to give Zulfa visibility to survey the carnage on two fronts. The remnants of the Moreland charge still lay to the east, where they had fallen two hours earlier. Cries of wounded horses and men could still be heard. The scene would have been satisfying to Aivacs Zulfa, if it were not for the equally grim visage to the south where the Narthani right had been.

Gone were the screening Eywellese cavalry, the anchoring infantry block, the western artillery redoubt, and one other block. Another block had been so depleted the men were distributed to other units. His forward-facing deployment toward the Caedelli horse army had contracted to a rough square with infantry blocks and the remaining artillery on two sides, the east ridgeline shielding a third side, and all of the remaining cavalry guarding the fourth and western side. The area where his right wing had been was now dotted with the bodies of his infantry and artillerymen. Aides estimated he had lost a thousand dead, plus two hundred wounded. The disparity between dead and wounded was testament to how quickly the islanders overran his men and finished the wounded before they withdrew.

A Caedelli rider carrying a white flag rode halfway between their positions, likely to request a ceasefire long enough to recover the wounded. Zulfa didn't respond. He might have his own wounded who could be saved, but from the appearance of the battlefield, there were more Caedellium wounded than Narthani, so he saw no reason to agree to a ceasefire benefiting the enemy more than his army. If several hundred islanders died of wounds, it was a justified tradeoff for a few score Narthani.

The last action had ceased more than an hour ago. He had waited to see whether the islanders had any further action in mind this day. The evidence and his intuition said no. The fighting evidently being over for today, he could no longer put off the bad taste in his mouth. The clever plan to deal a crushing blow to the Caedellium clans and hasten the island's subjugation lay in tatters.

Their success in trapping the central clan charge in no manner compensated for the collapse of their right wing. He had lost almost a fifth of his Narthani infantry, most of the Eywell auxiliary light cavalry, and as much as half of his artillery. With seven intact infantry blocks, the Narthani heavy cavalry, thirty cannon, and the Selfcellese horsemen, he was confident they could repel any Caedellium direct attack in the open field, but not as supremely confident as previously. Something new had been added that their assessment of the clans hadn't accounted for. The islander horse charge had cost the clans dearly but had focused the Narthani attention to their front so much, they hadn't recognized the danger to their flank until too late. It wasn't that Zulfa was appalled by the willingness to sacrifice so many men as a diversion; he would have done the same under the circumstances. It was the unanticipated willingness of the Caedelli to make that sacrifice, in addition to the coordination needed for their flank attack.

Zulfa listened to updates from his staff and weighed their next move. He saw little choice.

"We'll withdraw back to Preddi Province," he announced. A few of his staff appeared shocked to hear they would retreat from the islanders, though most understood the necessity. A hundred and fifty miles separated them from the Preddi border. They had suffered serious losses, including half of their cavalry screen, and would be outnumbered by a more mobile enemy showing unexpected tactical sense. Galling though it might feel, they needed to retreat to a more defendable position.

"Erdelin, how many of the Eywellese are still with us?"

The grim-faced commander of the broken right wing answered. "Somewhere between a hundred and a hundred and fifty. There may be another couple of hundred scattered to the rear, and many may be running for home."

Some Narthani commanders would have replaced Erdelin by now or even had him arrested for criminal incompetence to deflect blame from themselves. However, Zulfa knew that Akuyun demanded honest reports, and Zulfa's evaluation of Erdelin's performance would be positive, much to even Zulfa's surprise. He had had low expectations of Erdelin, but it had been Zulfa's plan, albeit approved by General Akuyun, that failed so badly. Erdelin, given the plan and their understanding of the Caedelli, had done about as well as anyone else could have in his place. Although more initiative in responding to the threat to his right might have saved the day, initiative wasn't encouraged by the Narthani military culture.

"Colonel Erdelin, you're most familiar with Eywell and still have some of them with us. They'll know more of the terrain on the way back to Eywell territory. Therefore, you're in charge of the lead van. The remaining Eywellese horses will scout and screen to our direction of movement west. We'll keep to open territory to maximize our fire discipline, and it will be a forced march. If the Caedelli are smart, they'll harass us all the way back, so we need to move quickly. I'll leave you one infantry block and half the artillery. Be sure to keep the artillery moving. We also need to send riders back to both Eywell and General Akuyun. The Eywellese are to gather the rest of their horsemen and provide an obstacle for clan cavalry trying to get in front of us. I don't expect the Eywellese to fight if greatly outnumbered, but they are to get at least five hundred horsemen to us, if at all possible. No dithering is to be tolerated."

Erdelin was about the say something, when Zulfa raised a restraining hand. "I know they will argue that such a mobilization to reinforce us will strip their province of protection from the other clans, but I doubt the clans will focus on anything except us. I'll send riders to Parthmal to warn our garrison there to be alert. Their position is good enough to stop the islanders for a few days until either the Eywellese are gathered in strength or we arrive. I also expect General Akuyun will dispatch what forces he can to meet us."

Zulfa looked down at the map spread before them. "We'll head northwest to the Bayrin River and hit it about here." His finger indicated a bend where the river turned sharply west. "This point is thirty miles to our rear. Once we reach the river, we can use it to protect one flank. The river is too wide for their horsemen to charge across before we could react. That will let our infantry march in a three-sided defensive formation with wounded, supply wagons, and other auxiliaries in the middle. The river will also provide water, so it won't have to be carried with us. This route will add twenty to thirty miles but will be the safest."

Zulfa turned to his other two immediate sub-commanders. "Ketin, you'll take half of the remaining infantry to screen our left column of march and oversee the auxiliaries within our formation. Metan, you have the rest of the infantry and the other half of the artillery. Your infantry will be on our right, with the artillery following behind the auxiliaries. Once we reach the river, you'll fall back as our rear guard. We'll also keep our heavy cavalry to the rear to discourage direct attacks by clan horsemen and keep the dust out of our infantry's lungs as much as possible. They'll be stressed enough moving as fast as we need to."

Zulfa looked around, waiting for questions. There were none, and he concluded. "Colonels, I expect this army to be repositioned and moving in twenty minutes."

The clans didn't yet realize it, but the battle of Moreland City was over.

# CHAPTER 33

# VICTORY?

**Or Standoff?**

The Tri-Alliance men reassembled, once well out of Narthani cannon range. Horseless riders were matched to riderless horses, ownership to be determined later. Scattered men found their clans and assigned groups, and medicants finished retrieving the wounded. They were exuberant from the extent of their victory, and adrenaline had yet to flush from their veins—until they passed within view of the Moreland charge results. Acre after acre of Moreland men's and horses' bodies littered the ground. The Narthani had finally stopped shelling any attempts to retrieve the dead and the wounded, and medicants searched among the carnage.

Fortunately, Seabiscuit needed no guidance to follow the other horses. Yozef accompanied the withdrawal and reassembly, oblivious to his surroundings. He felt drained, his body coming down from the last hours, and his head throbbed under the makeshift bandage. Carnigan grabbed a medicant, who checked Yozef's head laceration, pronounced it minor, and closed the gash with eight stitches, each of which hurt more than the original wound.

They found Culich and the other Keelan leaders gathered at their original position. Culich saw Yozef and started toward him. Then a rider pulled up, leaned down from his saddle, and handed Culich a message. He read it once, then revealed the contents.

"From Hetman Stent. His observers on the northern ridgeline report the Narthani are withdrawing to the west back toward Eywell. Clan leaders are called to Hetman Orosz's flag." Culich looked up, his eyes full of wonder. "I can hardly believe it. I confess I doubted we could drive them back. May God forgive me my doubts."

Shouts of jubilation rang out among all within earshot, and the word quickly spread throughout the Keelanders and continued several minutes before Culich quieted those around him.

"There are still things to do. Let's see to the men and horses. Vortig, Pedr, Denes, and Yozef, come with me to the hetman meeting Orosz has called." Culich glanced at Yozef, eyed the uncovered stitched gash still seeping blood, and nodded.

Half an hour later, they met at the same building as the day before. Clansmen clustered around the structure, along with horses held or staked farther away. All the men talked among themselves until the Keelanders and their allies rode up, then voices trailed away. Culich's guards held the Keelanders' horses, while they went inside. As they walked to the front door, men stepped aside, word having spread how the Tri-Alliance portion of the battle had been decisive.

The Keelanders and their allies were the last to arrive. Several hetmen rose to shake Culich's hand or clasp forearms and slap him on the back. Orosz waited until Culich sat. "You've all heard the news that the Narthani are withdrawing. Unless there are objections, I suggest we hear summaries of today's battle, first from Hetman Stent and then Hetman Keelan."

"I'll report what my clansmen and I observed," Hetman Stent began. "First, the charge toward the Narthani line this morning. You remember we were to pretend to carry out a mass attack at three points on their line to see how the Narthani would react and also whether the Eywellese could be lured out of their position, thus exposing the Narthani left. Our position was to the right of Moreland, who led the center group. We charged as planned, and I was to take my cue from Moreland. When we reached where we should turn and ride back and forth across their front, just outside musket and canister range, I watched Moreland for his signal. At first, I thought the signal would come any second, then I saw him raise his sword toward the Narthani. That's when I realized he intended to carry out the charge."

Despite most of the men already knowing what had happened, hearing it from Stent brought forth curses.

"I hesitated too long, then signaled my clansmen and we turned as planned. However, my delay put us in range of the Narthani fire, and some of my men were too far to the front and didn't see my signal. I'm afraid some watched the Morelanders more than our own leadership. As a result, Stent suffered forty casualties from the first Narthani volleys."

Grim-faced Hetman Hewell spoke up. "Hewell had seventy casualties. I didn't respond as fast as Hetman Stent."

"I've spoken with the senior Moreland leaders still alive," Stent continued. "Gynfor Moreland and both of his sons are dead, and the surviving leaders are afraid there are also more than a thousand Moreland men dead."

"Merciful God!" and "Oh God!" were among the exclamations, along with more gasps of shock and anger.

"Damn Gynfor Moreland to eternal darkness!" shouted a bitter Hetman Bultecki. "Moreland getting killed due to stupidity and arrogance is nothing but a blessing, but to take so many of his clansmen with him, damn him!"

Orosz spat to one side in agreement. "No Moreland representative is here because they're trying to deal with this catastrophe and decide who *can* represent them."

The recriminations and anger continued until Orosz brought them back to the moment. "Let's finish the reports. Hetman Stent, please continue."

"The second report is from observers I placed on top of the high ridgeline. The Narthani are withdrawing as fast as their infantry can march toward Eywell and Preddi. Obviously, for them the invasion of Moreland is over." With that, Stent sat.

"Thank you. Hetman Keelan?" said Orosz.

Culich rose. "As bad as the news is about the Moreland charge, I think we can take solace that we drove the Narthani back to their base territory. The effort to see if we could entice the Eywellese screening the Narthani right flank to leave their position worked better than I expected, and about two-thirds of them followed Hetman Eywell into an ambush commanded by Denes Vegga." Culich gestured to Denes standing behind him. "At this point I had little direct observation of the action, so I'll let Ser Vegga describe what happened."

Denes, still begrimed with dirt and powder from the day's fighting, cleared his throat. "Hetman Keelan led the Eywellese into our ambush. We opened fire with muskets and three new artillery pieces made by Yozef Kolsko. We took the Eywellese completely by surprise, and many of the Eywellese chasing our hetman died in the ambush. More were killed by Tri-Alliance horsemen who cut off their retreat. Our mounted clansmen then killed or dispersed the rest of the Eywellese guarding the Narthani flank. We had planned that if the opportunity arose, we'd attack the end Narthani block. I'll not go into detail, but our attack was successful, and we annihilated that block of infantry. Our horsemen then overran their artillery position, and we turned some of those guns against the next Narthani block, destroying it and possibly one other block. We estimate the Eywellese dead at a thousand and about the same number of Narthani. At this point, the Narthani pulled back other blocks to form a new line facing us, and we could see their artillery setting up and cavalry approaching, so we withdrew."

Denes quit speaking. The room was silent while the clan leaders absorbed the report, their previous dismay morphing into grim satisfaction.

"Somehow I suspect this summary doesn't do Ser Vegga and his men enough credit," Hetman Adris said. "To accomplish what they did in so short a time I find amazing, and we all owe Keelan, Gwillamer, Mittack, and especially Denes Vegga our deepest thanks."

"Here, here," voiced sitting hetmen and standing men, to the accompaniment of fists pounding the table and feet the floor.

Denes appeared to want to say something but looked to Culich for permission. Culich nodded.

"Thank you for your comment, Hetman Adris. Naturally, I accept them for all the Tri-Alliance men who fought this day. I also must point out that the original ideas for our plan came from Yozef Kolsko." Denes gestured to Yozef standing beside him. "It was both his advice on the plan and his actions with ours and the Narthani artillery that deserve major credit for the victory today."

Many in the room looked with curiosity at Yozef. A number knew something of him, some only from rumors, and the rest had never heard of him.

"I agree with Ser Vegga's comments about Yozef Kolsko," Culich concurred. "His advice turned out to be uncannily accurate, both in the attempt to lure the Eywellese and to attack the Narthani's unprotected flank. And don't forget his warning about a direct attack on the Narthani line. We all saw the result when Moreland tried it."

"That was Moreland attacking alone," interjected Hetman Pewitt. "That allowed the Narthani to concentrate all their fire on one clan. What if we had attacked across the entire front? Might not the entire Narthani line have collapsed, and we could have killed them all and ended their threat forever?"

Several hetmen dismissed or belittled Pewitt's question, but it was Stent who snarled an answer.

"Did you see what happened to Moreland?! They were not just shot from their horses, but most horses and men were hit multiple times. I saw men's bodies hit five or more times. If we had all charged, they would have had to spread their fire out over a broader front, which means those killed might have been hit only two or three times, instead of five or six. And, remember, their horsemen never came into play. If they had fired at all the clans at once, I suspected their horses, plus the Selfcellese and the Eywellese, would have rolled through our survivors, and our total losses would have been so bad, we might never have recovered."

Culich interrupted before an argument started. "We can argue such points forever. For now, we should discuss what to do next."

"What's to do next?" questioned Hetman Hewell. "The Narthani are retreating, which was our objective. Are you suggesting we should try to engage them in more battles?"

Culich grunted. "I understand your question, Lordum. For myself, and I believe most or all of you, there was never any thought for what we would do in the situation we find ourselves. Our focus was just surviving this day."

He stopped and glanced behind him. "Ser Kolsko has given priceless advice so far, so I now wonder if he might have more insights or suggestions to share with us?"

Culich turned in his seat to the men standing behind him.

Yozef was still recovering: from the adrenaline that had coursed through his veins, first in fear, then as he became obsessed with details of the battle and especially the artillery, and finally in reaction to the head wound. He stood beside Denes and right behind Culich, concentrating on his throbbing head. Nothing said so far at the meeting had penetrated the fog. All eyes were on him, and there was silence. After a few moments, Denes elbowed him sharply.

Yozef's eyes cleared, and he looked questioningly at Denes. "What?"

"Hetman Keelan asked you if you had any thoughts about the victory today and what might come next."

Yozef looked surprised at Culich and then around the room. He had heard the earlier reports, but they hadn't registered with his consciousness, until now. He licked his lips and tried to focus.

"The Narthani are withdrawing but aren't destroyed. I suspect they're surprised, even a little shocked at what happened today. Although today was a great victory, it's not the end of the Narthani."

He stopped talking and looked uneasily around the room, feeling the eyes of clan leaders pressing on him.

*I wonder if I should tell them we might have used up all of our luck? Or perhaps that idiot Moreland deserves most of the credit? If the Narthani hadn't focused on the*

*Morelanders, they likely would have responded faster, and the results could have been far different.*

He decided there was no reason for gloom—yet. The clans could use some confidence. They would need it for the next Narthani moves.

"They're returning to secure territory. We still can't face them in a field battle, because they have more experience and cannon. What should be done is to harass them as long as possible. With your greater mobility, you can easily get ahead of them to set ambushes and pick off scouts and small patrols. Anything you can do to reduce their numbers will help in the future and further dishearten their men. The more they respect you as fighters, the less effective they'll be. I also wonder if there's an opportunity to damage some of their infrastructure, such as supplies or smaller outposts."

"Parthmal," asserted Stent. "We know they have a base at Parthmal in Eywell a few miles from the Moreland border. I've secretly had men scouting the area. There's a small Narthani force there, along with Eywellese, and it appears to be the supply base for this invasion. If a large enough number of clansmen could get there before the Narthani army arrives, we might be able to destroy it and force the Narthani farther back into Eywell territory. There may also be supplies, such as weapons that could be captured for our use. Hanslow, the Eywellese capital, is not much farther, but there'll likely be too many Narthani, plus fortifications, for us to attempt an attack there."

Two hours of argument and discussion followed, taking into account Yozef's suggestions and *who* would do *what* under *whose* command. He didn't contribute more to the planning and instead leaned against the back wall, then sat on a chair when Denes noticed him unsteady on his feet. However, he listened with discouragement at the lack of an overall command structure. Committees would not defeat the Narthani.

Finally, the hetmen decided Stent and Hewell would take Yozef's three hybrid field pieces and three of the captured Narthani 12-pounder cannon, along with enough volunteers from the surviving artillerymen to train others en route and push hard to Parthmal to take the town before either the Narthani army got there or the forces there knew what was happening. Both clans had suffered needless losses, due to Moreland's lack of control, and, since they didn't have Moreland to take it out on, they were eager for another target. Meanwhile, Adris, Bultecki, Orosz, and Pewitt would slow the Narthani army and pick off stragglers and small groups, as opportunities occurred. All the clans agreed that the Tri-Alliance contingent had more than fulfilled a contribution and should retire to their provinces. What was left of the Moreland men of fighting capability would maintain order within Moreland Province, while surviving elders sorted out the clan's future.

## Back to Abersford, Betrayed by Carnigan

Yozef and the others from the Abersford area left the main Keelan column when their turn came to peel off for home. Culich thanked him again and said to expect meetings and planning for the future, though not for a while, to let the men have time with their families.

When they crested a hill and first saw Abersford and St. Sidryn's in the distance, Yozef's spirits leaped.

*Home.*

He had been on Anyar approaching three years and had thought he'd accepted that this was where he would spend the rest of his life, but something was different.

*Is it the battle? Coming close to death? Somehow, I have a greater sense of having a stake here. And, of course, there's Maera and the baby.*

News of the victory had gone ahead before they left Moreland City, with no details. More important, Culich had insisted the casualty list be sent as soon as possible. All of the clan's people deserved to know whether family and friends had survived. Of the dead, mourning could begin. Of the wounded, it would be known they were alive. And for the majority, news that their men would return unscathed lessened fear in thousands of hearts.

The Abersford area was hit hard by the casualties, especially from the artillery crews. Maera had been active in checking that families of the dead were honored for their sacrifice and ensured that the widows and the children would be cared for. It was similar for the wounded. Families would be provided for, until the men recovered enough to resume their normal lives, and for those whose wounds would not allow that, provisions were made. Maera never doubted Yozef would agree with the obligation.

Maera was sitting on their veranda swing when Yozef and Seabiscuit came into view. She rose when she recognized him and walked to the front walk, where Brak took his horse. The elderly man grunted and nodded to Yozef, an unusual gesture of respect from the hardscrabble man. Although Yozef smelled of sweat, horse, dust, and who knew what, Maera hugged him with a fierceness that surprised him. She said nothing for several minutes as he held her gently, her belly pressed up against him.

"Come into the house. You smell like a cesspool. A bath and fresh clothes are waiting. Then some food, and I want to hear all about it."

She eyed the compression bandage held in place on his head by a cloth wrap. "How did you get that and how bad is it?"

"A fluke accident. The battle was over when a stray Narthani cannon shot hit a carriage I was near, and a piece of wood hit me. It's minor."

With his arm around her shoulder and hers around his waist, they walked into their home.

Three days later Yozef came home from his shops and found Maera sitting on the same swing, this time with pursed lips and an expression that elicited a *Whoops, what did I do wrong?* thought. Yozef was ten feet away when she snapped, "You somehow forgot to mention exactly what *you* did during the battle!"

"I told you I advised and helped with artillery."

"Yes, but you didn't say you were at the front of the fighting and could easily have been killed! Denes wouldn't give me any details, but Carnigan told me everything."

*Traitor.*

"You were supposed to stay back and not get that far forward. You're too valuable to our people to risk yourself that way! And what about our baby, who would never know a father! I can hardly believe you were so irresponsible."

Yozef sat down beside her on the swing and placed a hand gently on her knee. *She's acting mad at me, but it's because she was worried. She really does care for me.* He patted her leg.

She didn't respond, just sat there eying him angrily.

"That was my intention, as I promised," said Yozef. "But when Denes and his men attacked the Narthani infantry, our artillerymen were confused in all of the chaos. No matter how much we'd practiced or how hard they'd tried, it's totally different in the middle of a battle. It looked as if the Narthani might stop the attack, which would have meant we failed and likely many more of our men would die before we could withdraw."

"Why did it have to be you?"

"Because I was there and saw the danger and opportunity. Believe me, it wasn't something I wanted to do or planned. One minute I was scared and trying to stay back, and without thinking, the next minute I was with the guns and even more scared."

Maera was silent, then seemed to relax. The angry set to her face melted away, replaced by confusion and softness. She placed one hand over his on her knee. They sat that way for several minutes.

"I'm still angry with you," she said, with more resignation than fury. "And I don't know what you should have done. Just please don't do it again."

"Believe me, Maera, I've no desire to be a hero, and if I never get near a battle again, no one will be happier than me."

She leaned her head against him, and they didn't speak for the next hour, both holding tight to the other.

*She's never said she loves me, but then, neither have I said I love her. What a pair we are.*

During the next two sixdays, there was sporadic news of the retreating Narthani army, which withdrew into safer confines deeper into Eywellese territory. Miles of Eywell province were more a no-man's land than firmly in Narthani control. The clans shadowing the Narthani inflicted several hundred more casualties in an endless parade of ambushes and night attacks, always keeping under cover and retreating on horseback whenever the Narthani tried to counterattack. As many clan casualties resulted from accidents and friendly fire as from the Narthani.

The greater news was how Stent and Hewell took the town of Parthmal and the Narthani garrison by surprise. They allowed Eywell civilians to leave the town with what they could carry and then burned the town. All the 150 Narthani, mainly guard units and support staff, were killed, to a man. Any supplies and stores the clansmen couldn't take with them by horse or commandeered wagon were burned. They confiscated close to six hundred muskets, either those of the fallen Narthani garrison or intended replacements for the army, along with eight cannon, which were never fired during the surprise assault.

## What Now?

Evening meal was finished. He and Maera sat on the veranda swing, watching the last light in the east fade. Elian and a servant girl finished cleaning up and left them alone. The faint squeak of the swing, the wind in trees around the house, and the distant breaking of waves lulled their senses for half an hour.

"What's going to happen, Yozef? With the Narthani. They're coming again, aren't they?"

He put an arm around her. "Yes. I'm afraid so. We pushed them back, but they weren't defeated, in spite of what many of your . . . *our* . . . people believe. I think they were surprised and withdrew from uncertainty and caution, more than feeling defeated."

"What's next? Do they come again like before? Try to force a battle again? Use their navy to attack clans anywhere around Caedellium? How could we stop them?"

"This time, the Narthani allowed the clans to gather, but if they attack from the sea, a clan would be overwhelmed before help could come. I'm sorry, Maera, I just don't know what they'll do next. What I *do* know is that the clans have to prepare for anything, as hard as that may be. One good result of the Battle of Moreland City is that most clans should now not be able to use the excuse that all of this will pass them by. Hopefully, the clans can unite in ways they haven't done before."

"That's also what Father believes, though he doesn't know how it will happen. What about you? We've all come to think of Yozef the Mysterious coming up with new ideas. Is there anything you can do?"

"We need more cannon. There's no way we can fight the Narthani on even terms as long as they have such superiority in artillery. I've got to find a way to cast bigger barrels than the swivels."

Maera smiled and hugged him. "I'm sure you'll find a way. You always do."

He frowned, sat back, and released her. "Don't say that, Maera. I'm not a miracle worker. Yes, I know things not known on Caedellium, but it's dangerous to start thinking I have answers to every problem."

She saw that he was upset at her comment. Culich and Diera had cautioned her not to press her husband too hard. Somehow, he managed to solve problems, even when others hadn't realized the problems existed, but he was loath to assume responsibility. It had bothered her at first. Her father grabbed responsibility with both hands; Yozef pushed it away.

"Remember, Maera," Diera had warned, "the important thing is not how *you* expect Yozef to behave, but *what* he accomplishes. The *Word* tells us to judge by deeds and not words."

She worked hard to remember, although it wasn't always easy.

He put his arm back around her. "I don't know what's coming. All I can say is I'll do what I can to protect you and the baby."

She unconsciously put a hand on her stomach. "I'm afraid for our child. What kind of future will we bring it into?"

"I wish I could be more reassuring. Your people are strong. Great sacrifices might be needed, but somehow I believe they'll rise to whatever is required. As fearful as I often am, I somehow intuit that great events are coming and that, in the end, there's hope."

Yozef sighed, looking over the sea. "And here I am, working on ways to kill people, when what I really want to do is give Caedellium what knowledge I have. I want to work on the university, write up more notes to share, establish more trades to help the people. It's a version of the conundrum of the quill and the sword. I subscribe to the belief that the quill should be more important. The quill may be mightier long term, but the sword wins short term. Maybe the belief should be more that it takes the sword to protect the quill, I don't know."

"Or maybe it's both and not either," Maera said, hooking her arm into his and pulling him closer. "Father says all we can do is our best. If it's both quill and sword, then I believe you'll do what you can with both for all of us."


# END OF BOOK 2

# MAJOR CHARACTERS

*Akuyun, Okan.* Commander of Narthani mission to conquer Caedellium.

*Akuyun, Rabia.* Wife of Okan.

*Bakalacs, Feren.* Hetman of Farkesh Clan.

*Balcan, Mamduk.* Narthani religious prelate.

*Beynom, Cadwulf.* Mathematics scholastic. Son of Diera and Sistian. Friend and employee of Yozef.

*Beynom, Diera.* A medicant. Abbess of St. Sidryn's abbey. Wife of Sistian.

*Beynom, Sistian.* A theophist. Abbot of St. Sidryn's abbey. Husband of Diera.

*Bolwyn, Elton.* A medicant at St. Sidryn's abbey.

*Bultecki, Teresz.* Hetman of Bultecki Clan.

*Dyllis, Saoul.* A medicant at St. Sidryn's abbey.

*Erdelin, Memas.* Narthani colonel.

*Eywell, Brandor.* Hetman of Eywell Clan.

*Eywell, Biltin.* Son of Brandor Eywell.

*Faughns, Brak and Elian.* Elderly home staff couple of Yozef.

*Fitham, Petros.* Elderly theophist at St. Sidryn's abbey.

*Fuller, Filtin.* Skilled worker and friend to Yozef.

*Gwillamer, Cadoc.* Hetman of Gwillamer Clan.

*Harlie.* Name given by Yozef to alien artificial intelligence created to interact with Yozef.

*Hewell, Lordum.* Hetman of Hewell Clan.

*Hizer, Sadek.* Narthani Assessor reporting direct to Narthani High Command.

*Kalcan, Morfred.* Narthani naval commander.

*Kales, Wyfor.* Abersford citizen. Tutor to Yozef for blade fighting and occasional bodyguard.

*Keelan, Breda.* Wife of Culich. Mother of Maera.

*Keelan, Culich.* Hetman of Clan Keelan. Father of Maera.

*Keelan, Maera.* Eldest daughter of Culich and Breda.

*Kennrick, Pedr.* Advisor to Hetman Culich Keelan.

*Ketin, Erkan.* Narthani colonel.

*Kolsko, Yozef* (a.k.a. Joseph Colsco). California chemistry graduate student who boards an ill-fated flight to a conference and meets an unimagined future.

*Linton (Merton), Bronwyn.* Owner of farm near Abersford. Mother of Aragorn, Yozef's son.

*Metin, Nuthrat.* Narthani colonel.

*Mittack, Hulwyn.* Hetman of Mittack Clan.

*Moreland, Anarynd* (a.k.a. Ana). Friend of Maera Keelan. Related to Moreland Clan hetman.

*Moreland, Brym.* Father of Anarynd. Cousin to Moreland hetman.

*Moreland, Gynfor.* Hetman of Moreland Clan.

*Orosz, Tomis.* Hetman of Orosz Clan.

*Stent, Welman.* Hetman of Stent Clan.

*Puvey, Carnigan.* Physically imposing member of abbey staff. Friend of Yozef.

*Tuzere, Nizam.* Narthani civilian administrator.

*Vega, Denes.* Magistrate and sheriff-equivalent in town of Abersford. Commander of Abersford fighting levy.

*Vortig, Luwis.* Advisor to Hetman Culich Keelan.

*Vorwich, Longnor.* Keelan Clan boyerman (district chief) of Abersford and St. Sidryn's area.

*Watchers.* Name given by Yozef to alien creators of Harlie and whose spaceship destroyed Yozef's flight to Chicago.

*Zulfa, Aivacs.* Brigadier. Commander of Narthani ground troops on Caedellium.

# ABOUT THE AUTHOR

Olan Thorensen is a pen name. He's a long-time science fiction fan (emphasis on 'long') who has jumped into independent publication with all its pitfalls and unknowns. He thinks all colors go together: clash, what clash? A fan of Dilbert, Non Sequitur, Peanuts (even if old strips), and still think the end of The Far Side was a tragedy. In his youth, served in the US Special Forces (Vietnam:SOG). Has a Phd in Genetics, around 200 science publications as author and co-author, and is a Fellow of the American Association for the Advancement of Science (AAAS). Lives in the Blue Ridge country of Virginia. Thinks it's totally cool someone can read his stories and enjoy them. Loves fireflies, thunderstorms, is eclectic in music, and thinks four seasons are better than one. His web page is olanthorensen.com and hopes his books sell enough he can afford a better web site, better maps, and faster publication. All input from readers is appreciated.

Please email me with any comments at olanthorensen@gmail.com or through my web site at olanthorensen.com where color maps of Anyar are available. I promise to read all emails, though I won't be able to answer personally every one. Also, if you enjoyed the story, please leave a comment/review on appropriate venues, such as Amazon and Goodreads.

Made in the USA
San Bernardino, CA
27 July 2018